W9-BMD-975

ACCLAIM FOR ROBERT WHITLOW

"My verdict for Robert Whitlow's *Chosen People*: compelling, realistic, and inspiring. Robert combines the intensity of a legal battle against terrorists with a poignant depiction of Israel, with all of its tensions and grandeur. As a lawyer who handles cases for terrorism victims, I loved the realism of the novel and felt deeply the joys, disappoints and triumphs of its characters. But the matters of the law were eclipsed by matters of the heart—faith, love and hope in the midst of despair—this is where Whitlow truly shines."

—RANDY SINGER, BESTSELLING AUTHOR OF *RULE OF LAW*

"Whitlow writes a fast-paced legal suspense with amazing characters. There are twists and turns throughout, and a number of unexpected surprises to heighten the suspense. Whitlow is an amazing writer and he touches upon delicate topics with grit and respect."

—*RT BOOK REVIEWS*, 4 STARS, ON *A TIME TO STAND*

"Whitlow's timely story shines a spotlight on prejudice, race, and the pursuit of justice in a world bent on blind revenge. Fans of Greg Iles's *Natchez Burning* will find this just as compelling if not more so."

—*LIBRARY JOURNAL*, STARRED REVIEW, ON *A TIME TO STAND*

"Part mystery and part legal thriller, Whitlow's latest novel is definitely a must-read!"

—*RT BOOK REVIEWS*, 4 STARS, ON *THE WITNESSES*

"Whitlow's characters continuously prove that God loves the broken and that faith is a lot more than just showing up to church. [This] contemplative novel is a fine rumination on ethics, morality, and free will."

—*PUBLISHERS WEEKLY* ON *THE WITNESSES*

"Highlights not only Whitlow's considerable skills as an author of legal thrillers, but it is also a gripping story of family dynamics and the burden of alcoholism."

—*CBA Retailers + Resources* on *A House Divided*

"Attorney and Christy Award–winning author Whitlow pens a character-driven story once again showcasing his legal expertise . . . Corbin is highly relatable, leaving readers rooting for his redemption even after family and friends have written him off."

—*Publishers Weekly* on *A House Divided*

"Christy Award winner Whitlow's experience in the law is apparent in this well-crafted legal thriller. Holt's spiritual growth as he discovers his faith and questions his motives for hiding his secret is inspiring. Fans of John Grisham will find much to like here."

—*Library Journal* on *The Confession*

"Whitlow writes with the credence of a legal background and quite adeptly incorporates intrigue, romance, and redemption in its many forms into his book. Recommend to young adults and older readers with a penchant for unexpected twists and unanticipated outcomes."

—*CBA Retailers + Resources* on *The Confession*

"Whitlow has weaved a well-constructed and engaging mystery with a crisp, concise style of storytelling, authentic, gritty characters, and a well-defined plot. Strong tension and steady pacing add to this stellar read."

—*RT Book Reviews*, 4½ stars, on *The Confession*

"Readers will find plenty to love about this suspenseful novel as they watch its appealing main character juggle personal, professional, and spiritual crises with a combination of vulnerability and strength."

—*CBA Retailers + Resources* on *The Living Room*

". . . an intensely good read."

"In *The Choice*, Robert Whitlow crafts a moving tale of a mother's love for her unborn children cast against the specter of the culture wars. Fans of Whitlow's courtroom drama will not be disappointed, but here, too, the human drama of which we all become a part takes center stage."

"Author Robert Whitlow combines Grisham's suspenseful legal-thriller style with the emotional connection of a Hallmark made-for-TV movie."

"Whitlow captures the struggle of many women trapped in the battle over abortion in a truly sympathetic and affecting way."

". . . a solid, suspenseful thriller."

CHOSEN
PEOPLE

ALSO BY ROBERT WHITLOW

A Time to Stand
The Witnesses
A House Divided
The Confession
The Living Room
The Choice
Water's Edge
Mountain Top
Jimmy
The Sacrifice
The Trial
The List

THE TIDES OF TRUTH SERIES

Deeper Water
Higher Hope
Greater Love

THE ALEXIA LINDALE SERIES

Life Everlasting
Life Support

CHOSEN PEOPLE

PEOPLE

ROBERT WHITLOW

THOMAS NELSON
Since 1798

Published in Nashville, Tennessee, by Thomas Nelson. Thomas Nelson is a registered trademark of HarperCollins Christian Publishing, Inc.

Thomas Nelson titles may be purchased in bulk for educational, business, fundraising, or sales promotional use. For information, please email SpecialMarkets@ ThomasNelson.com.

Library of Congress Cataloging-in-Publication Data

Names: Whitlow, Robert, 1954- author. | Whitlow, Robert, author.
Title: Chosen people / Robert Whitlow, Robert Whitlow.
Description: Nashville, Tennessee : Thomas Nelson, 2018.
Identifiers: LCCN 2018024091| ISBN 9780718083045 (trade paper) | ISBN 9780718083755 (epub)
Subjects: LCSH: Guilt--Fiction. | Georgia--Fiction. | Women lawyers--Fiction. | GSAFD: Legal stories. | Christian fiction.
Classification: LCC PS3573.H49837 C56 2018 | DDC 813/.54--dc23 LC record available at https://lccn.loc.gov/2018024091

Printed in the United States of America

18 19 20 21 22 M&G 5 4 3 2 1

*To those who desire to see people through
God's eyes, heart, and promises.*

You are a chosen people, a royal priesthood, a holy nation, God's special possession, that you may declare the praises of him who called you out of darkness into his wonderful light.

—1 PETER 2:9

PROLOGUE

"H ana!"

Hearing her name, Hana left her cousins and ran toward the canvas canopy where Uncle Anwar sat peeling an orange with a well-worn pocketknife. Accustomed to the Middle Eastern heat, six-year-old Hana didn't let the ninety-degree temperature keep her from playing outdoors. But when the family patriarch called, she stopped what she was doing and responded immediately.

Hana brushed a wayward strand of long black hair from her face as she stepped into the shade. Anwar, her seventy-four-year-old great-uncle, sat in a white plastic chair. The multicolored canopy was attached to the rambling three-story concrete structure that several generations of the Abboud family had called home.

"Yes, Uncle," she responded in the courteous tone of voice her mother had taught her to use when addressing her elders.

"Greetings, child."

Anwar cut a fresh piece of orange and handed it to Hana. Her uncle's brown thumb revealed weathered scars from decades of work in the olive groves on the hills surrounding Nazareth. Hana's father was a prosperous businessman who, along with his brothers, owned a factory that produced plastic irrigation pipe sold all over Israel and the West Bank. Their family lived in Reineh, an Arab town four miles north of Nazareth. Uncle Anwar still made his home in the much larger ancient city where Jesus spent most of his childhood.

"This is for you," Anwar said. "Tell me if it tastes sweet."

Hana knew the answer but bit into the orange flesh, releasing a cascade of warm juice in her mouth. The oranges of Israel were the best in the world.

"Yes, it is sweet and juicy."

"Did you know that the Lord says to 'taste and see' that he is good?"

"No, sir," Hana answered, her eyes big.

She'd watched in awe and fear as Anwar asked her older brothers and cousins questions that, to her mind, had no answers.

"He wants his goodness to be as real to you as the sweet juice in your mouth."

"Yes, sir." Hana nodded.

"Do you know why I called you by name to come to me?" Anwar asked.

"So you could give me a piece of orange?"

"Yes," Anwar replied with a smile. "And because you've been chosen by the Almighty to walk with him all the days of your life."

Hana thoughtfully swallowed the last morsel of the juicy fruit. "Like the boy Samuel," she said, remembering the story she'd heard the previous week at the small church the family attended. It was the first time Hana had realized her name appeared in the Scriptures. The biblical Hannah was Samuel's mother.

"That's right. When Pastor Sadr read the story, I thought of you."

"Not my brothers? They're boys like Samuel."

"God has a plan for Mikael and Nathanil, but this is about you," Anwar said, leaning forward. "If the Lord wakes you in the night, do you know what to say?"

Hana's precocious memory had already caught the attention of the adults in the family.

"Speak, Lord, for your servant is listening."

"Good." Anwar smiled as he sat back and carved off three more sections of fruit. "Take these to your cousins."

CHAPTER 1

Hana sang a few soft words as she organized the contract documents into separate file folders. Sensing someone's presence, she turned around. In the doorway stood Janet Dean, the assistant she shared with two other associates at the law firm.

"How many times have I told you that you sing like an angel?" Janet asked.

"A lot." Hana smiled. "And every time I feel embarrassed and encouraged."

"Was that Arabic or Hebrew? I want to guess. Let me hear a few more words."

In a slightly louder voice, Hana sang the next line of the song and stopped.

"It's Hebrew," Janet said emphatically. "I could tell because you were making that noise in your throat. Even that sounds beautiful when you do it."

"Arabic," Hana answered. "But don't feel bad. There is some similarity between the two languages."

"I'll keep guessing if you keep singing," Janet replied. "In the meantime, take that voice and brain of yours to conference room A for a meeting with Mr. Lowenstein."

"I'm supposed to be meeting in ten minutes with Mr. Collins and his group."

"Where you'll be listening, not participating. Gladys Applewhite says it's imperative you join Mr. Lowenstein. I'll take care of Mr. Collins."

"Okay. Who is going to be in conference room A?"

"You, Mr. Lowenstein, and a lawyer named Jakob Brodsky. I don't know why Lowenstein demanded you come at the drop of a hat."

Hana had adjusted to the assistant's Maine accent but still occasionally stumbled when the cheery woman threw in idiomatic American terms. It took her a moment to figure out what "drop of a hat" meant.

Janet continued, "Gladys says Brodsky wants to associate the firm in some kind of international personal injury case."

"Personal injury?" Hana asked. "Did a ship sink and injure someone?"

Leon Lowenstein's admiralty law practice often involved insurance claims for millions of dollars if cargo was lost or a ship damaged.

"Gloria didn't say," Janet answered. She lowered her voice. "But it sounds like pirates to me, which would be supercool so long as no one was killed or anything. They're going to show a video, and Mr. Lowenstein wants you there to see it. You'd better scoot if you don't want to be late. Don't worry about Mr. Collins."

The idea of a lawsuit involving pirates wasn't far-fetched. Shortly after Hana joined the firm, Mr. Lowenstein settled a claim for damages incurred in a piracy incident off the coast of Somalia. Hana brushed her hands across her dark gray skirt and adjusted her white blouse. Slender and fit, she was five feet six inches tall with long black hair, light brown skin, and dark brown eyes.

The exterior wall of conference room A was a continuous bank of windows that gave a panoramic view of the affluent Buckhead area of north Atlanta. A long glass table sat in the middle of the room.

Stocky and gray-haired, Leon Lowenstein stood in front of a large video screen attached to the wall. Beside him was a tall young man with short, curly black hair who wore a blue suit with snug European styling and a bright yellow tie. Mr. Lowenstein smiled when Hana appeared.

"Thanks for coming on short notice," he said. "This is Jakob Brodsky, a lawyer with a personal injury practice in Sandy Springs."

"Call me Jakob," the younger lawyer said, extending his hand to her.

"Hana Abboud."

"And you're Israeli?" Jakob asked with a puzzled glance at Mr. Lowenstein.

"But not Jewish," Mr. Lowenstein supplied. "Hana can explain."

"I'm an Arab Israeli who grew up near Nazareth in a town called Reineh and graduated from law school at Hebrew University in Jerusalem."

"And for the past year and a half she's worked in the international transaction section of the firm," Mr. Lowenstein added. "I thought about her after we spoke about your case."

"Are you sure this is a good idea for her to be here?" Jakob asked.

"Yes," the older lawyer said with a dismissive wave of his hand. "Hana isn't a Muslim. She has a Christian background."

This was familiar territory for Hana, but she had no clue why it was relevant to the meeting with Brodsky. She'd spent much of her life unraveling her history for people who immediately jumped to a long list of erroneous assumptions when first meeting her. She faced Jakob Brodsky.

"I'm a Christian who served two years in the national service program in lieu of military duty in the Israel Defense Forces," she said in a matter-of-fact tone of voice. "I'm an Israeli citizen who can vote, pay taxes, and receive benefits available to any other citizen of the country."

"Okay." Jakob shrugged and turned to Mr. Lowenstein. "Do I have your agreement that what I'm about to show you is subject to attorney-client privilege?"

"Certainly, but you've not been secretive about your involvement in this case," Mr. Lowenstein responded. "My assistant showed me the request you posted on the trial lawyers forum."

"I've had to cast a wide net looking for help."

Gladys Applewhite entered the room carrying a tray that held water, a pot of coffee, glasses, and cups. She placed the beverages in the middle of the table.

Jakob held up a flash drive. "The video footage is on here."

Mr. Lowenstein inserted the drive into a USB port. Hana poured a glass of water. The video contained a date and the names "Gloria and Sadie Neumann" alongside a frozen image that looked vaguely familiar to Hana. The senior lawyer handed the controller to Jakob.

"I'll run it through once without stopping," Jakob said. "We can back it up and do sections later. There's no audio." He pressed the play button.

"I know that place," Hana said after less than thirty seconds had passed. "It's Hurva Square in the Jewish Quarter of the Old City of Jerusalem."

"Correct," Jakob replied. "The video is from a surveillance camera outside a shop that sells snacks and ice cream. It was recorded in late May four years ago. The shop is located at the southwest corner of the square."

Jakob had memorized every second of the eleven-minute video, yet it still had the irresistible power to draw him in. The black-and-white images were captured late on a Friday afternoon. People filled the square. Ultra-Orthodox Jewish men with beards and side curls, wearing long black coats and old-fashioned hats, walked quickly through the camera's line of sight. The religious men wore similar but not identical black garments, and varied black hats identified their rabbinic allegiance. Jakob had seen Haredim in Brooklyn, but his connection with any form of faith was tenuous, and he'd never attended synagogue. During the five years since he'd moved to Georgia from New York, he'd built his practice handling difficult cases other lawyers wouldn't touch. What got him out of bed in the morning was the chance to tackle a tough legal challenge.

The camera tracked scores of other people who looked no different from those getting off a subway in a major city. Six young Israel Defense Forces soldiers appeared: three men and three women, all with machine guns slung over their shoulders. Jakob looked at the Arab lawyer, whose face didn't change expression at the sight of the troops. A few seconds later a group of fifteen to twenty teenagers stopped in front of the shop.

"Is that a Nefesh B'Nefesh group?" Hana asked.

"What?" Jakob replied.

"A birthright tour for young Jews to visit Israel."

"Maybe, I'm not sure."

Two young Arab men, one in his late teens, the other several years younger, watched the young people. One of the group's chaperones turned sideways and revealed a handgun in a holster strapped to his waist. Four young people emerged from the shop with ice cream. The entire group moved away. The two young Arab men disappeared, too. Three other figures approached the ice cream shop.

"That's the Neumann family," Jakob said. "Ben, Gloria, and three-year-old Sadie. They're going into the store."

As the family moved out of sight, a second group of younger ultra-Orthodox men came by with their arms linked together.

"Was this on a Shabbat evening?" Hana asked. "The Haredim look like they're on their way to the Kotel, the Western Wall."

"Yes," Jakob replied, impressed with the lawyer's obvious familiarity with what they were watching. "The Western Wall is only about a quarter mile away."

The Neumann family reappeared. Gloria sat down and held an ice cream cone in front of Sadie, who licked it. Her husband walked away.

"Ben is going into a nearby shop to buy a necklace Gloria saw earlier but wouldn't let him purchase because she said it was too expensive," Jakob said.

"Stop!" Hana suddenly exclaimed, standing up. "If this is what I think it is, I don't want to watch it!"

Jakob pressed a button on the controller, and the scene froze with Sadie's mouth open as she leaned toward the ice cream. He looked at Hana, who continued to stare at the still images on the screen.

"Is this a terrorist attack?" she asked.

"Yes, and you should see it for yourself," Jakob said in a voice that sounded more callous than he intended. "It's compelling."

"I agree with Hana," Mr. Lowenstein interjected, shaking his head. "It's one thing to talk about events like this on the phone, but another to witness them so directly."

"Do you remember this attack?" Jakob asked the Arab lawyer.

"Only that it involved an American tourist. I was living in the UK at the time. There were multiple terrorist incidents in Israel during the few months I was away."

Hana's willingness to use the terrorist label caught Jakob's attention.

Mr. Lowenstein turned to Jakob. "If you'll excuse us for a few minutes," he said.

Suspecting that he'd wasted a trip, Jakob stepped forward to retrieve the flash drive.

"Would you leave the flash drive?" Mr. Lowenstein asked.

"I went through a lot to get this," Jakob replied. "I have copies, of course, but I'm not going to risk—"

"After I talk with Hana, I'll ask Gladys to bring you back in for a chat."

Jakob hesitated, then shrugged. "Okay," he said.

Jakob poured a cup of coffee to take with him. Mr. Lowenstein pressed a button on a conference station in the middle of the table.

"Gladys, please take Mr. Brodsky to conference room D for a few minutes."

CHAPTER 2

The conference room door closed.

"Mr. Lowenstein, I'm sorry, but—" Hana began.

"No," the senior partner interrupted, holding up his hand. "I apologize for not advising you about the purpose of the meeting. A close friend who knows the Neumann family called last week and asked me to meet with Brodsky. Bringing you in didn't cross my mind until Gladys told me he was in our reception area."

Mr. Lowenstein had always been courteous to Hana and made her feel welcome at the firm. The older lawyer and his wife had invited her to dinner at their beautiful home within a week of Hana's arrival in Atlanta. Later, Mrs. Lowenstein insisted that Hana sit next to her at a lavish catered dinner for one of the firm's biggest clients. Hana looked at the screen. The image of the child and the ice cream disappeared as the video went into sleep mode.

"Who died?" she asked.

"Gloria Neumann was killed by a terrorist."

Hana pressed her lips together for a moment so she could regain her professional composure. "What does Mr. Brodsky want?"

"To associate Collins, Lowenstein, and Capella as cocounsel in the case. This firm doesn't normally take on personal injury claims, and we have no experience in suits brought under the US antiterrorist laws. But we have a lot of expertise in piercing the corporate veil to uncover hidden assets. Do you remember the Harkins litigation? We unraveled three dummy companies, one that was offshore, and recovered over five million dollars for our client."

Hana recalled the firm-wide celebration and bonus checks issued when the case was resolved. She'd been in Atlanta only three weeks, yet she received an extra $1,000.

"Yes, sir."

"That's where this case will end up—uncovering a murky money trail. Brodsky wants to bring in a law firm that can finance the litigation in return for a percentage of recovery. Whether he's willing to admit it or not, he doesn't have the skill set to pursue complex litigation. Today is a preliminary step. I've not mentioned it to the partnership committee, which would have the final word."

Hana knew little about firm politics, but she suspected Mr. Lowenstein would have his way no matter what the other partners desired.

"And I'm not sure it would be approved even if I want to do it," Mr. Lowenstein continued.

"Really?" Hana asked in surprise.

"My name at the top of the letterhead counts for something," Mr. Lowenstein said, "but there are eight equity partners who would share the loss if we agreed to underwrite the litigation and didn't recover any damages. Taking on risk is not in their nature."

Hana suspected Mr. Collins would fall in the risk-averse category. Frank Capella, who worked in the securities law area, was more of a gambler.

Mr. Lowenstein checked his watch. "I don't want to leave Brodsky in the conference room too long," he said.

"Are you going to watch the video?" Hana asked.

"I have to review it in order to make up my own mind about presenting the case to the rest of the firm. But there's no need for you to see it. The last thing I want to do is give you bad dreams."

"Thanks," Hana said.

"And again, please accept my apology for not notifying you in advance about the purpose of the meeting."

"That's not necessary, Mr. Lowenstein. Terrorist attacks can occur anyplace in the world, but Israel is such a small country that when it happens there it feels close to home for everyone."

The senior partner pointed to the screen with the controller. "And this one reached all the way from Jerusalem to Atlanta."

Hana stood to leave the conference room as the image of Sadie Neumann about to enjoy the ice cream cone reappeared. She glanced at Mr. Lowenstein and hesitated. She looked again at the mother and daughter.

"How old was Gloria Neumann?" she asked.

"Thirty-one when this took place."

Hana's thirty-first birthday was only four months away. To celebrate, she was flying to Israel so she could spend ten days with her family and friends.

"And Sadie is their only child?"

"Yes," Mr. Lowenstein said. "Brodsky sent over a written summary if you'd like to read it."

Hana's jaw tightened. Either through watching the video or conducting a quick online search, she'd know the pertinent details in a few minutes.

"I don't want to watch it, but I can't get away from the thought that I should," she said, slowly sitting down.

Mr. Lowenstein raised his bushy eyebrows. "Are you sure?" he asked.

"Yes," Hana replied and nodded grimly.

She gripped the arms of the chair as Mr. Lowenstein pressed the play button. The video resumed. Hana held her breath as Sadie leaned in for a lick of ice cream. Several more bites followed. Hana forced herself to breathe. A man walked quickly past mother and daughter. Hana flinched. Nothing happened.

There was movement as several people ran past the place where Gloria and Sadie sat. Gloria suddenly stood up, and the ice cream fell from her hand to the ground. Two dark-clad figures, one taller than the other, flashed into the picture. The taller man raised his right hand in the air and brought it down toward Sadie. Gloria was able to turn her body enough to absorb the blow. From the angle of the camera, Hana couldn't see what the man had in his hand. But when he raised it again, it was clear that he was holding a large knife. He slashed it down from right to left. Gloria bowed down as it raked across her neck. The man quickly stabbed her again and she fell to the ground with Sadie beneath her. Grabbing the knife with both hands, the man raised it high, but before he could plunge it into the mother or the daughter, he crumpled to the ground on top of Gloria.

The shorter male figure standing beside the taller man during the attack spun around so that his face came into clear focus. He was an Arab boy, a teenager. Hana suddenly realized he was wearing a coat even though the temperature in Jerusalem in May could be sticky-hot. "He's wearing a suicide vest!" she cried out.

The boy reached inside the coat with his right hand and raised his left hand in the air. Nothing happened, and in a split second three soldiers wearing border patrol uniforms appeared with their weapons drawn. The boy dropped to the ground and lay flat with his arms extended above his head. One of the soldiers pulled Gloria Neumann from beneath the body of the man who'd stabbed her and another picked up Sadie, whose mouth was open in a silent scream. Mother and daughter were both covered in a dark substance that Hana knew was blood. She wanted to look away but couldn't. The images abruptly ended.

"That's all," Mr. Lowenstein said in a somber voice. "Gloria died three hours later at Hadassah Medical Center. There's no doubt she sacrificed herself to save her daughter."

"Was the girl hurt?" Hana asked.

"Sadie suffered a cut to the right side of her face. Brodsky included a photo of Sadie in the packet he sent for my review. You can still see the scar. It was a deep wound."

Mr. Lowenstein removed a photo from a thin folder and slid it across the table to Hana. Sadie, a gorgeous child with black hair, had a scar running down her right cheek that created a crevice to the edge of her lips. The damage caused the little girl's face to be slightly asymmetrical, with her mouth sagging on the right side. Her soulful dark eyes grabbed Hana's attention.

"When was this taken?" she asked.

"Within the past few months. She's six now, almost seven."

"She looks older than that. Can they fix the damage to her face with plastic surgery?"

"I'm not sure about her medical status, but I do know she's being treated by a child psychologist."

After a final look at the photo and a quick, silent prayer for the motherless child, Hana returned the picture to Mr. Lowenstein.

"And the attackers?" she asked.

"Two brothers from the Ramallah area in the West Bank. I don't remember the name of the specific town, but you may recognize it. Brodsky indicated they were from a well-to-do family, which surprised me."

"Not me. It's often the better-educated people who buy into jihadist ideology."

Mr. Lowenstein took a sheet of paper from the folder and slipped on reading glasses. "Abdul Zadan, the older brother, was shot by the soldiers you saw at the end of the video. Tawfik Zadan, the younger brother, was wearing a suicide vest that failed to detonate. Tawfik was taken into custody."

"Did any group claim responsibility? Hamas, Hezbollah, al-Aqsa Brigade, ISIS?"

Mr. Lowenstein shook his head. "No. The well-known organizations all praised the bravery of the Zadan brothers but didn't take direct credit. Tawfik gave a statement claiming he and his brother were on a mission for Allah. If no link to a specific group is established, it will be hard to justify a lawsuit since the core purpose of the statute is to hit terrorists in the wallet."

Hana had a limited knowledge of the antiterrorism laws. "Like the cases filed against Middle Eastern banks that served as financial depositories for terrorist groups?" she asked.

"Exactly." Mr. Lowenstein nodded.

Hana's law license was from Israel, and her role at the firm was to interact as an Israeli lawyer with the firm's international clients. She wasn't familiar with the intricacies of US civil procedure, but she knew it would take a very long arm of the law to cross the Atlantic Ocean and the Mediterranean Sea and reach into the dark recesses of a terrorist cell. She shook her head.

"I understand why Brodsky hasn't found a firm to help him," she said.

"True, but I've untangled knotty situations in my career that looked like there was no string to pull. Some investigations begin with very little information to work with." Mr. Lowenstein paused. "Now that you've seen the video, do you want to stay while I talk some more with Brodsky?"

"If you want me to."

Mr. Lowenstein eyed her for a few seconds. "No, that won't be necessary," he said. "But I may have some follow-up questions for you later."

When Hana left the conference room, the route to her office took her past conference room D. Through the glass wall she saw Jakob Brodsky sitting in a chair with a cup of coffee on the table in front of him. He was checking something on his phone but looked up as she approached. Their eyes met. She looked away first.

Hana didn't log on to the internet and read about the attack on the Neumann family. In spite of Mr. Lowenstein's desire that she not have bad dreams, she couldn't shake from her mind the image of Sadie Neumann covered in blood, her mouth wide open in terror. Hana couldn't bear the thought of something horrible happening to one of her nieces or their mothers. She closed her eyes and prayed a one-word prayer for peace she'd first heard from older members of her family.

"*Shlama, shlama,*" she said in Aramaic, the language spoken on a day-to-day basis by Jesus himself and kept alive in scattered Arab and Assyrian Christian communities.

The soothing sound of the ancient petition brought a measure of peace to Hana's soul.

• • •

While he waited in conference room D, Jakob received negative responses from two other law firms he'd contacted about joining his fight for justice on behalf of the Neumann family. Both firms turned him down without explanation. So far, he'd failed to effectively communicate the passion and righteous indignation he felt concerning the tragedy. The case was more of a raisin than a plum. None of the big national firms that pioneered claims against terrorist organizations were willing to meet with him after conducting a preliminary investigation. But that hadn't deterred Jakob.

One of the first things Jakob and Ben had agreed upon when Jakob decided to take the case was the need to associate cocounsel. Jakob posted requests for help on twenty lawyer forums and provided additional information to almost fifty individuals and firms that contacted him. None of them panned out, mostly because of Jakob's inability to provide the name of a defendant that could be sued for significant money damages. Some of Jakob's queries escaped the attorney fishbowl and prompted a few emails from nonlawyers, including a literary agent who wanted to acquire the movie rights to Gloria Neumann's story. Now, the possibility of help from Collins,

Lowenstein, and Capella had given Jakob renewed impetus to uncover a link between the Zadan brothers and an identifiable terrorist organization with assets.

Jakob hadn't limited his investigation to the English-language web. Because he could speak and read Russian, he set up an account that enabled him to delve into the much darker internet world of the former Soviet Union. The Russian web was dangerous, a place filled with hackers, data thieves, and proponents of bizarre conspiracy theories.

Adopting a profile that identified him as a Russian sympathetic to fundamentalist Islamic causes, Jakob explored websites and read chilling blog entries. Searches that mentioned Islamic jihadists usually led to information originating from individuals and groups in south-central Asian countries with predominantly Muslim populations: Azerbaijan, Chechnya, Kazakhstan, Kyrgyzstan, Tajikistan, and Uzbekistan. Many of the people living in the region were cultural Muslims, but others had crossed over into radical fundamentalist beliefs. The bulk of the information Jakob found focused on antagonism toward Russia, which had dominated the region for millennia, but there was also vitriol directed against corrupt Western societies and Israel, the interloper state wrongfully squatting on land that should be under Islamic control and Sharia law. Whenever the topic of Israel appeared, Jakob dug deeper.

He'd read many poorly written diatribes urging true believers to rise up and die in jihad. But there were also more sophisticated videos and posts that hinted at better organization and more money. So far, he'd found eight specific references to terrorist activity directed at Jews in Israel. Three of those sites, one in Tajikistan and two in Chechnya, celebrated Gloria Neumann's death without claiming any direct responsibility. It had been sobering to read the name of the woman from Atlanta in a hate-filled diatribe written on the other side of the world. He'd also stumbled across a startling recruitment video from Chechnya. In the ten-minute piece, a tall, slender Caucasian man in his late thirties or early forties spoke passionately in American-accented English about the glories of jihad. The bearded man urged English-speaking Muslims to heed the call to leave the decadent societies of the West and give themselves fully to the advancement of the Islamic faith until it reigned supreme over the whole earth.

The previous year Jakob had won a lawsuit filed on behalf of a disabled Vietnamese woman wrongfully evicted from her apartment. Three law firms and the local legal aid office had turned down the woman's case. Jakob's attorney fee barely justified the hours required, but the jury verdict enabled the woman to afford the down payment on a small single-story house nearer to her son and daughter-in-law. The Neumann case, however, was in another legal universe.

Leon Lowenstein had been Jakob's most promising lead. The personal connection between Mr. Lowenstein and a friend of Ben Neumann sent Jakob's hopes soaring. Everything he'd learned researching Lowenstein's experience and background prior to the meeting increased his optimism. The older Jewish lawyer was a generous philanthropist who'd made enough money that he could risk a few dollars in a righteous crusade. And more importantly, Lowenstein had encountered terrorist activity in the practice of admiralty law. In Jakob's optimistic mind, it was a small step from pursuing Somali pirates in high-speed skiffs to suing knife-wielding jihadists in Jerusalem.

The unexpected appearance of the female Arab lawyer was a huge red flag, and when she demanded he stop the video, Jakob was afraid he'd wasted his time. It would be tough breaking the news to Ben that he'd struck out again. Jakob glanced up as Hana walked quickly past the conference room. Her face was inscrutable.

Jakob's knowledge of the conflict between Arabs and Jews in the Middle East was limited to sound bites, but it didn't take a political scientist to realize the battle lines between the groups were hard and fixed. The Arab lawyer's reference to her Israeli citizenship and government service as evidence of neutrality sounded positive, but he wasn't sure how much weight to give it.

The older woman who'd escorted Jakob to the conference room returned. "Mr. Lowenstein is ready to see you," she said.

CHAPTER 3

M s. Abboud and I watched the rest of the video," the older lawyer said. "Ben and Sadie Neumann have suffered a great loss and deserve a chance for justice."

"You want to help?" Jakob asked in surprise.

"I'm willing to present the case to the firm's equity partners as a next step," Mr. Lowenstein said, touching the slim folder on the table. "But I'm going to need more than what you included in here to convince our firm to join the fight. What are the terms of your contract with Mr. Neumann?"

"One-third contingency if settled prior to trial; forty percent if we try the case."

"That's fair given the challenges. How much will you and the Neumann family invest in the case toward the costs of litigation?"

Jakob cleared his throat. "Mr. Lowenstein, that's the main reason I'm here. My client and I can't finance this type of lawsuit."

"And Collins, Lowenstein, and Capella is a law firm, not a bank. Your side will have to bring funds to the table, too."

Jakob's mind went into overdrive. A door cracked open was better than one closed and locked. He spoke rapidly and honestly: "Ben Neumann is the branch manager of a men's clothing store and doesn't have significant resources. Sadie is in private school. With education costs, childcare, and medical bills, I'm not sure Ben could contribute more than a few thousand dollars."

"Did he receive any life insurance proceeds from Gloria's death?"

Jakob was glad he'd asked Ben that question at their last meeting. "Yes, he was able to cover burial costs, pay off Gloria's student loans, and buy a new minivan."

"I would still want him to put in at least forty thousand dollars toward out-of-pocket costs. Of course, your firm could contribute as well. We'd use those funds first before this firm starts bankrolling the case."

Jakob swallowed. He had student loan debt, four credit cards with balances he juggled like a clown tossing flaming torches into the air at the circus, and a new apartment. He had virtually no reserves at the law firm, but one good case on his docket was on the verge of settling and would net a fee in the $20,000 range. Maybe he and Ben could contribute an equal amount.

"If we do that, how much would your firm fund over the initial forty thousand?"

"The figure I'd present to my partners would be $250,000," Lowenstein replied. "With the attorney fee split seventy-thirty."

Jakob nodded. "I think that's fair. I'd be satisfied with seventy percent."

"No," Lowenstein corrected him. "That's seventy percent to us and thirty percent to you."

"But I'd be doing all the legal work!" Jakob protested.

"Mr. Brodsky," Lowenstein replied evenly, "if we agree to provide the majority of the funding for the case, we'll also be involved in every aspect of the litigation, from investigation to trial to any appeals."

"I want to be involved in the case," Jakob said. "This isn't a handoff."

"You'll earn your portion of the attorney fee. It's unethical to agree to a split based solely on your role as a rainmaker."

Jakob was familiar with the ethical rule, but he and the other lawyers in his building routinely ignored it. Each one of them had a different legal niche, and funneling matters to the right lawyer was worth a kickback of ten to fifteen percent as long as it didn't result in overcharging a client.

"You'd work with lawyers on my team," Lowenstein continued. "And I'd oversee everyone."

Graduating in the middle of his law school class, Jakob had no chance for employment at a firm like Collins, Lowenstein, and Capella, which interviewed only students in the top ten percent of their class. To work with an attorney like Leon Lowenstein and see how his firm litigated a big case would not only be good for Ben Neumann, it would be an invaluable experience for Jakob, regardless of the attorney fee earned.

"That's worth a lot," he admitted, pressing his lips together for a moment and quickly considering his options. There were none. "Agreed," he said.

"Contingent on approval by our partnership committee."

"Understood, and by Mr. Neumann as well."

"You do your job; we'll do ours," Mr. Lowenstein said. "Ben and Sadie Neumann deserve the best representation available."

"Yes, they do."

Lowenstein gave Jakob a steely look. "And I mean that with every fiber of my being. Otherwise, we wouldn't be having this conversation. Gloria's life mattered, and those who took it from her must be held responsible."

Leon Lowenstein's words and tone of voice elevated Jakob's confidence to its highest level yet.

"I feel exactly the same way," he said.

• • •

Hana closed the screen displaying the acquisition agreement initiated by a Silicon Valley investment firm for an Israeli software company based in Ra'anana, a city about twenty kilometers north of Tel Aviv. Bouncing back and forth between English and Hebrew in such a complex way was exhausting. Hana needed a break and stepped out to Janet's desk. Her assistant hadn't been at her workstation when Hana returned from the meeting with Mr. Lowenstein and Jakob Brodsky.

"Was it pirates?" Janet asked.

"No, much worse."

"Can you tell me or should I not ask?"

Hana hesitated. Janet was a good soul who didn't deserve to be needlessly burdened by what had happened in Hurva Square.

"Let me spare you the details for now," Hana replied. "Mr. Lowenstein has to talk to the equity partners about the case."

"Wow!" Janet's eyes grew big.

Hana regretted revealing that detail. "Keep that between us," she quickly added.

"Of course. Are you off to lunch?"

"Yes."

"By yourself again?"

"Yes."

"There's a group of female associates in Mr. Capella's group that go to lunch together on a regular basis. Let me check with Thalia Botts who works over there. I bet they'd love to have you—"

"Thank you, but no," Hana said with a smile. "I need to relax more than anything else. Sorting out a tableful of female conversations would not be a break for me."

"Whatever you say," Janet said with a shrug. "But you need a social life coordinator in the worst way. I was less than half a person until I met Donnie. And he was less than a quarter of the person he's become since meeting me. Together, we're close to a whole person."

Hana chuckled. "I'm going to dinner with someone later this week," she said.

"A man?" Janet's eyebrows shot up.

"Yes, I met him at a big church I visited a few weeks ago. He's interested in learning more about Arab culture."

"I bet." Janet nodded knowingly and added, "Especially from someone like you."

Shaking her head, Hana walked away and took the elevator to the parking deck. She'd never owned a car in Israel, where public transportation via buses crisscrossed virtually every inch of the small country. However, shortly after moving to Atlanta, she'd signed a three-year lease for a small German import.

Five or six nearby restaurants were on Hana's regular rotation for a midday meal. Today, she opted for a tiny deli run by an Arab man whose family had come to the United States from Lebanon. The deli was crowded with people lining up at the counter. Entering, Hana greeted Mahmoud Akbar in rapid-fire Arabic.

"Hana, don't do that to me," the balding middle-aged man replied in English. "I moved to Baltimore from Beirut when I was thirteen. All I understood about what you just said was something about the sun shining on me, and it's been cloudy all morning."

Arabic is a rich language with a myriad of options for even simple greetings.

"That's close," Hana answered in English. "It was a greeting and a blessing for the sun to rise on you with a warmth that comforts your aching bones."

Mr. Akbar smiled. He was cutting slices for shawarma sandwiches from a large roll of meat turning on a spit in front of an exposed vertical cooking element. Another worker quickly scooped up the meat for the deli's most popular lunchtime offering. Mr. Akbar wiped his forehead with a small towel he kept tucked in his apron strings.

"What would you like?" he asked.

"Breakfast and lunch, please," she answered. "But not too much. I have to work this afternoon, not take a nap."

"Labneh and makanek?"

Hana nodded. "Yes."

The owner handed the long knife to his son, Gadi, a sour young man who never seemed interested in talking with Hana in any language. Mr. Akbar scooped labneh dip, a yogurt seasoned with cucumbers, dill, garlic, and salt, into a small bowl along with a few thinly sliced strips of fresh cucumber. Hana dipped a cucumber strip into the yogurt and waited as the owner dropped several two-inch makanek sausages, a combination of lamb and beef, onto a grill top.

Mr. Akbar yelled at one of his workers, "Rusty! Drop more fries!"

"You'd think they'd realize when the fries are running low," Mr. Akbar grumbled when he faced Hana.

He turned the miniature sausages on the grill. A few moments later, he placed them in a small bowl and drizzled pomegranate molasses over them. Hana placed a twenty-dollar bill on the counter. While she waited for her change, she ate a bite of savory sausage enhanced by the sweetness of the molasses.

"Your makanek are delicious," Hana said, wiping her lips with a thin paper napkin. "As good as the ones I ate in Lebanon when I went to the American School for a high school debate competition."

Mr. Akbar leaned over and spoke in a low voice to Hana. "I'm sure your father was very proud of you then and now," he said. "But I'm worried about Gadi. He's going out at night to meetings and won't tell me what they're about. And I've caught him looking at religious stuff on his phone that I don't like or agree with."

"What sort of things?" Hana asked, her heart sinking.

"Not good." Mr. Akbar glanced over his shoulder at his son. "I know it's Wahhabi-influenced, and when I mentioned it he insisted I call it Salafism. We had a big blowup over it this morning when we were getting ready to open the restaurant."

Hana looked at Gadi, who was now expertly slicing shawarma meat. Seeing a long, sharp knife in his hands so soon after watching the Neumann video made her shiver.

Mr. Akbar continued, "He says the Saudis believe it, and Allah has blessed them so much that they're the richest people in the world."

"They have the most oil in the world."

Mr. Akbar pointed up. "Who put the oil under the sands where the Prophet lived?"

Hana had never revealed her Christian faith to the owner of the restaurant, and she knew he assumed she was a secular Muslim like himself. She hesitated. Rusty, the boy cooking the French fries, called out to Mr. Akbar.

"I'll pray for Gadi and for you," Hana said quickly.

Mr. Akbar gave her a puzzled look as he scurried off. Hana never wore a head covering, and in Islam, no woman could pray without one. Thus, for her to offer to pray made no sense to him.

Hana finished her meal, all the time watching Gadi. Her head might be uncovered, but her heart was wide open, and she prayed to the God of heaven and earth for this father and his son.

CHAPTER 4

Jakob stopped for a fast-food cheeseburger on the way back to his office. A first-generation immigrant from the former Soviet Union, he reveled in every aspect of freedom and had no interest in restricting himself by following Jewish dietary rules. However, when eating out with other Jews, he didn't intentionally offend them. Instead, he waited to see what they ordered before making a selection. He loved all different kinds of food, and finding something he liked wasn't a challenge.

Jakob inherited his fierce love of freedom from his father, a Jewish refusenik who sought for years to flee communism but was denied exit visas for himself and his family. Because of his open desire to emigrate, Anatoly Brodsky suffered persecution, including being sentenced to a six-month stint in jail. The elder Brodsky had passed along his broad stubborn streak to his youngest son. Only after the Berlin Wall fell was the family able to leave the Soviet Union and settle in New York City. A large, framed photo of the Statue of Liberty hung in the living room of the house on Long Island where Jakob lived from age ten forward. Jakob's father was a skilled aeronautics worker, and his mother, a classically trained musician, found part-time employment with a second-tier orchestra. Once immersed in America, Jakob quickly lost his Russian accent, and the intonations of New York took over.

Jakob's representation of Ben Neumann came through the recommendation of a former client named Ken Smith. Jakob agreed to meet with Ben and listened sympathetically to what took place in Hurva Square, but it wasn't until he watched the surveillance video on Ben's laptop that a familiar fire had begun to burn in Jakob's belly. To him, it was a sign that he should consider taking the case. But there was one question he had to ask before allowing himself to take the next step.

"Why do you want to file a lawsuit?" he asked Ben. "It's just going to make you think more about your loss."

"Do you think that isn't already the case?" Ben asked. "Every time I look at my daughter I see her mother's face. And when I kiss Sadie's cheek, my lips touch the scar left by my wife's murderer. The love of my life is gone, but she would want me to do something, anything, that might make it less likely for another family to suffer like we have. When I read about the antiterrorism laws and this type of lawsuit, I knew I had to pursue it as far as I could."

As Jakob listened, he reached one conclusion: if given the chance, Ben Neumann could share his story in a way that would soften the heart of the most callous juror.

"Ken said you weren't intimidated by a challenge," Ben continued. "He told me how you dug and dug until you found out who was responsible for the injuries to his son. The other lawyers I've talked to tell me that's what I need—someone who can dig and find out if the murderers acted alone or not."

"I have no experience in this area of the law," Jakob said. "And it would be very expensive to investigate and litigate this type of claim."

"I understand," Ben said with obvious disappointment. "Thanks for agreeing to meet with me." He closed his laptop and stood up.

"Don't leave," Jakob said, holding up his hand. "Not until you look over a proposed attorney-client contract."

• • •

Traffic was snarled due to an accident, so it took Jakob twice as long as it should have to reach his office located in a two-story building that contained eight suites. One of the downstairs offices served as a common conference room. Five of the eight tenants were lawyers.

The nonlawyers included an insurance agent, a financial planner, and a naturopath.

A receptionist on the main floor answered the phone for all the tenants. Maddie had the impressive ability to instantly give the right greeting depending on which light blinked on the phone.

"Jakob Brodsky, attorney at law," she said to a caller as Jakob entered the building. Then, after a short pause, "I'll put you right through to him."

"That was mean!" Jakob called out as he dashed up the stairs, taking two at a time.

His voice mail would turn on by the fifth ring. Often, people looking for a personal injury lawyer were working their way down a list of attorneys and wouldn't leave a message. He fumbled his key for a second, but managing to open the door, he lunged for the phone on the corner of his desk and pressed the receive button.

"This is Jakob Brodsky," he said, slightly out of breath. "How may I help you?"

"I'm calling to help you, Mr. Brodsky," a perky female voice replied. "I was looking at your firm website, and we can take it to the next level. Are you in a position to take on more clients?"

"Yes, but not more overhead expense," Jakob replied, sitting down in the leather chair behind his desk.

"A detailed website analysis by our firm won't cost you anything," the woman responded quickly. "Aren't you interested in learning how to increase your internet marketing footprint for pennies a month?"

"How many pennies?"

"Fewer than you think. We've worked with other Atlanta-area law firms that have increased monthly contacts by fifty to sixty percent. And we guarantee our results. How often do you hear the word 'guarantee' from a marketing firm?"

"Not often." Jakob felt himself being drawn in like a fish on a lure. Guaranteed results might let him avoid flushing precious dollars down a marketing black hole. Competition for new business was intense, and any edge was worth exploring.

"One of our sales representatives is going to be in your area on Wednesday afternoon and would love to meet with you," the woman continued confidently. "He'll bring a free gift that I'm sure you'll find—"

The other phone line to Jakob's office blinked, signaling a new call.

"Gotta go," Jakob said as he swam away from the hook. Hoping it wasn't someone else wanting to sell him something, he pressed the button to accept the new call.

"Mr. Brodsky?" asked a female voice.

"Yes."

"This is Amanda Brooks with Brookstone Adjusting Services. You've been talking with Natalie Fletchall in our office about the Harrison case."

Jakob sat up straighter. It was the case he'd hoped would generate the fee he could use to fund his share of the costs in the Neumann litigation. Mr. Harrison had been defrauded by a disability insurance company after an agent forged Harrison's initials on a medical questionnaire.

"Yes," he said. "I sent a demand of eighty thousand dollars to Natalie in an email last week along with a copy of the complaint I'll file in Fulton County Superior Court if we can't reach a settlement. That's as low as I can go to get this case resolved prior to litigation."

"We have a deal. The insurance company wants to put this claim in the rearview mirror. You'll have our standard release in your in-box within the hour. Once we receive a signed copy of the release, we'll overnight the check, payable to you and your client."

Jakob called to give his client the good news, then unsuccessfully tried to reach Ben Neumann. He left Ben a succinct voice mail: "Good news. Call me."

. . .

Hana brushed her teeth to avoid sharing the pungent garlic in the labneh dip and the spices in the makanek with her coworkers. She then worked on legal documents written in Hebrew and sent them to a client in Ra'anana. Just as she was about to take a break there was a knock on her door. She answered in Hebrew before correcting herself. Mr. Collins entered. The bald, overweight lawyer in his midsixties rarely came to her office.

"Sorry," Hana began. "I've been going back and forth between English and Hebrew."

"Which is a good thing for the law firm. You said, 'Yes, please.' Correct?"

"That's right."

Mr. Collins closed the door and sat down in the single chair across from Hana's desk.

"Did you think of something else I should have included in the Jezreel Software agreement?" she asked. "I sent the revised contract to the management team in Israel a few minutes ago. It's not too late to make changes—"

"No, I wanted to talk to you about your meeting this morning with Leon."

Jim Collins was more turtle than rabbit, and Hana knew it might take him awhile to get to the point of his visit.

"Did he ask you to research Jakob Brodsky's background and experience?" the senior partner asked.

"No, but he mentioned that he might have some follow-up questions later."

"And you watched the surveillance tape of the terrorist attack in Jerusalem?"

"At first I said no to watching it and then changed my mind."

"Why is that?"

Hana thought the answer should be obvious. "A woman was stabbed to death, and her little girl's face slashed with a knife. The young Arab man who did it was shot and killed. It wasn't something I wanted to see or have as a memory."

"Leon didn't give you a heads-up about the meeting?"

"Heads-up?"

"Inform you in advance."

"No, but he apologized and told me I was a last-minute addition after Mr. Brodsky arrived at the office."

Hana felt uneasy. It seemed Mr. Collins was accumulating information to oppose his colleague in the partners' meeting.

"What else did Leon say to you about the case?"

"He mentioned the challenges that existed to finding a solvent defendant who could pay monetary damages, and that it would be up to the equity partners to decide whether the law firm became involved."

Mr. Collins nodded and then looked Hana directly in the eyes. "If you had a vote, would you be in favor or opposed?"

"Mr. Collins," Hana protested. "It isn't my place—"

"It is if I ask you a direct question." The senior partner spoke more emphatically than normal. "And that's exactly what I'm doing. You're an Arab and a citizen of Israel. You have a perspective on this none of the other lawyers in the firm can share. I came to see you because I want to know what you think."

Images of Gloria Neumann falling to the ground and Abdul Zadan crumpling on top of her flashed through Hana's mind. "I'd vote no," Hana answered.

"Why?"

Hana was tempted to use the difficulty of finding a defendant with money as her primary reason, but she knew that wasn't true. "In Israel, we always talk about not letting the violence that surrounds us keep us from living normal lives," she said. "I didn't move to Atlanta to try to escape that world, but I thought I would leave it behind while working here. That's the best answer I can give."

Jim Collins was silent for a moment and then stood up. "Thanks, I respect your perspective," he said, leaving the room and shutting the door behind him.

Hana took a deep breath. For several moments, she stared out her window. However, she didn't see the normal skyline view of modern buildings against a clear blue sky. Instead, in her mind's eye she traveled from north Atlanta to Hurva Square in Jerusalem.

CHAPTER 5

Jakob stepped into the hallway outside his office for a drink from the water fountain as Butch Watson, one of the other lawyers in the building, trudged up the stairs with a heavy catalog case in his hands. Butch was building a trusts and estates practice, and he often met with clients at the office of their financial planner or stockbroker.

"Why didn't you take the elevator?" Jakob asked, pointing at the heavy case.

"I promised my wife I'd begin walking more," replied the broad-shouldered young lawyer. "I've gained more weight since we found out she was pregnant with the twins than she has."

"When are they due?"

"Three weeks," Butch said as he reached the top of the steps. "And I'm hoping the boys can play offensive line like I did and get a free ride through college."

Butch's extra pounds hung on a physique that still remembered when he could bench-press 450 pounds. Occasionally, Jakob and Butch went to a sports bar for a beer. Jakob never bet against Butch if someone challenged him to an arm-wrestling match.

Jakob pointed to the catalog case. "Good client?"

Butch's face lit up with a broad smile. "Yes. And not just one. I met with a stockbroker who played against me when I was in college. Luckily, we hit it off better today than when we butted heads ten years ago. I'd forgotten the details of the game, but he remembered I received a personal foul penalty for grabbing his face mask and trying to separate his skull from his neck. He laughed about it because his team won the game. He's promised to start steering as many clients as he can my way."

"Awesome."

"How about you? Any progress in finding a moneybags cocounsel for your antiterrorism case?"

"I just had my best meeting yet." Jakob summarized his conversation with Leon Lowenstein.

"You're the big-risk, big-reward guy who tosses the fifty-yard pass downfield into double coverage," Butch responded. "I'm more three yards and a cloud of dust. I wish I could buy in for a tiny piece of the action, but I'm tapped out getting ready for the boys to arrive."

Jakob remembered his conversation with Mr. Lowenstein, who held a much stricter view of cocounsel relationships than the frathouse camaraderie of the lawyers who shared space with Jakob in the modest office building.

"It's the thought that counts," he replied.

"No, it isn't," Butch grunted as he continued toward his office. "I've got to see if these stubby fingers can still crank out sixty words a minute on a set of trust documents."

Ten minutes later, Maddie buzzed Jakob. "Mr. Ben Neumann and a beautiful young lady are here to see you. He says he doesn't have an appointment—"

"It's okay. Send them up."

Ascending the stairs were Ben and Sadie Neumann. Sadie was wearing her school uniform: white blouse, sky blue jumper, and dark blue Mary Jane shoes. Her black hair was in a ponytail that flopped on top of a small orange backpack. Her father wore a nicely tailored suit. Random strands of gray were sprinkled throughout his dark hair.

"I received your message while on my way to take Sadie to a therapy appointment," Ben said. "We have to pass by here on the way."

"Perfect timing," Jakob answered. "Come in."

Jakob's office was spacious, with top-quality furniture that had been selected by an interior decorator. He had a large wooden desk with a leather inlay top and several leather chairs.

Sadie picked out a burgundy chair in one corner of the room and climbed into it. Her feet dangled a couple of inches above the floor.

Ben took a tablet from the little girl's backpack. She plugged in earbuds, and in a few seconds her eyes were glued to the tablet screen.

"And she won't listen to us?" Jakob asked.

Ben smiled. "You don't have kids yet, do you?"

"No."

"They have no problem leaving the real world for an imaginary one, especially when they have an electronic device to take them there."

Jakob sat down behind his desk. "I had a productive meeting earlier today with Leon Lowenstein," he began. "Thanks for making that connection. His firm is interested in joining the case as cocounsel."

"Really?" Ben sat up straighter.

"He watched the video and agrees that you and Sadie deserve representation." Jakob explained the process that included Mr. Lowenstein's presenting the case to the law firm's equity partners.

Ben frowned. "That doesn't sound so good."

"But we have a chance," Jakob said optimistically. "However, there's a second precondition to moving forward. You and I have to commit to deposit forty thousand dollars into their trust account toward out-of-pocket costs for the case. I'm willing to pay twenty thousand if you can come up with an equal amount. I believe that much in the case."

Jakob waited for Ben to respond. Instead, the client glanced over at Sadie, who remained focused on the tablet.

"You know how much I want to pursue this," Ben said. "And I appreciate more than I can say what you're willing to do, but that's a lot of cash to come up with all at once. I have some money left over from the life insurance, but it's going to be awhile before I can build up my savings. Gloria always kept a tight lid on our family finances.

I'm more impulsive. Over the past couple of years, I've spent every penny trying to make Sadie's world as happy as possible."

Jakob was relieved that his client hadn't totally depleted the insurance money. "What should I tell Mr. Lowenstein?" he asked.

"I'd been thinking the firm you brought in as cocounsel would be able to fund the case," Ben answered, avoiding the question.

"That was our goal, but it hasn't worked out that way," Jakob admitted. "Mr. Lowenstein is going to recommend to his partners that they put in an additional $250,000 to fund the litigation. That should cover the cost of experts, investigators, depositions, and travel to other parts of the world. Anyone named as a defendant is going to fight as hard as possible because if they pay us, they might have to pay other terror victims and their families." This was territory Jakob had covered with Ben in the past, but it seemed right to revisit it. "One rule of litigation is that it always takes more time and costs more money than you think. And in addition to the funds to finance the claim, Mr. Lowenstein has multiple lawyers at his firm who will assist me."

"What will you do?" Ben asked.

"I'll be in the middle of everything as the main attorney," Jakob answered confidently.

"Be patient with me," Ben said after a few moments of silence passed. "It's a big decision, and I need to think this through."

"Daddy," a little girl's voice said, "I need to go potty." Sadie hopped down from the chair and took out the earbuds.

"It's down the hall near the elevator," Jakob said. "The code for the door is 1-2-3."

• • •

A spirit of heaviness descended on Hana for the rest of the afternoon. Her words to Jim Collins about the terrorist attack in Jerusalem revealed as much to her as they had to the firm's senior partner. She hadn't considered the move to the United States an escape. In her mind, it was simply a chance to work in a new environment where she could hone her legal skills and proficiency in the English language. Now she had to rethink her motives and uncover hidden places in her soul.

Finding it difficult to concentrate on work, Hana was glad when she received a positive answer from the Jezreel leadership team to the changes she'd suggested in the agreement. She forwarded the information to Mr. Collins. After sending the email, she went downstairs to a coffee shop on the first floor of their building. The people on the sidewalk in front of the plate-glass window and sitting next to her sipping lattes didn't live under a constant threat of imminent harm. There was a bus stop twenty feet down the street that had no concrete barricades protecting it from a jihadist intent on driving a car or truck into the people waiting for public transportation. If Hana looked up and down the street, she wouldn't see any border patrol soldiers or police armed with machine guns. No metal detectors manned by security guards were set up at all the entrances to the high-end shopping mall across the street.

At the end of the day, Hana came up two and a half hours short of the billing quota needed to meet the benchmarks established by the law firm.

"See you tomorrow," she said to Janet when she left the office.

"Have a good evening. You were awfully quiet after Mr. Collins dropped in. Is everything okay?"

"How did you know I was quiet?"

Janet pointed to her computer. "You send me a copy of your billable time when it's forwarded to the accounting department."

"Yes, I'm okay," Hana said, then shook her head. "I didn't meet my goal."

"Did it have anything to do with the meeting you had with Mr. Lowenstein this morning? We joked about pirates, but it must have been something else. Gladys says Mr. Lowenstein kept her out of the loop, which almost never happens. And then Mr. Collins shows up asking if you're in your office. You're not in hot water, are you?"

"You mean in trouble?"

"Right."

"No, I didn't do anything wrong."

"Good," Janet said with relief. "I feel responsible for protecting you."

Hana had been trained in Krav Maga, the hand-to-hand self-defense technique used by the Israeli army. A would-be mugger on the streets of Atlanta would likely end up with a broken arm or dislocated shoulder if he attacked her. But Hana knew that wasn't the kind of protection Janet had in mind.

"That's very kind, and I really appreciate it," Hana said gratefully. "But I'm doing okay. Don't stay too late yourself."

"I was approved for a couple of hours of overtime and need the money. The bill for my teenage son's car insurance is due this month, and I agreed to pay half if he handles the rest."

• • •

It was a fifteen-minute drive from the office to Hana's home at the end of a quiet residential street in an older neighborhood. The tiny house was built decades earlier as a mother-in-law residence by a couple who themselves had long since died. The residence came fully furnished. The interior consisted of an open area that served as the living and dining room, with a compact but fully equipped kitchen and a spacious bedroom with an en suite bathroom. Most of the furniture pieces were genuine antiques or high-quality reproductions.

The house was radically different from the massive home where Hana grew up in Reineh. In Arab families, the additions caused by marriage and children simply meant adding rooms and floors onto an existing structure. When she was a child, Hana occupied a house with her mother, father, two brothers, one set of grandparents, a great-aunt, and two uncles and aunts and their eight children. It was a rowdy, roiling chaos.

The quiet solitude of the Atlanta house was a jolt she'd learned to love. She especially liked summer evenings when crickets that didn't realize they were surrounded by millions of people called to one another at dusk. The windows in the living area were screened and Hana, who didn't mind warm weather, would turn off the air conditioner, open the four windows, and listen to the sounds of the night.

She parked her car beneath a maple tree that exploded with vibrant red leaves in autumn. The first fall Hana spent in the house, she sent photos of the changing leaves to her family every few days. One of her nephews called it the "candy tree."

Hana fixed a pot of tea that she drank in English fashion with milk and sugar. While she waited for the tea to brew, she turned on her laptop with an Arabic keyboard, responded to personal emails, and reviewed her social media accounts in Israel. Tonight, she received an immediate greeting on social media from Farah, one of her first cousins and the mother of two small boys. Another cousin, Fabia, was the mother of a five-year-old girl named Khadijah. The sisters had similar names but starkly different personalities. Fabia was fiery, while Farah was calm. Hana typed a quick question to Farah in Arabic, which, like Hebrew, is written right to left:

What are you doing up so late?
Barak has a fever. I gave him medicine and I am waiting for him to go to sleep.

Barak was the younger of her boys. Farah continued:

I was going to write you tomorrow. We visited Uncle Anwar this morning. He's feeble but spoke your name several times.

Anwar and Hana's great-grandfather Mathiu were brothers. Her great-grandfather was dead, and ninety-eight-year-old Anwar was the last of his generation still living. Together, the two men were the spiritual pillars of the entire clan. In the 1950s, they had led the family out of the orthodox Christian faith that had been their spiritual home for centuries to join a new Protestant group founded by Scottish missionaries who came to Nazareth from the Hebrides islands. Anwar had always held a special place in Hana's heart. It touched her that he was thinking of her out of all his many relatives as he prepared to leave earth for heaven. She typed a simple response:

Why?
I do not know, but when he said your name I felt the presence of God.

Hana typed a quick response:

What does it mean?

She waited, but no response came. Hana stepped into the kitchen and fixed her tea. Returning to the computer, she saw that Farah had answered:

I believe he was praying for you.

In her heart, she sensed Farah was right, but then a different possibility flashed across her mind. Hana's fingers flew across the keyboard:

Maybe he was thinking about Anna who recognized Jesus as the Messiah when his parents brought him to the temple.

A man who knew the Bible well might live in its pages as his connection with this life weakened.

No. You always try to direct attention away from yourself.

Hana smiled. Her cousin knew her well. Hana had achieved extraordinary academic and professional success as a modern Arab woman, yet she kept herself veiled—not on the outside, but on the inside.

If that is true, what was the reason for his prayers?
I am going back to see him in a few days so he can lay his
hands on the boys and bless them. I will ask him about you.

Farah typed another question:

When Anwar passes will you return for the time of mourning?

Burial of the dead in Hana's family took place as soon as possible, much like the practice of their Jewish neighbors. Relatives weren't expected at the grave if the circumstances made it difficult. There followed a period of concentrated mourning lasting seven to ten days. Custom and respect for the departed made an appearance at the family house during this period mandatory.

Yes.

Her cousin replied:

Barak is asleep. Sometimes I think about our talks in the night.
Be blessed.

Farah signed off.

As preteen girls, Hana, Farah, Fabia, and another cousin, Palma, shared the same bedroom on the third floor of the family house. On hot summer nights they would lie in the dark and share the whispered fantasies of girls dreaming about the future. Farah always wanted to be a mother and a homemaker. Fabia proclaimed she would travel the globe, but she'd never gone farther than Beirut or Beersheba. Hana had aspired to be a schoolteacher in Nazareth and voiced no great ambition to see the wider world. Now she was the one living alone in a faraway city that none of the girls had known existed when they stared out their bedroom windows at the distant stars.

CHAPTER 6

Jakob sat alone at the raucous sports bar drinking an icy mug of draft beer. The NBA play-offs were underway, but Jakob wasn't interested. His European roots were deep enough that he was a die-hard soccer fan. Ben Neumann had left their meeting without committing to help fund the lawsuit. Trying to convince an unwilling client to pursue litigation was harder than pushing a rope up a ramp. Jakob's phone lit up with an incoming call. It was Ben.

Forgetting about his beer, Jakob went outside and raised the phone to his ear. "Ben?"

"Hey, I'm sorry to call after business hours, but I know you need an answer for Mr. Lowenstein. I called Gloria's father and mother and talked over the situation with them. Her dad has been in favor of suing from the beginning, but her mother is more practical like Gloria was. Also, she's worried that if we stir up a bunch of trouble with a terrorist organization, it might put Sadie in danger."

Sadie's safety was an issue Jakob had considered but dismissed as remote. He was a warrior who wanted to take the fight to the enemy. Let them experience fear, even if it was limited to their bank accounts.

"Her father had a question," Ben continued. "Would the federal government get involved if we uncover a terrorist cell that isn't already on their list of dangerous groups?"

"Maybe, but I doubt they'd directly help with our case. Their interest would be in national security."

A clearly intoxicated couple walked past Jakob toward a yellow sports car. Whichever one drove out of the parking lot was a DWI waiting to happen.

"Gloria's father is willing to contribute ten thousand dollars toward the costs of the case," Ben said. "If he does that, I'll use part of the remaining life insurance money to come up with the rest. Sadie's college fund will have to wait."

"That's great."

"There's one stipulation," Ben added. "Gloria's parents don't want Sadie's name to appear on any of the paperwork filed in court."

"We can't agree to that," Jakob answered quickly. "A huge part of any damage model would be Sadie's loss. If we take that out, we're left with only you."

"I lost a lot."

"And I don't want to minimize that in any way. But there's no substitute for the sympathy a jury will have for a small child whose mother has been cruelly taken from her. And Sadie is the one who has the physical scars that speak louder than—"

"This is nonnegotiable," Ben cut in. "After listening to my mother-in-law, I agree with her. I want Sadie as far away from the case as possible. Her name can't be mentioned when you play the surveillance video."

"The jury will want to know what happened to her in the attack," Jakob protested.

"You can ask me about it when I'm on the witness stand."

Jakob paused and tried to quickly formulate a counterargument. Nothing came to mind.

"I'll have to let Leon Lowenstein know about this," he warned. "Remember, the partners of his firm have to approve moving forward, and there's a good chance leaving Sadie out will influence their decision on whether or not to help."

"Then it's better for this to come out now instead of later."

Jakob beat a tactical retreat. "Okay, you're the boss. As soon as I have the twenty thousand dollars from you and Gloria's parents in my trust account, I'll call Mr. Lowenstein."

"Send me a text with wiring instructions, and you'll have the money tomorrow," Ben said. "Thanks again for being patient with me and understanding my need to process everything."

The call ended. Jakob sent the bank routing and account numbers. Returning to the bar, he discovered his beer gone, the table wiped clean.

. . .

True to the word Anwar had given her when she was a little girl, Hana often woke up in the night to pray and seek the Lord. She didn't worry that she might be tired in the morning. Instead, she slipped out of bed in anticipation of what the night watch might hold in store for her.

There was also historical precedent for Hana's middle-of-the-night wakefulness. Throughout much of human history, divided sleep was the norm for most people. The invention of electric lights pushed bedtimes later and later, and humanity shifted toward a single installment of sleep in a twenty-four-hour period. Hana preferred the ancient rhythm.

It was 2:22 a.m. when Hana awoke. The street outside her house was deserted. The voices of the insects had fallen silent. Refreshed by several hours of sleep, her mind was uncluttered, her spirit clear. Sometimes she prayed while walking through the house. Other nights, she sat on the sofa in the living room and read the Bible or listened to music. Often, she simply sat in expectant silence.

Tonight she thought about Mathiu and Anwar. Both men had a deep relationship with God and brought an atmosphere of respect with them wherever they went. Hana had witnessed the power of their spoken and unspoken influence. Proud men became more humble; humble men received confidence.

Hana slipped a robe over her nightgown and sat on a short sofa covered with a velvety dark blue fabric. She curled her legs beneath her and turned on a lamp. The lamp provided a soft, diffuse light. She picked up the journal she kept on an end table and opened to a blank page. She wrote Anwar's name at the top and began to write and to pray that he would live out the fullness of his days and peacefully transition to the timeless realm. She also prayed that the reason he'd spoken her name to Farah would come to light. Hana then moved to Farah and Fabia and their children. There was a long list of family members waiting in line for prayer, but Hana stopped after lifting up Khadijah and thought about another little girl—Sadie Neumann.

Tears welled up in Hana's eyes as the image of Sadie on the surveillance tape replayed in her mind. Anyone with a sensitive heart would feel sympathy for Sadie, but Hana's grief felt personal. She tightly gripped the pen in her hand but didn't write a prayer. Instead, she reached out with imaginary arms to embrace a little girl she'd never met in person. She pressed her lips together and closed her eyes for a moment. With a sigh of compassion, she released a final prayer and made a simple notation in her journal: "Prayed for Sadie Neumann—may she find healing, comfort, and a peace that passes understanding."

Awaking the second time shortly after dawn, Hana ground coffee beans for a cup of strong espresso. Occasionally, she brewed traditional Arab coffee flavored with cardamom, but usually she preferred just a simple jolt of caffeine. She might drink another cup later at the office, but the coffee at the office was a different beverage from what she fixed at home. Hana watched Israeli news reports on her computer while eating a breakfast of yogurt, fresh fruit, and sweet pastry. By 7:10 she was out the door and on her way to the office. If she waited another fifteen minutes to leave, the twenty-minute commute would take thirty minutes longer.

A normal workweek for an associate attorney like Hana ran fifty to sixty hours. With the Jezreel Software acquisition moving off the front burner, Hana focused on a project for an Israeli oil and gas company that was seeking to cut a deal with an American partner. Shortly before noon, she stood up and rubbed her eyes. Her phone buzzed. It was Janet.

"Do you want me to pick up something for your lunch?" the

secretary asked. "You've been holed up in there all morning. I can lower your food to you in a basket."

"No, thanks," Hana answered. "I'm going out for a salad."

"You should try that new place beside the Hughes Building. They have a big spread with lots of options."

"Are you going there?"

"I'm in the mood for wood-fired pizza, and I'm meeting a high school friend I haven't seen in fifteen years."

Hana lowered the phone receiver. There was a knock on her door. It was Gladys Applewhite.

"I'm glad you're still here," said the plump, gray-haired woman with the aristocratic southern accent. "I hope you don't have lunch plans."

"Not yet. I was just talking to Janet about where I should go."

"Mr. Lowenstein and Mr. Collins want you to join them. They're finishing brunch in conference room D."

"Do I need my laptop?"

"My only instructions were to bring you." Gladys led the way to a smaller conference room in the interior of the office. It was a windowless space decorated in a spare style. Abstract art adorned the walls. There were ten chairs around a glass-topped conference table. Against one wall was a sleek sideboard with breakfast foods arranged on silver platters beside china plates, cloth napkins, and silver utensils. A young man was loading dirty dishes onto a cart. The only lawyers in the room were Mr. Lowenstein and Mr. Collins.

"Hana, I'm glad Gladys caught you," Mr. Lowenstein said when she appeared. "Join us. Fix a plate. It's self-serve."

"You want me to eat?"

"It would be rude to take you away from lunch and not offer you something. There's plenty."

Hana picked up a plate and placed a few pieces of freshly cut fruit on it.

"Make sure you get a piece of the cinnamon French toast," Mr. Collins added. "It's made from a sliced baguette that tastes like Paris."

Hana found half a piece of the toast and added it to her plate.

"Sit at the head of the table," Mr. Lowenstein said. "Jim and I will sit on either side."

Feeling awkward, Hana sat down in a large chair that threatened to swallow her. She eyed Mr. Collins, whose expression revealed nothing about his thoughts.

"You eat while we talk," Mr. Lowenstein said.

Hana put a piece of pineapple in her mouth.

"The equity partners met this morning," Mr. Collins said. "One of the items on the agenda was the Neumann case."

The news wasn't a shock to Hana, but she was surprised at how quickly things were developing. She swallowed the pineapple and nodded in acknowledgment as she cut off a small piece of French toast.

"Jakob Brodsky and his client met the financial terms I laid out for him the other day after you left the conference room," Mr. Lowenstein said, explaining the cost advance deposit requirements.

"But that wasn't the end of the conversation," Mr. Collins said, glancing at his law partner. "Following a lengthy discussion, the consensus around the table was that the firm shouldn't become involved unless you are willing to take a major role in the case."

Hana swallowed even though her bite of French toast wasn't thoroughly chewed. She drank a few sips of water. "Sorry," she said hoarsely.

"Other lawyers here at the firm will also assist in the case," Mr. Lowenstein said. "But you're the key. I know it was hard for you to watch the surveillance video of the attack. It was tough on me, too. And the way both of us reacted proves why those who are responsible for Gloria Neumann's death and the serious injury to her daughter should be held accountable."

Hana's throat cleared, but she took another quick sip of water to be sure.

"We don't think we should order you to do it," Mr. Collins said. "This type of case wasn't included in your job description. We often tell associates what to do regardless of their personal feelings, but that would be wrong here."

Hana was calm and professional on the outside. Inside, her heart was beating so hard that it echoed in her ears.

"So, I have a choice?" she asked with a glance at Mr. Lowenstein.

"Yes," Mr. Collins replied. "Even though Leon, who only goes to synagogue on the high holy days, mentioned something about God bringing you to the law firm for just this situation."

"And how much time do you spend in church?" Mr. Lowenstein shot back.

"Not enough to invoke God's name in our partner meetings," Mr. Collins replied gruffly.

The exchange between the two men gave Hana a moment to compose herself. "What do you mean by a major role?" she asked.

"Mostly in the investigative stage," Mr. Lowenstein answered. "Once we haul a solvent defendant into a US courtroom, the case is on home turf, and our litigators can take over. You speak Arabic, Hebrew, and English—"

"And French," Mr. Collins added. "Americans are so pathetic in their linguistic limitations."

"I barely know enough French to guess what's on the menu at a fancy restaurant," Mr. Lowenstein said with a smile. "Anyway, you would oversee the legal aspects of the investigation and file any actions or pleadings necessary in Israel to uncover information."

"When I practiced law in Israel I was a solicitor, not a barrister," Hana replied, using the English distinction between a business lawyer and a litigator.

"Then you can hire local Israeli counsel to help you," Mr. Lowenstein said.

Hana felt like she was standing in a tank of water that was inching toward her chin. The emotional stress of working on the Neumann case would be amplified by an unfamiliar legal landscape.

"And I'm sure we'd hire one or more private investigators," Mr. Lowenstein said. "They would report to you."

"What would Jakob Brodsky do?" she asked.

Mr. Lowenstein coughed and cleared his throat. "Stay out of our way as much as possible, with just enough involvement to justify paying him a fee. After our meeting yesterday, I asked Gladys to find out everything she could about him. He handles a lot of cases no lawyer with a decent book of business would touch."

"Nobody wanted to help Ben Neumann," Hana pointed out.

"Brodsky is also in debt up to his eyeballs and barely scraping by financially. I'm surprised he was able to come up with the cost advance deposit we required before we'd consider joining the case."

"I think the client put up all the money," Mr. Collins said.

Hana was puzzled by the level of negativity directed toward Jakob Brodsky by the older lawyers. Mr. Collins checked his watch.

Hana glanced down at her plate. She'd not gone beyond the single bite of French toast and sampling the fruit. Her appetite was gone. "May I have some time to think about it?" she asked.

"Yes, we don't think Brodsky can convince another law firm to help him," Mr. Lowenstein replied. "How much time do you need?"

"A couple of days?"

Lowenstein and Collins looked at each other. "That's fine," Mr. Lowenstein answered.

"There's one thing I need to do before I give an answer," Hana continued.

"What's that?" Mr. Collins asked.

"Meet with Sadie Neumann and her father."

CHAPTER 7

Jakob paced back and forth in front of his desk. He'd notified Leon Lowenstein via email that he had the necessary funds in his trust account, but what really made Jakob nervous was how to communicate the news that Sadie Neumann wouldn't be a party to any lawsuit. Gutting half the damage model might be a deal breaker for a potential cocounsel arrangement that was already as fragile as an antique teacup. Now he was arguing with himself about delaying disclosure of the change.

"It won't be an issue for months," he muttered. "And the investigation will give me time to talk Ben into changing his mind."

His phone buzzed. "Hello," he said.

"Mr. Jakob Brodsky, please," said a woman with a slight accent.

"Speaking."

"This is Hana Abboud at Collins, Lowenstein, and Capella. Is this a convenient time to talk?"

"As good as any," Jakob replied, puzzled as to why an associate lawyer was contacting him. "Have the partners made a decision? I have the money in my trust account."

"Not yet," she replied. "I'd like to meet with Mr. Neumann and his daughter as part of the firm's consideration of the case. Can you make the arrangements for that to happen?"

Jakob hesitated.

"I'm flexible as to time and place," Hana continued. "You would be present, of course. Why don't you look at your calendar so we can coordinate a meeting?"

"Will Mr. Lowenstein be there?" Jakob asked, stalling for time.

"That's not necessary. If the firm agrees to join the case, I'm going to play a major role in the investigative phase."

"Why?" Jakob blurted out. "I got the impression this wasn't something you wanted to have anything to do with."

The phone was silent for several moments.

"Are you there?" Jakob asked.

"Yes."

Another period of silence followed. Ms. Abboud obviously wasn't going to explain her change of mind. Jakob turned to his computer and looked at his calendar.

"Uh, I have openings tomorrow in the afternoon after Sadie gets out of school and again next Monday."

"Tomorrow afternoon works for me."

"Ben can usually leave the store for an hour or so. But I'll have to confirm anything with him first."

"Would you like to meet at your office or mine?"

Impressing Ben with the office layout at Collins, Lowenstein, and Capella would be helpful. "Your office would be better," Jakob replied. "Ben needs to know where it is since we may be spending a lot of time there in the future."

"I'll send my contact information as soon as we hang up."

The call ended. Five seconds later Hana Abboud's name popped up on Jakob's computer screen. He went to the law firm's website, clicked open her biography page, and read every word in an effort to squeeze out any hidden agendas or motivations. One interesting point emerged: the lawyer had worked for two years as a security officer for the Israeli government at Ben Gurion Airport, which must have been the national service activity Hana mentioned during the meeting with Leon Lowenstein. Jakob jotted a few notes on a legal pad.

Ten minutes later, he'd arranged for Ben to meet him in the

reception area of Collins, Lowenstein, and Capella at four forty-five the following afternoon. Ben didn't question Hana Abboud's potential involvement in the case. Instead, he immediately saw that an Arab lawyer might be able to open doors an American Jewish Israeli attorney couldn't.

"It makes me believe they're taking us seriously," Ben said. "And she will know something about the court system in Israel."

"True," Jakob acknowledged. "It could also save a bunch of money by removing the need to hire an Israeli lawyer on an hourly basis since the Lowenstein firm is working on a contingency basis."

Jakob paused before stating what he knew would be the biggest hurdle. "Ms. Abboud wants you to bring Sadie, too," he said.

"To the meeting at the law office? Why is that necessary since she's not going to be involved?"

"She didn't say," Jakob answered. "I was so caught off guard by the call that I didn't ask her. Do you want me to call her back and tell her that Sadie can't come?"

Jakob held his breath.

"No," Ben replied. "She has to be with me anyway since Gloria's mother isn't available to babysit, but I don't want her listening to anything about the attack."

"Understood," Jakob replied with relief. "We'll handle it like we did the other day in my office. Sadie can watch a movie on her tablet while we talk. That seemed to work okay."

"Sometimes it does; sometimes it doesn't."

After the call ended, Jakob leaned back in his chair and rubbed his eyes. Ben sounded much more cooperative today. If Jakob could get past the meeting tomorrow with Hana Abboud in good shape, his plan to convince Ben that Sadie's claims should be included in a potential lawsuit might work.

• • •

Setting aside her other projects, Hana embarked on a crash course in US antiterrorism laws. The Anti-Terrorism Act, enacted by Congress in 1990, enabled an individual who had been "injured in his or her person, property, or business by reason of an act of international terrorism" to file an action in US federal court for recovery of three times their actual damages. "International terrorism" was defined as "activities that . . . involve violent acts or acts dangerous to human life that are in violation of the criminal laws of the United States."

Prior to the September 11, 2001, attacks by al-Qaeda in New York, Washington, DC, and the skies over Pennsylvania, legal actions under the ATA were rare. After that, people started filing lawsuits against organizations that allegedly gave "material support" to those who committed terrorist acts. The most highly publicized claims were against the banks used by terrorist organizations. At first, the courts were reluctant to hold banks responsible for the acts of depositors.

Then a few cases began to go the other way, with the most famous being against Arab Bank, a huge financial institution based in Jordan with offices all over the world. Arab Bank served as the conduit for cash payments made to the families of Hamas suicide terrorists who died while carrying out attacks that killed and maimed hundreds of people. And more importantly, the bank didn't try to hide its actions; rather, it publicly trumpeted them. Ultimately, it paid millions of dollars to settle 527 claims. Living in Israel, Hana knew about Arab Bank's activities, but she'd never examined the cases in detail. She was able to go behind the information available in English and read background data written in Arabic. It was dark and sinister.

Late in the afternoon she took a break and stepped out of her office. There was no current evidence in Jakob Brodsky's thin file of involvement by a bank in the Neumann case. In fact, nothing indicated that Abdul and Tawfik Zadan were anything other than "lone wolf" terrorists.

"Is tonight when you're going to meet the young man from

the church?" Janet asked. "I saw a reminder on your calendar this morning."

"Yes."

"What's his name?"

"Bart Kendall. He works in media, something to do with commercials for women's beauty products."

Janet nodded knowingly. "And you're going to be featured in his next project." She added, "I can totally see you in a hair commercial. Do you know how many women would give a year of their lives for hair like yours?"

"I'm no different from many of the women in my family."

"And we're jealous of them, too." Janet ran her fingers through her mousy brown hair.

"Don't criticize your curls," Hana replied, checking her watch. "I'm not sure if I should go home to change outfits or keep working and wear these clothes—"

"Go home," Janet said. "I mean, there's nothing wrong with what you have on, but that dark blue suit and white blouse is like hanging a huge sign around your neck that shouts, 'I'm a lawyer! I'm a lawyer!'"

Hana smiled. "I am a lawyer."

"Not twenty-four/seven. Tonight, you need to be more feminine."

"You win," Hana said.

"Send me a selfie, please. And include Bart in the photo unless it's too awkward to pull it off."

"This is not really a date. He's interested in learning about Arab culture."

"You're not going to convince me of that," Janet said and rolled her eyes. "Where are you going to dinner?"

"It's in my phone, but I don't remember the name of the restaurant. I checked the menu. It serves gourmet food."

"Don't let him talk you into ordering something exotic that you feel like you have to choke down even if it makes you gag."

"What time should I be home?" Hana asked with a smile.

"How would your real mother answer that question?"

Hana thought about dating protocol in the household in Reineh. "Unless a man lived far away from Reineh, his first meal might be at our house so he could meet my family."

Janet nodded. "I like that. I always wanted to know my father's opinion about the men I dated. He could smell a rat quicker than I could."

• • •

Hana stood in front of her closet trying to decide what to wear. She'd bought a lot of clothes since coming to the United States. Israeli fashion was more European than American, and Hana had accumulated a conservative but stylish wardrobe. She selected a predominantly green outfit with sleek pants and a cream-colored top that let her show off a silk scarf she'd brought with her from Israel. The scarf was over forty years old yet still retained its vibrant colors. She took a selfie and sent it to Janet, who replied with a thumbs-up.

While in law school, Hana had a steady boyfriend who was training to be a radiologist. A lot of doctors and nurses in Israel came from the Christian Arab community, and Hana's family was thrilled that their picky daughter had found a man worthy of her affections. Ibrahim Ghanem grew up in a suburb of East Jerusalem.

Ibrahim and Hana had shared many common interests, including matters of faith, and they began making plans to marry. In more traditional Arab Christian families, even for young professionals, parents communicated betrothal plans via an intermediary who had been mutually agreed upon. An intermediary had been selected and plans set in place for Ibrahim and Hana's wedding in Nazareth followed by a honeymoon in Spain.

But then Ibrahim's father insisted that Hana drop out of law school prior to the wedding and not return until Ibrahim was working as a doctor. Mr. Ghanem argued that it was a necessary move so the young couple could concentrate on their marriage without outside distractions. Hana knew that in reality, her future father-in-law wanted her to abandon her career, start a family, and devote herself to raising a houseful of children. Hana loved children and wanted a family, but the resulting tension with Ibrahim, who wouldn't stand up to his father, soured the relationship. To make matters worse, Hana's mother agreed with Ibrahim's father, thus adding another layer of conflict. Then Hana's father, a quiet man, announced one Saturday evening that he was going to suspend marriage negotiations. Shocked, Hana dissolved in tears of relief. Six months later, Ibrahim was engaged to another woman.

Hana knew there was gossip in Reineh that by taking the job in America she had resigned herself to singleness. Nothing had happened since her arrival to prove the gossipers wrong. Most of the men she'd met had revealed a level of immaturity and self-centeredness that made going to the next level of romance impossible. For the past few months, Hana had stopped mentioning dates when talking to her mother.

The restaurant for her dinner with Bart was located in an older neighborhood close to the center of the city. The tiny parking lot was full, and Hana found an open space a couple of blocks away alongside the curb.

It had been a warm afternoon, but after sunset the air cooled, and it was a pleasant walk up a gradual incline to the restaurant, which was in a 1930s vintage house with painted brick and windows framed in black shutters. The entrance featured a broad porch with seating for those waiting on a table. Bart Kendall was sitting in a chair on the porch waiting for her. He stood as she approached. The stocky young man with a well-groomed sandy beard and kind blue eyes was wearing a casual shirt, sport coat, and olive trousers.

"Did you have any trouble finding the restaurant?" he asked.

"No. Just a parking space, but I'm close by."

The front door opened, and a young woman appeared. "Mr. Kendall? Your table is ready."

Bart held the door for Hana, who followed the hostess to a table for two beside a window that looked out onto a small flower garden. Even in the fading light, Hana could see an array of late spring colors.

"This is nice," she said as they sat down. "Have you been here before?"

"Yes, I discovered it during a photo shoot," Bart answered. "We used the flower garden as a location for a commercial a few weeks ago. I came back for dinner and liked it."

A waiter brought water and handed them menus.

"Any recommendations?" she asked Bart.

"The calamari is the best I've eaten in Atlanta. It's cooked in a Thai chili sauce with red peppers that really make it pop."

Hana's eyes went to a miso-glazed sea bass.

"What would you like this evening?" the waiter asked when he brought them water to drink.

"Calamari with the house special salad," she answered.

"And I'll have the sea bass," Bart said.

"I thought about that too."

"Which means I can share." He grinned at her.

"Thanks for agreeing to come," Bart said after the waiter left. "Make sure you let me know if I say anything stupid."

"What do you mean?"

"I've traveled enough to know that it's a mistake to assume everyone views things the same way as Americans. I embarrassed myself so many times during a trip to Europe a couple of years ago that I was afraid the French were going to kick me out of the country."

"What did you do?"

Bart told Hana two stories, one of which made her laugh so hard she had to cover her mouth. With her knowledge of French, she could appreciate his subtle but significant error.

"It must be crazy switching back and forth between all the languages on your computer keyboards," he said.

"Yes, it wears me out."

"But your English is great."

"Except for the idioms," she answered with a shake of her head. "I've made mistakes as bad as the one you stumbled into in southern France."

Hana told him about her response when first hearing the term "going cold turkey" and seeing "chicken fingers" on a restaurant menu.

"And then there are what I call the positional idioms," she continued. "Things like 'face the music,' 'sit tight,' 'lose touch,' and 'up in the air.'"

"Have you been to France?"

"Only Paris for a short stay, but I've visited Beirut many times, and my family is originally from Lebanon. It was under French control for years, and there's an area in Beirut along the Mediterranean that's like a miniature Paris. But Lebanon and Beirut are much different now than when one of my grandfathers studied at the American School. The political situation has been a mess for years."

"Is there a part of the Middle East where that isn't true?" Bart asked. "Did your family have to leave Lebanon because of the political unrest?"

"No, my ancestors left four hundred years ago and moved to Nazareth when the whole area from Istanbul to Cairo was controlled by the Ottoman Empire."

"Wow. That's a long time ago."

"Not by Middle Eastern standards. 'Old' there means thousands, not hundreds of years."

"Why Nazareth?"

"It was a natural landing spot. There were Christians in Beirut and Christians in Nazareth. Religious affiliation influenced everything. Under Ottoman rule, Arab Christians had dhimmi status as second-class citizens in a Muslim-controlled society. They had to pay a special tax and couldn't ride horses, own weapons, or hold certain jobs. It was less oppressive in areas with a higher percentage of Christians."

The waiter brought the salads, and Hana spent several minutes giving a thumbnail history lesson she'd shared many times with Westerners. She paused. "Are you interested in this?" she asked.

"Totally. This is exactly what I wanted to know more about. And from what I've read, the treatment of non-Christians in Europe during the Middle Ages was just as bad or worse."

When the food arrived, Bart prayed a quick blessing for the meal and cut off a piece of sea bass for Hana before he sampled it himself. She gave him a couple of calamari rings. The sea bass was delicious, and Hana jealously eyed the piece of fish on Bart's plate. She ate a bite of the spicy calamari. To her relief, it was also good.

"I was a European history major in college," Bart said. "Which wasn't exactly perfect preparation for what I do now."

Hana asked about his work, and Bart explained the basic duties of a producer.

"What's the most challenging part of your job?" she asked.

"Dealing with creative people," he replied immediately. "Learning how to play well with others isn't common in the media world, which leads me back to the situation for you and your family in Israel. What kind of oppression and discrimination do you face? And how does the current situation for Arabs compare to life under the Ottoman Turks?"

Hana swallowed a bite of calamari. "How much do you already know about life today in Israel?" she asked.

"Mostly what I've read online. It's clear that the two sides have been going around in circles for decades with no real change in the situation."

"That's true," Hana said with a nod. "But more and more Christian Arabs, especially in my generation, identify as Israelis even though we're not Jewish."

"Really?" Bart asked in surprise.

Hana told him about her two years in national service at the airport, and the educational benefits and free health care she'd received from the government as an Israeli citizen.

"Our family is entrepreneurial," she said. "My father and his brothers own their own business, and my parents could have paid for my upper-level schooling, but it was great not to place that burden on them."

"You're the exception, right?" Bart asked. "Most Arabs don't support the presence of a Jewish state in the Middle East."

"There are four hundred million Arabs in the world, and I'm sure the vast majority oppose the existence of Israel. But if you mean the Arabs who actually live in Israel as citizens, many of them, Christian and Muslim, recognize the benefits of living there. The Western media focus entirely on the people who don't want Israel to exist at all. But if you were given a choice between living in a country ruled by a secular Arab dictator, a government that implemented strict Islamic Sharia law over all aspects of life, and a democracy with freedom of religion, press, speech, et cetera, which would you choose?"

"The democracy."

"And that's especially true for Christian Arabs like me."

Hana ate another bite of calamari. "Are you sure this isn't more than you wanted to hear?" she asked.

"I told you I wanted to learn when I asked you to dinner. You've put a different spin on things."

"It doesn't mean Israel is perfect," Hana said after she'd taken a sip of water. "Arab areas of the country don't always receive services at the same level as Jewish ones, which is wrong. And sometimes I've experienced negative looks and comments when I step into situations where Jews are in the majority. That hurts a lot because I've been a loyal citizen. But even with its faults, Israel is the only country in the entire Middle East where the overall Christian population is growing. The number of Christians in Gaza is tiny, and the Christian population in the area of the West Bank controlled by the Palestinian Authority, like Bethlehem, has been shrinking for years. Christian Arabs in the PA areas are leaving in droves for a better life in Europe or the United States."

"Like you?"

"No," Hana answered emphatically. "My stay in America is temporary. I enjoy my work, but my roots are in Israel."

They ate in silence. Bart seemed troubled.

"This is so different from what the assistant minister at my church has indicated," he said.

Hana instantly suspected what the minister believed. "Does he think the Jews are irrelevant in God's current purposes and future plans?" she asked.

"Yeah, something like that."

"That's not the way I read the Bible. There are promises with multiple applications: to the Jews first and then to the church. Anything else tortures the truth. Imagine how tough it is for an Arab like me to admit there are ways in which the Jews continue to be his chosen people. The beautiful thing is that because I put my faith in the Jewish Messiah, I'm chosen, too."

Bart shook his head. "So much for stereotypes."

"Hearing you say that makes me happy," Hana replied with a smile. "Regardless of what people say about the influence of mass media, human understanding takes place one person at a time."

"Enough," Bart said, holding up his hand. "I know I asked for it, but talking to you is like drinking from a fire hydrant."

"I'm sorry—"

"No, I can just tell you've given this a lot of thought."

"I've had to. For me, it's not theoretical. It touches my whole life." Hana paused. "Tell me more about you and your family."

Hana enjoyed hearing stories about Bart's years growing up in central Ohio. He came from a family of farmers who lived in the same area for multiple generations. Bart was a kind, sensitive man, and the continuity of his family background resonated with Hana. She realized she'd like to get to know him better.

After the meal, Bart walked her down the street to her car. In the back of her mind, Hana rehearsed how she would respond if he asked to see her again. She knew she'd say yes. They reached her car parked beneath an old streetlight with a soft yellow glow.

"You've provided me with much to think about," Bart said.

"And I've enjoyed talking with you—"

"No, you don't understand what I mean. I asked you to dinner because I wanted your help in putting together a video I'm producing for a BDS group based in Atlanta. I thought the project would be a nice change of pace from pumping beauty products. The assistant pastor I mentioned supports Palestinian rights to self-determination and encouraged me to do it. I've studied all this stuff more than I let on, but I played dumb to get you to talk. As an articulate, attractive Arab woman who's lived in Israel, I thought you'd be a perfect spokesperson for my video."

Hana's mouth dropped open. The Boycott, Divestment, and Sanctions movement promoted activities designed to damage the Israeli economy and thus pressure the Israeli government. It was a worldwide phenomenon that, to Hana, smacked of anti-Semitism. In many instances it hurt Arab workers more than Jewish ones. What immediately stung Hana was the producer's silent deception.

"A BDS video?" she managed. "I wouldn't do that."

"I know. The pay is good, but now I'm questioning whether it's the right thing to do." With that, Bart abruptly said good night and walked away.

Hana got in her car and sat for a couple of minutes, wondering if she would have said anything differently if she'd known what was lurking in the back of the producer's mind. She'd shared openly and honestly, even if he hadn't.

CHAPTER 8

Jakob tapped his right foot nervously against the floor. The Neumanns were twenty minutes late, and Ben hadn't responded to repeated texts and two phone calls. There had to be a good reason why they hadn't arrived. A young receptionist sitting behind a sleek glass-and-steel desk turned toward him.

"Ms. Abboud wants to know if you need to reschedule?" she asked.

"Let's give it a few more minutes," Jakob answered.

While he waited, Jakob role-played different ways the meeting might unfold. Sadie was a cute little girl who engendered instant sympathy when she didn't have her nose buried in her tablet. However, the tablet and earbuds would be her babysitter during the meeting. Several more minutes passed.

"Mr. Brodsky," the receptionist said. "I'll be glad to check with Ms. Abboud about rescheduling."

"No!" Jakob replied more forcibly than he intended.

At that moment the door opened, and a harried Ben Neumann entered. He was holding Sadie by the hand.

"Don't ask," he said, holding up his other hand to Jakob. "I felt like I was transported back to 1980, which I don't even remember. I was letting Sadie play on my phone before we left the house, and she dropped it in the toilet. Now it's sitting in a bag of rice. Then a water hose in my new minivan burst and the engine overheated on the way over here. I couldn't let you know I'd be late."

"I know about overheating cars," Jakob replied. He turned to the receptionist. "Please let Ms. Abboud know we're here."

Ben plopped down in a chair. Sadie, wearing her school uniform, crawled into her father's lap and laid her head against his chest.

"Sadie is worn out," Ben said, stroking the little girl's black hair that was sticky with perspiration.

Hana Abboud entered the reception area. She extended her hand to Jakob, who shook it, and then turned toward Ben and Sadie. Ben held his daughter in his arms when he stood. Jakob introduced them. Sadie looked shyly at the Arab lawyer.

"She has pretty hair, like mine," Sadie whispered so loudly in her father's ear that even the receptionist could hear her.

"Thank you," Hana said with a smile. "This way, please."

Instead of going to the large conference room where they'd met with Mr. Lowenstein, they entered a much smaller room with seating for six people around a chrome-and-glass table. One outside wall was glass from floor to ceiling and gave a spectacular view. Sadie scrambled out of her father's arms and stood in front of the transparent wall. The Arab lawyer knelt down on the floor beside the little girl and began pointing out landmarks to her. Jakob and Ben watched.

"And over there on a clear day you can see Stone Mountain," Hana said, pointing to the east. "Have you been there?"

"Yes," Ben answered. "I took her to the top in the big cable car a few months ago."

Sadie made a couple of comments about the outing. Her most vivid memory centered on a blue-colored frozen drink.

"Which was pure sugar and turned her tongue aqua until the next day," Ben said.

Jakob cleared his throat in anticipation of a change in the conversation. He turned to Ben. "Did you remember to bring Sadie's tablet?" he asked.

Ben struck his forehead with his hand. "That's why she was playing on my phone. I let the battery on the tablet run down."

"That's not a problem," Hana said.

Sadie was leaning against the lawyer and resting her hand on Hana's shoulder.

"But we can't talk about anything substantive with the child in the room," Jakob protested.

Hana didn't say anything. Instead, she returned to her conversation with Sadie. This was one of the more unusual client conferences of Jakob's career, and it was getting stranger by the second.

"Mr. Neumann," Hana began.

"Please, call me Ben," the client responded.

"And I'm Hana," the lawyer said.

"Hana," Sadie repeated with the same intonation, strongly emphasizing the final "a."

"Children are such incredible mimics," Hana said with a smile.

"Yeah, she's not yet seven, but I believe Sadie is going to have a knack for languages," Ben replied. "Verbally, she's off the charts."

"When will they start teaching her another language?" Hana asked.

"She's learning Hebrew at school, and they'll add Spanish next year in second grade."

"She goes to a Jewish school?"

"Yes."

Hana said something to Sadie that Jakob didn't understand. The child immediately replied. Hana followed up with a longer sentence that produced another answer. They went back and forth for a minute.

"You're right," Hana said to Ben. "She has linguistic ability."

"How many languages do you speak?" Ben asked.

"Arabic, Hebrew, English, and French," Hana answered, getting to her feet. "And I used them all when I worked as a security officer at Ben Gurion Airport. French is my weakest, but it was good enough that I could question travelers coming in from French-speaking parts of the world."

Hana sat in a chair. Instead of returning to her father, Sadie started to climb onto the lawyer's lap.

"No, Sadie," Ben said. "Come here."

"It's okay," Hana answered as Sadie confidently positioned herself. "Holding her makes me think about my nieces in Israel. I miss them a lot."

Jakob had given up trying to figure out the direction of the conversation, but he was glad it seemed positive. He stayed silent and waited.

"What questions do you have?" Hana asked Ben.

Sadie turned and gently pulled Hana's face close to hers and whispered in her ear. Hana smiled.

"What did she say to you?" Ben asked.

"You tell," Hana said to the little girl. "But say it in English, not Hebrew."

"I asked if Hana would eat ice cream with us," Sadie answered.

Ben smiled. "Fine with me."

Hana stroked the little girl's hair. Sadie was leaning against the female lawyer with her eyes closed. Jakob felt like he'd parachuted into a therapy session.

"Why are we meeting with you instead of Mr. Lowenstein?" Ben asked Hana.

"The partners left it up to me to decide whether the firm is going to become cocounsel on the case. I wanted to meet with you and Sadie before giving my recommendation." Hana gently touched Sadie's back. "Seeing her is all the encouragement I need."

Jakob was completely mystified.

"I think I understand," Ben replied slowly. "But tell me exactly why you would be willing to get involved in the lawsuit. Not on behalf of the firm, but you."

"I am an Arab, and I am an Israeli. What took place that day in Jerusalem was inexcusable and horrible. No amount of money will compensate you and Sadie for your loss, but I'm willing to work to see justice done even if it's unpopular for me to do so." Hana placed her hand on the top of Sadie's head. "Above all else, I want her to know that a person like me was willing to help and bless her, not hurt or harm her."

"That's—" Ben started and then stopped before finishing, "more than I could have hoped for."

"I'm good with it," Jakob interjected. He was interested in results, not rationale.

"It's amazing," Ben continued, "to find two lawyers like you and Jakob who want to help not just with a lawsuit, but because you care about us as a family. That means a lot. It's the sort of thing that would please Gloria."

"Gloria is my mama," Sadie said to Hana. "A bad man killed her and hurt me."

"I know," Hana answered. "But I think part of her is alive in you."

"That's what my grammy says," Sadie replied.

"Gloria's mother," Ben explained.

Ben turned to Jakob. "I'm satisfied if you are."

Jakob looked at Hana, who was watching him with intent black eyes that seemed to bore into his soul. "We need to let Hana know about your decision regarding Sadie," he said to Ben.

"What about me?" Sadie asked, sitting up straighter and staring at her father. "Are you going to send me to that other school? I don't want to leave my friends."

"No, no," Ben replied.

"Ben doesn't want Sadie to be a party to the lawsuit," Jakob said, trying to make it sound like a minor point.

"Daddy, he's not talking about my birthday party, is he?" Sadie asked anxiously.

"No, sweetie. It's something else."

"Can Hana come to my party?"

"Maybe, but that's something we'll talk about later."

"It's okay," Hana said to Sadie before turning to Ben and Jakob. "But this is a new development that I'll have to discuss with Mr. Lowenstein."

"It's all about her safety," Ben said. "Which I can explain later if you like."

Hana nodded. "I understand, but this is outside the scope of my authority to accept."

Jakob felt a wave of disappointment threaten to sweep over him. He fended it off by changing the subject. "We're ready to pay our portion of the cost advance immediately upon signing the cocounsel agreement," he offered.

"Mr. Lowenstein sent me a memo about that prior to our meeting," Hana answered. "Let me see if he's available to discuss this change in the scope of the claim. I'd like to give you an answer today if possible."

There was a phone on a side table in the conference room. Hana picked it up and pressed several numbers. "Is Mr. Lowenstein available?" she asked. "It's about the Neumann matter."

"Thanks," she said after a pause. "I'll be right there."

"Can I come?" Sadie asked.

"Not this time," Hana answered. "I need to talk to my boss."

"I hope he's nicer than Daddy's boss," Sadie said. "He makes him work even if we're supposed to go someplace fun."

• • •

From the moment she first saw the little girl in the reception area, Hana felt a deep tenderness well up in her heart for the motherless child. It was both intensely sweet and disturbingly confusing. She knew from her experience in the night that she was supposed to meet Sadie, but she hadn't anticipated the depth of her reaction. It had taken every ounce of willpower she possessed not to burst into tears.

She reached Mr. Lowenstein's office. The senior partner was sitting behind his desk with his necktie loosened and his hair slightly mussed. Leon Lowenstein collected miniature antique sailing ships that he displayed under glass covers. Some of the rigging for the ships seemed so fragile that it would dissolve if exposed to the atmosphere. He spoke before she did.

"Hana, we represent a shipping company caught between two feuding underwriters who can't agree on allocation of risk for a shipment bound for Mumbai. Two vessels have to leave Antwerp within the next twenty-four hours. The value of the cargo is over fifty million dollars. Our client wants to go through the Suez Canal instead of around Cape Horn. That means they'll have to run the Somalia gauntlet. We're scrambling to bring on extra security and obtain approval for the route. Anyway, there's nothing I can do now but wait on a return phone call. What's on your mind? Gladys said it was important."

Hana summarized her conversation with Jakob Brodsky and Ben Neumann. Mr. Lowenstein listened with his chin almost touching his chest. He raised his head when she mentioned the requirement that they leave Sadie out of the lawsuit.

"Do you think the best thing to do is shut this down before we get started?" Mr. Lowenstein asked.

"That's why I'm here. To ask you."

"Who has the better claim? The father or the daughter?"

Ben lost a wife. Sadie lost a mother. Both had scars on the inside, but Sadie bore one on the outside.

"The daughter," Hana said.

"I disagree," the senior partner replied.

"You do?" Hana's eyes widened. "Why?"

"Ben Neumann lost his wife, which will justify a substantial damage claim. And common decency says it's prudent to minimize a small child's exposure to the kind of publicity a case like this will generate. Remember, I have granddaughters of my own, so I understand where the father is coming from. The question is whether there is enough left to warrant proceeding."

"I want to do it," Hana said.

"I've seen that in your eyes the whole time you've been sitting here," Mr. Lowenstein said. "And when I see that determination in a lawyer's eyes, it gets my attention. Let's take the next step, which is an investigation. Brodsky and the client will fund that part of the litigation. Except for your time, the risk to the firm is low."

"Do the partners have to agree?"

"I'll send around a memo, but I think it will be fine. Go ahead and sign a cocounsel agreement."

"Thank you," Hana said.

Mr. Lowenstein ran his fingers through his gray hair. "I hope you can say that to me a year from now."

Hana returned to the conference room and delivered the good news. Ben didn't seem surprised, but Jakob was clearly shocked.

"What did you say to convince him?" he blurted out.

"He's a grandfather with granddaughters. I think that was as important as anything. If you're ready, I'll modify the cocounsel agreement and bring it in for your signatures."

Jakob and Ben looked at each other and nodded. Hana turned toward the door.

"I want to go with you," Sadie said. "You can show me where you work."

"It's up to you," Ben said to Hana with a wave of his hand.

Hana squeezed Sadie's hand as they walked down the hallway. The child seemed completely at peace. They reached Janet's desk.

"Janet, this is Sadie Neumann," Hana said.

"Hi, Sadie," Janet replied, laying her dictation earbuds on the desk. "It looks like you've found a new friend."

Hana explained to Janet the changes needed in the cocounsel agreement.

"I'm on it," Janet replied.

Hana took Sadie into her office. The little girl walked around the desk and climbed into the modern executive chair.

"Does this chair go in circles?" Sadie asked.

"Yes." Hana spun her around a few times.

"Faster, please," Sadie said.

Hana spun the chair slightly faster. Sadie put her head down and closed her eyes.

"Okay, the ride is over," Hana said as the chair slowed.

Sadie looked around the room and spotted the picture of Khadijah on the corner of the desk. "Is that your little girl?" she asked.

"No, my niece. Her name is Khadijah."

Sadie repeated the name. Hana added the Arabic for "She is my niece," which Sadie mimicked perfectly.

"Maybe you should add Arabic to Hebrew and Spanish," Hana said.

Janet brought in the cocounsel agreement. "It was a quick fix," the assistant said and then turned to Sadie. "You're a doll baby."

"No, I'm a girl," Sadie replied.

"That's right," Hana said to Janet. "A very smart girl."

Sadie sat in Hana's lap while Hana checked the revisions in the document. They then retraced their steps to the small conference room.

"Here you go," Hana said, handing the agreement to Jakob.

Sadie resumed her place on Hana's lap. Hana turned the chair so that she and the child could look out the wall window again.

"Do you see how small the people look on the sidewalk?" Hana asked.

Sadie leaned forward and peered down. "Can they see us?" she asked.

"No, there's something on the outside of the window that lets us see out but makes it hard for them to see in during the daytime."

"But they can see us if it's dark outside and the light is on in here?"

"Yes."

"That's the way it is at my house. I keep the blinds closed so that no bad people can see into my room. Daddy bought a box that calls the police if any bad people try to come inside our house."

"That's because he cares about you."

"Do you have one of those boxes at your house?"

"No," Hana said. "I rent my house. Do you know what that means?"

Sadie shook her head.

"I don't own the house. Someone else does, and I pay them money every month so I can stay there."

"You could stay at our house for free," Sadie noted. "We have two bedrooms that no one sleeps in except when my nana or my grammy spends the night. My favorite room has light blue walls. Would you like to come over and see it?"

"Sadie," Ben cut in. "You need to let Ms. Abboud decide where she wants to live."

"Ms. Abboud?" Sadie asked. "I thought your name was Hana."

"It is for you."

"The agreement looks fine," Jakob said.

Hana swiveled around in the chair and faced Ben. "Any questions?"

"No, I'll leave the paperwork up to you lawyers. I'm trying to figure out how I'm going to explain to Sadie that she shouldn't invite you to live with us without asking me first."

"Could you come to my birthday party?" Sadie asked.

"I'm not sure," Hana answered, looking toward Ben for help.

"I'll send you an invitation as soon as I finish coloring it," Sadie continued. "Daddy, I have two left in the box you bought me."

After adding his signature to the document, Jakob slid the cocounsel agreement across the table to Hana. "Would you make a copy for me?"

"Of course." Hana gently lifted Sadie off her lap and quickly left the room as tears threatened her eyes. Through bleared vision she signed the agreement on a small worktable next to the copy machine nearest the conference room. No child, regardless of the reason or supposed justification, was a legitimate object of terror. Absent Gloria Neumann's instinctive, sacrificial love, this could have been a double death case.

As she slipped copies of the agreement into separate envelopes for Jakob and Ben, Hana thought about how Sadie represented the many other children maimed or killed or orphaned over the past seventy years since the founding of Israel. Jewish, Arab, Christian, Muslim, Druze—children in the wrong place at the wrong time when bullets were fired, rockets flew, or bombs dropped.

Children who bore no guilt yet suffered great loss.

Hana returned to the conference room. Sadie beamed when she appeared. Hana managed a slight smile but couldn't escape how severely Sadie's own smile dwindled when it reached the scar at the corner of her mouth. It was the smile of an overcomer who didn't fully understand what she had to overcome.

CHAPTER 9

Before leaving Collins, Lowenstein, and Capella, Sadie insisted that her father take a photo of her with Hana on Jakob's phone and then send it to the lawyer so Hana could "remember what I look like."

"I'll be glad to give you and Sadie a ride wherever you need to go," Jakob said when they were standing in front of the elevator. "I don't need to go back to the office."

"Are you sure?" Ben asked. "We'll be trapped in rush-hour traffic."

"That's true in every direction."

"If you could drop us off at the mall near my in-laws' house, that would be great," Ben said. "Gloria's father can pick us up there."

"You mean Poppy?" Sadie asked as the elevator doors opened.

"Yes."

"I want to see him," Sadie said. "And tell him about Hana."

"Ms. Abboud made quite an impression on Sadie," Jakob said as they walked toward the parking garage.

"Yes," Ben agreed. "It's happened before. Women meet Sadie and are instantly drawn to her. This time, the feeling was mutual." Leaning over and speaking in a voice only Jakob could hear, he continued, "The birthday party thing really threw me for a loop. If Hana shows up, people will immediately assume we're dating. Right or wrong, that would create a whole lot of other questions."

They reached Jakob's car.

"Where's my booster seat?" Sadie asked her father.

"In our car. You'll still be buckled in and safe."

After exiting the parking garage, Jakob eventually turned right into a stream of slow-moving traffic. The navigation app on his phone predicted a forty-five-minute drive to the rendezvous spot with Ben's father-in-law.

"How long will it take your father-in-law to drive to the mall?"

"Five minutes."

"I could take you directly to his house."

"No, Sadie will enjoy grabbing a bite to eat with her poppy."

"I want fried chicken," the little girl said.

"She loves fried chicken," Ben said to Jakob. "And not just the ordinary kind. She wants it spicy."

"I like spicy chicken, too," Jakob said, glancing in the rearview mirror at Sadie.

Sadie was staring out the window. "What is Hana doing now?" she asked.

"She's a lawyer like Mr. Jakob," Ben said. "She's probably talking to people she helps or writing letters to judges."

"Or entering her time for the day," Jakob said to Ben. "Most lawyers at firms like that bill by the hour. It's rare for them to work on a contingency case."

"Would you please call Hana for me?" Sadie asked her father. "I want to FaceTime."

"No, we need to let her work," Ben said and then turned to Jakob. "She FaceTimes a lot with her poppy, nana, grammy, and grandad. If I'd let them, they'd buy her a phone and put it on their plan, but she's only six."

"I'm almost seven," Sadie responded. "Liza has a phone. She uses it to talk to her nana."

"While you're at school?" Ben asked sharply.

"Yes, it's okay. The teacher doesn't know about it."

Ben turned sideways in his seat so he could look directly into

Sadie's eyes. "I know what we're going to talk about tonight when it's bedtime."

. . .

Hana opened the photo of herself and Sadie. In the picture Hana was sitting in a conference room chair with the little girl standing beside her and resting her hand casually on Hana's shoulder. Janet appeared in the doorway.

"Was Mr. Neumann smitten with you as much as his daughter was?"

Janet's question raised an issue Hana hadn't considered. She showed Janet the photo on her phone.

"No, it was all about me and Sadie."

"It would be for me, too," Janet admitted as she stared at the photo and touched her own face at the place where Sadie's scar began and ran her finger to the corner of her mouth.

"Yes," Hana said, acknowledging Janet's empathy. "And then there are the invisible scars on the inside that no one can see."

"Maybe you can be part of her healing."

"I hope so."

"Oh, how was your date last night?" Janet asked.

Hana told her about her conversation with Bart Kendall. When she got to the end, the assistant gasped. "What? I would have slapped his face off!"

"Maybe I'm making it sound worse than it was."

"No, it was worse than you're telling," Janet said. "I'm going to mark his name off the list."

"You have a list?"

"Not yet, but if I do, his name won't be on it." Janet turned and left with a huff aimed at Bart.

Hana's phone buzzed. It was Mr. Lowenstein, who asked, "Any other surprises on the Neumann matter?"

"No. Sadie is adorable, and I think Ben will be easy to work with. The cocounsel agreement is signed, and Jakob Brodsky is going to transfer the cost advance money tomorrow."

"I sent an email to the equity partners after you left my office, and a majority wrote back and gave approval to proceed. Hire a private investigator and book a flight to Israel to get things moving."

"Go to Israel now?"

"I trust your eyes and your brain to give me reliable information. Also, begin developing your own relationship with the client independent of Jakob Brodsky. I'm not sold on his contribution to the claim, and I want you to be on solid footing with Ben Neumann if we need to cut ties with Brodsky later on."

Mr. Lowenstein's mind was rapidly moving in unexpected directions. Hana wasn't sure exactly how to react.

"Sadie wants me to join them for ice cream as soon as possible and attend her birthday party."

"Excellent. You won her over quickly."

"It was mutual."

"Set up an ice cream date. Pay for it as a business expense." Mr. Lowenstein paused. "Do you have any initial thoughts about an individual investigator or a firm to interview?"

"No," Hana said. "But I can begin with the contacts I made when I worked at the airport."

"Sounds good. Provide me with regular updates when there's something worth passing along."

• • •

During the stop-and-go commute to the mall, Sadie fell asleep in the rear seat of the car.

"What happens next in the case?" Ben asked.

"There will be strategy meetings," Jakob answered vaguely. "I have ideas for the investigative stage that I'll pass along to Hana and

Leon Lowenstein. We'll divide the labor, but I'll have more time to work on the case than they do. The fact that Hana speaks Arabic and Hebrew should be a plus."

"She's passionate about helping."

"Yeah, and that's good. I'd hoped we'd cover next steps in the case today, but this was a meet-and-greet session."

Ben turned in his seat and glanced at Sadie. "Especially for Sadie. She's going to bug me about calling Hana. Once Sadie fixates on something, I think she's tougher to distract than a typical six-year-old."

"Or almost seven as she puts it," Jakob said.

"Over there is fine," Ben said as he pointed to the south side of the mall. "That's close to the place where Sadie and her grandfather like to eat."

Jakob waited for a pickup truck to get out of the way so he could move forward.

Ben leaned over the seat and patted Sadie on the knee. "Ready to see Poppy?" he asked.

Sadie opened her eyes and stretched her arms. "Yes."

Jakob handed Ben the envelope containing an extra copy of the cocounsel agreement.

"Thanks for going out of your way to give us a ride," Ben said.

Jakob watched father and daughter walk hand in hand toward the mall. Hearing Hana's words and watching her reaction to Sadie had reinforced something Jakob already knew—there was something unique about the Neumann case.

• • •

Hana arrived home and set a pot of homemade soup she'd made a few days earlier on the stove to warm. While she waited, she went outside to refill a finch feeder she'd recently hung from a tree limb. She'd been able to attract a steady stream of bright yellow finches with an occasional purple one thrown in.

The sun dipped below the tree line and cast long shadows across the small yard in front of her house. While she was pouring tiny black seeds into the plastic tube, she heard a rustle in the heavily wooded area at the edge of the property. She peered in the direction of the sound, expecting a squirrel to emerge and scamper up a nearby tree with a nut in its mouth. The sound grew louder, followed by a long, low moan that made the hair on the back of Hana's neck stand up.

One of her neighbors had recently posted signs on several nearby telephone poles warning of a rabid fox and giving the phone number for the city animal control unit. Hana glanced over her shoulder toward the door of the house and prepared to run if a crazed fox dashed out into the open. With a louder crash and scuffle, a furry animal rolled out of the woods into the fading sunlight. It wasn't a fox; it was a black-and-white puppy.

The dog shook some dead leaves and twigs from its fur and walked over to Hana. It was a male, with a thick coat and oversize feet that promised an impending growth spurt. Hana rubbed the dog's neck. There was no collar. It had either wandered away from home or been abandoned.

Individual pet ownership was less common in Israel than in the US, and there were no domestic animals in the large house in Reineh where Hana grew up. Most of the dogs she saw as a child were half-wild animals that foraged on household garbage. The puppy began to furiously lick Hana's fingers with his thick pink tongue.

"Okay, okay," Hana said in English. "It is nice to meet you, too."

Thoughts of the rabid fox on the loose in the neighborhood made Hana feel protective. She carried the puppy into the house. Taking a bowl from the cupboard, she filled it with water and placed it on the kitchen floor. The dog buried its nose in the bowl and rapidly lapped up the water.

"You're thirsty," Hana said.

There was a drainage ditch at the rear of the neighborhood, but it filled with water only during rainstorms. If she turned him loose, Hana wasn't sure where the lost animal would find his next drink of water, much less something to eat. The puppy lifted a paw and placed it in the middle of the remaining water in the bowl. The water turned slightly brown.

Hana carried the puppy into the bathroom and placed him in the tub. To her surprise the dog didn't try to escape but sat down and waited for the water level to rise.

"You've had a bath before and liked it," she said.

When the dog's fur was damp, Hana squeezed out a generous portion of expensive shampoo and made a thick lather. Once the puppy had been thoroughly washed, she used a handheld shower nozzle to rinse off the suds. The dog seemed to love every opportunity to interact with water. Hana used an old towel to dry him, but that didn't keep the puppy from vigorously shaking himself from head to tail. The fragrance of the shampoo filled the bathroom.

Returning to the kitchen, Hana found a few pieces of thin-sliced roast beef and placed them on a plate on the floor. The dog scarfed down the meat. Hana realized she was woefully unprepared for a four-legged guest. Grabbing her purse, she picked up the dog and walked outside to her car. It was now dark. When she flipped on the car's headlamps, she thought she saw a pair of glowing eyes in the wooded area the puppy had emerged from. The eyes disappeared, but not before causing Hana to decide there was no way she could send the puppy back into the forbidding forest, even if it was only a hundred feet deep.

The dog curled up on the passenger seat as Hana drove out of the neighborhood. It was a five-minute drive to the local supermarket. Leaving the puppy in the car with the windows cracked open, Hana bought several types of dry dog food, cans of processed food, a metal bowl, a red collar, a nylon leash, and an orange chew toy. Returning, she found the puppy still curled up on the seat. His nose twitched and he let out a quick bark when she placed the bags of dog food in front of him on the floor of the car.

Once home, Hana poured a generous portion of dry food into a metal bowl. The puppy noisily munched the nuggets, which was a relief because Hana didn't relish the odor of canned dog food. When he finished, the dog trotted to the front door of the house and scratched. Hana put the collar around his neck and attached the leash. They went outside, and the puppy promptly did his business in the grass a couple of feet from the door. Inside, the little dog flipped over onto his back and wiggled back and forth on an area rug that covered part of the living room floor. His actions reminded Hana that she didn't know if there was a prohibition in her lease regarding pets.

Hana kept her important papers in an antique desk. Pulling out the lease, she found what she was looking for on page 3 beneath the heading "Pets." By the end of the paragraph, she knew there was no problem having a bird in a cage, but the presence of a dog or a cat on the premises triggered a hefty deposit. Hana knew it would be the first of many costs if she began the adventure of pet ownership.

The dog had moved from wiggling on the rug to sniffing every piece of furniture. Hana knelt down and scratched his belly. The dog was adorable. Hana's heart melted, and her head surrendered. However, before adopting him she knew she should post flyers on the telephone poles beneath the rabid fox notices and ask if anyone had lost a black-and-white puppy. She took a photo of the dog on her phone and printed out the flyers. Twenty minutes later, she returned to the house, finding the dog asleep. He popped up when she entered, gave a sharp bark, and wiggled excitedly in greeting.

"What will I call you?" Hana asked as the dog barked again, softer this time.

Hana knelt and scratched the puppy behind his ears. She smiled as inspiration came. "Leon," she said. "I'm sure Mr. Lowenstein won't mind letting you borrow his name."

...

After spending a couple of hours researching terrorist networks through both English- and Russian-language portals, Jakob logged off his computer. He'd located another reference to Gloria Neumann's murder originating in Chechnya. The writer of the blog extolled the brave acts of Abdul and Tawfik Zadan and called for the death of "all Jews and other infidel dogs." However, once again, the comment was by an individual who didn't claim any allegiance or membership to a group.

To relax in the evenings, Jakob usually watched soccer on TV. He subscribed to a service that let him follow matches in the English Premier League, Spanish La Liga, German Bundesliga, Italian Serie A, Russian Premier League, and US Major League Soccer. Jakob kept his Russian comprehension sharp by listening to the fast-talking announcers. He didn't understand Spanish or Italian, but when a player in those leagues scored a goal, the announcers celebrated with the enthusiasm usually reserved for a winning lottery ticket.

Spartak Moscow was a perennial contender for the national championship, and tonight was a big match between Spartak and CSKA Moscow, another powerful squad. Jakob knew the names of all the starting players on both teams. Because the game was broadcast on delay, he had to resist the urge to check online for the eventual winner.

He ate a bite of pizza and propped up his feet on a small table. His black leather couch was positioned perfectly in front of the massive video screen mounted on the wall. Sound bombarded him from multiple angles in the room and produced a realistic experience of being present in the stadium. The fans for the teams were yelling familiar chants.

Jakob's phone lit up with an incoming call. It was Butch Watson.

"Jakob, the twins are here!"

"Congratulations. Is everyone okay?"

"Yeah, awesome. One boy is six pounds ten ounces, and the other is six pounds four ounces. Can you believe Nelle was carrying that much beef around in her belly?"

Jakob didn't want to go where Butch's description beckoned him. The last time Jakob saw Nelle, he'd wondered how the petite blonde could walk upright without tipping over.

"That's amazing," Jakob said and pumped his fist as the goalie for Spartak knocked away a shot. "Thanks for calling."

Butch continued, "They were born this morning, and I've not been able to get away from the hospital since then. Nelle's parents are supposed to be here to help out, but they've been delayed until tomorrow. I hate to ask you to do this, but a four-hundred-dollar baby monitoring system was delivered to our house thirty minutes ago, and I'm worried somebody might swipe it if it's left outside the door. We've lost a couple of packages to thieves recently."

"Did you file a police report?"

"Yeah, but you know how that goes. Is there any way you could run over there and put it inside the apartment for us? I tracked the delivery and confirmed it's there. I'd go over myself, but when one of the boys is asleep the other one is wide awake. The nurses want us to start getting used to double trouble from the beginning."

Butch and Nelle lived twenty minutes away from Jakob's new apartment, in a much sketchier neighborhood.

"Sure," Jakob replied. "I was just watching soccer on TV, but I can take a break."

"Thanks. You know where we hide the spare key, right?"

"Behind the holly bush at the corner of the building?"

"Yeah. Thanks a bunch. Nelle is really worried about the monitoring stuff."

"I'm on my way," Jakob said. "I'll text you when I've put it inside."

Jakob walked quickly down three flights of steps to the underground garage where he parked his car.

Four blocks south of his apartment complex the neighborhoods deteriorated and then improved for several blocks before going back down again, revealing the uneven nature of city renewal. Built in the 1940s, the apartments where Butch and Nelle lived would probably be slated for destruction within a few years. The Watsons' unit was at the back side of the complex. Jakob pulled in beside Nelle's minivan. Someone had tied two blue balloons to one of the side mirrors to welcome the babies. Jakob took a quick picture of the balloons on his phone and sent it to Butch.

Jakob identified the holly bush, squeezed behind it, and dug through the pine needles in the dark until he found a tiny metal box that contained Butch's spare key. He walked up the steps to the apartment. A large cardboard box covered the welcome mat. Unlocking the door, he placed the box inside. It was bulky but not very heavy.

The inside of the apartment was chaotic, probably due to a quick departure for the hospital. Jakob checked the kitchen. The sink overflowed with dirty dishes. There wasn't a dishwasher in the unit, and he concluded that Butch and Nelle had better find a new place to live fast.

Jakob filled the sink with hot soapy water and began to wash the dishes. He spent the next thirty minutes cleaning the kitchen, including running a mop over the floor. He kept his own apartment meticulously clean. Butch's law office was always a mess, and neither he nor Nelle valued tidiness at home. Maybe that would make them the perfect parents for twins. When he finished, Jakob moved the box into the living room. There were piles of clean clothes on the couch, but he left them where they lay. He wasn't going to fold Butch's underwear.

Leaving the apartment, Jakob locked the door and stepped to the top of the stairway. The security light was out, and he had to feel his way forward a couple of steps. Suddenly, everything went black.

CHAPTER 10

When Hana slipped out of bed to pray in the middle of the night, Leon groaned and twitched but didn't wake up. When she returned an hour later, he'd inched his way up the bed and buried his head beneath the edge of her pillow. She gently moved him to the side. Listening to his breathing, she lay awake longer than usual. She woke up with a start when a wet tongue licked her left cheek. Leon let out a good-morning bark. Slipping on a robe, Hana took him outside on his leash and then filled his food bowl before brewing a cup of coffee. Checking her email, she found she hadn't received any responses to the notices she'd posted on the telephone poles.

In the light of a new day there were plans to implement if she was going to keep a pet. While she drank her coffee, she checked dog boarders in the area and quickly discovered admittance was contingent on proof of up-to-date vaccinations and a certification of health from a veterinarian. She fired off a quick email to Mr. Collins and Mr. Lowenstein letting them know she would be a few hours late to work to attend to a personal matter but would make up the time before the end of the week. She sent a second email to Janet informing her of what was really going on.

Four hours later, Hana dropped off a disgruntled Leon, still pouting at the insult of multiple needles piercing his skin, at a pricey day boarder for dogs. The vet informed Hana that the rescued animal had a multi-limbed family tree, which included doses of golden retriever, Saint Bernard, Labrador, and other yet-to-be discerned breeds that would result in a full-grown animal weighing at least eighty pounds.

"He wasn't living in the woods very long," the vet said after he'd examined Leon. "It's a good thing he found you. A puppy this young would only last a few days."

Hana looked into Leon's soulful eyes that seemed filled with unspoken gratitude.

"But he's healthy," the vet continued. "No hip problems or anything else I can see. There's a lot to be said for hybrid vigor."

Armed with free pamphlets and proof of vaccinations in her purse, Hana filled out paperwork at the dog boarder, which seemed more like a preschool for kids than a kennel for dogs. She passed on the invitation for a free tour and quickly left with an app loaded on her phone that would allow her to watch Leon throughout the day. It was almost noon when she arrived at the office.

"You're a mommy!" Janet exclaimed when Hana appeared.

"Quiet!" Hana held her index finger to her lips. "That sounds wrong."

"You may as well be," Janet replied in a loud whisper. "First, a cute little girl falls in love with you, and now you have a puppy! Your world is getting a lot more crowded in a beautiful way. Did you take a bunch of pictures of the dog? I want to see them."

"Of course! I can even show you what he's doing right now."

Within thirty seconds, she and Janet had their heads close together watching Leon play with a rope chew toy. He was sucking the frayed ends like a baby's pacifier.

"He's adorable," Janet said. "I totally get why you fell for him. He looks a lot like a dog our family owned when I was a child. We called him Buddy. Have you named your pup?"

Hana glanced over her shoulder before replying. "Leon," she whispered.

Janet's eyes widened. "In honor of Mr. Lowenstein? Are you going to tell him?"

"Maybe," Hana answered slowly.

The phone on Hana's desk buzzed, and she quickly stepped into her office to answer it.

"Ben Neumann calling," the receptionist said.

Before answering, Hana clicked open the calendar on her computer so she could schedule the ice cream date.

"I'm calling about Jakob Brodsky," Ben began. "He was mugged last night and is in the hospital."

Hana didn't know the meaning of "mugged" except that it was clearly bad. "What happened?" she asked.

"He was attacked and robbed. His receptionist told me when I called the office a few minutes ago."

"Attacked and robbed?" Hana repeated as she absorbed the news.

"Yes, but I don't know the extent of his injuries." Ben paused. "He's in Piedmont Hospital. I'm going to try to see him, but it's going to be tough because I don't have a babysitter for Sadie."

"Thanks for letting me know," Hana replied. "Please keep me updated."

"Will do."

No matter where a person lived, the world could, in a split second, become a dangerous, life-threatening place. Hana delivered the news to Janet.

"I'll find out what happened," Janet responded. "I have a close friend who works with the Atlanta Police Department. She can pull the incident report and fill me in on the details."

"Where does the word 'mugging' come from?"

"I have no idea about the history of the word," Janet answered. "Except that it means a person has been assaulted and sometimes robbed in a public place."

Hana spent the next three hours working on matters assigned to her by Mr. Collins. It was mentally taxing as she jumped back and forth between English, Hebrew, and Arabic. When she finally took a break, she logged on to the app for the doggie day care and checked on Leon. He was in a pen with two other puppies. The youngsters were chasing each other in happy circles. Janet appeared in her doorway.

"I heard back from my friend at the APD. Brodsky was attacked at an apartment complex not far from the midtown area. The file indicates he suffered head injuries from 'blunt force trauma.' No one has been arrested."

"How serious was the head injury?"

"Undetermined. Piedmont Hospital isn't far from where you live. Are you thinking about visiting him?"

"No, I've only met him twice and barely know him. I don't think it would be proper for me to do that."

"Proper? This is America. You can do whatever you like."

Janet returned to her desk, and Hana resumed working on a highly technical specification sheet that all parties to a multinational agreement had to approve. By five o'clock she felt like she'd worked eight hours when in fact she'd billed only five and a half. She considered pushing on into the night, but the new responsibility for Leon made her hesitate. If she picked the dog up later than six o'clock, she had to pay an extra service charge.

"You were really grinding away in there today," Janet said. "Did you generate a lot of work for me?"

"Not until you learn how to type on an Arabic keyboard."

"That's a steep learning curve for a girl who grew up in Portland, Maine." Janet's computer screen went blank. "Are you going by the hospital to see Jakob Brodsky?"

"You think I should?"

"Yeah. I'm not saying God told me or anything, but I can't get it out of my mind."

Hana hesitated. "I have to pick up Leon and buy a few more things. No one has come forward to claim him."

"Sure, that's your first priority."

• • •

With a new metal kennel wedged in the back seat of her car, Hana pulled into the parking lot for the doggie day care center. Any concerns she'd had about Leon recognizing her or not wanting to leave his new friends evaporated when she saw him. His entire body began to wiggle and shake, causing the young girl who was leading him to laugh out loud.

"He knows his mama," the girl said.

"You're the second person to say that to me today," Hana responded with a smile. "I guess it must be true."

It was less than a ten-minute drive to Hana's house. On the way, she could see one of the taller buildings of the Piedmont Hospital complex over a low hill. She offered up a quick prayer for Jakob Brodsky. At home, she set up Leon's kennel near the front door. The dog sniffed it and then went into the bedroom and whined until Hana lifted him onto the bed.

"This is temporary," Hana warned as the dog curled into a furry ball on the bedspread and immediately fell asleep after his busy day.

• • •

Jakob dutifully answered the questions posed to him by the nurse practitioner who worked for his treating neurologist. She'd spent close to an hour administering a battery of tests that fatigued Jakob more than he wanted to admit.

"I feel a lot better," Jakob said confidently. "Would you check with Dr. Bedford about releasing me in the morning? I don't want to spend another day in the hospital."

"I'll mention it to him along with the results of my testing, which show ongoing deficits in higher reasoning skills."

"Deficits?" Jakob shot back. "I answered every question correctly, didn't I?"

"I'll note your compliance and best efforts," the nurse answered cryptically. "We have a good picture of your current status that I hope will steadily improve."

"What do I need to do to improve?" Jakob asked in frustration.

"Rest and take your medication, Mr. Brodsky. You suffered three significant blows to the head. The one near your right temple could have been life-threatening."

Even through the bandages, Jakob could feel the three knots on the right side of his skull. He remembered nothing from the attack and could only vaguely recall talking to the officer who took a statement from him shortly after he arrived at the hospital. Two of the blows had required stitches to stop the bleeding. The third created an area of massive swelling that was creeping toward Jakob's eye. He shifted his head and turned it slightly. A searing pain caused him to wince.

"I guess I'm going to lose this argument," he said.

"There's nothing to argue about," the nurse replied. "You'll be kept under observation here at the hospital until we're sure the intracranial swelling goes down and know you're not at risk for a seizure or other severe reaction."

Jakob remembered a lawsuit he'd filed a couple of years earlier that involved a construction worker who fell from a defective scaffold and landed on his head.

"I've represented clients with traumatic brain injuries who experienced personality changes. Do you think I'm at risk for that sort of thing?"

"We don't have a baseline for purposes of comparison. Those types of problems don't usually manifest immediately. If you notice any changes, or if friends or family members observe differences, mention it to Dr. Bedford."

Jakob waited for the nurse to leave before pounding his fist into the mattress in frustration. He turned on the TV and tried to lose himself in a sitcom with a piped-in laugh track.

A few minutes later, there was a knock on the door. So far, his only visitor had been Butch Watson, who had walked over from the maternity wing and spent most of his visit apologizing for asking Jakob to go to the apartment. Jakob reassured the new father that he didn't blame him for anything that happened.

"Come in," Jakob said.

The door opened, and a dark-haired woman emerged from the shadows. It was Hana Abboud.

"Are you feeling well enough for a visit?" she asked in her accented English.

"Yes, I was just talking to the nurse practitioner from my neurologist's office about going home."

"That's encouraging."

"Not really. She put me off. How did you find out I was here?"

"Ben Neumann called."

With the amount of crime that took place in a city like Atlanta, Jakob was surprised that his assault had been singled out for special attention.

"It was on the news?"

"No, your receptionist told him when he called your office. How bad is it?"

Jakob could see Hana staring at the right side of his head, which was totally swathed in a bandage.

"The assailant hit me three times, knocking me unconscious. I also have some sore ribs. He stole my wallet but didn't ransack the apartment I'd just left. Even if he had, I doubt he would have wanted a fancy new baby monitor."

Hana didn't smile at his feeble attempt at humor. "Did you see the attacker?" she asked. "Are you sure it was a man?"

Hana's question raised an issue Jakob hadn't considered. "No. I assumed it was a man. It could have been a woman. I'm sure I'll be back at work within the next few days. Tell Ben I'm going to be okay."

While he talked, Jakob felt himself become light-headed and disoriented. He tried to focus his eyes on a generic painting of a seascape on the wall opposite the bed.

"What's wrong?" he heard Hana ask from what seemed like a great distance away.

Jakob tried to answer, but gibberish came out of his mouth. He could see alarm sweep across Hana's face. She opened her mouth and began to speak in words as incomprehensible to him as what he'd said himself. Jakob closed his eyes for a moment and exerted all his willpower to bring the chaos of his world into order. When he opened his eyes, Hana was reaching for the call button that was on the bedside table.

"No, no," Jakob managed as the room came back into focus. "It's nothing. The doctor said I might have short moments of confusion due to the swelling of my brain."

Hana looked at him skeptically. "Are you sure? I thought you were about to faint or have a seizure."

Jakob's mouth felt dry. He reached for a cup of water on the tray table and watched as his hand unsteadily made its way forward. Hana picked up the cup and held it close to his mouth. He took one drink through a straw followed by another one. Hana returned the cup of water to the tray.

"Thanks," Jakob said. "That was weird. I couldn't understand what I was saying or what you said."

"There's an explanation for why you couldn't understand me," Hana answered. "I was praying for you in Arabic. After that you went to sleep or passed out for at least a minute before coming around."

"A minute?" Jakob asked in shock. "It was only a couple of seconds."

"I was here. I know."

Jakob reached up and gently touched the right side of his head. "Maybe I'm in worse shape than I'd like to admit. I don't think I have any court appearances for the next few days." He paused. "But I don't trust my memory on that. Where's my cell phone?"

Jakob sat up straighter in bed and turned to the right. A wave of nausea swept over him, and he quickly resumed his previous position. Hana found the phone in the small drawer of the table beside the bed and handed it to him. The phone was almost dead. Relieved that he remembered his password, Jakob checked his calendar. It was clear except for appointments with clients and reminders for things that needed to be done.

"I'm good," he said. "One of the guys who practices in my building can bring my laptop. I won't be functioning at one hundred percent, but I can make it work."

"How many episodes have you had like the one that just happened?" Hana asked.

"None. My brain is adjusting to the trauma. And in the meantime, let Ben Neumann know that I'm recovering."

"You already said that."

"Right. What's our next step in his case?"

"I'm going to locate a private investigator in Israel. But we can talk about that later. You need to rest."

"Come up with a list of candidates, and I'll jump in for the interview process. Once I have my computer, I can look into possible investigators, too. I've done a lot of research on terrorist groups and found links to posts that mention Gloria Neumann's death."

"Okay, take care." Hana stood and moved toward the door.

"Thanks for stopping by," Jakob said.

After Hana left, Jakob glanced at a small clock on the nightstand. It was nine forty-five, late for a visit from a virtual stranger.

CHAPTER 11

L eon whimpered and complained when Hana deposited him in his wire kennel for the night. She'd spruced up the space with a host of toys positioned around soft bedding.

"This is better than my bed," she said to the dog as she closed and latched the door. "Janet says your wolf ancestors loved sleeping in a secure den where they would be aware of any enemies who approached in the night."

Leon wasn't persuaded by Hana's appeal to his remote canine ancestry. While he yelped, she tossed and turned in her bed and debated whether to surrender to his cries and bring him into her bedroom. She covered her head with her pillow, turned away from the door, and squeezed her eyes shut. When nothing worked, she slipped out of bed to open the kennel, only to be met by silence before she reached her bedroom door. She froze in place. The dog remained quiet. Worried, she peeked through the door and in the pale light from a full moon saw Leon curled up in a ball in the middle of the padding on the bottom of the cage. Within minutes, Hana herself was asleep.

When she awoke in the middle of the night, she stayed in her bedroom to pray instead of spending time in the living room. One of the main concerns on her heart was Jakob Brodsky. The lawyer was more seriously injured in the attack than he realized or was willing to admit. Upon returning home, she'd researched the complications from a serious blow to the head. And Jakob was struck not once, but three times. Because Ben Neumann was now a client of Collins,

Lowenstein, and Capella, Hana had an obligation to make sure the client's interests were protected, and in a morbid way, the injury to Jakob made Mr. Lowenstein's instruction that Hana assume primary responsibility for the case easier to implement. Even thinking in those terms made Hana uncomfortable.

She awoke for the second time as the first rays of sun peeked around the edges of the plantation shutters that covered her bedroom windows. She checked on Leon, who opened one eye, saw her, and hopped to his feet. She opened the door of the kennel to greet him. The puppy's entire body communicated a hearty hello. After taking him outside, Hana watched him lap water while she fixed her morning coffee. When she dropped him off at the doggie day care center, Leon clearly remembered the fun he'd had the previous day and trotted off with the attendant to his assigned area.

"Should I bet a month's house payment that you went to the hospital to visit lawyer Brodsky?" Janet asked when Hana stopped by the assistant's desk to greet her.

"I have aunts who play the Israeli lotto every week," Hana answered.

"Do they ever win?"

"Not as often as you would if you bet that I went to the hospital to visit Jakob Brodsky."

Janet's eyes widened. "I can't believe you did it. I even prayed you'd go on the way home. What convinced you?"

"I needed to see for myself how seriously injured he is, in part because of the impact it could have on the Neumann case, but mostly because Jakob seems like a decent man who was viciously attacked."

Hana summarized what she'd seen and observed.

"That's a shame," Janet said, shaking her head. "I have a nephew who wasn't wearing a helmet when he wrecked his dirt bike. He hit his head against a tree and hasn't been the same since."

"Dirt bike?"

"A motorcycle that people ride on trails in the woods."

Hana sipped the strong black coffee she'd brewed in the law office break room. "I'm not sure if I should mention the possible complication to Ben Neumann now or wait to see if Jakob gets better. I read a couple of articles about severe concussions, and it seems the person often gets worse rather than better."

"It's hard to predict is all I know."

Coffee in hand, Hana went into her office. Her first item for the day was to contact one of her former colleagues, a Jewish woman named Anat Naphtali who had worked with Hana at the airport. They'd talked a couple of times since Hana started working in Atlanta. Less than five minutes after sending an email, Hana received a phone call.

"I am at home trying not to throw up," Anat said in Hebrew. "Ari and I just found out that I'm pregnant, and I will never joke again when someone tells me she is suffering from morning sickness. It's terrible."

Anat and Ari had been together for five years, but they were not religious and the last Hana knew had never married. Jewish marriages in Israel were heavily regulated by the ultra-Orthodox religious establishment, and it was difficult for secular Israelis to obtain a marriage license. Often, couples like Anat and Ari traveled outside the country to marry because the Israeli civil government would then recognize their foreign marriage licenses. Cyprus was a popular wedding destination.

"And before you ask," Anat continued, "Ari and I went to Cyprus a week after I saw the doctor. We are officially a married couple. Finding out he's going to be a father has had a big impact on him. He's trying to get a promotion at work and promised to use the extra money to buy things for the baby, not a fancier surfboard."

Hana smiled. Ari loved the ocean. It seemed like every picture of the couple on Instagram had been taken on one of the many Israeli beaches along the Mediterranean.

"Send pictures as soon as you have an ultrasound," Hana said.

"Will do. And I have a few names to suggest for your private investigator. Do you want a Jew or an Arab?"

"You know me. I can work with anyone. I'm not sure it matters."

"Hana, it always matters," Anat replied. "Can you tell me what you want this person to do?"

Hana hadn't provided any details about the Neumann case in her email. "The reason for the investigation is confidential, but he will need to interview Arab men if I can't do it."

"That's your answer. You need an Arab. As a woman, you would have a tough time convincing a conservative Arab man to talk to you."

Anat was right, especially in light of the likely connection between the Zadan brothers and Islamic radicalism.

"Agreed."

"Just a minute," Anat said. "I have to go to the bathroom."

A couple of minutes passed before she returned. "Sorry. That should be it for hugging the toilet today. It is no longer called morning sickness if I get sick in the afternoon. I'll send along two names for you along with their contact information and a little bit about them. They have different personalities and skill sets, so it will be up to you to decide which one is a better fit for your needs. Both of them are determined and work hard."

"Thanks so much, and congratulations. You're going to be a wonderful mom."

"Tell Ari's mother that. She's given me four books on parenting and acts like I don't know how to change a diaper."

Anat didn't come from a large family like Hana. "How are your diapering skills?"

"Excellent. I changed a diaper on a friend's baby a few weeks ago. And I'm not going to use cloth diapers, even though Ari's mother thinks it's more sanitary. I mean, what woman living in the twenty-first century washes diapers?"

After the call ended, Hana printed out the email containing names and contact information for the two investigators: Daud Hasan and Sahir Benali. According to Anat, both men had performed security work for the government in the past and now sold their services in the private sector. When Hana checked their websites, she saw that neither furnished a photograph, which made sense if they didn't want to be easily identified. Benali was more experienced and had worked for years in law enforcement, both as a police officer and as a detective in several Arab towns. Hasan's qualifications emphasized education and training. His name sounded vaguely familiar, but Hana decided to contact the more experienced Benali first. She dialed the number in East Jerusalem, and a receptionist answered in Arabic-accented Hebrew.

"This is Hana Abboud, a lawyer in America," Hana replied in Hebrew.

The receptionist immediately switched to broken English. Hana interrupted her. "Hebrew or Arabic is better for me," she said in Arabic.

The receptionist then spoke in Arabic with a Jordanian accent. "We require submission of an online information form prior to discussing Mr. Benali's services," the woman said.

"That's fine," Hana replied. "Anat Naphtali, a former colleague of mine, recommended Mr. Benali to me, and I have a few background questions. This matter involves investigation as part of a lawsuit that would be filed in the United States against persons or companies based in Israel, and I need to know if he has experience working with American clients."

"Yes. He also has his private investigator license in New York and Florida."

"Does he have an area of particular expertise?"

"Mr. Denali handles a lot of missing person cases and domestic disputes, and he locates people who don't want to be found."

The third item on the list was exactly what Hana was looking for.

She needed someone who could track down and interview people to determine possible connections with the attack on the Neumann family.

"And he has contacts within law enforcement from his time working with local police departments?" Hana asked.

"Yes, many."

"Does he have Israeli citizenship?"

"Yes, but he also carries a Jordanian passport."

It wasn't unusual for people within Israel to have passports from multiple countries. When she worked at the airport, Hana had often interviewed people who could lay down passports like playing cards.

"That helps," Hana responded. "I'll fill out the information sheet and send it to you. I work for the American law firm of Collins, Lowenstein, and Capella."

"Lowenstein?" the woman asked.

"Yes."

"And your name again?"

"Hana Abboud. I'm from Reineh, but I live and work in Atlanta, Georgia, in the United States."

There was a brief moment of silence. Hana suspected the receptionist was processing assumptions about a woman who spoke Hebrew, Arabic, and English, grew up in a Christian town in northern Israel, and now worked in the United States.

"I'll pass the information sheet to Mr. Benali. He's out of the office this afternoon but will return in the morning."

"Thanks."

The call ended. Hana stared at Daud Hasan's contact information and decided to fully evaluate Mr. Benali first.

• • •

Jakob ate the final bite of breakfast. He'd awakened feeling more normal. His face looked terrible because the bruising had finally reached his right eye. The door opened and Dr. Bedford entered.

"Good morning," Jakob said before the neurologist spoke. "I slept well and feel great."

"Let me check you out."

The doctor examined Jakob's eyes. Jakob tried to open his right eye, but it was impossible to do more than squint.

"My eye looks bad, but I can see well enough. I just can't open it all the way."

The doctor didn't respond. He removed the bandages from Jakob's skull and gently touched the knots with his fingers. Jakob stoically kept himself rigid. He'd not yet seen the damage, but he knew someone had shaved the hair on the right side of his head. The doctor then checked the muscles in Jakob's neck and asked him to move his head.

"How does my head look?" Jakob asked.

"Like a man who was beaten severely with a blunt object yet survived. Whistle for me."

It was the fourth time Jakob had jumped through the neurological hoops to determine the presence and severity of a concussion. After whistling, he smiled, clenched his teeth, and moved his hands into various positions to prove he didn't have any tremors. Jakob then began answering the standard questions in a mini mental-status exam without being asked. Dr. Bedford held up his right hand to stop him.

"Do you want to be discharged?" the doctor asked.

"Yes," Jakob answered.

"You've suffered a significant concussion," the doctor continued. "If you played professional football, you'd be on the sidelines in the concussion protocol."

"But I'm a lawyer who uses the inside of his head, not the outside," Jakob responded confidently.

"It's the inside I'm most concerned about," Dr. Bedford said as he put the bandages back in place. "Have you experienced any problems besides headaches?"

"No," Jakob answered. "And the medication knocks the edge off the pain without any side effects. I'd be willing to transition to over-the-counter meds."

Jakob had concluded that the altered consciousness and confusion he experienced during Hana Abboud's visit was most likely due to low blood sugar. Dr. Bedford flipped through the medical file.

"All right, I'll let you go home so long as you come into the office tomorrow. Fill the prescription for pain medication even if you're determined not to take them. You'll thank me later."

"No problem."

"Have you heard anything else from the police about the attack?"

"No, and I'll be surprised if I do. I notified my credit card companies and ordered a new driver's license."

"Take it easy and stay away from the office for a few days," the doctor added. "Rest is the best medicine."

"Will do. That will be easier at home than in here."

"Oh, and avoid straining your eyes. Limit TV viewing and reading to short periods of time. My nurse will call and give you an appointment time for tomorrow."

Jakob nodded. Dr. Bedford made a note on a sheet of paper and closed the medical file.

"Thanks," Jakob said. "What about driving?"

"Keep it to a minimum and stop immediately if you start having dizzy spells or feel faint. Make sure you notify my office right away if you experience any additional symptoms. Your brain is weeks away from stabilizing."

The doctor left. Jakob sighed with relief and closed his eyes. When he opened them the opposite side of the room began jumping around. He shook his head. That didn't help, and he closed his eyes again. When he opened them this time, the wall remained firmly in place.

After he showered, Jakob put on the clothes he was wearing at the time of the attack. There was blood on the upper portion of his shirt, but he was able to remove most of it by holding the shirt under hot water in the bathroom sink and scrubbing it with hand soap. He placed the shirt on the windowsill to dry as much as possible before putting it on. He'd decided to catch a cab to Butch Watson's apartment and retrieve his car. He was holding his shirt up to the light when there was a knock on his door and Butch entered.

"Are you going home?" the new father asked.

"Yes. How about Nelle and the twins?"

"Maybe tomorrow, but we're lobbying hard to stay an extra day. Nelle's parents finally rolled into town. This twin thing is going to be way tougher than we imagined."

"You'll figure it out."

Jakob saw Butch eyeing his still slightly bloody shirt. The estate lawyer's eyes were bloodshot from lack of sleep.

"I should have offered to swing by your place and bring you some clean clothes," Butch said with a big yawn.

"This will work until I get home for a real shower and change."

"Who's picking you up from the hospital?"

"I'll call a cab."

"No way," Butch said and held up his hand. "Did the police leave your car at our apartment?"

"Yes."

"I'll take you. I need a break."

"I'm not sure exactly when I'm getting out—"

"Text me. I'm a five-minute walk away."

An hour later, the duty nurse told Jakob that he was cleared for discharge. He texted Butch, who walked alongside him for the obligatory wheelchair ride to the main entrance of the hospital. It was around noon on a sunny day. With the bandages on his head, Jakob attracted more than his fair share of stares.

"I need to make up a better story than getting blindsided by a mugger," Jakob said to Butch when they rolled out of the elevator on the main floor.

"Nelle and I are just relieved you're okay," Butch responded. "She cried when I told her you were being discharged to go home."

"Aw, that's nice."

"Don't feel too special. She also cried when they messed up her breakfast order and her eggs were scrambled, not poached."

Jakob sat in the wheelchair while he waited for Butch to arrive with the car. As soon as his friend pulled up to the curb, Jakob stood. When he did, the scene in front of the hospital swirled around a few times. The elderly male volunteer who'd pushed the wheelchair reached out and touched him on the shoulder.

"Are you okay?" the white-haired man asked.

"Just need to get oriented." Jakob placed his hand on the back of the wheelchair to steady himself. "Everything's good to go."

He got in Butch's vehicle, a two-seat sports car that was a hold-over from his college days. Until the arrival of the twins, the car had been Butch's baby.

"I wanted to ride in Nelle's new minivan," Jakob said.

"No such luck."

Jakob was surprised at the anxiety that rose up in his chest when they pulled into the parking lot for the apartment complex. He took several deep breaths.

"The police had the area roped off with yellow tape for the first twenty-four hours," Butch said.

"The guy who knocked me out was in a hurry," Jakob said. "All he took was my wallet. He could have grabbed my keys and figured out which vehicle responded to the key fob."

"Getting rid of a stolen car is a lot tougher than spending cash or using a credit card for a couple of days. And do you really think someone would want to steal your car?"

"Don't criticize my car. It's paid for."

They parked beside Jakob's vehicle.

"I want to walk upstairs and look around," he said.

"Are you sure?" Butch asked in surprise. "There's nothing to see."

"Except my blood."

"That's gone. The maintenance guy cleaned it up as soon as the cops left."

Jakob had no physical problem following Butch up the steps to the landing. There were several dark splotches on the concrete area, but they looked like the effect of weathering, not blood.

"I guess I was standing here when he decked me," Jakob said, moving two feet to the left. "But I really don't know."

"And then he dragged you down the stairs, which seems unnecessary if all he wanted was your wallet."

"No, I was up here when the ambulance came."

"That's not what the detective told me when he interviewed me at the hospital."

"Nobody mentioned that to me."

Jakob had noticed scrapes on his lower back and right side when he took his morning shower. He'd assumed they occurred when he fell to the concrete on the landing.

"But I didn't regain consciousness until I was at the hospital," Jakob said. "So I don't know what really happened."

The two men stood next to each other in silence for a few moments. "Well, thanks for the ride," Jakob said.

"It's the least I can do. I needed to come over here anyway. Nelle forgot her favorite pair of socks she likes to wear at night. Her feet can be like ice cubes, even in the summer."

"Mm," Jakob replied without really listening.

"When will you be able to go back to the office?" Butch continued. "I'd offer to help out, but I'm out of commission myself—"

"Probably tomorrow," Jakob broke in. "I just need to take it easy until I'm at the top of my game again."

After trading good-byes, Butch disappeared into the apartment. As a precaution, Jakob held on to the handrail while he descended the steps. He felt slightly light-headed, but nothing like the two instances at the hospital. Reaching the sidewalk, he stuck his right hand into his pocket to retrieve his car keys. When he did, he felt Butch's spare apartment key. He started to go back upstairs, but then he decided to return it to its place behind the holly bush. As he did so, his eyes caught sight of something long and brown camouflaged in the dark pine straw near the edge of the sidewalk. He poked it with his foot to make sure it wasn't a snake. The object moved, but it wasn't alive. Jakob picked it up. It was a brown beaded necklace. The beads were wooden and uniform except for two black beads next to each other on a piece of strong leather. It had an African look and feel to it. Jakob slipped it into his pocket.

CHAPTER 12

The drive home from Butch's apartment was more of an adventure than Jakob had anticipated. Twice, his vision became blurry, and when the sun shone in his eyes, it gave him an instant headache. Inside his apartment, he changed into clean clothes and lay down on the couch for a rare afternoon nap. One sign of a concussion was increased drowsiness. When he woke up, it took him a second to realize he wasn't in the hospital. He went to the kitchen and drank a glass of water.

Sitting on his couch, he signed into his office computer and began answering emails. Thankfully, it had been a slow couple of days, and an hour later he'd reached the end of new communications. Then he listened to his voice-mail messages. That was a longer process. A third of the way down the list was a call from Ben Neumann, who said he hoped Jakob was recovering quickly. He didn't request a return phone call, but Jakob hit the redial button.

"Thanks for checking up on me," Jakob said after Ben answered. "I'm home now. I was surprised when Hana Abboud stopped by the hospital to visit me. She told me that you let her know what happened."

"How are you feeling?"

Jakob gave an overly optimistic diagnosis and prognosis.

"That's good," Ben replied. "Any word from the police?"

"Nothing. There wasn't a surveillance camera in the stairwell of the apartment, and it was pitch-dark."

Ben started talking, but Jakob felt like he was slightly detached from the conversation and had trouble following him.

"I'm going to be fine," Jakob said, hoping the words made sense.

"Hana is pressing on with the case and has called me several times," Ben said. "Her firm is really taking it seriously. She's going to book a flight to Israel within the next few days."

"What?" Jakob managed.

"She wants to personally interview potential investigators and do some initial work on her own."

Jakob sat up straighter. "She didn't mention any of that when she came by the hospital."

"Probably because you're in no shape to go anywhere right now. You need to focus on getting better."

"Oh, I'll be on that plane," Jakob said, summoning a strong tone of voice. "It's not an option."

"Please, be careful," Ben replied. "You just got out of the hospital. Talk to your doctor."

"I will. But first I'm going to call Hana."

"Don't get upset with her. She's come along at the perfect time."

"Yeah," Jakob muttered.

The call ended. Jakob decided to rest for a few minutes before calling Hana. He lay down on his left side and stared at the combination of light and shadow on the carpeted floor. And soon drifted off to sleep.

• • •

Janet buzzed Hana's phone.

"There's a Mr. Mebali or Denali or something like that on the phone," the assistant said. "I try to get these names right, but when they start talking so fast, I'm left in the dust like a camel racing a sports car."

Hana chuckled at the comparison. "It's Benali. He's a private investigator I contacted in the Neumann case. I'll take it."

Hana glanced at the clock. It was 7:30 p.m. in Jerusalem. She answered the call in Arabic.

"Good evening," she said. "I haven't had a chance to submit my request for assistance in writing, but I intend to do so within the next day or so."

"Forget about formalities," the investigator replied. "I checked you out on the law firm website, and there's no need to send a written request. What sort of help are you looking for? Whatever it is, I'm the man for the job."

Listening to Benali reminded Hana of a merchant in a local market, or souk, inviting a customer into his shop. It was easy to imagine the former police officer communicating with ordinary people on the street.

"Based on what your assistant told me, our case is different from what you usually handle."

"Maybe not. She's only been working for me a couple of months. It's hard to find a young person willing to put in the hours needed to succeed. I may be out of the office two or three days straight when I'm on a big case. I bet you have to put in a lot of hours working for an American law firm. You look about the same age as my daughters, and they don't seem to want to—"

"It can be busy," Hana broke in. "I need help with a lawsuit based on the death of an American tourist in Jerusalem four years ago. We represent the husband and daughter of a woman who was killed."

"Car wreck?" Benali asked. "American drivers don't realize what they're getting into when they rent a car in Israel."

"No, it was a terrorist attack in Hurva Square. The woman was an American Jew stabbed to death by a twenty-year-old named Abdul Zadan. Abdul was shot and killed by border patrol officers, and his younger brother, Tawfik, was taken into custody as an accomplice. The brothers came from a village near Ramallah."

Hana's summary of the case put the brakes on Benali's loquaciousness.

"And what would you hire me to do?" the investigator asked in a subdued tone of voice.

Hana explained the basis for a damage claim under the US Anti-Terrorism Act. "Before filing a lawsuit in the United States, we need to locate a defendant or defendants who could pay the money awarded by a jury. My guess is the Zadan brothers don't have significant assets, but that would have to be checked out to be sure. Are you familiar with the Arab Bank litigation filed in the US?"

"Yes, my ex-brother-in-law used to work for a branch of the bank in Amman. Did any group with links to a bank claim responsibility for the attack?"

"No. It appears to have been an attack by two brothers un-affiliated with a known terrorist network."

Benali was silent for a moment. "This isn't a matter of a few phone calls," he said. "It's more like a formal police investigation. It would take a lot of time, and I would have to be extra cautious."

"I understand. How much experience do you have in obtaining financial records?"

"That part would be easy. I have contacts who can unlock doors that don't have keys."

Hana knew low-level bribery would likely be part of any investigation. Locals treated it like an unwritten fee for services.

"We can't be directly involved in—"

"No problem," Benali said before Hana could finish. "I know how Americans operate. They care about appearances even though they do the same thing on a larger scale on Wall Street. But the answer to your question is yes. I uncover financial assets and information in divorce cases. This would be similar. Finding out where to look would be the challenge."

"Exactly. And we can't jeopardize the admissibility in court of the information obtained."

"No problem. I deal with that issue all the time. What's the rate of pay? This will have to be hourly, not a flat fee."

Hana had considered asking Mr. Lowenstein for guidance on this point but knew the senior partner would defer to her. She'd prepared a rough budget for the investigation. Knowing she would have to negotiate, Hana tossed out an hourly figure below the amount she'd allocated.

"I'd need at least twice that much," Benali answered immediately. "I don't have to tell you this will have to be handled delicately."

"There's room for negotiation," Hana replied. "This is just a preliminary call. I'm planning on coming to Israel to talk more before making a final decision."

"Perfect. I'll look forward to meeting with you. But you can save yourself a trip if that's the only reason you're coming. I'm your man."

"I'll take that into consideration."

The phone call ended. Hana stared at Sahir Benali's website. The fact that Anat Naphtali vouched for Benali was important, but it wasn't enough to sway her. She needed more input and remembered Jakob's request that she keep him in the loop of information. Even though Mr. Lowenstein had told her to marginalize the young lawyer, Hana couldn't justify not letting Jakob know about such an important decision. She placed the call. Jakob didn't answer, and Hana didn't leave a message. She then unsuccessfully tried to reach the other investigator, Daud Hasan.

• • •

Jakob awoke with a start. The sunbeams on the floor were gone, and the room was dark. He grappled for his phone, which had fallen behind one of the seat cushions on the couch. It was after nine. He sat up and rubbed his eyes. His head was throbbing. He went into the kitchen and took one of the pain pills. Checking his phone again, he saw that he'd missed four calls and multiple texts. One of the phone calls was from Collins, Lowenstein, and Capella. Within a few minutes, the strong pain pills made him drowsy, and he went to bed.

In the morning, Jakob gingerly moved his head. The hospital staff had sent him home with dressing material, and it took several minutes to fashion a bandage that didn't make him look like a mummy who'd escaped from a tomb. During the drive to Dr. Bedford's office, he noticed the brown necklace in the tray behind the shifter and slipped it into his pocket. He tried to call Hana Abboud but had to leave a message.

At 9:10 a.m. Jakob was sitting in a treatment room at Dr. Bedford's office.

"Tell me how you've been feeling," the doctor said after he'd entered and shaken Jakob's hand. "Any headaches?"

"Yes."

"Good."

"Why is that good?" Jakob asked in surprise.

"Every human being with a functioning brain would experience headaches after undergoing the trauma you've suffered. It was a credibility question. How bad are the headaches?"

"Rough enough that I've taken the prescription pain meds."

"Any other symptoms?"

"Yes," he admitted. "I've had several spells when I zoned out for a few seconds, perhaps longer."

"Nothing while driving?"

"No, but are you going to recommend that I stop driving?"

"It depends on the seriousness of what you've experienced. Tell me more."

Jakob felt like a witness trapped in his testimony. He described what had happened in the hospital room with Hana Abboud and the incident on the phone with Ben Neumann when he had trouble staying focused during the conversation.

"I tried to chalk up what happened at the hospital to low blood sugar because I'd lost my appetite and hadn't eaten. Now I'm not so sure."

"If you don't try to self-diagnose your medical condition, I won't try to practice law," the doctor replied.

The physician scrolled through the tablet in his right hand. "Your EEG and MRI studies were normal, and your heart is healthy," he said. "You may have experienced a syncopal episode at the hospital. Are you sure it hasn't happened again?"

"Positive."

Dr. Bedford looked into Jakob's eyes. "Since I'm not a lawyer, may I ask you a legal question?"

"Sure."

"Assume you have a blackout spell that causes a car wreck in which another person is seriously injured or killed. Would a good lawyer investigate your medical history and sue the neurologist who failed to recommend that you stop driving for three to six months?"

Jakob's hands felt sweaty. "That's possible. And I wouldn't want to hurt or kill someone anyway."

"Then we're in agreement. Don't drive for ninety days. I think that's a reasonable time period since you didn't have a seizure and your other tests are normal. I'll repeat the brain studies in three months. If they're clear and you don't have another serious episode, you should be okay. Schedule your next appointment in four weeks, but call sooner if you need to."

"Ninety days? That's a long time."

"It's less than six months, which would be the case if you'd suffered a full-blown seizure."

"Okay. What about flying overseas?"

Dr. Bedford paused. "If you're talking about a vacation where you relax on a beach, I'd write a prescription if we thought your insurance company would pay the bill. But no sports or recreational activity that would pose the risk of a blow to your head."

"This would be a business trip without much chance of beach time, but I don't foresee any physical activity, either."

"Just be smart and treat your skull like you would an egg that's in danger of cracking open."

Jakob frowned. "That's disturbing."

"It's meant to be."

Jakob left the office. On the way home he debated whether to follow the physician's advice. Georgia wasn't a state where a doctor had the duty of notifying the department of transportation to recommend suspension of a patient's driver's license. That responsibility rested on Jakob. He sat in the car for a few moments, took out everything he might need in the near future, and trudged up the steps to his apartment. He tossed his car keys in the top drawer of the dresser of his bedroom and closed it. For the next three months, he'd be spending money on taxis and Uber.

• • •

Hana arrived a few minutes early at the ice cream parlor and parked her car in the shade of a large oak tree. Per Mr. Lowenstein's instructions, an entry would appear on her work activity sheet for "Client Meeting/ Ice Cream." Sadie arrived wearing her school uniform. She waved excitedly when she saw Hana. In the little girl's other hand was a doll.

"Thanks for coming," Ben said, "even though eating ice cream isn't the best way to prepare a child for a good supper."

"Ice cream is made from milk that comes from cows," Sadie replied. "And milk is good for making strong bones."

"Then my bones are going to grow stronger from something with chocolate in it," Hana answered. "Tell me about your doll."

Sadie held up the lifelike doll. It had an olive complexion, dark eyes, and straight black hair and was wearing a long blue gown that fell from her neck to her feet.

"She's an Arab doll," Sadie replied.

Hana nodded. "I can see. My cousin Fabia wore a dress like that when she graduated from high school."

"Fabia?" Sadie repeated. "That's going to be my doll's name."

Hana took out her phone. "May I take a picture of Sadie with the doll and send it to my cousin?" she asked Ben. "I wouldn't mention Sadie's name or anything other than that she's a new friend."

Ben glanced down at Sadie for a moment before responding. "So long as she doesn't post it on any form of social media."

"What do you mean, Daddy?" Sadie asked.

"He's right," Hana responded before Ben spoke. "Hold Fabia so I can take a good picture."

Hana knelt, took five photos, and then let Sadie pick her favorite.

"That's the one I like, too," Hana said.

The shop featured ice cream blended together on a thick marble slab. Sadie asked for strawberry mixed with peach in a cake cone. Ben and Hana both ordered a vanilla sundae with hot fudge. Hana added toasted almonds to hers.

Ben took his wallet from his pocket.

"No," Hana said, placing her purse on the counter. "Mr. Lowenstein specifically instructed me to pay for Sadie's ice cream."

"Why?" Ben asked with a puzzled look on his face.

"He wants Sadie to grow up liking lawyers."

They sat at a small round table toward the rear of the shop. They were the only customers.

Sadie handed the doll to Hana. "Fabia likes what you ordered."

Hana placed the doll in her lap and pretended to give her a bite before placing it in her own mouth.

"The last thing I did with my mommy was eat ice cream," Sadie said.

Hana, who was raising her spoon to her mouth, quickly lowered it. Sadie looked forlornly at her father.

"Here, Daddy," she said, handing him her cone. "I'm not hungry."

"I thought you were in the mood for ice cream," he said gently.

"Not anymore," Sadie replied, looking down into her lap. "You can throw it away."

Ben gave Hana a look that communicated a silent plea for help. Hana didn't have anything to offer.

"I'll see if Fabia likes it," she said, taking the cone from Ben and placing it in front of the doll's lips. "I think she does."

Sadie watched through the tops of her eyelashes. She held out her hand, and Hana returned the ice cream cone to her. Sadie took one more lick, stood up, and dropped the rest of it in a trash bin.

"I licked it one more time to show that I could," she announced when she returned to her chair.

"What do you mean, sweetie?" Ben asked.

"Poppy says that when he gets sad about Mommy being gone, he does something like put a dirty plate in the dishwasher before letting himself be sad."

Hana wasn't exactly sure what Sadie meant or the lesson intended by her grandfather but left it alone. She held the doll out to Sadie.

"Fabia wants a hug," she said.

Sadie took the doll and wrapped her in a tight embrace. "That works, too," she said. "Daddy hugs me when I'm sad."

Hana's appetite was gone, but she made herself eat a few more bites, too. Ben's ice cream had remained untouched since Sadie's announcement.

"I guess we'd better go," he said after a few moments passed.

They walked outside. There were clouds in the sky and a cool breeze that hinted of a thunderstorm.

"Thanks so much for inviting me," Hana said to Sadie.

Ben opened the rear door of the car. Before Sadie hopped in, she came over to Hana. "Would you hug me?"

"Of course." Hana knelt and wrapped her arms around the little girl, who nestled in as close as possible.

"You smell nice," Sadie said when she finally stepped away. "Do you wear perfume?"

"A little bit."

Sadie turned to her father. "I want to smell like Hana."

"We'll talk about that later," Ben answered, managing a slight smile.

"That means 'no,'" Sadie said to Hana. "But I'll change his mind."

"Not every time," Ben replied.

Sadie slipped into her car booster seat, and Ben closed the door. He turned to Hana. "Maybe she was talking today about Hurva Square with her counselor," he said. "It comes up quick sometimes."

"I'm glad she asked me to hug her. It made me feel better."

"There will be more hugs at home."

. . .

Back at the office Hana had a note from Jakob requesting a meeting with her and Ben at his office the following day at noon about the status of the case. Hana checked her calendar and accepted. As she scrolled down, she saw an email from an unfamiliar address. Because it had made it past the law firm firewall, she opened it. It was from Bart Kendall.

Hana,

Thanks again for meeting and talking with me. I considered what you said and decided to proceed with the BDS project. My church is going to be one of the sponsors. I recently met with a young Arab man who grew up in Bethlehem. He has a compelling story of suffering under Israeli occupation and will be the spokesperson in the video. Because of my conversation with you, I'd like to include a brief statement that not all Arabs share his perspective. Would you be willing to do that part of the video?

Bart Kendall

Hana read the email several times as she processed it at different levels. The first was the personal hurt she felt from Bart rejecting what she'd said. Second, she dealt with anger that the producer was going to place another pebble on the mountain of offense that existed between Arabs and Jews. Third, she grieved that Bart's church was going to perpetuate the problem, not be part of a solution that could occur only through the power of the gospel.

She started to type a quick response turning him down but decided she needed to ask God what to do first.

CHAPTER 13

The following morning Jakob requested an Uber driver to take him from his apartment to the office. Four responses popped up, and he selected one. On the way to the front of the apartment complex, he stopped by his car to retrieve a spare office key from the glove box. The dome light didn't come on when he opened the car door, and he realized that he hadn't turned off the headlamps the previous evening. The car's battery was dead. Jakob had been too busy to take the vehicle in for needed maintenance, and he quickly decided this would be an ideal time to take care of it. He called Tony, his mechanic, who agreed to send a tow truck to pick up the disabled car.

"No rush," Jakob said. "I'm not going to be driving for a while. I'll leave the keys under the front mat."

"I'll check it over from bumper to bumper and let you know what I find."

Jakob stood on the sidewalk near the entrance of the apartments. A MARTA bus lumbered by. Riding the bus to his office would require a couple of transfers. The Uber driver arrived in a bright yellow subcompact.

Behind the wheel was a young woman in her late twenties or early thirties with short blond hair and multiple piercings in both ears. Her car was immaculately clean. Without asking Jakob why his head was swathed in bandages, she handed him her card as he got in the rear seat. The driver's name was Emily Johnson. The car was a five-speed manual transmission with startling power. Classical music blared through the car's speakers.

"Is that Tchaikovsky's Violin Concerto, opus 35?" Jakob asked.

The car came to a halt as a traffic light turned red.

"Yes," the driver answered.

"Julia Fischer or Itzhak Perlman?"

"Perlman, but I like Fischer, too," the young woman said, glancing in the rearview mirror at Jakob. "Are you a musician?"

"No, but my mother plays viola for the Long Island Symphony. Our family immigrated to the US from Russia when I was eight years old. My mom made my sisters and me listen to classical music all the time when I was a kid."

The light turned green. The driver skillfully navigated her way through traffic to Jakob's office.

"Would you be available later today?" Jakob asked when they reached his building.

"When and where?" the driver responded. "I go to music school in the evenings, but I try to stay in the loop for the north side of town until four o'clock."

Jakob didn't anticipate the deposition that would start at two o'clock taking more than an hour and a half. "Let's say three thirty," he said.

"Okay," the young woman replied. "I'll text a reminder ten minutes before the time to pick you up."

"Don't be late."

"No worries. I know how to come in on cue."

• • •

Hana stepped out to Janet's desk. Her assistant was putting labels on subfiles for one of Mr. Collins's clients. Hana glanced around to make sure the two of them were alone.

"Do you think you can get me a copy of Mr. Lowenstein's investigation of Jakob Brodsky?" she asked. "I know he checked him out, but I'm not sure what that includes."

"It could mean a lot of things. Did Mr. Lowenstein refuse to let you see it?"

"No, otherwise I wouldn't ask you to help me."

"You're so honest," Janet sighed. "What does that feel like?"

Hana rolled her eyes.

"Don't answer," Janet continued. "Let me see what I can find out without getting either one of us in trouble."

Hana returned to her office and closed the door. Twenty minutes later there was a knock and Janet entered. She placed a thin stack of papers on Hana's desk.

"Here's the dossier on Mr. Brodsky, courtesy of Gladys Applewhite."

"Did she ask Mr. Lowenstein if it was okay to give it to me?"

"He's busy. Mr. Lowenstein values people who can think for themselves and make independent decisions. Gladys and I decided you can read the papers and then shred them, leaving no trail on your computer."

Hana didn't touch the stack. "This makes me nervous," she said.

"I'm ramping up the drama," Janet answered. "Gladys didn't see a problem with it since you're going to be working with the guy, and she has your back if Mr. Lowenstein raises a question about it."

It took Hana a few seconds to catch up to Janet's meaning. "I think I understand," she said.

"Read away," Janet said, turning to leave. "I thought it was very interesting. Brodsky isn't your typical young sole practitioner scraping out a living. He has ideals. He's handled a bunch of cases no other lawyer would touch for people who deserved representation. The more I read, the more I liked him."

Thirty minutes later, Hana agreed with Janet's conclusion. Jakob Brodsky was the kind of lawyer who chose to fight for justice, even when it might not be in his financial interest to do so.

• • •

Jakob washed his hands and looked in the mirror. The area around his right eye was now a vivid purple. When he touched the knots on his skull, they were rock-hard and didn't yield to gentle pressure from his fingertips. When he returned to his office, his phone buzzed. Ben and Hana were there to see him. Jakob went downstairs and introduced Hana to Maddie. The receptionist eyed the female lawyer closely.

"How are you feeling?" Hana asked Jakob as soon as they were in his office.

"Better if you weren't keeping me in the dark about what's going on with Ben's case."

"I told Jakob about your plan to travel to Israel," Ben interjected.

"I thought we could discuss it today," Hana replied.

Prepared to vent his frustration, Jakob was stopped by Hana's tone of voice when she responded.

"You did?" he asked.

"Yes. I've talked to one candidate, but Mr. Lowenstein recommended I conduct further evaluations in person while beginning our own investigation. I've not bought a plane ticket but want to leave soon."

Jakob touched the bandages on his head. "When I asked my neurologist about traveling overseas, he said it was fine so long as I avoided contact sports or extreme recreational activities. I'll be ready to go when we fly to Israel, but I need the date as soon as possible."

"Let me tell you about my conversation with the first investigator," Hana said.

"Did you record it?" Jakob asked.

"Yes, but we spoke in Arabic."

"Then you'd better translate into English for Jakob and me," Ben said with a smile.

As Hana summarized her conversation with Sahir Benali, Jakob thought about a local investigator he'd hired a couple of times. The man was a former police officer with extensive contacts and the ability to navigate shady situations.

"He sounds legitimate," Jakob said when Hana finished.

"I agree," Ben added. "We need someone who isn't afraid to tackle the situation."

"He sent me a follow-up email." Hana reached into her purse and took out a sheet of paper.

Jakob extended his hand, but Hana didn't give it to him.

"The email is in Arabic, too," she said.

Hana went on to describe how, in the email, Benali had explained that he would conduct his investigation under pretense, similar to an undercover police operation. That meant he would adopt a fake identity as a man interested in helping to fund terrorist activity.

"That's so he can gain access and protect his safety," Hana said.

"Do you think that would work?" Ben asked.

"It could," Hana replied. "Mr. Benali certainly doesn't lack confidence."

"The recommendation from your former colleague at the airport is important," Jakob said.

"I agree. She also gave me the name of another man. I've tried unsuccessfully to talk to him a couple of times, but he sent an email saying he was interested in the job."

"He doesn't sound very interested to me," Jakob said. "What's his name?"

"Daud Hasan," she replied. "His name is vaguely familiar to me, but I can't place him. He has an office in Beit Hanina, a large Arab suburb of Jerusalem. He forwarded a half-page résumé that left out more than it told, but he did serve in an intelligence unit in the IDF. Not the famous 8200 group, but one that deals with terrorist activity directed at soldiers."

"And he's an Arab?" Jakob asked.

"With a name like Daud Hasan, the answer would be yes," Hana replied.

The room started spinning, and Jakob shut his eyes. He heard Ben speak his name.

"Jakob, why don't you pull up his website?" he said.

"For who?"

"Daud Hasan."

Jakob shook his head to clear it, but the room didn't stabilize. "Listen," he said. "I haven't eaten anything today except two cups of coffee, and I need a snack. Maddie keeps stuff at her desk. Would you like me to get you a pack of crackers or a piece of fruit? She usually has bananas and apples."

"No thanks," Ben replied.

"I'm fine," Hana added.

Using his right hand to steady himself, Jakob stood. Thankfully, he was able to walk normally to the door and leave. Once in the hallway, he leaned against the wall until he trusted himself to descend the stairs.

Hana turned to Ben as soon as Jakob left the room and closed the door. "That's what happened at the hospital, only it lasted longer," she said. "I've researched the effects of a severe concussion, which can include fainting spells called syncope."

"He was wobbly when he stood up," Ben noted. "His doctor told him not to drive a car, and I don't see any way he can go with you to Israel."

The door opened and Jakob entered. He returned to his desk and took a bite from an apple.

"I feel rude eating in front of you," he began. "Are you sure you aren't hungry?"

"No, it's okay," Ben answered. "You have to take care of yourself."

"Would you like a water?" Jakob asked.

"Sure," Hana replied.

Jakob opened a drawer of his large desk and took out a bottle of water. He started to get up.

"No, I'll come to you," Hana said as she quickly stepped over and retrieved the water from his hand. "Thanks."

Hana unscrewed the top of the water bottle and took a drink. When she set it down on the small table beside her chair, she noticed a brown necklace in front of the brass lamp. Picking it up, she examined it and held it up. "Do you know what this is?" she asked.

"It's a necklace," Jakob answered. "I found it the other day."

"It's a misbaha—prayer beads," Hana said. "They're also called subha beads."

"Prayer beads," Jakob said.

"Yes. A misbaha is used by religious men in Islam when they glorify Allah. The beads help them keep track of where they are in the ritual. Most misbaha have ninety-nine beads, but some, like this one, have thirty-three. They're also used as stress relievers or 'worry beads.' Some of the most expensive are made of amber and give off a fragrance when touched."

Ben nodded. "I've seen them hanging in shops in the Arab market in Jerusalem. At first I thought they were rosary beads for sale to Catholics, but one of the guys in our group explained the difference."

"Where did you buy this?" Hana asked Jakob. "I hope you didn't pay much for it."

Jakob's face looked pale. "I didn't buy it," he said. "It was in the bushes by the apartment where I was attacked."

Hana glanced at Ben, who was now staring wide-eyed at the misbaha. "Do you think there might be a link between the attack on Jakob and my case?" he asked Hana.

"Don't jump to conclusions," Jakob quickly said. "I was knocked out at the top of the stairs by a mugger who stole my wallet. I found the—whatever you called it—in the bushes."

"Is that all you remember about the attack?" Hana asked.

Jakob rubbed his left temple. "The police report claims the assailant dragged me down the stairs, but I didn't learn that part until the other day."

"It could have been an attempted kidnapping," Hana said. "And something caused the man who attacked you to flee."

"No, no," Jakob said and held up his hands. "We're not going all conspiracy theory here."

Hana glanced down at the misbaha. The beads were wooden and irregular in shape. The necklace was crudely fashioned, perhaps even homemade. That thought made a chill run down her spine. Anyone who went to the trouble to construct his own misbaha was serious about its use.

"Carrying around prayer beads doesn't prove anything," Hana said, reining in her imagination. "A lot of peaceful old men and women sit in the sun and chat while fingering the beads. But where you found these might be important."

"Maybe you should show that to the police," Ben suggested.

"Probably won't do much good after Hana and I have handled it like we owned it," Jakob said.

Hana quickly returned the misbaha to the lamp table.

"If someone was targeting me, do you really think it would be someone who lived near my friend's apartment?" Jakob asked. "That's too random."

"That argument doesn't make me feel any better," Ben replied. "Especially in regard to Sadie."

The mention of the little girl caused Hana's thoughts to take a U-turn. "Ben's right," she said slowly. "It's one thing to consider the risk to us, but Sadie is another matter."

CHAPTER 14

Hana barely noticed her surroundings as she drove back to her office. It was possible, but not likely, that a terrorist network would target Jakob Brodsky. Most groups were regional and didn't have the level of organization to operate on the other side of the world. Al-Qaeda had been the exception. An even bigger question was how Jakob had shown up on someone's radar in the first place.

"I like Mr. Humid in Israel," Janet bubbled as soon as Hana appeared. "He called, and I talked to him for a few minutes. He has a dreamy voice, so deep and masculine. Why isn't there a photo on his website? I'm dying to see what he looks like."

"It's Hasan," Hana replied. "And he doesn't want to be easily identified."

"I think you should meet with him before you talk to anyone else. Take a photo on your phone when he's not looking and send it to me so—"

"Janet, please."

"Okay, sorry. I'm a lousy matchmaker, but my motives are pure. I want people to be as happy as I am."

"I appreciate that."

Ten minutes later Hana made her way to Mr. Lowenstein's office to tell him about Jakob Brodsky's status and the Islamic prayer beads.

"Do you think there might be a connection between these beads and the attack?" the senior partner asked.

"I don't know."

"It sounds far-fetched to me, except for the fact that Brodsky cast a broad net trying to find cocounsel in the case. Lawyer forums aren't as private as some attorneys think they are. A savvy internet researcher who's keeping tabs on anyone expressing interest in Gloria Neumann's death could have picked up on his post, and he'd never know it."

"What about Ben and Sadie? I'm worried about their safety."

Mr. Lowenstein eyed Hana for a moment. "What are you really asking? Get to the root of it."

Hana cleared her throat before answering. "If Ben wants to continue with the investigation, I'm ready to proceed," she said. "But that has to be his decision more than mine."

"I agree."

Hana spent the rest of the afternoon working on a project for Mr. Collins and barely made it to the doggie day care center in time to avoid a late fee. Leon weakly wagged his tail when he saw her.

"Is he okay?" Hana asked the young woman attendant who brought the dog to her.

"Did you watch him any on the spy cam today?" the woman replied. "He plays as hard as any dog here. I'm surprised you're not carrying him to the car like a child in the middle of a nap."

Hana smiled and picked up the puppy. His fur was damp.

"Did he have a bath?" she asked.

"Yes," the woman said, pointing to the daily summary in Hana's hand. "Read about it. Part of the play with a couple of other dogs ended up being messy."

Leon lay on the passenger seat of the car and struggled to keep his eyelids open during the drive home. He revived when Hana poured dog food into his metal dish but soon fell asleep for good.

When Hana slipped out of bed around three thirty in the morning, her first thoughts went to the Neumann case and the attack on Jakob Brodsky. Thinking about it in the dark of night made her nervous for her own safety. She tiptoed into the kitchen to make sure she'd locked the front door and then turned on the outside lights for a few seconds to make sure no one was in the small yard. Leon didn't stir in his kennel.

Hana hated giving in to fear, but she couldn't help it. She spent thirty minutes reading scriptures on the topic. The most help came from the Psalms and Isaiah. She returned to bed repeating Isaiah 12:2: "Surely God is my salvation; I will trust and not be afraid. The LORD, the LORD himself, is my strength and my defense; he has become my salvation." It was a beautiful promise, but she couldn't escape passages with a different message. Daniel spent a night in the lions' den; Paul was whipped and beaten. Sometimes God delivered people from danger; other times he was with them as they passed through it.

• • •

The following morning one of the other lawyers in their office building gave Jakob a ride to work. Jakob had been seated at his desk for only a few minutes when there was a knock on his door.

"Come in!" he said.

It was Butch Watson. The beefy lawyer's eyes revealed deep fatigue.

"You look terrible," Jakob said.

"Did you check yourself in the mirror before you left for work?" Butch replied. "You look like a potato about to sprout and bud."

Jakob shrugged. "You win that argument. How are the boys?"

"I don't want to say they're too healthy because that's not possible. But they have the appetites of hikers on the Appalachian Trail. Nelle continually stays in the red zone. I spend my time getting one of the babies ready for her to feed and then cleaning up the other one. Her folks are there today, and I received a hall pass so I can earn enough money to pay for diapers." Butch rubbed his eyes. "By the way, Nelle was blown away by your cleanup job in the kitchen. The only problem is that now she's going to expect me to do it."

"A few more sleepless nights should drive that out of her mind."

"There's something else I need to tell you," Butch said. "A woman who lives in our apartment complex stopped by yesterday. She was at home the evening of your attack."

"Did she see anything?" Jakob asked.

"Not directly. She lives in the next building and heard all the sirens from the police and ambulance. About an hour earlier, she was taking trash to the Dumpster when a car flew around the corner and almost hit her. Garbage went everywhere. She yelled for the driver to stop. Someone got out on the passenger side and shined a flashlight at her. He said something in a language she didn't understand and got back in the car."

"What's the connection?" Jakob asked.

"How long were you in our apartment providing maid service?"

"I don't know. It could have been thirty minutes, maybe forty. Do you think the guys in the car were the ones who knocked me in the head?"

"Possibly. Nelle told our neighbor to get in touch with the police. It might create a lead."

"Did she describe the car?"

"She thinks it was big and blue."

"That's a large universe."

"Yeah. She didn't remember the make or model, license plate, or anything more helpful. But to be fair, she was up to her elbows in garbage."

Jakob glanced down at the desk drawer where he'd stored the misbaha beads after the meeting with Ben and Hana. He decided not to show the beads to Butch. The new father had enough to worry about.

"Even if there's nothing to it, it will give me a good reason to check with the detective working the investigation and ask how it's going," he said.

After Butch left, Jakob called the detective and left a voice mail.

A moment later an email from Hana Abboud appeared. She wanted to meet again as soon as possible with Jakob and Ben. Jakob called her office. Hana wasn't available, and the receptionist directed him to her assistant.

"Would you be available at four o'clock?" the woman asked.

Jakob glanced at his computer. "I can make it, but I'm not sure about Ben Neumann."

"He accepted an email invite a few minutes ago."

"Okay, I'll be there."

Jakob took a smelly taxi to Collins, Lowenstein, and Capella. When he got out, he made up his mind to contact Emily Johnson for future rides. The sporty yellow car was clean and the driver skilled.

Ben and Sadie came through the door a few minutes after Jakob arrived. The little girl's face was flushed and her hair disheveled. As soon as Ben sat down, she brushed a loose strand away from her face, climbed into her father's lap, and closed her eyes.

"Is she sick?" Jakob asked.

"No," Ben said, stroking her head. "It was field day at school, and she's been running around outside. She fell asleep during the car ride."

The door to the office suites opened, and a middle-aged woman came out. "I'm Hana's assistant," she said. "Please come with me."

Ben carried Sadie, who rested her head on his right shoulder. When Sadie saw Hana, she raised her head and extended her arms toward her. Ben transferred the child to the female lawyer. Sadie promptly laid her head on Hana's shoulder and closed her eyes.

"Does she have a fever?" Hana asked.

Ben told Hana about field day, which included a much lengthier explanation than the one he'd given Jakob. While Ben talked, Jakob saw a folder labeled "Neumann v. Doe et al." on the table beside Hana's laptop. The folder was much thicker than the last time they'd met.

"Do you think she'll sleep through this meeting?" Hana asked as she sat down with Sadie in her arms.

"We'll see," Ben answered. "She can be cranky when she wakes up."

"How are you feeling?" Hana asked Jakob.

"Traveling at the speed of light on the road to recovery," Jakob replied. "Ready to book a flight to Israel."

"Before we get to that, I need to know what Ben thinks about the possibility that he and Sadie are in danger. I talked to Mr. Lowenstein, and while we aren't convinced there is a terrorist connection to the attack at the apartment, it raises an issue we should discuss now. I know we're leaving Sadie's name out of any lawsuit, but is that enough?"

Jakob turned to Ben, who was staring at his daughter in Hana's arms. "That's why I lay awake last night and couldn't sleep," he answered. "I thought about calling Gloria's parents this morning, but it's not right to put this decision on them. Sadie is my responsibility."

"And you're the most important person in her life," Hana added.

Jakob started to speak but decided to keep his mouth shut. Ben had entered territory where only he could go.

"I'm going to stick with the choice I made when I decided to pursue a lawsuit in the first place," Ben said. "I want to keep going."

"Okay," Hana replied.

"I'm good with that," Jakob said.

Hana turned toward Jakob. "Do you think you've publicized the case too much?" she asked. "Mr. Lowenstein said the lawyer forums where you posted requests for assistance aren't always private."

"I'm sure he's right," Jakob answered. "But it's a huge leap from a trial lawyers' list server to me being mugged in north Atlanta."

"We should all be careful where and how we communicate," Hana said.

Jakob and Ben nodded in agreement.

"My assistant is completing a memo for you that will bring you up-to-date on everything we've done," Hana said. "I'll check to see if it's finished."

When Hana stood, Sadie visibly tightened her grip on the lawyer's neck.

"Looks like Sadie wants to go with you," Ben said. "I don't want her to be a distraction."

"It's fine. All I have to do is proofread the memo when it's complete."

After Hana and Sadie left, Jakob shut his eyes. He felt a headache building. When he opened his eyes, Ben was staring at him.

"Headache," Jakob said.

"It's not just that," Ben replied. "You need time to recover, and taking a trip to Israel right now doesn't make sense to me. It was obvious that you were struggling yesterday at your office."

"It looked that bad?"

"It was that bad. Look, I don't think Hana is trying to squeeze you out of the case, and I'll be glad to confront her about it if you want me to."

Jakob was used to being the one who acted forcibly on behalf of his clients, so it felt strange being on the receiving end of an offer of help.

"Thanks, but I can talk for myself," he said.

"Of course you can, but as the client I have the right to an opinion. You've told me that from the beginning of your representation."

"True, but I didn't expect you to take me seriously." Jakob managed a pained smile. In the back of his mind, though, he knew Ben was right.

Ben waited.

"Okay," Jakob said. "You win. I'll hold off on this initial trip to Israel."

"You know it's the smart move, don't you?"

Jakob nodded. "Yeah. But let me tell Hana."

• • •

While she waited for Janet, Hana sat in her office chair with Sadie in her arms. She softly hummed a melody from her own childhood. Sadie stirred and raised her head slightly.

"Does that song have words?" she asked.

"Yes." Hana began to sing softly in Arabic. Sadie lowered her head. The song had a haunting melody. It was about a shepherd boy who searched for a lost sheep under the light of the stars. Exhausted, he fell asleep, and when he awoke, he discovered the lamb curled up beside him. Hana's eyes were usually too heavy to stay open by the time her mother reached the part about the boy falling asleep. Sadie's breathing was slow and steady. Hana's door opened, and Janet peeked inside. Hana nodded, and the assistant quietly came in. Hana transitioned to a melody without words. Janet sat across the desk from her and listened. She didn't speak until Hana stopped.

"That gave me chill bumps," Janet whispered, rubbing her arms.

Hana patted Sadie's back. "She brings out the best in me."

"The mothering instinct if you ask me," Janet replied in a soft voice. "It's remarkable how quickly she's connected with you."

Hana pointed up. "He's doing it, but I'm not sure exactly why."

"God loves the orphan," Janet answered. "Here's the memo. I double-checked it because I knew you were spending time in here with Sadie."

Hana held the sheets of paper in her hand resting lightly on Sadie's back.

"Looks good," she said. "Please make three copies."

Hana softly talked to Sadie while carrying her back to the conference room. The little girl stirred and raised her head. Her eyes blinked open.

"Where's my daddy?" she asked.

"Waiting for us," Hana answered. "I'm taking you to him."

Sadie wiggled to the floor. "I can walk now," she announced.

They held hands. The little girl's grip was strong. Upon reaching the conference room, Sadie ran over to her father. Hana handed the two men copies of the memo.

"Thanks," Jakob said. "Ben and I talked, and I'm not going to join you on this trip to Israel. I'm not in shape to do so, but I want to remain in the loop of information."

"Yes—" Hana began.

"And I insist on it," Ben added before she could continue. "Jakob took my case when no one else would give me a call back. He's my lawyer."

"I understand. I'll communicate with both of you."

"Hana sang to me," Sadie cut in.

"What did she sing about?" Ben asked.

"I don't know," Sadie said with a shake of her head. "But I liked it." Hana explained the history and meaning of the song.

Ben smiled. "I'm sorry I missed that," he said.

"It made me feel all warm and cozy in here." Sadie touched her chest.

CHAPTER 15

Ben gave Jakob a ride home from Collins, Lowenstein, and Capella. Jakob's head was pounding, and as soon as he was inside his apartment, he took two pain pills, wolfed down a few saltine crackers, and lay on the sofa with a hot rag on his forehead. After about thirty minutes the pain began to subside as the potent medicine kicked in. He repositioned himself on the couch and wondered how much longer he was going to be plagued with side effects from the injuries he'd received in the attack. He'd never been sick for more than a few days in his life. His phone, which was on the coffee table in front of the sofa, vibrated. Jakob's first impulse was to ignore it, but when he saw the call was from the Atlanta Police Department, he answered.

"This is Detective Freeman, returning your call," the man on the other end of the line said.

Jakob told him about the conversation between Butch's wife, Nelle, and the woman at the apartment complex.

"Do you have the name and phone number for the neighbor?"

Jakob realized he hadn't asked Butch for this basic data. "No, but I can give you Butch Watson's number."

"The incident with the car fits other information we've uncovered," the detective replied.

"What other information?" Jakob asked, sitting up straighter on the couch.

"It's an ongoing investigation," Freeman said in a matter-of-fact voice. "I can't reveal any specifics to you, even though you're the victim. But this case isn't sitting dead in a filing cabinet."

Jakob's headache had retreated under the assault of the strong pain medication, and he felt more lucid. "There's something else that might be relevant," he said and then told Freeman about finding the misbaha beads and his involvement in the Neumann case.

"Where are these prayer beads now?"

"At my office."

"I'll send a patrol officer to pick them up tomorrow."

After the call ended, Jakob went downstairs to the small room where all the tenants had post office boxes. As he thumbed through a stack of advertising flyers, he heard a noise and saw movement through the glass top half of the exit door. The door was locked on the inside, barring any entrance. Holding the mail in his hand, Jakob looked out. It was dark, and he could see only as far as a security light a few feet from the door. No one was there. A flying object flashed through the circle cast by the light. It was a fruit bat. Jakob had seen the bats hunting insects on warm evenings. He returned upstairs with his mail.

• • •

The following morning, Hana sent a short memo to Mr. Lowenstein about the meeting with Jakob and Ben. She also sent an email to Anat Naphtali asking her friend about a good time to call. It was early afternoon in Tel Aviv. Anat answered with a single word: Now!

Hana placed the call, and Anat answered in Arabic.

"How are you feeling?" Hana replied in the same language.

Anat switched to Hebrew. "Okay, but not well enough to practice my Arabic with you. I'll mix up words like scrambled eggs."

"Your Arabic worked at the airport."

"Not good enough. That's why we needed you. But this has been a good day, even though I have zero appetite in the morning and can't use words like 'pickled fish' in a sentence before noon. What's new in your world?"

Hana told her friend about her new puppy.

"I would have predicted you'd adopt a cat, not a dog," Anat replied. "Make sure he understands you in multiple languages. That will come in handy if you have to order him to attack someone to protect you."

"My dog is a lover, not a fighter," Hana said. "Can you keep this conversation between us?"

"Sure."

Hana told Anat about the Neumann case without violating the attorney-client confidentiality rules. However, she did include the attack on Jakob Brodsky and his finding the misbaha prayer beads.

"I remember when the American was murdered," Anat said. "I was sitting in a café in Dizengoff Square when I heard the news. I never knew what happened to the child except that she was injured. I'm glad she's okay."

Hana didn't respond. Sadie was alive, but no one could claim she was okay.

Anat continued, speaking more rapidly. "And I don't think you should get involved in this. You may be living in America, but you will eventually come home. It only takes one crazy person to find out what you're doing and make you his next target. Does your family know about this?"

"No."

"They would drag you to Reineh and lock you up until they could find a proper husband for you. They could be at risk, too. This is a terrible idea."

Anat was a smart, opinionated person. Hana inwardly repeated Isaiah 12:2.

"I'd only put myself in potential danger for a good reason," Hana said, but she instantly knew that hadn't sounded persuasive.

"Listen to yourself!" Anat shot back. "Just because you didn't serve in a combat unit in the IDF is no reason to do something stupid now. You did a lot more for the country serving in security at the airport than you could have sitting in a tent on the Golan watching the snow melt on Mount Hermon. It's the cowards in charge who send the young men out to die in jihad. The leaders talk tough but stay behind."

Hana could tell Anat wasn't going to stop unless interrupted, so she cut in. "You're right, and I'm glad you care about my safety. Will you at least let me tell you why I wanted to talk to you today?"

"Okay, but that's not going to shut me up."

"I know," Hana said, then continued, "I'm coming to Israel to interview investigators and do preliminary research. I've talked to Sahir Benali but not Daud Hasan. Now that you know the facts, are there any larger firms that might be better equipped to help me?"

"My opinion is that you should get out of this mess before your name is linked to it."

"I understand."

Anat was silent for so long that Hana checked her phone to make sure her friend hadn't hung up on her. "Are you there?" she finally asked.

"Yes, yes, yes," Anat replied in the common Israeli fashion of rapidly repeating short answers to questions. "Let me think about it and make a few phone calls. As to Sahir and Daud, Sahir is a grinder who will dig until he comes up with an answer. Daud is younger and more up-to-date on technology. Also—" Anat was silent again for a moment.

"What?" Hana asked.

"If you were ever in danger, I'd want Daud looking after you. He never talks about some of his training, but I think he can do things most people only see in movies."

A shudder ran down Hana's spine. "I'll consider that," she replied.

"Make the smart move and let someone else go down this dark hole in the ground. The units assigned to Gaza tunnel duty have the scariest job in the army. They don't need any competition from you."

The phone call ended. Hana stared out her small window for several moments. She didn't see the Atlanta skyline; she saw Reineh and the deep concern she knew would be on the faces of her family members if they knew what she was doing.

• • •

It had been two days since Jakob's meeting with Ben Neumann and Hana Abboud. He'd transitioned to a smaller bandage that barely covered the knots on his skull. The bumps were getting softer, and the area of bruising more yellow than purple. He eased into the rear seat of Emily Johnson's car after making arrangements with her to serve as his driver for the day. As promised, the blond driver had arrived exactly on time to pick him up for work. She pushed the passenger seat forward to increase his legroom.

"How's traffic between here and my office?" Jakob asked as he closed the door.

"No wrecks or delays unless they happen while we're en route," she replied as she lowered the volume of the music that was blasting from the speakers.

"That's from *Swan Lake*, isn't it?" Jakob asked.

"Yes." Emily glanced at him in the rearview mirror. "You're good."

Emily zigzagged through traffic and beat a light just as it was turning yellow. Jakob was thrown back and forth in his seat. He checked to make sure his seat belt was securely fastened. His cell phone vibrated with a call from Detective Freeman. He held the phone to his ear and answered. Emily turned down the volume of the music.

"We've identified a possible suspect in your case," the detective began.

"Who?" Jakob asked as Emily failed to make a light and the car came to a sudden stop.

"We're not sure about his real name, but based on facial recognition software, he turned up as a person of interest for the customs branch of Homeland Security."

"Homeland Security?"

"Yes."

"And how did you get a picture of his face?"

"At your apartment complex two nights ago. He was driving a car matching the description of the vehicle that almost ran over the woman the night of the attack. After we interviewed her, we were able to narrow down the car to a late-model Buick from her description of the taillights. And the camera located by the barrier gate at your complex entrance gave us a screenshot of the suspect."

Jakob was speechless. He vaguely remembered seeing the camera on a metal pole.

"You're watching my apartment?" he managed.

"Not all the time, but aspects of the assault bore the marks of a hit, not a robbery. We weren't sure, of course, but we placed your case in a protocol that allocates resources to check on you for a few weeks to make sure you're not an ongoing target."

Jakob tried to calm his rapidly beating heart. Emily turned onto Roswell Road. They were ten minutes away from Jakob's office.

He looked at the back of Emily's head. The blond music student didn't need to know his business.

"What else can you tell me?" he asked in a low voice.

"Homeland Security believes the man we identified left the country yesterday. They were in position to apprehend him in the southwest part of the city on other charges, but he evaded capture and used a fake passport to book a flight to Venezuela where we can't touch him."

"He's from Venezuela?"

"No, somewhere in the Middle East. The feds wouldn't give us a specific country of origin. But there's no question he was here illegally and involved in smuggling untaxed cigarettes."

"I'm not following this."

"The suspect was making money selling bootleg cigarettes and then funneling the profits overseas."

Jakob sat up straighter in the seat. "What's his name? And the identity of the organization he's linked to. That could be important to me in a civil case I'm handling."

"They wouldn't tell me any of that information. Once they had the image of his face and identified him, my contact told me they'd take it from there."

Emily pulled in front of the office building and stopped.

"Hold on," Jakob said to the detective. "I have another question for you."

Jakob got out and waved bye to Emily. His thoughts flashed to how his father must have felt when under constant threat from the KGB. "What precautions should I take?" he asked.

"Exercise common sense and keep your eyes open," the detective replied. "We're an open society. The address of an ordinary citizen can be located within seconds with the right online program."

"I guess I'm looking for an Arab?"

"Most likely, but there's no guarantee. Terrorists come in all nationalities. Terrorism is based on belief, not ethnicity. I'll call again as soon as I have relevant information to pass along."

The call ended. Jakob stepped inside the two-story building.

"You look better," Maddie said brightly. "How do you feel?"

"Worse," Jakob mumbled as he continued up the stairs.

• • •

Hana ordered a tabbouleh salad at Mr. Akbar's restaurant. The spicy dish woke up her taste buds.

"Where's Gadi?" Hana asked when she didn't see Mr. Akbar's son at his usual place in front of the flattop grill.

"He left yesterday for Beirut," Mr. Akbar replied. "He feels chained down here at the restaurant and doesn't appreciate the opportunity for his future. When I tried to stop him we had an argument, and he left the house without saying good-bye."

Hana's heart went out to the grieving father. "Maybe he'll appreciate America and a future in the family business when he returns."

"I'm worried about more than that."

"I know," Hana said, not wanting to verbalize the possibility that Gadi might join a militant Islamic group and never return.

The restaurant was busy, but Mr. Akbar lingered. "I thought about you praying for Gadi," the older man said anxiously in a softer voice. "What do you pray except 'if Allah wills it'?"

Hana offered up a quick plea for heavenly help. Before she could speak, one of the other workers called out to Mr. Akbar, and he stepped away. Hana's heart was beating so hard she wondered if the woman standing next to her in the noisy restaurant could hear it. It was several minutes before the owner returned. Hana's salad was almost gone when he did.

"You enjoyed the food?" he asked.

"Yes," Hana answered. "I loved it. And that's what I pray for you and Gadi. That you will experience God's goodness and love."

"Experience love?" Mr. Akbar asked, a puzzled expression on his face.

Hana looked directly into the older man's eyes. "Mr. Akbar, I come from a Christian family. We've believed in Jesus Christ for hundreds of years."

"Oh, I see," the restaurant owner said and nodded slowly with a serious expression on his face. "I would not want you to dishonor the faith of your fathers. I had Christian friends when I was a boy. We played together all the time. That was during the time when we believed the different groups could live together in peace."

Hana knew all about the valiant attempts by Maronite Christians and the two branches of Islam in the country to coexist after World War I.

"And you are welcome here at my restaurant as an honored guest,"

Mr. Akbar continued. "Hearing your words makes me wish for the old days. And please, keep praying to your God."

After leaving the restaurant, Hana spent most of the time during the short drive to her office building thinking about Mr. Akbar and his son. The concept of God's mercy was common in Islam, but the Qur'an contained only a few references to divine love, all linked to the performance of religious duties. God's unconditional love didn't exist in the Islamic world. Hana's heart ached. She reached Janet's desk.

"Do you know that God loves you?" Hana blurted out.

"Uh, yes," her assistant replied, her eyes big. "That's what it says in John 3:16. I memorized that verse when I was just a girl, and it was one of the first things I taught my kids."

"Right, I didn't mean to—"

"It's okay. Did something happen at lunch?"

"Yes," Hana answered, knowing she shouldn't relate her conversation at the restaurant with Mr. Akbar. "And be glad you live in America."

"I am," Janet said. "Mr. Collins, one of your American bosses, wants to see you."

When she returned to her office after an hour-long meeting with Mr. Collins, Hana had an email from Anat Naphtali providing information about three more investigative firms. Hana spent the rest of the afternoon checking them out and setting up appointments. She also sent emails to Sahir Benali and Daud Hasan requesting times for face-to-face interviews while she was in Jerusalem. She wrote a group email to members of her family letting them know she wouldn't have time for more than a brief visit in Reineh.

As she was shutting down her computer for the evening, she received a response from Daud Hasan. It was after midnight in Israel. The investigator wanted to talk with her on the phone the following afternoon. Hana sent an email agreeing to a call and copied Jakob, inviting him to join them.

CHAPTER 16

The police officer sent to collect the misbaha beads left Jakob's office. Thirty minutes later, Jakob was in the rear seat of Emily's car on his way to a deposition.

"The insurance defense lawyer wants to start a few minutes earlier," Jakob said.

Emily floored the accelerator, and the car shot forward. She turned up the volume of her music, a Bach fugue played on a massive pipe organ. She took an unexpected turn away from the main thoroughfare onto a side street. Jakob knew the best route to their destination.

"Why did you turn there?" he asked in a loud voice.

Without answering, Emily braked hard and turned onto another side street. Thrown to the right, Jakob glanced around. They were in a run-down residential neighborhood. He repeated his question.

"Trust me," she said.

They passed a boarded-up convenience store and took another sharp left. They reached a traffic light as it turned green, and Emily turned onto a familiar main road that was surprisingly close to where Jakob needed to go. The serpentine detour had enabled them to avoid two well-known traffic bottlenecks. Then they left the main road again. This time, Jakob tried to keep track of the detour but couldn't. Emily turned left into the back of a parking lot and stopped.

"Here we are," she announced as she turned off the music. "Fourteen minutes early."

Jakob hadn't approached the office building from this direction before, but he quickly recognized it and grabbed his laptop and brief-case. "That was impressive driving," he said. "How did you know those side routes?"

"I used to be a cop who worked this part of the city."

Not sure if the eclectic blonde was telling him the truth or attempting a joke, Jakob got out of the car. Emily turned sharply and left the parking lot.

An hour and a half later, Jakob and the defense lawyer settled the case on terms favorable to Jakob's client. When he stepped outside, Emily was waiting. It was exactly one thirty.

"You play it tight, don't you?" the driver said as she put the car in gear and took off. "I wasn't going to cut you any slack."

"It's been a good day. I hope nothing ruins it."

After Emily let him out in front of Hana's office building, Jakob glanced up and down the street. A man with an olive complexion approached and looked directly into Jakob's face before glancing away. Jakob watched him continue down the street. The man disappeared around a corner. Jakob entered the building, glad to see an armed security guard positioned near a fountain in the center of the large atrium.

• • •

Janet buzzed Hana's phone. "Mr. Brodsky is here," she said. "I reserved conference room J."

"Okay, tell him I'll be there shortly."

Hana took her laptop to the conference room. Jakob was facing the large window that provided a panoramic view of Buckhead. While they waited for Daud Hasan to call, she updated him on her plans.

The speakerphone in the middle of the table buzzed. It was Janet. "Mr. Hasan is on the phone."

"Thanks," Hana responded and turned to Jakob. "I know Hasan speaks English, but we'll need to check his level of fluency."

The phone buzzed and Hana answered in English. "Hello."

"Hasan, here," a male voice said in Hebrew.

"This is Hana Abboud," Hana replied, continuing in English. "I'm here with Jakob Brodsky, one of the other lawyers representing the Neumann family. Are you available for a meeting when I am in Israel?"

"No problem," Daud answered in heavily accented English. "I am calling now because I spoke with Anat earlier, and she wanted me to call you immediately."

"For what reason?" Hana asked.

Daud responded in Arabic. "Anat is concerned about your safety. Is the lawyer with you the one who was attacked?"

"Yes," Hana replied in Arabic. She held up her finger for Jakob to be patient. "But the police haven't established a connection."

"Okay, tell me more about the lawsuit."

"Can I switch to English?" Hana asked. "That way Jakob can understand."

"I'd prefer Hebrew or Arabic."

Hana turned to Jakob. "I'm going to explain the basis for the lawsuit to him in Arabic."

"Did he answer your question about Anat?"

"I'll explain later," she replied and then spoke to Daud in Arabic. "We are at the beginning stages of the investigation and want to pursue a lawsuit under the US Anti-Terrorism statutes."

Hana launched into a quick tutorial in Arabic about the legal basis for a cause of action. They went back and forth as she explained what they needed and how the investigator might be able to help.

"Are you working with the US government?" Daud asked when she paused.

"No," Hana answered, surprised by the question. "Why?"

"A man from New York City who said he worked for the US government called me about the Neumann murder two days after I received your first email. I thought there might be a connection with you. He wanted to hire me."

"What did he want you to do?" Hana asked. "And before you answer, let me translate for Jakob."

Jakob's eyes widened as he listened. "Which branch of the US government?" he asked.

"He did not tell me," Daud answered in English. "At first I thought he was looking for a translator, but he told me they were investigating the terrorist attack on Gloria Neumann and wanted my professional help. He did not answer when I asked if someone within the Israeli government gave him my name."

Daud Hasan's English seemed better than he'd initially let on.

"Did he hire you?" she asked.

"No, I turned him down."

"Why?"

"I am not a mercenary. If you do one job for a foreign government, they will come back and ask you to do another. Then, if you turn them down, they will blow your cover," Hasan said.

Jakob nodded at Hana and mouthed, "That's good."

"What kind of cover?" Hana asked.

"Investigative."

Hana wasn't sure what Daud meant but left it alone. "What do you already know about Gloria Neumann's murder?" she asked.

"It was described as a lone-wolf attack in the Israeli press," the investigator said, switching back to Arabic. "That may not be true. If the man who contacted me works for the CIA, he wouldn't have tried to hire me unless the US believes the Zadan brothers had links to a terrorist network."

"Is the Palestinian Authority paying money to the Zadan family?" she asked.

"Probably, but I'll confirm it. They make payments even in the case of an attack by an unaffiliated terrorist. It's easy to get an answer on that."

"I also need to find out if the younger Zadan brother is still in custody and interview him. Can you locate him?"

"Yes, but whether he will talk is unknown. I doubt he'll talk to you. But there are alternative ways to obtain information."

Hana could see Jakob checking his watch. So far, except for brief moments, he'd been cut out of much of the conversation.

"Would you be willing to do some preliminary work before I arrive in Israel?" she asked.

"Without a retainer contract or being paid?"

"No, of course not," Hana answered, embarrassed. "But I definitely want to meet with you."

Daud gave her his personal cell phone number. She did the same.

"Anat mentioned you would be talking to other investigative firms," Daud said. "Who is on your list?"

"Why do you ask?"

"So I can tell you if they're suited for this type of work."

"I'll make up my own mind on that."

"Okay. See you in Jerusalem."

Hana pressed the button on the speaker to end the call. "Sorry, we were able to communicate much better in Arabic," she said to Jakob.

"I understand," he said, then quickly added, "Actually, I didn't understand it at all. What's the bottom line?"

Hana summarized the Arabic portion of the conversation.

"He's not telling you everything he knows."

"You're right," Hana agreed. "I had the same feeling."

"And do you really believe he'd give you an honest opinion about his competition?"

"No."

Jakob told Hana about his conversation with Detective Freeman.

"That's real evidence showing you were targeted," she said soberly. "How do you feel about it?"

"Right now, it's an adrenaline rush. Tomorrow morning, I may have a different opinion. There's no need to mention it to anyone else except Ben and Mr. Lowenstein."

"Why not?"

"Because we don't know who we can trust."

After Jakob left, Hana returned to her office, and Janet ambushed her.

"How was the call?" Janet asked. "And what did you think about Daud Hasan? Even his name has an air of mystery. What does it mean? You've told me before how important that is in your culture."

Hana thought for a moment. "Daud is David, which means 'beloved.' It's pronounced with an emphasis on the last two letters. Hasan indicates that the person is handsome."

Janet nodded. "I like that. Very much. Maybe you should have named your dog Hasan instead of Leon."

Hana laughed. "I'm going to meet with Daud Hasan in Israel."

"I approve."

"And several other investigators, including Sahir Benali."

"You know my vote."

"Yes, and it will be counted."

• • •

After fixing a sandwich for supper, Jakob logged on to his home computer and then the link to his office account. He took a bite of Lebanon bologna and Swiss cheese on rye bread. Before he checked anything on the computer, his phone on the coffee table vibrated. It was Detective Freeman.

"We found the dark blue car and made an arrest," the detective began. "A patrol officer saw the car in a residential neighborhood off Piedmont Road and pulled it over. The driver didn't offer any resistance. He's been in a holding cell for a couple of hours."

The location wasn't near where either Jakob or Ben Neumann lived.

"What can you tell me about the driver?" Jakob asked.

"He's not Middle Eastern. His driver's license, which is a fake, listed his name as John Smith."

"John Smith?"

"Actually, John M. Smith. But his fingerprints match a thirty-two-year-old man named Andre Sarkasian arrested two years ago in Raleigh for auto theft. He jumped bond and has been on the run ever since."

"Sarkasian?" Jakob repeated.

"Yes, he's from Dearborn, Michigan, and has a rap sheet going back to when he was a juvenile. He came to the US as a kid from one of those countries in the former Soviet Union that I can't pronounce," Detective Freeman replied.

Jakob sat up straighter. "Do you think he was at the apartment complex the night I was attacked?" he asked.

"Not according to his alibi. He's worked at a local restaurant for three months as a dishwasher. It's not far from our precinct, and I went over there with his picture. Four people in the kitchen and the general manager are one hundred percent sure Sarkasian, or Johnny as they know him, was working at the time you were attacked."

"Any connections with the man who came to my apartment complex and then fled the country?"

"Too soon to know. Sarkasian has had lawyers before, so he didn't tell us anything except his alibi story. Other than that, he's kept his mouth shut. He doesn't know we have a match on his fingerprints on the case in North Carolina. He's probably hoping bail will be set so he can take off again. That's not happening."

"What will you do now?"

"Johnny will lawyer up with a public defender, and we'll go from there until he's extradited to North Carolina."

While finishing his sandwich after the call ended, Jakob thought about what the detective had told him. A link to one of the Islamic republics to the south of Russia made Jakob's skin crawl. He called Ben Neumann.

"You're working late," Ben said.

"Yes, is Sadie in bed?"

"For over an hour. I received an email from Hana a few minutes ago. She mentioned what the detective told you about the man who fled the country."

"Yes, and that's not all." Jakob told him about the follow-up call from Detective Freeman. "With the one guy gone and the arrest of Sarkasian, it's clear the police are bringing light to the situation. That should cut down on the risk."

"Our townhome is in a gated community," Ben said slowly. "But we leave every morning when Sadie goes to school or day care and I go to work. After that, we're as vulnerable as anyone else."

CHAPTER 17

Hana woke up suddenly from a deep sleep, grateful she'd escaped from a nightmare in which she was in Reineh but couldn't find her way home. Walking faster and faster, she glanced over her shoulder to make sure she wasn't being followed or chased. Out of the corner of her eye, she saw shadowy figures that didn't materialize in human form. A deadly vapor came from their faces. Hana started running as fast as she could up a hill, even though she didn't know what lay at the top. Just as she crested the hill she jerked awake. Her heart was pounding, and there was perspiration on her forehead.

Getting out of bed, she splashed water on her face before going into the living room to read and pray. Leon was lying in the kennel on his back with his legs in the air. Hana had no idea a dog could sleep in such an unusual position. He didn't stir when she sat on the couch and turned on a lamp. She opened her Bible to Psalm 46. The chapter began with an earthquake and toward the end quoted the famous words "Be still, and know that I am God."

One of Hana's faith goals was to quickly bring herself to a place of internal rest regardless of her outward circumstances. Even with the psalmist's help, it took a full hour to dispel the nagging wisps of the nightmare from her soul. There was no doubt that since she'd become involved in the Neumann case, the level of spiritual warfare swirling around her had increased.

In the morning, Hana brewed her coffee Middle Eastern–strong and poured an extra cup to take in the car. After dropping Leon off, she arrived at the office earlier than usual and began working.

Morning was her most productive time of the day. When she finally took a break at ten o'clock, she'd accomplished a lot. She stepped out to Janet's desk.

"I could feel the brain activity seeping out from beneath your door," her assistant said. "When you're in the zone like that, it makes my IQ go up a couple of points."

Hana stretched and smiled. "I have to complete several projects before I leave for Israel. Did anyone important want to disturb me?"

"Does Jakob Brodsky make the cut?"

"Yes."

"Also, Mr. Lowenstein wants to see you in five minutes."

"Five minutes!"

"I was about to interrupt you when you came out."

Hana entered the senior partner's office, and he motioned for her to sit down. "What's the status of the Neumann case?" Mr. Lowenstein asked.

Hana told him about her conversation with Daud Hasan. When she mentioned Hasan being contacted by an American governmental official from New York, Mr. Lowenstein's eyes widened, and he held up his hand to stop her.

"That's what I wanted to talk to you about. The US Attorney's Office for the Southern District of New York has an open file on Gloria Neumann's murder, and I talked with an assistant US attorney a few minutes ago. She wanted to know what we were up to."

"How did they know about us?"

"I assume your investigator spoke with them after talking to you yesterday. The woman who called me is named Sylvia Armstrong." Mr. Lowenstein looked down at his desk. "She wanted to find out information, not give it, but she told me it's a criminal investigation."

"Have they identified a suspect besides Tawfik Zadan?" Hana asked.

"I don't know. But the presence of a federal investigation could certainly work in our favor. They have capabilities far beyond ours to obtain information."

"If they're willing to share, but it doesn't sound like that's part of their plan."

"Don't give up so easily," the senior partner replied. "They haven't met you yet. Ms. Armstrong was very interested when I mentioned that we have an Israeli Arab lawyer working on our case and that you'll be in Israel later this week. I think you may be able to broker an exchange of information at the right time, which is another reason for you to get on a plane as soon as possible."

"And complicates the investigator issue," Hana said. "Daud Hasan plainly told me the American tried to hire him, but he refused the offer. Then he talks to the US attorney after getting information from me. What you're telling me makes me wonder who he'd be working for. Jakob Brodsky had a sense Hasan was hiding something. I think we should move on from him."

Mr. Lowenstein shrugged. "When it comes down to it, how much difference is that going to make? In the big picture we're all on the same team—we want to catch and hurt the bad guys—both financially and by locking them up. The way I view it, you should be able to ride Hasan's coattails and use it to our advantage."

"Ride his coattails?"

"Utilize information and guidance he receives from the feds and their other sources. I'm optimistic this can be a breakthrough opportunity."

Once again, Hana had to adjust to Mr. Lowenstein's ability to evaluate a situation differently from the way it first appeared.

"Looking at it that way helps," she said slowly. "But should I confront Hasan?"

"Only as a door for discussion as to how much collaborative communication you can expect. I also want you to call Sylvia Armstrong. I'm sending you her contact information. Try to establish a level of quid pro quo with her. She gives you something; you give her something."

"I'm not sure I'm up for this," Hana sighed.

"View it as a sophisticated form of haggling in the marketplace."

"I'll try, but we're not dealing with oranges or cucumbers."

Hana returned to her office. Janet was on the phone and motioned for her to wait a moment.

"Let me check," the assistant said as she put the caller on hold.

"It's Jakob Brodsky. He wants to know if you're free for lunch. He says it's important."

"Why lunch?"

"He's hungry," Janet offered.

Hana went into her office and picked up the phone. "What's going on, Jakob?" she asked.

"I have news about the criminal investigation into the assault at the apartment complex, and I want to talk to you about our case before you leave. I know it's an imposition, but could you pick me up? I'm not far from your office and can text you the address."

"Okay. I'll leave here in about fifteen minutes."

"I'll be waiting in front of the building so you won't have to park."

• • •

Jakob stood at the curb. It was a warm day. In a few weeks the humid summer heat would descend on Atlanta and cause the pavement and concrete to reach scorching temperatures. He'd taken off his suit jacket and slung it over his shoulder. A car pulled to the curb and stopped. It was Hana. The air-conditioning system was blasting cold air.

"Thanks for picking me up and having the AC on max," Jakob said, leaning over so that the cool air blew directly into his face.

"Where I come from, we consider air-conditioning one of the greatest inventions of all time," Hana replied. "Where would you like to eat?"

"You decide."

"Do you have any dietary restrictions?"

"No, I eat barbecue, bacon, lobster, and shrimp."

"My conscience doesn't prohibit pork, but I rarely eat it. I thought we would go to an Indian place. It's not far from here."

"Fine with me. Do Arabs avoid pork?"

"Islam prohibits pork as strongly as Judaism. That means it's not a common part of Arab diets, even for Christians like me. The Jewish Christians I know usually don't eat pork either."

"Jewish Christians? How is that possible?"

"It's becoming more common all the time."

The car slowed, and Hana pulled into a small public parking lot with several open spaces. "The restaurant is only a couple of blocks from here."

Jakob left his suit jacket in the car and loosened his tie as they walked down the street. Hana was wearing a gray skirt and a light blue blouse. Her black shoes had low heels. They waited at a corner for a streetlight to change. The sun momentarily slipped behind a large cloud.

"It's in the middle of the next block," Hana said when the light changed.

As Hana stepped off the curb, Jakob saw a car running the red light and turning directly in front of them. He instinctively grabbed Hana by the arm and jerked her back. She stumbled, and he had to catch her to keep her from falling.

"Thanks," she said when she'd regained her footing. "I only looked at the red light and didn't see that car coming."

"I've been in hypervigilance mode for several days," Jakob replied. "That's one of the things I wanted to talk to you about at lunch."

The restaurant was tucked into a space between a shoe repair shop and a nail salon.

"How did you find this place?" Jakob asked as he held the door for Hana.

"If you research good Indian food restaurants in Atlanta, this one is at the top of the list. I don't go a month without curry."

There were twelve to fifteen tables arranged in a long, rectangular room. The pungent smells of Indian cuisine met them at the door. All the tables were set up for four people. It was a business crowd. A redheaded woman in her twenties brought them water and a list of the items on the lunch buffet. Jakob had very little experience with Indian food.

"What do you recommend?" he asked Hana.

"I usually go with the lamb curry, vegetable root curry, or rabbit curry," Hana said as she pointed to a section of the buffet. "There are other dishes that don't have a strong curry taste. I know the chilli paneer is popular."

Curry wasn't Jakob's favorite spice, so he piled a generous portion of chilli paneer on his plate.

Before eating, Hana excused herself to the ladies' room. While she was gone, Jakob switched chairs so that his back was to the wall and he could see everything and everyone in front of him. He checked his phone to see if he'd missed a call or text message.

• • •

Hana gave her hair a couple of quick brushes and reapplied a touch of lipstick before leaving the restroom. She'd inwardly kicked herself over the missed opportunity to respond in greater detail to Jakob's question about Jews believing in Jesus. Jakob Brodsky seemed to have a spiritual blank slate. She returned to the table. Jakob had changed seats and now sat to her left instead of across from her.

"Why did you move?" Hana asked.

"Like I said, I've been a bit skittish since the attack."

Hana listened as Jakob told her about his most recent conversation with the police detective, the flight of one of the attackers, and the arrest of Andre Sarkasian.

"Was he from Dagestan, Uzbekistan, Chechnya, or one of the other Islamic countries?" she asked. "The Islamic fundamentalists recruit heavily from there."

"Detective Freeman wasn't sure of his ethnic origin, but I wanted to inform you before you left for Israel. I called Ben about it last night."

Hana thought for a moment. On rare occasions she carried a Jericho 9 mm pistol. Perhaps it was time to take the gun out of its case and put it in her purse.

Jakob ate another bite of his food. "This chilli paneer has a kick," he said. "Maybe that's why they put an extra 'l' in chilli."

Hana was eating a baby turnip with the greens still attached. She took a sip of Indian chai.

"You need to know about the conversation I had with Mr. Lowenstein this morning," she said. Hana then told Jakob about the interest by the US Attorney's Office in Gloria Neumann's murder and the connection with Daud Hasan.

"I doubt the US Attorney's Office would be investigating the case unless they believed someone or something bigger than the Zadan brothers was involved," she concluded. "And in my mind, that makes it more likely there are individuals with a connection to the terrorists aware of your efforts to help Ben Neumann."

"That blows my mind," Jakob said. "When I did my initial legal research, I ran across references to US Attorney Offices in both the Eastern and Southern Districts of New York that have prosecuted terrorists. They didn't sit back and wait for a military drone attack to take out the bad guys. They acted within the scope of their authority and faced the same problems we have in identifying the right persons and then bringing them within the jurisdiction of US courts. They've had success. Several people have gone to prison, including some who were extradited from foreign countries after an indictment was issued by a grand jury in the United States. I've saved my findings and can forward them to you."

"Yes. I saw references to that, but I don't have a lot of details."

Jakob ate another bite of food followed by a quick sip of water. "But I'm not sure I agree with Leon Lowenstein about Daud Hasan. Mr. Lowenstein makes it sound like Hasan would function like a double agent. That seems naive to me."

Hana had harbored similar thoughts, but her job at the moment was to defend her boss. "His point is that our interests would parallel those of the US Attorney's Office and give us access to levels of intelligence beyond our capabilities."

"I'm not buying that argument. It implies a level of trust in a man who's lied to you already." Jakob paused and wiped his forehead with a napkin. "I must be getting better. Anyone who can eat this dish without having to call an ambulance or the fire department is healthy."

"Your face is red," Hana said.

"That happens to me when I eat spicy food."

Jakob left to go to the restroom. Hana glanced around the room at the other people eating lunch. At least two-thirds were from the Indian subcontinent, which validated the authenticity of the food. When Jakob returned his cheeks were less rosy. He insisted on paying for lunch.

"Do you want me to drop you off?" she asked when they reached her car.

"No, thanks. The Uber driver I'm using should be here in a couple of minutes. I sent her a text as soon as we finished eating."

A small yellow car zipped into the parking lot and stopped directly in front of them. Hana could see a young blond-haired woman wearing very dark sunglasses in the driver's seat. Jakob got in the passenger seat, and the car took off. The driver squeezed into traffic and accelerated without waiting for a clear opening.

"Is it okay if I ride up front?" Jakob asked as he fastened his seat belt.

"It brings you closer to the action," Emily replied as she spurted into traffic. "Who's the woman in the parking lot? She has an interesting look."

"She's an Arab Israeli lawyer who is working for an international law firm with offices in Buckhead. Oh, and she's a Christian."

"That's different."

"Very."

Emily was taking Jakob back to his office. The music, which featured a flute, wasn't as loud as before.

"Haydn?" Jakob guessed after he listened for a minute.

"Yes. Symphony no. 104, his last major work."

They turned off the main roadway.

"Is this another one of your detours?" Jakob asked.

"Only so we can avoid a broken water main. Normally, it's not any quicker."

They went through two residential neighborhoods before emerging onto a familiar road.

"Were you kidding or did you really work for the police department?" Jakob asked.

"Dead serious. I have the commendations in the bottom drawer of my dresser to prove it."

"Did you ever come across a detective named Caleb Freeman? He's the detective in charge of the investigation into the mugging that sent me to the hospital and into your car."

"Not that I can remember. It's a huge police force, and the last few years I worked in a small unit."

"Drug enforcement?" Jakob asked, confident in his deduction but doubtful she'd confirm it. He could easily see Emily blending in as an undercover officer on a drug buy.

"No," Emily said as she made it through a light that was turning yellow. "Human sex trafficking. We worked with the feds trying to cut down on the exploitation of women brought in to Atlanta from all over the world. The Hartsfield Airport is busy for a lot of negative reasons as well as the good ones. You wouldn't believe the scope of the problem."

Jakob remembered a criminal court case in which he represented a man charged with his third DUI, and also on the docket that day was a defendant who didn't speak English and faced multiple counts of kidnapping related to sex trafficking. He mentioned it to Emily.

"Yeah, the biggest problem is convincing the girls to testify. Most of them are minors and scared to death. Now I volunteer for a nonprofit that works with the women who are trafficked."

They rode in silence for a few minutes. Jakob spoke again. "Why did you stop?" he asked.

"That's what a red light means," Emily answered, pointing up at the traffic signal.

"No, I mean working for the police department."

"Two years as a patrol officer and four years in the special unit taxed me beyond my limit. I saw a lot that I'd like to forget. Music takes me to a much happier place."

Emily whipped the car into the parking lot for Jakob's office building and stopped. Jakob opened the door.

"Thanks. I'm going to catch a ride home with one of the guys in my building today. I'm staying home in the morning, but I'll text you my schedule for coming into the office in the afternoon."

"Just remember that I turn into a pumpkin at four o'clock."

As Jakob walked into the building, he thought about the terrorism that had snuffed out Gloria Neumann's life and the sex trafficking of young girls. The world was an evil place that needed as much justice as he could give it.

CHAPTER 18

"How was lunch?" Janet asked in a conspiratorial tone when Hana returned to the office.

"He found it spicy," Hana answered.

"Really?" Janet raised her eyebrows. "That doesn't sound like you, but I'm willing to listen."

"Oh, it wasn't me. He selected chilli paneer, one of the hottest things on the buffet at the Indian restaurant where we ate. I lost track of the number of glasses of water he drank. It must have been at least five."

"Indian food?"

"Yes, it influenced Middle Eastern cooking. Arabs and Jews like similar dishes."

"So, he's a foodie?"

"What?" Hana asked.

"A person who's interested in different types and kinds of food."

"I don't know. We mostly talked about the Neumann case."

"Scintillating," Janet replied. "But I know lawyers enjoy acting smart when they get together. It's like sharing a secret handshake. What's next?"

"I'll try to bill a few more hours before picking up Leon," Hana replied.

"You know what I mean. What's the next step with Jakob Brodsky? Is he going to Israel? You never told me if he's recovered enough to make the trip."

"Not this time," Hana replied. "His doctor hasn't released him to drive. But when Jakob does go to Israel with me, it will be a working relationship, nothing more. There is no romantic attraction between us. My parents fell in love and knew they were going to marry a week after they met. I want the same thing for myself."

"We call that love at first sight."

"I like that," Hana replied, repeating the phrase.

"But I'm not sure you're the spontaneous type," Janet said doubtfully as she reinserted her dictation buds in her ears.

Janet was getting ready to leave for the day when Hana emerged from her office. "I sent Donnie a text about the Indian restaurant, and he made arrangements for a babysitter so we can go there tonight. He claims to love Indian food. How can I be married to a man for seventeen years and not know that he has a passion for Indian food? He wants to try the chili thing you mentioned. I have no idea what I'll order."

"The dinner menu has pictures. And tell Donnie to order goat's milk. It cuts the heat from the chilli paneer."

Janet gave Hana a skeptical look. "Goat's milk?"

"Yes."

Janet checked her watch. "What time do you have to be at the airport?"

"Around six. I'll arrive in Jerusalem late in the afternoon."

"Will you be emailing me twenty times a day like you did when you went to Germany last year?"

"At least," Hana answered. "Actually, though, you might not hear much from me since I'll only be gone for three days."

"Okay, but tell me you're going to be very careful and not go to places that aren't safe. This has a different feel to it than the times when you've gone to see your family or to Tel Aviv for a business meeting."

"I'm not going to take any risks out of line with my role as a lawyer. And I know my way around the country. Remember, it's my home."

"Tell your father about my idea that you bring all potential husbands to him and line them up so he can pick one for you, just in case your love-at-first-sight strategy doesn't work out. That can be your backup plan."

"He will think that is a good idea." Hana laughed.

Janet touched her heart. "I can't deny what's in here. You're too beautiful in every way to live a solitary life."

Hana leaned over and gave Janet a hug.

"Please send pictures," the assistant said when Hana stood up. "And you know who I want to see more than anyone else."

• • •

Hana flew from Atlanta to Reagan Airport in Washington, DC, and after a layover was on a plane to Israel. She had an aisle seat, and the woman to her right was an Arab from East Jerusalem returning to Israel after visiting a son and grandchildren who lived in Baltimore. They spoke in Arabic. The woman's son was enrolled in a PhD program in computer science at Johns Hopkins University and hoped to find a permanent job in the United States upon graduation. The woman asked Hana a lot of questions about life in the US. One of her chief concerns for her family was the loss of ethnic identity and assimilation into American culture. They were nominal Muslims. When Hana explained that she was a Christian, the woman nodded.

"It's easier for you because America is a Christian nation."

"Not as much as you might think," Hana answered. "It depends on who you're with."

Hana was no Alexis de Tocqueville, but she did her best to summarize contemporary American life. As she talked, she realized how much she'd come to love her temporary home. It reminded her of the command in Jeremiah 29:7 to pray for the peace and prosperity of the place where you live.

Halfway through the flight, the older woman yawned and soon took a long nap. Hana closed her eyes but didn't sleep. She wanted to sync her biological clock to Israeli time as soon as possible. They landed at Ben Gurion Airport. The woman kissed Hana on both cheeks before they parted ways.

Hana rented a car and drove to Jerusalem. She'd considered staying with friends, but she wanted to focus on business and so selected a hotel that catered to business travelers in the modern western part of the city. Both investigators knew where she was staying. As soon as she was in her room, she checked her office email for messages. At the top of the list were ones from Sahir Benali and Daud Hasan. Hana read the one from Benali first, stopped, and read it again. The experienced investigator was withdrawing his name from consideration for the job. The only reason he gave was "new circumstances that have come to my attention."

Hana opened the email from Daud Hasan. His reply in English was shorter and puzzling in a different way: "I will pick you up at your hotel at seven and take you to dinner." He left a different phone number than the one on his office website. It would be efficient to interview Daud over a meal as soon as possible. If she hired him, he could begin working immediately. If not, she could move on to other firms in the morning. However, one thing was certain: Daud Hasan wasn't going to pick her up at her hotel. Hana typed a quick reply: "Tell me the name of the restaurant and I will meet you there at seven thirty."

• • •

It was early in the morning when Jakob woke up and brewed a pot of coffee. Dr. Bedford had recommended limited intake of caffeine, so Jakob nursed a cup of weak coffee as he began investigating Andre Sarkasian. All the initial hits on the internet were related to Sarkasian's activities in the United States, including references to petty offenses committed when he was a teenager in Dearborn. Jakob suspected that the rap sheet in Detective Freeman's file was more comprehensive. There were two photographs of Sarkasian taken within the past five years. In the pictures an unsmiling young man in his mid- to late twenties stared coldly into the camera.

As Jakob went deeper, more and more Russian-language references began to surface. Lifted from the ethos of the search engine algorithms, most of them had no obvious connection to Sarkasian, and Jakob spent two hours without uncovering anything relevant. While taking a break, he tuned in to a classical music station featuring Beethoven as the composer of the week. He resumed his search to the strident opening of Beethoven's Fifth Symphony. The notes sounded like hammer blows that could crack rock.

Ten minutes later, Jakob opened a link to a blog originating from Dagestan that advocated Islamic purity. Included on the page was a photograph of ten Islamic fundamentalists swearing allegiance to jihad. Almost all of the faces in the photo were Caucasian. Standing slightly off to the side of the group was a face that appeared familiar. Jakob looked closer. It wasn't Sarkasian. Checking his saved files, Jakob pulled up the recruitment video filmed by the tall, slender white man with the American accent. It was the same individual.

Returning to the blog from Dagestan, Jakob carefully searched everything on the website. There were a total of ten blogs, and he read them all. Much of the language was repetitive. There were only so many ways to say the same thing. The message of militant Islam was clear—Dar al-Salam and Dar al-Harb—house of peace and house of war. The former were the areas of the world under Islamic control; the latter were parts yet to be conquered either through conversion or by force.

Tired, Jakob lay down for a nap. Before he did, he sent a text to Emily Johnson asking if she was available to take him to the office at noon.

• • •

Hana put on the nicest dress she'd brought on the trip. The restaurant was located in the swankiest new area of the city. The prices on the à la carte menu would put a big dent in the food budget she'd set for the entire trip. She inspected herself in the full-length mirror on the bathroom door and adjusted her sleek black dress. Going downstairs, she asked the concierge to order a cab. When the concierge asked where she was going, he rubbed his fingers together to signal that the restaurant was expensive. The driver of the cab was an Israeli, and Hana gave him her destination in Hebrew. She arrived at the restaurant a few minutes early, and the maître d' escorted her into the bar to wait. It was a Jewish crowd, and Hana didn't see any other Arabs besides the bartender.

Five minutes after she sat down, an Arab man hurriedly entered the bar. Hana instantly knew it had to be Daud Hasan. The investigator was about six feet tall with broad shoulders, black hair, and a square chin. He saw Hana and came over to her. He lowered his head slightly and greeted her formally in Arabic.

"And nice to meet you," Hana answered in the same language.

"Do you have a brother named Mikael?" Daud asked. "I played club football with a man named Mikael Abboud about six or seven years ago."

Hana nodded. "That's my older brother. He lived in Jerusalem back then and worked for a food wholesaler."

"That makes sense. He always brought snacks to the matches. Where is he now?"

"Working with my father and uncles in the family irrigation pipe company. Mikael handles sales to Africa and India where they are trying to expand the business. He's out of the country a lot."

"He was a good football player and scored at least half our goals. I stayed on the defensive end of the field."

Mikael was the best athlete in the Abboud family.

"I thought your name sounded familiar when Anat mentioned you to me," Hana said. "Mikael must have mentioned you back then."

The investigator had an engaging smile and came across as less serious than Hana had anticipated.

"Are you ready to eat?" he asked.

"Yes. I've never been here before."

"It's new and has the best steaks in Jerusalem."

The maître d' took them to a table for two in a back corner of the restaurant. Hana was aware of the attention they received as they passed through the restaurant.

"If we want to be inconspicuous and talk about business, this isn't the place to do it," she said after they sat down.

"I disagree," Daud replied. "Would it be better to discuss investigating a terrorist attack while eating at a restaurant in East Jerusalem or surrounded by Jews?"

"Good point," Hana admitted.

A waiter took their drink orders. Daud spoke knowledgeably with him about the wine list.

"Will it offend you if I order a glass of wine?" Daud asked.

"No, go ahead." Hana avoided alcohol and ordered tonic water with a twist of lime.

The waiter left, and Daud faced Hana. "I'm also friends with Ibrahim Ghanem," he said. "We've known each other since we were teenagers."

The mention of Hana's former fiancé caused a light to come on in her mind. That was how she'd heard Daud's name. Several times Ibrahim had mentioned a longtime friend who served in a secret branch of the Israel Defense Forces.

"How is Ibrahim?" Hana asked somewhat awkwardly.

"He and his wife just had their fourth child, a boy after three girls. He works in the radiology department at St. Louis French Hospital."

"Tell him congratulations on the birth of his son," Hana said, then immediately added, "without revealing why we talked."

"I'll save your congratulations for an appropriate time."

Hana wondered what Ibrahim had said to Daud Hasan about her. The waiter returned with a glass of wine for Daud and tonic water for Hana. Daud waited until the waiter had stepped away from their table before continuing.

"I know you're here to interview me," Daud said. "But I'd like to volunteer some information to save time. The first has to do with my fees if you decide to hire me. Given the circumstances of the case, I'm willing to charge fifty percent less than my usual rate."

Stunned, Hana didn't immediately respond. "What circumstances?" she managed.

"Two factors," Daud said as he leaned forward slightly. "Working on a matter involving a terrorist attack is a rare opportunity."

"And that's good?" Hana asked. "You already mentioned how risky and dangerous it will be."

"Risk isn't necessarily a bad thing. Why did you agree to become involved?"

Hana thought about Sadie, but she wasn't comfortable revealing her feelings for the little girl to a man she'd just met. "Could we leave that to the side for now?"

"No problem, you're here to find out about me," Daud replied. "This is my chance to work on an important case, not just for the client, but for the country. Terrorism is everyone's enemy. Second, I don't often get to work with an Arab attorney who is a Christian."

The investigator's second statement was even more surprising than his first.

"Really?" Hana managed.

Daud leaned forward and smiled again. "To be completely honest, I've been curious to meet you ever since you ended your engagement to Ibrahim. I even asked your brother about you when we played on the football team. He told me you were totally dedicated to your career."

"That's not entirely true," Hana responded. "But I guess it could look that way to members of my family."

The server arrived with salads. In typical Middle Eastern fashion, it wasn't a bed of lettuce but rather a variety of olives, cheeses, and fresh fruit.

"Do you mind if I pray?" Daud asked.

"That would be great."

Hana watched as the investigator unashamedly bowed his head and closed his eyes.

"Father, I thank you for this meal and the opportunity to meet Hana. I pray that you will comfort Ben and Sadie Neumann in the loss of a wife and mother and bring healing to their lives in the ways that only you can do. May you direct the steps of everyone who helps them. In Jesus' name, amen."

Hearing the words of the prayer in Arabic for Ben and Sadie deeply touched Hana. She looked up into Daud's face. There was an intensity and tenderness in his gaze.

"Thank you," she said.

"Now, in between bites, I'll tell you about me," he said.

Daud was the third of four children, and his mother lived in the fast-growing Negev city of Beersheba. Most of the Arabs in Beersheba were Bedouins, but Daud's great-grandfather had come to Israel from Egypt after the end of World War I.

"We were Coptic Christians for many, many generations," he said. "But my father met Jesus in a deeper way before his death ten years ago. That changed everything in our family. His encounter with God sent me on a journey of my own."

Hana felt tears well up in her eyes as Daud described his realization that Jesus wasn't merely a historical figure but a personal Savior and Lord. It had been a watershed moment that impacted his life from that point forward. He read the Bible, prayed, and looked for chances to share his faith with others.

The investigator lived in a modern apartment building in the Arab area of East Jerusalem. He attended a church Hana had heard about but never visited. She shared the story of her grandfather and Uncle Anwar.

"Why did your family leave Egypt for the Negev?" she asked.

"My great-grandfather worked with horses and mules, and in those days people still used a lot of draft animals in the desert because the roads were so poor. My father was a civil engineer. Did your family come from Syria or Lebanon? I never asked Mikael or Ibrahim."

"Lebanon. Four hundred years ago to Nazareth and sixty years ago to Reineh."

They continued to share family history. When Hana checked her phone, she saw they'd been at the restaurant for over two hours. The time had flown by. Hana remembered one of the negative questions she had for Daud.

"I have to ask: Why did you tell me you'd turned down a job offer from the US Attorney's Office in New York to work on the Neumann case and then call your contact there as soon as we talked?"

Daud shook his head. "I didn't tell anyone about our conversation except Anat Naphtali. Who claims that I did?"

"An assistant US attorney in New York City phoned my boss and said her office was looking into the Gloria Neumann murder. How would a prosecutor in New York know to call my law firm if you didn't tell someone about our interest?"

"Did the lawyer claim I provided the information?"

"No."

"What's her name?"

"Sylvia Armstrong."

"Never heard of her."

"Okay, my boss and I jumped to a wrong conclusion, not that we believed there would be a problem with you working for the US government along with us. Our interests are parallel."

"It's clear that the United States government either hired somebody to keep very close tabs on this situation or has access to conversations originating from your phone or mine."

Hana stared at her phone for a second. It had always seemed a benign part of her life.

Daud continued, "I always assume that my phone calls are recorded. And that my computer is subject to being hacked."

Hana knew for certain she wasn't equipped to move forward into such alien, potentially hostile territory. And after meeting Daud, she couldn't imagine hiring anyone other than the man sitting across the table to be her guide.

"I want your help," she said. "I need your help."

"Good." Daud beamed. "May I start by buying your dinner and giving you a ride to your hotel?"

"No to dinner because you're already agreeing to cut your fees, but yes to a ride."

They stepped outside into the cooler air of nighttime in Jerusalem. The Holy City is over two thousand feet above sea level and enjoys a more temperate climate than lower-lying areas like Galilee and the Dead Sea. The valet brought up a dark green Land Rover. It wasn't a common vehicle in Israel. Daud held Hana's hand as she climbed into the passenger seat. His light touch couldn't hide his strength.

"I travel off-road a lot in the Negev, for both business and recreation," he said when they were seated.

Hana enjoyed sitting high above the roadway as Daud smoothly navigated his way through the winding streets. She couldn't remember when she'd felt so instantly comfortable with a man.

"I'd like to see you tomorrow," Daud said when they reached the hotel.

"Yes," Hana said more eagerly than she intended.

"I have information about the Neumann murder to pass along," Daud continued. "I started working on the case even though I told you I wouldn't. We could meet in one of the conference rooms at your hotel."

"Okay. Would you like to join me for breakfast?"

"No, I'm meeting someone in Tel Aviv. Why don't we get together around two o'clock?"

They confirmed that they had each other's correct cell phone numbers. As she entered the hotel, Hana glanced over her shoulder at the receding taillights of Daud's vehicle. That night, she tossed and turned, replaying everything Daud had said over their dinner. She tried to calm her heart, but it was no use.

Early the next morning, Hana was up and on her computer. She canceled the appointments with the other investigative firms and composed a memo to Mr. Lowenstein notifying him that she was retaining Daud Hasan as their investigator. She also let him know about Daud's denial of any involvement with the US government. After sending the memo to the senior partner, she forwarded it to Jakob Brodsky and Ben Neumann. Circling back, she sent Janet a few sentences about Daud Hasan. She concluded with

No photos—yet.

CHAPTER 19

Jakob read the memo from Hana. Rather than sending a reply, he called her.

"You acted with lightning speed in hiring Daud Hasan," he said when she answered. "I didn't take you as a person who would make a snap decision."

Jakob thus joined Janet in expressing his opinion about Hana, albeit in a different context.

"Two things changed," Hana said. "Sahir Benali withdrew his name for some unknown reason, and Daud offered to cut his normal rate by fifty percent. It was too good to pass up, especially since he has the same sense of call to the case that we do."

"You could tell that after one meeting?"

"Yes."

"And you're one hundred percent satisfied with his explanation about no follow-up contact with the US Attorney's Office in New York? He's not secretly working for the US government?"

"No, he's not. And we share the same faith."

"What does that have to do with anything?"

"Religion plays a big part in everything that occurs in the Middle East."

"Well, if it saves us a bunch of money, I'm all for it. What now?"

"We're meeting again this afternoon. He's already pulled together some information to pass along."

"I wish I could be there for that," Jakob said.

"I'll put together another memo for you and Mr. Lowenstein."

"What else can you tell me about Hasan that won't be in the memo?"

"I learned a lot last night at dinner."

"He took you out to dinner? Was this an interview or a date?"

"We have several common connections with people, which isn't unusual in Israel, especially in the Christian Arab world. We talked a lot about that, too. He played on a soccer team with one of my brothers several years ago."

"If he's a soccer player, that's a positive sign for me. Did he pick you up and take you back to your hotel?"

"I took a taxi to the restaurant, and he drove me back after dinner."

"It was a date," Jakob said confidently. "If you meet a woman in a bar and drive her home, it's a date."

"Please don't—"

"I'm kidding," Jakob cut in. "I think you made the right choice with Hasan. Does he speak other languages?"

"I haven't asked, but he speaks the ones we need: Arabic, Hebrew, and decent English."

"What will you do today?"

"I'm going to Hurva Square before Daud arrives this afternoon. I know the Jewish Quarter well, but I want to see it through the eyes of the case."

After hanging up, Jakob prepared to call a prospective client. But before he could, Maddie buzzed him.

"You'd better take this," she said. "It's your mechanic. He says he really needs to talk to you."

"What's up, Tony?" Jakob asked, puzzled at the urgency of the message.

"I've been waiting for you to call me back all morning," the mechanic responded. "Didn't you get the text message and photos from Diane?"

"I have no idea what you're talking about."

"Your car was destroyed by a fire."

"What?" Jakob asked in shock.

"The damage will be covered by our shop insurance policy, and as a lawyer I'm sure you can make them pay what they should. I'll help in any way I can as to valuation, but there's no question that it's a total loss."

"How did it happen?" Jakob managed.

Tony paused for a second. Jakob could hear him yell instructions at someone else.

"I had your car up on a lift first thing this morning. I found an aftermarket device that I didn't recognize installed next to your fuel line. I assumed it was a gimmicky product that's supposed to save gas mileage. I took a picture of it on my phone and tried to move it around to see how it was mounted. I left for a minute to see if I could identify it online, and the next thing I knew, one of my mechanics was yelling that your car was on fire. I'm waiting on a call from an investigator with the insurance company. He's going to come out today or tomorrow to see if he can determine what happened. I can't believe you didn't get the news. I'm sitting in the office right now. Let me check the phone number we have on file for you."

A couple of seconds later Tony rattled off a number that was one digit off from Jakob's cell.

"That's wrong," Jakob replied and gave the correct number.

"Then somebody else received the text and photos. I hope you didn't have anything valuable in the car."

"No, I cleaned it out. But it was paid for, and I wasn't planning on buying a new one anytime soon, especially if you could fix the problem it had with overheating."

The irony of the car overheating hit Jakob and he stopped.

"Did you install an add-on to supposedly increase gas mileage?" Tony asked. "I checked our repair records, and we didn't find anything. Have you taken it anyplace else for service?"

"Not in years. Do you think the thing you saw in the engine compartment could be the problem?"

"I don't know. I never could figure out what it was. It wasn't that big, maybe six to eight inches long."

"I'm glad no one was hurt. Did the fire damage your shop?"

"No, the guys covered the car with foam, but the engine is a mess. There's no doubt the insurance company will consider it a total loss. I'll send the photos to the correct cell number as soon as we hang up, and I will let you know when the insurance investigator is coming. Do you need a loaner? I'll give you one and make the insurance company reimburse me directly."

"Uh, no, I've been using a private driver because of a health issue. This won't change that."

"You could still turn in the cost of the driver. That's probably cheaper than the daily rental on a loaner."

"Yeah," Jakob answered absentmindedly as he continued to absorb the news. "Let me know about the investigator. I'd like to be there."

The call ended. Jakob waited for the buzz that signaled the arrival of the photos. It took several seconds for the pictures to download. His jaw dropped open. The engine compartment of the car was unrecognizable. The compact vehicle looked like an eyeless skull. The photo of the blackened box showed only part of a small rectangular piece hidden by other engine parts. Fifteen minutes later Jakob received a text from Tony telling him the insurance investigator was on his way to the garage. Jakob immediately contacted Emily.

• • •

Hana exited a taxi and walked up a slight hill into the Jewish Quarter of the Old City. Much of the thirty-acre area had been destroyed by the Jordanian army in 1948, leaving only one of its thirty-five synagogues standing. After Israel captured all of Jerusalem in the 1967 war, an extensive rebuilding program began. Relying on old photographs and historical records, care was taken to rebuild what was destroyed.

Hurva Square, named after a large synagogue originally built in the early 1700s, was a major landmark. A small open plaza surrounded by shops and restaurants, the square was part of a common route to the Western Wall. Hana reached one entrance and stopped. Across the plaza was the snack and ice cream shop. It was odd watching normal activity take place at a crime scene where a woman had died and a small child was scarred, both inside and out. Blocking out the normal hustle and bustle, Hana moved to a secluded spot near a stone building and closed her eyes.

In her spirit she heard the final cries of Gloria Neumann and the screams of three-year-old Sadie. The surveillance video was silent, but as with the blood of Abel after he was slain by his brother Cain, the blood of Gloria and Sadie cried out for justice. A tear escaped Hana's eye and rolled down her cheek. But it wasn't a tear of sorrow; it was a tear of righteous rage.

. . .

Jakob got in the front seat of Emily's car. "I'm more dependent on you than ever now," he said.

"What do you mean? You look way better today than you did last week."

Jakob told her about the loss of his car during the ride to the garage.

"You've had a string of bad luck," Emily said when he finished.

"I'm not sure it's just bad luck."

"How long will this take?" Emily asked as they arrived at the garage fifteen minutes later. "I can't wait long."

"Let me see what the insurance investigator has to say."

Jakob entered the office and recognized Diane, who worked for Tony. Another man was also present.

"This is Mr. Brodsky," Diane said. "He's the owner of the car that burned."

A middle-aged man wearing a white shirt and dark pants introduced himself. He handed Jakob a scuffed business card. His name was Tom Murdoch. A camera hung on a strap around his neck, and a battered black briefcase rested on the floor beside his feet.

"I'm with Independent Adjusting Consultants," he said. "Let's take a look at the car."

"Just a minute; I need to tell my ride to leave," Jakob said.

The door opened just then and Emily entered. "Can I tag along?" she asked.

"I thought you couldn't wait."

"The former cop in me got curious."

Murdoch led the way. Jakob walked behind with Emily. They entered the service area, which had six bays. Jakob's car was in the last one. Tony saw them and approached.

"Sorry again about what happened," the mechanic said, wiping his hands on a shop towel.

They reached Jakob's car that sat on the concrete floor. Up close, the damage was even more devastating than in the photos. The engine compartment was a tangle of charred metal, missing hoses, and material burned beyond recognition. Murdoch didn't say anything as he walked around snapping photos. When he finished, he laid his briefcase on the floor and took out plastic gloves.

"Let me see the picture your mechanic took of the aftermarket add-on," the investigator said to Tony.

Tony pulled up the image and showed it to Murdoch, who stared at it for no more than a couple of seconds.

"Did you watch the video of the fire caught on my security camera?" Tony asked.

"Yeah," Murdoch replied. "Can you raise the vehicle up on the lift?"

"Yes, but I'm not sure how steady it will be."

"I'll assume the risk. I'd rather not scoot around on my back."

The frame of the car creaked as it rose higher. It shifted slightly to the right, causing Jakob to take a step back.

"That's enough," Murdoch said.

The car was about five feet above the shop floor. The investigator retrieved a small flashlight from his briefcase and crouched beneath the car. He reached up and tapped something with the end of the flashlight.

"What are you looking for?" Jakob asked, leaning over.

"The cause of the fire."

Jakob glanced at Emily, who rolled her eyes.

"I need a crowbar," Murdoch said, coming out from beneath the car.

Tony found one and handed it to the investigator. The car shifted back and forth as Murdoch used the crowbar. It reminded Jakob of a dentist pulling a tooth.

"I don't think you should do that," Tony called out.

"I'm done," Murdoch answered.

A few seconds later, he emerged. There were black streaks on his white shirt and a line of soot across his forehead. He had something the size of an eyeglasses case in his hand. It was black and misshapen. He laid it on the ground and took several pictures.

"What is it?" Jakob asked.

"The cause of the fire," Murdoch replied. "It's a crude phosphorous explosive device. I haven't seen anything like this since I served in a demolition unit in Iraq. The bomb was connected to the fuel line and detonated after the mechanic messed with it."

CHAPTER 20

Hana dressed casually for her meeting with Daud Hasan. As it grew closer to two o'clock, she wondered why she hadn't heard from him confirming their meeting. When the clock showed 2:01 p.m., a text arrived from Daud:

In the lobby. Reserved conference room 4.

Daud removed dark sunglasses and put them in the pocket of his short-sleeved shirt as she approached. He had a small leather satchel under his right arm. Hana carried her laptop.

"Good afternoon," he said to her in Hebrew.

"Are we speaking Hebrew today?" she asked.

"Yes, it will be easier because all the information I have is in Hebrew. The conference room is on the other side of the elevators."

Daud led the way to a small conference room with two computer stations against one wall. He positioned a small table in the center of the room and brought up two chairs. Laying the satchel on the table, he flipped it open and took out a stack of papers.

"The two sheets on top are my retainer agreement," he said. "Please see if it's okay and sign before we proceed."

Daud was all business, and Hana adjusted her expectation that they might engage in small talk for a few minutes. She read the agreement. It wasn't skillfully drafted and didn't protect Daud to the extent it would if she represented him. The key provisions were the investigator's fees and the scope of services he would provide. Both of those paragraphs were clear.

"Who prepared this for you?" she asked.

"A paralegal with a law firm in East Jerusalem. Is there a problem?"

"No, it's adequate for our purposes, but after this case is over, you might want someone else to take a look at it."

They signed the agreement. The investigator had a flamboyant signature. He slipped the agreement into the satchel.

"I'll need a copy for my file," Hana said.

"Of course," he replied. "I'm a little distracted. There's one in here."

Wondering why the investigator was distracted, Hana signed the copy. Daud pushed the remaining stack of papers across the table to her.

"This is a summary of the attack on Gloria and Sadie Neumann," he said. "It's probably easier for you to read it and ask questions. The redacted information was blacked out by the Shin Bet investigator who gave it to me, but since so much time has passed, I can probably get a cleaner copy soon."

"What information did they delete?"

"Names of all witnesses and the identity of the border patrol soldiers who killed Abdul Zadan and arrested Tawfik."

Hana started reading. The document contained a minute-by-minute time line of events. Included was information about the actions of two officers, one male and one female, who fired the shots that killed Abdul Zadan. Multiple photographs were mentioned but none included. "Where are the photographs?" she asked.

"Archived and available with more digging. There's also a police file, but I don't have it yet."

Hana continued reading. Of particular interest to her was information about the Zadan brothers. They came from a village named Deir Dibwan that Hana had heard of but never visited. An uncle of the brothers was a suicide bomber who'd blown himself up and killed three other people at a Jerusalem bus stop during the First Intifada, or uprising, which lasted from 1987 to 1993. It was a familiar pattern. Because of his death by suicide for the cause, the uncle would be revered as a martyr and it was believed his actions would have a profound impact not only on his generation, but on children born into the extended family.

"What else do you know about the uncle who was a suicide bomber? Was he connected to any terrorist organization?"

"The al-Aqsa Brigade. But as you'll read later on, there isn't a link between the Zadan brothers and any specific group."

Following the death of Gloria Neumann, the Zadan family home in Deir Dibwan was bulldozed to the ground by the IDF. Hana had always questioned the merit of destroying a house. It didn't seem like a viable deterrent, especially since Abdul Zadan's family received ongoing payments from the Palestinian Authority in appreciation for the sacrificial death of their older son. Houses destroyed could be rebuilt. Checks could be issued in compensation for a suicidal death. Lives lost were gone forever. It was a vicious cycle.

"We can't sue the PA," Hana said. "The US courts have thrown out all attempts to sue the Palestinian Authority for paying money to the families of terrorists based on its status as a quasi-governmental entity. We have to find a nongovernmental defendant to sue for damages."

"Like a bank."

"Exactly."

The next section revealed that after his arrest, Tawfik went to the Ofer Prison facility not far from Ramallah. Following a quick trial in a military court, he had received a nine-month sentence. Most juveniles didn't serve their full sentences. The report didn't reveal Tawfik's current whereabouts.

"What happened to Tawfik after his release?"

"He was welcomed home as a hero in Deir Dibwan with his photo on posters plastered to the walls of buildings all over town. Locating him will be at the top of my list."

The next pages contained information about the Neumann family. The basic data was familiar to Hana, but there was much she didn't know, including details of their itinerary in Israel. As she read, Hana desperately wished that a brief stop in Hurva Square for ice cream could be erased. Specific details of Gloria's injuries were set forth in a medical report. The young mother survived the trip to the hospital but didn't make it to the operating room. The internal injuries and resulting blood loss were simply too much to overcome. An autopsy revealed three major organs slashed by the long knife. Sadie's injury and medical care in the children's wing was documented by several paragraphs. It had taken thirty-seven tiny stitches to close the wound on the side of her face.

"Sadie Neumann has a deep scar on her face," Hana said.

"Do you have a photo?"

Hana turned on her laptop and showed Daud the photograph Jakob had included in the original packet brought to Collins, Lowenstein, and Capella. She added a few current pictures taken with her phone.

"You've spent time socially with the child and her father?" Daud asked when he saw the photos from the trip to the ice cream parlor.

"Just because of Sadie. She touched my heart the first day I heard about what happened to her and her mother. I didn't mention it last night, but she's the main reason I'm involved in the case." Hana paused. "I went to Hurva Square earlier today. I'm determined to fight in every way I can against what happened there."

Daud nodded. "That makes sense to me. When an investigation becomes personal, it takes me to a much deeper level of commitment beyond simply doing my job."

Reading further, Hana learned that military police had seized three computers from the Zadan home in Deir Dibwan; however, the report didn't contain a summary of what, if anything, was found on them. Following this entry was a list of publicized responses to the attack from several well-known terrorist organizations. They uniformly praised the Zadan brothers but none took credit for training or sending them. Normally, groups didn't hesitate to acknowledge culpability in an attack, and their silence pointed to its being a lone-wolf act. This was the conclusion reached by the Israeli authorities.

"Not a very helpful analysis," Hana said, pushing back her chair. "And it's been almost four years since the attack."

"But now I'm working on the case," Daud said with a confident expression on his face. "The trail may be stale, but that can mean those responsible are no longer as careful as they should be."

• • •

Jakob called Detective Freeman, who said he would come as soon as he could to the garage. Murdoch wanted to talk to the detective, too.

"Are you still willing to serve as my driver?" Jakob asked Emily as they walked to her car. "I don't know what kind of risk I am to those around me."

"Let me get back to you on that," she answered as she opened the driver's door. "I'm a music student now."

Emily drove away, and Freeman arrived forty-five minutes later accompanied by an officer named Rob Colbert from the police department bomb squad. Murdoch placed the blackened object he'd removed from the vehicle on a metal desk in Tony's office. Colbert picked it up and turned it over a few times.

"I'd like to see the video, but it seems plausible that this is a phosphorous explosive device," Colbert said, pointing to a small hole in one end of the box. "This is for the antenna designed to receive a remote signal to ignite the phosphorus. The antenna was probably just a wire and would have melted in the fire. The larger hole in the side of the box funneled the phosphorus to the fuel line. That part of the box is degraded to a higher degree than the rest of the container."

Jakob now saw that the rectangular box was more crinkled on one side than the top or bottom.

"It isn't very complicated," Colbert said, turning to Jakob. "It's likely the mechanic caused the wires to close a circuit when he touched the device. This isn't like a car bomb that blows up suddenly in the movies, but once triggered it would cause a fire that spreads quickly."

"Sorry, man," Tony said to Jakob. "I had no idea."

"Of course you didn't. I'd asked you to check out the whole car."

Murdoch spoke up. "In my experience an incendiary device like this is more suited to destroying property than endangering life, assuming the occupants of the vehicle are conscious and capable of getting out once the fire started."

"That's true," Colbert said with a nod. "Let's watch the video."

Jakob could feel a headache beginning to spread from the place where he'd been struck.

"I rewound it to the correct spot," the garage owner said.

The date and time were at the bottom of the screen. It was 7:08 a.m. The camera angle was wide and showed the entire shop. At the end of the row was Jakob's car elevated on a lift. Tony came out from under the car and walked away. Even from the other end of the shop, Jakob clearly saw the sudden appearance of a white cloud of smoke billowing up from the engine compartment. Within five seconds flames peeked up through the crack between the hood and the right fender. The flame quickly spread and shot up three or four feet into the air.

"That was fast," Jakob blurted out.

"Yes, it's potent," Colbert answered.

Suddenly, one of the mechanics who worked for Tony appeared in the video. He grabbed a fire extinguisher from the wall and began spraying it on the car with little immediate effect. A second mechanic came into the frame and sprayed foam on the car.

Tony returned with a third extinguisher and all three aimed their extinguishers at the fire, which finally retreated, leaving the car a smoldering wreck.

"Back it up and play it again," Colbert said to Tony.

"I don't want to see it," Jakob said.

He left the garage office. It was early evening, and the air had cooled down. He should be relaxing on the deck at his apartment, not watching a surveillance video of his car burning up. Detective Freeman joined him.

"I'll report this to the FBI and Homeland Security to see if they want to get involved," Freeman said.

"Do you believe they will?"

"They'll open a file. Beyond that I don't know."

"And the guy caught driving the blue car is still in jail, right?" Jakob asked.

"Yes, with no bond set because he fled North Carolina."

Jakob stared across the lot at what was left of his car. "What would you do if you were me?" he asked the detective.

"Circumstances point to more than a run of bad luck, but it's still a big jump to conclude everything is linked to the antiterrorism case you mentioned. Let me ask you a question: Is there anything else going on, either professionally or personally, that might explain why someone is mad at you?"

Jakob ran through a quick inventory of his cases. "A former client filed a grievance against me last year after we lost his case at trial, but the state bar association found the complaint without merit. The guy came from a rough background and sent me nasty emails for several more months."

"Any threats?"

"None except that he wished I would go bankrupt, develop cancer, and never be happily married."

"He said all that?"

"No, he wasn't that articulate. I can't think of anyone who has a serious personal or professional grudge against me."

The two men were silent for a moment.

"The destruction of the car could be more harassment than direct threat," Freeman said.

"Those flames looked threatening to me."

Jakob's head was hurting, but the dizziness had passed after standing in the cool air.

After the police officers and the insurance investigator left, Tony joined Jakob outside. "I know you're not driving, but if you want a loaner until tomorrow, I have an old Mazda you could use—"

"No, thanks. Let me text my driver. If she's not available, I'll get someone else."

Jakob sent a message to Emily:

Initial investigation complete. Can you pick me up at the garage and drive me to my apartment? If not, I won't hold it against you.

Within seconds he received a response.

Be there in eighteen minutes, and I don't mean nineteen.

Jakob turned to Tony. "My ride is on the way."

CHAPTER 21

"These are your copies," Daud said, pushing the report across the table. "I'm going to focus on Tawfik, and anyone associated with him. The members of terrorist cells can't resist hanging out with one another. It's a close brotherhood. That may let me know if he and Abdul truly acted alone or not. What are you going to do?"

"I won't be interviewing any more private investigators so my schedule is flexible. Is there anything we could do together?"

As soon as she asked the question, Hana wished she had phrased it differently. "I mean, joint activity on the case," she corrected herself.

"That's what I thought you meant." Daud smiled. "Why don't I call you tomorrow afternoon? Would you like to eat dinner again?"

"Yes." Hana nodded, feeling an excited flutter in her stomach.

Daud picked up his leather satchel. They walked together to the lobby.

"I look forward to seeing you," Daud said.

The investigator left. Hana glanced at one of the desk clerks, a young Arab man who had watched their brief exchange. He pointed at Daud and smiled broadly. Hana fled to her room.

Even though the time difference between the United States and Israel was seven hours, Hana took a chance and called Jakob.

"Were you awake?" she asked when he answered the phone.

"Yes, but I'm tired. It's been a busy day."

"I wanted to tell you about my meeting with Daud Hasan."

"Go ahead."

A copy of the report in front of her, Hana went through it, translating from Hebrew into English.

"You didn't mention the date it was prepared," Jakob said when she paused. "How close in time was it to the attack?"

"That part was deleted, but it has to be several weeks later because it included the jail sentence given to Tawfik Zadan for his role."

"Several weeks? He would be tried and sentenced in so short a period of time?"

"Yes, it was handled in the military courts. And there wouldn't have been any dispute about the facts."

"There's always a dispute about the facts. I wouldn't want to be the lawyer who defended him, but that's a rush to judgment." Jakob paused. "He would have been provided a lawyer, wouldn't he?"

"Yes, but no jury trial."

"I get that," Jakob said. "Juveniles don't receive a jury trial in the US unless they are charged as adults. What's on your agenda for today?"

"I'll work on the case independently of Daud and then drive up to visit my family for a few hours. Daud and I will meet again tomorrow evening."

Jakob was silent for a moment. Hana braced herself for a teasing comment or question.

"Something serious happened here today," Jakob said.

He told her about the destruction of his car and results of the initial investigation. Hana, who had been walking around the room, sat down on the bed to listen.

"I'm sorry," she said. Then another thought flashed through her mind. "Does Ben know?"

"No."

"He needs to have his car inspected."

"You're right," Jakob responded. "I'll call him as soon as we hang up."

The call ended. Before going to sleep for the night, Hana spent time praying for Ben's and Sadie's safety. She woke up at 3:30 a.m. with the same theme running through her mind. She slipped out of bed and sat in a chair in front of the window in her room. Leaving the lights out, she opened the curtain. The view wasn't anything spectacular or historic, but she could see lights on the hills surrounding the city. A verse from Psalm 125 rose up in her spirit: "As the mountains surround Jerusalem, so the LORD surrounds his people both now and forevermore." While the primary focus of the promise rested on the Jewish people, God's hands are filled with goodness and blessing for all the people of the earth who belong to him. Hana felt safe in the all-encompassing embrace of the Lord and prayed the same reality would extend to Sadie, Ben, and Jakob. She paused. And included Daud Hasan.

The following morning, Hana ordered breakfast via room service and spent a couple of hours poring over the report Daud had given her. She ended up with several pages of notes and questions. Many of the action points fell on the investigator, but she had her own list, too. Picking one item, she called *Yamout News*, one of the most widely read sources of information about events in Israel, the West Bank, and Gaza. Written from an anti-Israel perspective, the articles published in English and Arabic advanced a sophisticated and consistent narrative of Israeli oppression.

Speaking again in Arabic, Hana identified herself as a researcher and asked to speak to someone who worked in archives. After waiting for ten minutes, she was about to hang up when a man answered the phone.

"This is Farad," he said.

"I'm trying to reach any journalists who wrote articles about the death of an American Jewish woman four years ago in Hurva Square. The man who killed her, Abdul Zadan from Deir Dibwan, was shot by Israeli border police. I tried to locate the articles myself, but the website doesn't support a search over two years old."

"Expanding the database is one of our goals for the year," Farad replied. "Do you have the specific date?"

Hana gave it to him along with the name of Gloria Neumann.

"I will check," the man said.

Hana held for another ten minutes before Farad returned.

"There were eight articles about the attack and Abdul Zadan's martyrdom. Most of them were written by a man who worked here full-time. He died six months ago, but I have a batch file of the articles. I can provide you a link to access them directly."

Hana scribbled down the link. "What about any nonpublished information?" she asked. "Is it still available, and if so, how would I gain access to it?"

Farad was silent for a moment. Hana held her breath.

"What sort of research are you doing?" Farad asked.

Hana was ready for that question. "To understand what motivated Abdul Zadan and others like him to serve Allah in jihad."

Hana wouldn't lie, even in pursuit of the truth, and she hoped the vague sentence with a few friendly buzzwords would produce results.

"You would have to speak to someone with the authority to grant you that kind of access," Farad replied.

"Who would that be?" Hana asked.

Farad gave her a name and added, "But he's not here. He's on an assignment in the UAE for the next two weeks."

"Thanks."

Hana clicked open the link to the *Yamout* articles. True to form, they categorized Gloria Neumann as a person visiting the region in support of Israeli occupation, as proved by a visit she and Ben had made to two settlement towns in the West Bank. It was a new detail, and Hana made a note to ask Ben about it. There was also a piece about Tawfik's conviction following the brutal execution of his brother Abdul by Israeli soldiers. A final article, written upon Tawfik's release from custody and return to Deir Dibwan, included photos. Tawfik was a tall, lanky teenager who looked no different than many young Arab men Hana had known. Her phone vibrated to signal a text message. It was from Daud in Arabic:

> Will not be back in Jerusalem until tomorrow. Can we schedule
> our dinner then?

Hana's return flight to the United States was not until noon of the following day.

> Yes.

With so much free time available, she knew what she wanted to do—see her family in Reineh.

• • •

Jakob waited outside his apartment building. He held two cups of coffee.

"Black with one sugar," he said to Emily when he handed her the drink. "Extra hot. Correct?"

Emily took a large sip. "Perfect," she said, placing the cup in a holder. "How did you sleep last night?"

"Not the best," Jakob admitted. "But at least I didn't dream about burning cars."

"Hold on to your coffee," the driver said.

She accelerated away from the curb. They reached the exit from the apartment complex, and she shot into a small gap in traffic. Jakob hurriedly sipped his coffee and balanced it in his right hand.

"I guess you can tell I'm a bit of an adrenaline junky," Emily said as they made it through a traffic light just before it turned red. "Hanging out with you isn't as much danger as when I worked under-cover, but I realized yesterday that in a crazy way I enjoy the feeling that comes when a threat exists. Most folks would run the other way, but people like you and me embrace it because it means we're doing something significant."

"I feel more stubborn than brave," he replied.

"There's really not much difference between the two."

"You deserve to know some of the background for what's happened," Jakob said and told her a bit about the Neumann case without mentioning any names.

"I get it," she said, nodding as she turned into the parking lot for Jakob's office. "First you get mugged. Then your mechanic finds a crude bomb in your car. Do the cops have any leads on the mugging?"

A Brahms piano concerto started playing. Jakob told her what he'd learned from Detective Freeman.

"He sounds like a good one," she said. "Would you mind if I called him?"

"Go ahead. I talked to the client last night, and he's getting his car checked out this morning," Jakob said.

"Makes sense. I might do the same."

"Really?" Jakob asked.

"It would be foolish not to, although I suspect the bad guys are out of the picture after one fled the country and another was arrested. Any who are left are likely to be supercautious."

"That's what I was thinking before my car burned up. Now I'm not so sure."

Emily shrugged. "It's impossible to know. I try to stay ready for all contingencies."

She reached under the driver's seat and pulled out one of the biggest revolvers Jakob had ever seen. It reminded him of something from an old Clint Eastwood movie. The appearance of the long-barreled gun during a delicate section of the Brahms musical piece created an odd irony.

"It takes two hands to hold this, but one shot does the job," Emily continued, returning the gun to its hiding place.

"I've tried to be a good customer," Jakob said.

Emily laughed. It was the first time she'd shown any humor. Jakob grinned.

"What's your schedule today?" she asked. "I have classes this evening."

"I'll send it to you as soon as I log on to my office computer."

As he prepared to get out of the car, Emily handed him the empty coffee cup. "Thanks again for the coffee," she said. "Send the schedule ASAP. I need as many rides as possible today. There's a tuition payment due next week."

As soon as he reached his office, Jakob ordered a check for $250 from his bookkeeper payable to Emily Johnson for "professional transportation services." The bookkeeper's office was in one of the other buildings in the same office complex. As soon as he sent the request, he had second thoughts and increased the amount to $500.

Shortly before noon, Maddie buzzed him. "Ben Neumann is calling."

Jakob quickly answered the call. Ben said, "Officer Colbert inspected my minivan for a bomb and didn't find anything unusual except for a cracked boot in the front end that's leaking grease and needs to be replaced. I didn't want to upset Sadie; she would have asked a hundred questions, so I waited to call until she was at school."

"That's good news," Jakob replied.

"And I'm not going to tell Gloria's parents or my family about what happened to your car," Ben said. "There's enough to worry about in the world without adding something new."

"Agreed."

"Any update from Hana? I received the memo about the report the investigator gave her."

"Not this morning, but she should be having dinner with Hasan soon. I hope to hear from her tonight or tomorrow."

CHAPTER 22

It was a 150-kilometer drive from Jerusalem to Reineh. Hana spent the two-hour trip debating whether to say anything about Daud and, if so, what that should be. Thirty minutes after she arrived in Reineh, she was alone with Fabia and Farah and blurted out the news.

"I've met someone," she began.

"I knew it from the look on your face when you got out of the car," Fabia responded.

"Farah, didn't I say something to you when we took the boys into the kitchen for a drink?"

"Yes," Farah replied with a kind smile directed at Hana. "Where does he live?"

"Beit Hanina in East Jerusalem."

"He's not in the US?" Fabia asked. "How did this happen? Did you meet him on the internet? I know some of those relationships work out, but I'm always suspicious."

"Do you remember Anat Naphtali who worked with me at the airport?" Hana asked. "She introduced us, and we started talking from there. He's working with me on a case that has connections here in Israel."

"Is he a Christian?" Farah asked.

"And a lawyer?" Fabia added before Hana could answer.

"Yes and no. He's a private investigator."

Fabia and Farah exchanged a look. "Why do you need to hire a private investigator?" Farah asked.

"For the case. I can't provide any details because of attorney-client confidentiality rules."

"Rubbish!" Fabia retorted. "We share everything!"

"No, I really can't. But I have a lot more to share about Daud," Hana said, and continued, "He played on a football team with Mikael six or seven years ago—and he's friends with Ibrahim Ghanem."

The other two women exchanged a glance. "Keep going," Farah said.

Hana told them all she could remember from the dinner. It took awhile because of frequent interruptions and demands for more details.

"Have you talked to Mikael about him?" Farah asked.

"No, I decided not to bother him while he's in Africa."

"You should," Fabia responded. "He has good discernment."

"Okay," Hana answered tentatively.

"Promise," Fabia pressed. "I know you've been looking for a man who steps into your life with a light from heaven shining above his head."

"I never said that."

"Not exactly, but it's what you've wanted."

"Show us a picture of Daud," Farah said.

"I don't have any," Hana replied. "There isn't one on his business website."

"Describe him anyway."

While Hana talked, Fabia was busy on her phone. "Is this him?" she asked, showing the phone to Hana.

Daud, his dark hair slightly mussed by what must have been a stout breeze, was standing on top of Mount Hermon. The picture appeared to have been taken in the springtime, after the snow had melted and the flowers had leapt from their hiding places beneath the soil. Carrying a small backpack, he leaned on a hiking pole.

"Yes," Hana said. "That's him."

"Three months ago," Fabia said, reading the caption.

"Wow," Farah said. "He's handsome."

"Gorgeous is more appropriate," Fabia said.

"And he's a perfect gentleman," Hana said. "Very polite and respectful."

Fabia ran her fingers through her long black hair. "Talk to Mikael, but I don't think you should say anything to your father or mother. Not yet."

"How will I know you won't talk to them after I'm gone?" Hana replied. "We're all terrible at keeping secrets."

"We'll share with each other," Farah said. "That will satisfy us."

"But only if you promise to keep giving us regular updates," Fabia said. "That will buy our silence."

"Deal," Hana answered.

Now that Fabia and Farah knew about Daud, Hana was able to easily navigate the rest of the day. Her nieces and nephews were fascinated with Leon, and repeatedly asked Hana to pull up the video feed for the doggie day care website. Images of the puppy playing with his friends became a focal point of the trip for the younger generation. Hana's mother demanded and gave multiple hugs, and her father seemed satisfied with updates about Hana's activities at the law firm.

Late in the afternoon, Hana was sitting on a long veranda that stretched the length of the house when a car pulled up and an old, wizened man got out of the passenger seat. It was Anwar.

"Did he know I was here?" Hana asked her mother.

"No."

"How's his health?"

"He's rallied recently."

Stooped over from the weight of ninety-eight summers and winters lived within five miles of where he was born, the old man approached the veranda. All the adults stood in respect. The children grew silent and stared for a few moments before running off to continue playing. Leaning on a walking stick, Anwar carefully surveyed the assembled adults before his eyes stopped on Hana. She felt his gaze and sharply inhaled a breath she didn't immediately let out.

Anwar pointed at her with a slightly crooked finger. "Hana," he said. "I've come to see you. Will you sit with me?"

Two chairs were hurriedly provided. Hana and Farah looked at each other. Farah's eyes were as big as saucers. Hana sat down, and the male cousin who'd driven Anwar to Reineh from Nazareth helped the old man to his chair. Most of the other adults hovered around close by. Hana's mother offered to get Anwar a glass of lemonade, but he declined with a wave of his hand.

"Leave us alone," he said.

Within seconds only Hana and Anwar remained on the open veranda. Hana glanced over her shoulder. She suspected family members would try to eavesdrop from nearby windows cracked open to let in the cooler air that arrived as the sun set.

"Alone, I said!" Anwar repeated in a louder voice.

Hana heard footsteps moving away from the closest window. Anwar looked at her thoughtfully. "Even though I'm an old man and can't see or hear as I once could, I still hear the voice that matters the most."

Hana knew what he meant.

"Do you remember when I told you about Samuel when you were a little girl?" Anwar asked.

"Yes."

"Does the Lord awaken you in the night to listen?"

"Yes."

"Good." Anwar closed his eyes for a moment before continuing. "There's more. Sometimes when a promise is on the way, the Lord sends a Hana to welcome it."

They sat in silence for a few moments.

"Anna in the New Testament; Hannah in the Old Testament," Hana said.

"That's right," Anwar said, nodding with approval. "And you bring together their faith."

Hana waited for a fuller explanation. Instead, Anwar closed his eyes. A minute passed. Watching the old man's steady breathing, Hana suspected he was asleep. She reached out to gently touch his arm but pulled back before doing so. Suddenly, he snorted and appeared to be awake. He looked at Hana for a moment before recognition came into his eyes.

"Do you believe?" he asked.

"Yes, Uncle," she answered.

"That's true. You do. But all faith is tested. I've prayed that you'll pass the test."

"What kind of test?"

Anwar pointed up. "He's the teacher; he selects the test."

Hana felt the truth of what she was hearing, but also frustration at the ambiguity of the message.

"Come closer," Anwar said.

Hana moved her chair until it almost touched the one in which the old man sat.

"That's good," he said. Anwar put his hand on Hana's head. She bowed lower so his hand rested easily on her hair. Hana felt a slight tingling that ran along her shoulders and then lifted.

"There it is," Anwar said. "Amen and amen." He raised his hand and returned it to his lap.

"What have you done?" Hana asked.

"Given you what I can. Meditate on the promises of the Almighty."

"I already do that."

"Good. Do it more. Call for the children, please."

Hana left the veranda, and after relaying the old man's request, she went upstairs to a room where she could be alone. She didn't come down until after the old man had departed for Nazareth.

When asked what he'd told her on the veranda, Hana gave a simple response: "He blessed me."

Alone in the upper room, she'd realized she needed to store Anwar's words in her heart and not share them with others, even her loved ones. After supper, Hana read a story and sang a song to Khadijah. Once all the younger nieces and nephews were in bed, Hana gave her mother a final hug and returned to Jerusalem.

• • •

Jakob waited for Emily to pick him up and take him home before she had to leave for class. He'd scribbled "Tuition" on the outside of the envelope containing the check and slipped it into his jacket pocket. The driver pulled up to the curb. It was hot, and she had the air conditioner at full blast.

"Busy day?" Jakob asked as he closed the passenger door and fastened his seat belt.

"Not busy enough," Emily replied, wiping her forehead with the back of her hand. "I've had two rides stand me up. The penalty payments for no-shows don't help much."

Emily reached over and turned up the volume. Jakob didn't recognize the music. "Who is that?" he asked.

"Saed Haddad, a modern composer from Jordan who lives in Germany," she said in a clipped voice. "We've been studying him at school."

Sensing that she didn't want to talk, Jakob didn't try to start a conversation. When they reached his apartment, he laid the envelope on the seat as he got out of the car. Emily peeled away from the curb. He'd barely closed his apartment door when she called him.

"What's up with the check?" she demanded. "If you wanted to freak me out, it worked."

"You mentioned a tuition payment coming up tomorrow, and I wanted to help. I wasn't trying to freak you out."

Emily didn't respond for several moments. Jakob didn't know what to expect.

"Thanks," she said in a much softer tone of voice. "That was very generous. Having someone be nice to me just because they want to has been rare in my life."

Jakob wanted to ask why, but whether to explain the comment was up to Emily.

"What time should I pick you up in the morning?" she asked.

"I have an appointment with my neurologist at nine, and a deposition in midtown at eleven that should take a couple of hours."

"Where is the doctor's office?"

Jakob gave her the address.

"I'll pick you up at 8:22."

"Great."

Inside his apartment, Jakob took off his tie and draped it over a chair. There was a knock on his door. Thinking maybe Emily had forgotten to tell him something, he quickly neatened up the living area before opening the door. Butch Watson stood on the landing.

"Is something wrong?" Jakob asked.

"I'd say so. Is it true what I heard about your car burning up?"

"Every bit of it."

Butch drank a beer while Jakob gave his friend a greatly edited version of events that excluded any mention of an incendiary device. Butch carried enough information about the physical attack on Jakob the night the twins were born. He didn't need another layer of worry.

"You've had the worst string of setbacks," Butch said, shaking his head. "When that happens to me, there's always something good around the corner."

"I'll take it," Jakob said.

Butch started in with anecdotes about the twins. A half hour later, he finally got up to leave.

"Oh, one other thing," Butch said, pausing at the door. "If you ever need a ride home, I'll do it if there's any way I can swing it."

"Thanks," Jakob replied. "But I've hired a regular Uber driver who's on call."

"Is that the cute blonde with the hot yellow car? That car is sweet."

"Yes, I didn't realize you'd noticed."

"Oh yeah. Maddie has you under surveillance. Most of the guys in the building have checked out the pictures she took of you and the driver."

CHAPTER 23

Hana relaxed on the bed and thought about the previous day in Reineh. Her phone vibrated, and an unfamiliar number in the States appeared. She hesitated before accepting the call.

"Hana Abboud?" a female voice asked.

"Speaking," she said.

"This is Sylvia Armstrong with the US Attorney's Office for the Eastern District of New York. Leon Lowenstein gave me your cell phone number."

Hana sat up on the bed and grabbed a notepad and pen from the nightstand. "Yes," she said. "He told me you called about the Gloria Neumann murder."

"Right, and he says you're in Israel conducting an investigation."

"For a few days. It's a preliminary trip. Our goal is to find out as much as we can about the man who attacked and killed Mrs. Neumann and anyone who helped or supported him. The first step is to hire a private investigator."

As she talked, Hana racked her brain for the best way to answer any questions the US attorney asked and to counter with her own.

"US law enforcement personnel oversee the investigative phase under our supervision and then we prosecute. I might go to Israel if the Israeli authorities make an arrest, and I would negotiate extradition of a defendant to the US for prosecution. Have you located a private detective?"

"How much can you tell me about your investigation?" Hana asked, ignoring Armstrong's question.

"Not much because I can't jeopardize our ability to obtain an indictment and prosecute a defendant."

"Is there information you can reveal that won't jeopardize your case?"

"Maybe, but that discussion would need to be on a quid pro quo basis. Right now, it doesn't sound like you have anything to contribute."

"There may be a link between Gloria Neumann's murder and threats against the lawyer who brought the case to our firm."

"Jakob Brodsky?"

"Yes."

"I tried to call him a few minutes ago. What kind of threats, and why do you believe they're connected?"

"Nothing is confirmed," Hana replied. "But there's circumstantial evidence."

She summarized the assault that left Jakob with a concussion and the destruction of his car by an explosive device. Armstrong listened without interruption.

"The Atlanta Police Department contacted Homeland Security, and one of the men who may have attacked Mr. Brodsky recently fled the country," Hana concluded.

"There could be a connection, but it doesn't sound solid yet. What's the status of your search for an Israeli investigator? We found out about your law firm's interest in the Neumann murder from a man I interviewed to possibly help us."

"Daud Hasan?" Hana asked, her heart sinking at the thought he'd deceived her.

"No, an Arab Israeli named Sahir Benali."

"Right," Hana said with relief.

"I'm not going to contact Hasan independently, but I need to make sure you've not hired a mole who's working for the bad guys before we exchange any intel."

"A friend and colleague who worked with me in security at Ben Gurion Airport recommended Daud Hasan. He's also an Arab Israeli and served in the IDF. His qualifications are on his website."

"Got it. I assume he has the basic report of the attack prepared by the Israeli border patrol and the local police. It's twelve pages in Hebrew and dated forty-one days after the murder. It gives the chronology of events."

Hana quickly checked what Daud had given her. Sure enough, it was twelve pages but without the date.

"I have twelve pages but no date," she said.

Armstrong read the introductory paragraph in English. Hana followed along and did her own internal translation.

"Does that sound right?" Armstrong asked.

"Yes, but my copy has certain names redacted."

"I have a clean one, which I'll send you. What's your secure email address?"

Hana assumed her work email met the definition of secure. The law firm had a sophisticated firewall. She gave the information to Armstrong, who reciprocated. The call ended without Hana's having taken a single note. But from the initial call, Armstrong seemed like a hardworking ally, not a hindrance.

Hana spent the day working on her investigative to-do list. She visited the Jerusalem police station closest to Hurva Square to see if she could figure out the origin of the report she'd received from Daud. When Hana explained what she was doing, a helpful female clerk located several photographs of the crime scene. All of them were stored digitally, but several had been printed onto photo paper.

"You can review them here," the woman said in Hebrew. "But I can't release them without a court order or authorization from one of my superiors."

"I understand."

Hana stepped away from the counter and sat down in a plastic chair in the corner of the room. She didn't want to open the folder, but she knew she had to. The color pictures of Gloria taken as she was being prepared to leave in an ambulance were worse than she'd imagined. In some ways, the similarity in appearance between Gloria and Sadie made the photos of the mother more heartrending to see. Also included were graphic photos of Abdul's body. In death, the young man looked harmless, yet minutes before he'd been viciously stabbing a mother and child with a large knife. Hana held it together emotionally until she reached the last three photographs and saw Sadie.

Tears streamed down Hana's cheeks at the sight of the jagged cut on the little girl's face. Unlike her mother, whose eyes were closed, Sadie's eyes were open and filled with uncontrolled terror. Hana wiped away the tears with the back of her hand and tried to stop crying. More tears overwhelmed the flimsy dam and flowed down her face. Closing the folder, she knew the images would never leave her. Through blurred vision she saw the female clerk watching her. Hana placed the folder on the counter. The woman held out a handful of tissues.

"I've seen these," the clerk said. "I have a daughter about the same age as the little girl. I hope you find the people behind this and make them pay."

"We will."

Thankfully, the other items Hana checked off her list were less emotional. She obtained contact information for the border patrol unit that responded to the attack, as well as the identification and current address for the company that had placed the surveillance camera in Hurva Square.

She had time to return to the hotel and rest for a few minutes before getting ready for an early dinner with Daud. Putting on a simple skirt, blouse, and sandals, Hana was sitting in a chair in the lobby when Daud entered and greeted her in Arabic.

"You look nice," he said with a smile. "Let's go. I'm parked in a spot out front where I'll be towed if I don't move my vehicle."

In the daylight, Hana could see that Daud's Land Rover had a few dents and dings, but it was clean on the inside.

"Chinese or Ethiopian food?" he asked once they had snapped their seat belts.

Following the immigration to Israel of thousands of Ethiopian Jews in the 1980s and 1990s, restaurants featuring their cuisine had sprung up all over Israel. However, Hana loved Chinese food, and Israel had a lot of great Chinese restaurants. It was easy to keep a kosher Chinese kitchen because virtually no dairy products were used in South Asian cooking.

"Chinese," she said.

"Good choice."

Daud left the predominantly Jewish neighborhoods of West Jerusalem and made his way into Arab East Jerusalem. He turned down several residential streets and stopped in front of a two-story building with a simple neon sign featuring two Chinese pictographs.

"What does it say?" Hana asked, pointing at the sign.

"My best guess is 'Chinese Food Here,'" Daud answered.

Hana laughed. They left the bright sunlight and entered a tiny dark room with only five or six tables, all empty. An older Chinese woman greeted them in Arabic.

"Marhaban, Daud!"

"Ahlan wa sahlan, Mrs. Wong," Daud replied.

"Who is your honored guest?" the Chinese woman asked.

"Hana Abboud, from Reineh but currently living in the United States."

The woman eyed Hana closely and then nodded. "Sit wherever you like," she said with a broad gesture.

"Where are the other customers?" Hana asked Daud in a soft voice.

"They'll arrive after we leave. I reserved the whole restaurant for our meal."

"What?" Hana asked in surprise.

"So we can talk. It didn't cost much. The dinner crowd won't start trickling in for over an hour. But it's a good thing you chose Chinese."

The menu was in Arabic and featured multiple noodle-based dishes. A young Chinese waiter brought tea, and Hana started with a cold noodle salad.

"If you like spicy food, I recommend the zhajiangmian," Daud said.

Hana was familiar with the dish containing thick wheat noodles, chili bean sauce, French beans, and sweet soybean sauce. This version featured tofu instead of meat.

"May we talk business first?" Hana asked after they ordered.

"Yes."

"I found out why a prosecutor with the US Attorney's Office in New York called my boss." She told Daud about the link between Sahir Benali and Sylvia Armstrong.

"Would that explain why he didn't want to meet with me because new circumstances came up?" she asked when she finished.

"Maybe."

Hana paused as another thought crossed her mind. "Did you scare him away?" she asked, leaning forward.

"Not exactly." Daud smiled. "But I encouraged him to move aside so I could help you. I'll make it up to him. Sahir is a good guy and has plenty of business."

"There's more background you need to know," Hana said. She then told him about the attack on Jakob, the phosphorous device that destroyed his car, and the misbaha beads he found in the bushes. Their food arrived. Hana devoured the cold salad. Daud was ambidextrous with the chopsticks.

"It looks like he's being targeted," Hana said as she pushed her salad bowl to the side and turned toward the zhajiangmian.

Daud ate a bite of his zhajiangmian before he spoke. "A terrorist group might have the capability to do that if they wanted to devote resources to the effort, but it seems unlikely unless they believed Brodsky was close to uncovering something they very much wanted to keep hidden."

"I doubt it," Hana replied. "I know everything Jakob does about the case."

"How can you be sure about that?"

"We're cocounsel," Hana said, realizing that wasn't very persuasive.

"If he's already a target of a terrorist cell, it would be best if it appears that he's acting alone until you're ready to go public with the case," Daud said. "I wouldn't want him to let anyone know that I've been hired or the names of any of the people we eventually interview here in Israel or the West Bank. They talk to me because they know they can do so safely."

"I'll mention that to him."

"With emphasis."

"Okay."

"I found out more about Tawfik Zadan," Daud continued. "He's not been in jail since serving time for the Neumann murder, and he lives in a family house in Deir Dibwan. Finding someone in the Deir Dibwan area who doesn't like Tawfik, due to either jealousy or an unrelated feud, would be a possibility. They might pass along a rumor that turns out to be more real than the typical conspiracy theory swirling around on the street."

"How would you find such a person?" Hana asked.

"I may have to spend a little money to make that happen."

"Okay, but we don't want any bribes to governmental officials that—"

"Please," Daud cut her off. "Trust me to do the right thing."

Hana nodded. She then told him about her contacting *Yamout News* and the trip to the police station. When she mentioned the photos, her tears returned.

"I'm sorry," Daud said gently. "I was planning on doing that after you returned to America."

"I would have seen them eventually," Hana said and sighed. "The pictures will speak louder than words if the case ends up in a courtroom."

They ate in silence for a few moments.

"I'm ready to talk about something besides business," Daud suggested.

"Yes!" Hana said.

Daud asked Hana more questions about her life. He told her about a group of men he regularly met with to pray and read the Scriptures.

"They're guys I can be completely honest with," he said.

"Do they know about me?"

"Sure, and they're praying for both of us."

They finished the meal with lotus seed paste for dessert.

"I'd like to come back here," Hana said. "There are several other dishes on the menu that look delicious and sound interesting."

"I'm glad you liked it. What is your time line for a return trip?"

"I haven't confirmed anything with Mr. Lowenstein, but I'm thinking a month. Would that give you enough time to set things up? I know it's impossible to predict."

"That's reasonable," Daud said. "I don't have any major assignments on my agenda."

"Assignments?"

"Cases. Which means I can devote a lot of time to the Neumann matter."

"You're only charging half your usual rate!" Hana protested. "I don't feel right about that."

Daud smiled. "But it's worth it to me."

CHAPTER 24

Jakob spent the evening on his couch watching a Russian soccer match. Checking his office email before going to bed, he saw a memo Hana had sent earlier in the evening. As he read about her investigation and the conversations with Sylvia Armstrong and Daud Hasan, Jakob's desire to get into the middle of the case increased. He checked his calendar for the dates when Hana mentioned returning to Israel. There was nothing on his docket that would prevent him from joining her.

The following morning Emily drove Jakob to the neurologist's office.

"I have one of the first appointments of the day and hope I won't have to wait long," he said when they arrived.

"No problem."

Jakob checked in at the front desk. A few minutes later an assistant took him to an examining room. Dr. Bedford came in shortly.

"How are you feeling?" the physician asked.

Jakob raised his right hand in the air as if taking an oath. "No problems. I've had one bad headache that came on after my car was totally destroyed in a fire."

"I thought you weren't driving."

"I'm not. The car was at my mechanic's garage."

The neurologist checked the side of Jakob's skull. The knots were almost gone. While performing a physical exam, he ran through a series of questions about Jakob's mental status.

"You're looking stable, but come back to see me in thirty days."

Jakob hesitated. "I may be out of the country on a business trip around that time," he said.

"Where?"

"Israel. Is that okay?"

The doctor raised his eyebrows. "Yes, unless you have a fainting spell or mini seizure before then. If you do go, be careful in more ways than one. Keep your stress level low."

Outside, Emily had moved her car to a spot beneath a large shade tree. "That was quick," she said when Jakob returned.

"Good news and bad news," Jakob replied.

"What?"

"Good news is that I'm much better. Bad news is that I still have to hire a driver for at least another month."

"One man's bad news can be another woman's good news," Emily said with a smile.

"And the doctor told me to maintain my current low-stress routine."

"Good luck with that," Emily said as she put the car in reverse and zoomed out of the parking space.

• • •

Daud insisted on taking Hana to the airport, so she returned her rental vehicle in Jerusalem. It was a sunny morning, and they merged into the steady stream of morning traffic that ran between Jerusalem and Tel Aviv. Hana found herself taking pleasure in the simple act of riding in Daud's vehicle with him behind the wheel.

"How often do you want to stay in touch?" he asked in Arabic.

Hana glanced out the window for a moment as she considered her response. She was missing Daud even though still with him.

"As much as you like," she answered simply.

Daud glanced at her. "Based on how I feel, that would be a lot," he said.

A smile creased Hana's lips and remained there. She saw Daud look at her and smile, too. She hoped the expression on her face communicated what she felt in her heart. They engaged in small talk during the remainder of the ride to the airport. Daud pulled up to the curb and quickly got out to retrieve her suitcase.

"Thanks for everything," Hana said.

Daud reached out his right hand with his palm up, and Hana placed her hand in his. He placed his left hand on top of hers. Never in her life had Hana felt more accepted and secure with a man than at that moment.

"You know I will be thinking about you every day and looking forward to seeing you again," Daud said.

Hana was glad he was holding her hand because she suddenly felt wobbly. She placed her other hand on top of his. "And I'm going to remember this moment when I think about you," she said.

With a final gentle squeeze, Daud released her hand. Not wanting to look back, Hana grabbed her suitcase and rolled it into the airport. Once she was through the doors she couldn't resist glancing over her shoulder. Daud had remained in the same place with his eyes glued on her. She waved.

Due to the prevailing winds at thirty-eight thousand feet, the return flight from Israel to the United States is always over an hour longer than the flight in the other direction. The tiny plane tracking their progress on the world screen moved forward in infinitesimal increments. Hana was restless. Her seatmates both took pills and fell asleep shortly after takeoff. Wide awake, Hana tried to watch a movie, but it didn't hold her interest. She tried to read but couldn't concentrate. After several hours, she attempted to nap and failed. By the time the plane landed in Newark, she was exhausted. After a short layover, she boarded a flight to Atlanta and caught an hour's fitful sleep.

Upon disembarking, it was too late to pick up Leon at the doggie day care center, so Hana drove straight home. When her head hit her pillow, she fell into a deep sleep and didn't wake up in the middle of the night.

• • •

Up early and feeling better than he had at any time since the attack at Butch's apartment, Jakob went out for a walk. There was access to a greenway nearby, and he joined a throng of walkers and joggers making their way along the shaded path through a grove of hardwoods and a smattering of pines. Jakob walked at a brisk pace. North Atlanta rises from the banks of the Chattahoochee River, and the path followed the undulating terrain. As he reached the top of a small hill, a break in the tree line provided a narrow overlook toward the downtown area of the city. Jakob stepped off the path to look at the skyscrapers framed by leafy branches.

The contrast between the leaves and the buildings, the beauty of nature and the accomplishments of man, caused a moment of reflection. Jakob had never thought much about mortality or the fragility of life, but the events of the past weeks were enough to get anyone's attention. On at least two occasions, he could have died. Jakob held no firm beliefs about anything beyond what he wanted to accomplish in the time organized on his computer calendar. But for the first time in his adult life, he wondered if he should. After lingering a few extra minutes, he turned for home. This time, he walked at a much slower pace.

• • •

Hana lay in bed an extra thirty minutes so she could wake up slowly. She already missed her family, Israel, and Daud. Brief homesickness always marked her return to the United States, but the addition of Daud to the mix and her hopes for their future relationship made this time different.

Stretching once again, she got out of bed and fixed a strong cup of coffee. While sipping it, she checked on Leon. The puppy was already hard at play. Even though she'd been away only a few days, he seemed bigger. Hana looked forward to the end of the day when she could pick him up and bring him home. Janet glanced up excitedly when Hana arrived.

"Knowing you'd be here kept me from calling in sick," the assistant said.

"Are you feeling bad?" Hana asked in concern.

"No, but it kept me from pretending that I was so I could be first in line for a big sale at my favorite clothing store." Janet leaned forward. "It was almost cruel reading the few lines you sent me about Daud Hasan. Kind of like giving a woman who hasn't had a drink of water for three days a few drops on the tip of her tongue."

Hana laughed. "If you're that desperate, I need to satisfy your curiosity before I start billing any of our clients. I have one photo of us together and can show you several others from social media."

The two women went into Hana's office and closed the door. Forty-five minutes later a satisfied Janet stood to leave.

"I was wrong," the assistant said. "As a woman, you knew love at first sight was in your future, and I shouldn't have doubted your intuition."

"I didn't say we are going to get married."

"Details, details," Janet replied with a wave of her hand. "Daud is an idiot and doesn't deserve you if he lets you slip away. I especially like his old-school approach to romance. I bet he'd throw his jacket on top of a mud puddle so you wouldn't have to get your shoes dirty."

Hana smiled. "Yes, I think he would, too."

Mr. Lowenstein was out of the office until after lunch, which gave Hana time to work on her backlog of other cases. As she returned to the flow of her office routine, the longing for home began to subside, but when it was time to slip away for a quick lunch, her appetite led her to Mahmoud Akbar's restaurant. The owner rewarded her with a huge smile as soon as he saw her standing at the counter.

"What do you want today?" he asked. "Order anything on the menu and it's on the house."

Hana gave him a puzzled look.

"Your food is free," the restaurant owner explained. "Your American English is so good that sometimes I forget you may not know all our slang."

"I'll be glad to pay—"

"No," Mr. Akbar said as he raised his hand and leaned over the counter. "God has heard your prayers. Gadi is coming home. My fears were real. He left America to join a militant group, but once he saw how they treated one another, he came to his senses."

"That's great," Hana said with heartfelt relief. "Where is he now?"

"In Paris for a few days visiting my brother's family. He'll return to Atlanta next week."

Hana wanted to join in the celebration without reservation, but she couldn't shake a nagging concern. "I'll feel better when he's with you," she said.

Mr. Akbar nodded. "You and my wife agree. Now, tell me what you want to eat."

"Your manakish with minced lamb is the best," Hana said, referring to a flatbread topped with cheese, thyme, oregano, toasted sesame seeds, spices, and ground meat. It was similar to a pizza.

"Don't you want something more expensive? I have a perfect lamb rack."

"No, no, that's too fancy for lunch. Seeing your smiling face is the best thing on the menu."

While she ate the manakish, Hana prayed that Gadi would completely separate himself from militant Islam, not only in the Middle East but in the United States as well. Her phone vibrated. It was a text from Daud asking how she was doing. She took a picture of the meal and sent it to him. He immediately replied:

I would eat that manakish. Take me there.

Imagining Daud in the restaurant transformed it into another place. Hana answered:

I would like that.

Hana spent the rest of the meal messaging with the investigator. None of it had to do with business. Returning to the office, she continued plowing her way through a project for Mr. Collins.

Shortly after two o'clock, Janet buzzed her. "You told me to let you know when Mr. Lowenstein was in his office. Gladys says he's there and available for a few minutes if you go now."

After saving her work, Hana made her way to the senior partner's office. He was wearing a gray suit and sporting a green bow tie. He motioned for her to sit down. "I read your memos," he said. "Sounds like you hit the ground running."

"Yes, I was busy."

"And you really like this Hasan guy?"

Surprised, Hana paused before responding. "In what way?"

"As an investigator, of course," Mr. Lowenstein answered. "How in the world did you convince him to cut his fee in half? If you can do that consistently, I have a few cases that need your magic touch."

"It was his idea."

"Why?"

Hana made a split-second decision to keep the personal side of the situation out of the discussion. "Primarily because it's a case he wants to handle. I'm sure it's more important than some of his other work."

"What kind of work?"

Hana realized she and Daud hadn't discussed that topic. "General investigation," she offered.

"Okay," Mr. Lowenstein replied. "I agree with your returning to Israel in a month. That's a reasonable plan that can be modified if circumstances dictate."

"With Jakob Brodsky?" Hana asked.

"Yeah," Mr. Lowenstein replied dismissively. "But only if you keep it from being a tourist junket for him. I question whether he can bring anything substantive to the table."

"We'll work on that."

"In the meantime, make sure you keep Jim Collins happy. He considers you on loan to me from his group."

"I've worked exclusively on his projects since I returned this morning."

After leaving Mr. Lowenstein's office and working until five, Hana was feeling the effects of jet lag and left the office. She stopped by to pick up Leon, who had received two As, two Bs, and one C on his doggie day care report card. His low mark was for a relapse in potty training.

"Do you have any problems with him at home?" the young woman checking him out asked.

"No," Hana replied with the defensiveness of a mother whose child is criticized by a kindergarten teacher.

"I hope his bad habits here don't spill over," the woman responded.

Leon greeted Hana with loving exuberance. During the car ride home, he licked her hand every time she reached over to pat him. He did his business in the yard without a hiccup. Both woman and dog went to sleep early.

CHAPTER 25

The following afternoon, Jakob cleaned off his desk in preparation for a meeting with Hana and Ben. Maddie buzzed him to report they'd arrived. He greeted Hana with a Hebrew phrase he'd memorized.

"That's good," she replied in the same language.

Jakob recognized *tov*, the word for "good," but not the one before it.

"Don't press me," he answered in English. "I don't know how to ask where the restroom is."

Hana replied with a word that sounded like "mushroom." Jakob opened the door and let them enter the office before him. He had the chairs set up for them.

"Any updates from the detective on the criminal investigations?" Ben asked as soon as they were seated.

"Not since we last talked. I'm doing what Detective Freeman suggested—keeping my eyes open and staying aware of my surroundings."

Hana supplemented the information she'd furnished in her memos. As he listened, Jakob again wished he'd been at the center of the action. Ben had several questions. Jakob remained silent.

"Mr. Lowenstein gave preliminary approval for a return trip in a month," Hana said when she'd finished her update. "By then, I hope Daud will have been able to set up interviews and make progress in uncovering any connections the Zadan brothers might have had with an organized group."

"I've spent a lot of time looking online for tidbits of information," Jakob said. "There was internet chatter about the attack coming out of the Islamic republics in the Black Sea area."

"Anything specific?" Hana asked. "I wouldn't have thought to focus on that region."

Jakob pulled up a summary he kept on his computer and went over his English notes about the blog entries without mentioning that he'd translated the information from Russian. It clearly upset Ben to hear this type of communication about Gloria and her death.

"I'm sorry, Ben," Jakob said at one point. "I know I'm talking in a detached way about what happened."

"I understand," Ben replied. "I can't help how it makes me feel, but I want to know what's going on."

"One of the more interesting things I found was a recruitment video by an American living in the region," Jakob continued. "It's in English with Russian and Arabic subtitles."

"Do you know his name?" Hana asked.

"No, he's not identified. He never mentioned Gloria's murder specifically, but the video appears on a site that does." Jakob paused. "Did you talk to Mr. Lowenstein about me joining you on the next trip to Israel?"

Hana nodded. "Yes, and I told him I wanted you to be there. He gave his permission but then raised questions about how much you could contribute due to the language limitations. I told him that shouldn't disqualify you."

"Thanks," Jakob said gratefully.

"I'll call him myself if he tries to backtrack," Ben jumped in. "I want Jakob to go."

"That may not be necessary," Hana replied. "If it is, I'll let you know."

"What are you going to work on in the meantime?" Ben asked.

"Getting a better understanding of the law and what we need

from witnesses," Hana said. "There is a large research bank at the law firm concerning that sort of thing. Because of the other work in my queue, though, it will take me at least a week to get to it."

This was exactly the type of expertise Jakob was seeking when he associated a firm like Collins, Lowenstein, and Capella.

"I'll help," he offered. "Because there is a difference in approach between domestic and foreign transactions, I'd like to focus on the US part."

"That makes sense," Hana said. "If Mr. Lowenstein agrees, I'll forward the research to you."

Jakob knew Hana had to follow law firm protocol. After they talked for another fifteen minutes, she checked her watch. "I have to return to the office for a meeting," she said, standing up.

"Don't forget Sadie's birthday party on Saturday afternoon," Ben said.

"The invitation is stuck to the front of my refrigerator, and it's categorized as the highest priority on my calendar at work," Hana said with a big smile.

Ben stayed after Hana left. "Do you have any thoughts about the case that you didn't want to mention in front of Hana?" he asked Jakob.

"First, I was happy she went to bat for me with her boss. That's not common for an associate attorney dealing with a senior partner," Jakob said. "But the biggest concern is that she wants to include the private investigator in everything. He's not subject to the attorney-client confidentiality rules, and the fact that he played on a soccer team with her brother several years ago doesn't mean much to me. Hana didn't admit it, but it's clear there was an immediate chemistry between them. I mean, two of their meetings were dinner dates. Hana is a very smart woman, but whoever said love is blind had a reason to do so."

"That's what I was thinking, too," Ben said. "But when you didn't say anything, I kept quiet."

"She's working hard to keep me in the loop, and it would sound ungrateful if I tried to marginalize the investigator. I hope you and I are both wrong, and Daud Hasan has more integrity than an Eagle Scout."

Two hours later, Jakob sent a text to Emily to tell her he was ready to go home. Just before he shut off his computer, he received an email with an attachment from Hana Abboud. The attached file included more than four hundred pages of research, documents, discovery, and pleadings about piercing the corporate veil and uncovering fraudulent and secret transfers of assets and money in the United States. It was jaw-dropping in scope.

Please keep this information confidential. Will discuss later.

Hana

• • •

Hana and Daud settled into a routine that suited both their schedules. After Hana arose in the morning and dressed for work, they Skyped on their computers. Early afternoon in Israel was a convenient time for Daud, who often worked late into the night. Hana suspected the investigator still juggled his calendar to carve out time for their conversations. They always began their time with a brief prayer.

One of the most telling parts of the routine was how they both reacted when, a few days after Hana returned to the States, they skipped a session because Daud had to attend a meeting he couldn't reschedule.

The following morning Daud began the conversation. "Yesterday was terrible," he said in Arabic as soon as Hana's face appeared.

"Why?"

"Because we weren't able to talk."

"I felt it, too," Hana replied. "It left a hole in my heart. If something comes up for you, we will set another time, even if I have to wake up in the night to talk. I could call when I finish praying."

Daud knew about Hana's nighttime sessions with the Lord. His own devotional life was limited to fifteen to thirty minutes as soon as he woke up.

"I'm open to any option," he replied, adjusting his computer so that Hana could catch a glimpse of his kitchen in the background. "Do you have time this morning for a tour of my apartment?"

"Sure."

Hana leaned forward as Daud carried the laptop around his apartment. It was the first time she'd seen where he lived. It exceeded anything she would have imagined. The main living area was huge, the kitchen was filled with top-notch appliances, and there were three bedrooms, one of which served as Daud's office.

"I'm on the top floor of a five-story building," he said when he showed her his broad balcony.

"It's like a penthouse suite," she said.

"That's because it is," he answered. "I'm not sure if you can see it, but there's a nice garden below the balcony."

The camera didn't transmit a very clear picture, but Hana could tell that the building was perched on a hill. She already knew that Daud lived in Beit Hanina, one of the nicer Arab suburbs of Jerusalem. To afford a top-floor apartment in that area proved that his investigative business was flourishing.

"The furniture is modern, not traditional," he said, returning to the living area. "I hope that's okay with you."

Hana started to say that it was none of her business but didn't because Daud obviously cared about her opinion. He showed her a leather-and-chrome chair and matching sofa, along with glass-topped tables upon which art objects rested. It was like a mini-museum. Even the kitchen featured pottery crafted in the desert.

"It fits together," she said. "And you have some beautiful pieces from the Negev."

"Those are family items."

"I'll show you my house," Hana said. "It came furnished, so none of the furniture is mine. It won't take as long."

It was Hana's turn to carry around her laptop. Daud asked her to stop when she reached a collection of photos of her family in frames on top of the dresser in her bedroom. She brought the laptop closer and told him about them.

"I see your nieces and nephews, but where's Mikael?" Daud asked.

"He's not as cute as they are."

"Have you talked to him since we met?"

"No, he's still in Africa and won't be returning to Israel until next week."

Leon was lying on a rug in the kitchen. He raised his head when Hana came closer. Daud told the dog to sit up in Arabic. Leon yawned and lowered his head.

"He only understands a couple of words in English," Hana replied. "I'm not sure he's going to be bilingual."

She told Daud how Leon came to live with her.

"I adopted a stray when I was a boy," Daud replied. "He had a great nose and ears. He would lead us to scorpions in the desert."

"Why would you want to find scorpions?" Hana said and pulled back from the screen.

"To play with them. We'd catch them, cut off their tails with a knife, and let them climb all over us. I didn't show you my scorpion cage in the apartment, did I?"

"Seriously?"

Daud smiled. "No, no pets of any kind. My schedule wouldn't allow it."

Hana and Daud would usually end their conversations with a discussion about the Neumann case. Daud was compiling a list of people to interview and waiting on responses for requests to obtain additional documents and official reports.

"I have copies on a flash drive of the photos you saw at the police station near Hurva Square," Daud said. "I'll send them to you later today. One of the captains is an acquaintance and released them to me."

Hana shuddered at the memory of the images. "I'll forward the photos to Jakob Brodsky but not Ben Neumann," she said.

"You should ask Neumann about that," Daud replied.

"Why?"

"It's his decision. You're his lawyer, not his caretaker."

Hana wasn't convinced. "Maybe I'll leave that up to Jakob."

Daud moved away from the camera for a moment. "I have to go," he said when his face came back into view. "I'll be away all day tomorrow and won't be able to talk or respond to texts."

"Working on our case?"

"No, something else that is very time-sensitive. I'll miss seeing and talking to you."

"I'll miss you, too. Bye."

The screen went blank. Hana, who was sitting on the sofa, leaned back against the cushions. Talking was fine, but her heart ached at the physical separation between them.

• • •

Jakob was at the office when he received the photos from the murder scene in Hurva Square. In their stark detail, they were harder to look at than the fuzzy surveillance video. Per Hana's request, he sent a text to Ben asking the client if he wanted to see them. Ben didn't immediately respond.

After taking a call from a client, Jakob finished responding to emails before resuming his internet research. Based on what he'd received from Hana and Daud, he'd switched much of his focus to sites within the Middle East. However, the language barrier was proving formidable. Arabic was like hieroglyphics to him. A recurring thread he was able to follow had to do with recruitment videos in English aimed at budding or fully committed Islamic fundamentalists in the United Kingdom or the United States. Most of the English speakers had a British accent, but the lanky American Jakob had seen before made a brief appearance, shouting, "Allahu akbar," meaning "God is greater," at the conclusion of a speech in English by an older man with a gray beard and wearing a red sweater. Maddie buzzed him.

"Detective Freeman from the APD is calling," she said. "Are you in trouble?"

"No, you're in trouble," Jakob joked. "I'll talk to him."

"No fresh leads since the guy fled to Venezuela," the detective said. "We've confirmed the type of phosphorous device that triggered the car fire. It was homemade. There's no way to know how long it was there, and it's almost certain the mechanic set it off by jiggling the triggering wires, causing them to make contact."

"What about Sarkasian?" Jakob asked.

"He admitted who he is and isn't going to fight extradition to North Carolina. Once he's processed, he won't be on the street for a while."

"What happens now?"

"That's why I called. I'm keeping the file open, but we're at a dead end unless we receive new information."

Jakob touched the side of his head. The knots were almost gone. "How would you rate the ongoing danger to me?"

"I have to say there's a possibility, but once a few rats are flushed into the light, the rest usually go into hiding."

"I'm going to Israel in a few weeks. Any concerns about that?"

"It's easier to keep tabs on the bad guys in a small country than it is in a big one. Just be careful where you go."

CHAPTER 26

Saturday afternoon, Hana parked down the street from the town-home where Ben and Sadie lived. She and Leon passed four minivans alongside the sidewalk. Delayed by work that had forced her to go into the office, she was forty-five minutes late for the party. One of the workers at the day care center had been teaching Leon how to walk on a leash, and Hana was impressed by the dog's developing discipline.

"Trust me," Ben said when Hana called to ask permission to bring Leon. "A puppy will not add much to the chaos caused by a houseful of six- and seven-year-old girls. We have a small fenced-in backyard where your dog can take refuge from the mob if it gets to be too much for him."

Birthday balloons decorated the front porch of the townhome. A woman who looked to be in her sixties with beautiful white hair opened the door. Hana immediately recognized her as Gloria's mother. The facial resemblance between grandmother, daughter, and grand-daughter was unmistakable. Hana could hear high-pitched squeals inside the house.

"I'm Florence Dershowitz, one of Sadie's grandmothers," the woman said with a warm smile. "You must be Ms. Abboud."

"Hana, please."

Leon's manners disappeared at the sounds and smells coming from inside the house. He yelped and strained on the leash.

"And this is Leon," Hana added, jerking the leash backward. "He wants to join the party."

Hana followed Mrs. Dershowitz through a small foyer into a large living room-dining room combination. The furniture had been pushed against the walls to clear space for the party. A large banner proclaimed, "Happy Birthday, Sadie!" at one end of the room. Hana placed her present, an outfit for the doll Fabia, on a table covered with gifts.

The girls were playing a relay game in which they had to grab a balloon, run across the room to a chair, and pop the balloon by sitting down on it. There were two lines of girls. Sadie was next in line to pop a balloon. One of her friends tagged Sadie's hand. When Sadie turned around to sit in the chair, she saw Hana and hesitated.

"Pop the balloon, Sadie!" Hana called out.

Several adults who hadn't noticed Hana's entrance turned and saw her. The prolonged looks she received made her slightly uncomfortable. Ben, carrying Fabia in one hand, came out of the kitchen.

"Did you receive my text about being late?" Hana asked.

"Yes, and I told Sadie so she wouldn't be anxious about it."

"What are you doing with Fabia?"

"Babysitting," Ben said, handing the doll to Hana and turning back to the kitchen. "I need to put the candles on the cake."

Hana could tell that the doll had been receiving a lot of attention. Her clothes were disheveled, her hair matted. A new outfit would be the perfect remedy.

"Sadie and Fabia are inseparable," Mrs. Dershowitz said after Ben left. "She told me you have a niece with that name."

"Actually, Fabia is a cousin," Hana replied. "We spent a lot of time together when we were growing up."

Sadie's balloon popped, and she scampered back to her team.

"Sadie looks a lot like you," Hana said to Mrs. Dershowitz.

"And has her mother's personality."

After the final balloon popped, Sadie left her group and ran over to Hana and Leon. She knelt down so the puppy could lick her face. Hana started to pull the dog away.

"It's okay," Mrs. Dershowitz said. "To hear her laugh like that is worth a few dog germs."

"Can you let him go so we can play with him?" Sadie begged.

Hana unhooked the leash, and within seconds the puppy was surrounded by little girls. Leon wiggled with delight at the sensory overload of multiple hands on his fur. Ben reappeared with a large rectangular birthday cake.

Soon the partygoers crowded around in a tight circle and Sadie blew out the candles. Hana ended up standing next to a woman who looked to be about her own age. After the candles were out, the woman turned to Hana.

"I'm Marissa Cohen. Ben is my younger brother."

Hana introduced herself.

"You're the new lawyer representing Ben in his lawsuit, right?"

"Yes."

Ben began cutting small pieces of cake for the girls.

"Do you have experience suing terrorists?" Marissa asked.

Hana briefly explained her role in international business law. Even though Marissa was Ben's sister, she had to be careful not to violate attorney-client confidentiality.

"If that's your area of expertise, why get involved in a lawsuit about Gloria's murder?"

"The senior partners at the firm asked me to consider it, and I agreed to help."

At that moment, Hana saw a little girl let Leon lick icing from her fingers. "I'd better not let my puppy eat too much cake," Hana said.

She picked up Leon and took him into the kitchen. Ben was pouring punch into little pink cups.

"Is the garden still available for Leon?" she asked.

"Through that door," Ben said, pointing. "It's totally fenced in."

Hana deposited Leon on the green grass. The flower beds were neglected and filled with weedy interlopers. When she returned to the kitchen, Marissa was talking to Ben. She walked away when she saw Hana.

"I think your sister is suspicious of me," Hana said in a soft voice. "Is it personal or related to the lawsuit?"

"Maybe both," Ben said, lifting one shoulder in a shrug. "I'm sure I'll find out before she leaves for Cincinnati in the morning. Marissa has never been shy about sharing her opinions."

Over the next hour Hana met several mothers of the girls invited to the party. They didn't try to hide their curiosity about whether Hana and Ben's relationship had crossed the line from professional to personal. Hana tried to squelch speculation by emphasizing her interest in Sadie, but it didn't work. The look on the women's faces said, *What better way to get to a widower than through his little girl?*

Sadie's grandfather came over to Hana. Mr. Dershowitz was a tall, gray-haired man with wire-frame glasses. He told Hana about his conversation with Sadie at the doll store. "From the beginning you made quite an impression on her," the older man said.

Hana was feeling a bit on the defensive following her encounters with some of the women at the party. "Do you approve?" she asked.

"Yes," Mr. Dershowitz said, looking directly into Hana's eyes. "Because I believe you're playing a role in Sadie's life beyond representing Ben in the lawsuit."

Mr. Dershowitz reminded Hana of a wise, kind rabbi.

"Do you know what that role might be?" she asked.

Hana knew her words sounded formal, but she didn't know another way to phrase the question.

"That's up to Hashem," Mr. Dershowitz said and looked upward. "But his light shines in you. Both my wife and I can see it in your eyes."

"Thank you," Hana said gratefully. "That's one of the nicest compliments I've ever received."

Hana glanced over at Mrs. Dershowitz, who was playing with Sadie and her friends.

"Time doesn't heal wounds," the older man continued.

"No, it doesn't," Hana agreed. "There was a saying in our house that God appoints angels whose job is to change scars from frowns into smiles. The deeper meaning is that this occurs from the inside out, not the outside in."

"Tell it to me."

"Do you speak Arabic?" Hana asked in surprise.

Mr. Dershowitz shook his head. "No, but I'd still like to hear the sound of the words."

Hana repeated the proverb that contained alliteration in Arabic, making it sound like a poem.

"That's beautiful," Mr. Dershowitz said when she finished. "The doctors say that when she's a teenager Sadie can have surgery, which will make the scar on her face barely visible. I hope I get a chance to see that, but even more I want to see your proverb become a reality for her. We're all trying to do our part, but we welcome reinforcements."

Mr. Dershowitz stepped away. A few girls began to leave, and Hana knew it was time for her to do so, too. She went over to Sadie to tell her good-bye.

"Thanks for coming," Sadie said, giving her a hug. "I love the new dress for Fabia."

Hana went to the backyard to retrieve Leon. The dog's paws were muddy.

"Uh-oh," Ben said when he saw him. "The sprinkler system is broken, and Leon found the leak."

Ben washed the dog's paws in the sink. Another mother peeked in to say good-bye and saw Hana and Ben standing side by side. Ben handed Hana a dish towel to dry Leon's damp feet. "There, that should work," Ben said.

He handed Leon to Hana. "Go out that way if you like," he said, pointing to another exit from the kitchen.

"Okay, thanks again for letting me come."

The door led to a short hallway that connected the foyer with the bedrooms. Hana could see into the master bedroom. A picture of Gloria and Ben from their wedding rested on a tall chest of drawers. Hana couldn't keep an image from the folder at the Hurva Square police station from flashing through her mind. Needing a moment of happiness and hope to balance the brutality of pain and death, she spent a few extra seconds staring at the wedding photo.

• • •

Hana and Daud spent longer on Skype than usual and Hana arrived late at the office on Monday morning. Janet was already at her workstation.

"Did you go to the birthday party?" Janet asked as soon as Hana approached the secretary's desk.

"Yes, it was typical of birthday parties for seven-year-old girls."

"Not when you showed up," Janet said skeptically. "Any moms of the other kids around?"

"Yes, and they wanted to know about me and Ben. I guess I'm going to have to get used to that if I spend time with Sadie."

"Yeah, and I bet there was a lot more conversation among them after the party ended."

In her office, Hana translated and distributed Daud's latest report to Mr. Lowenstein, Jakob, and Ben. Posing as a job recruiter for a plastics factory, the investigator had made a trip to Deir Dibwan. He listed the names of the people he'd talked to. There were several Zadans. Nobody had much to say about Tawfik except that he spent most of his time away from town. Not surprisingly, Abdul and Tawfik were considered local heroes for taking the fight to the Jews.

After she sent the report, the receptionist buzzed her.

"Mr. Bart Kendall would like to speak to you."

. . .

Emily picked up Jakob to take him to work. They'd developed a comfortable working relationship. He handed her a cup of coffee.

"I need to stop by my bank to deposit a check," he said. "The insurance company paid me for the loss of my car."

"Okay. How are you feeling?"

"I had a bad headache last night, but I'm feeling better this morning."

Emily navigated her way through a stream of traffic toward the bank. Jakob noticed that no music was playing.

"Why the silence?" he asked.

"After seeing the explosive device planted on your car, I wanted to know more about your mugging at Butch Watson's apartment. The cop in me rose up and so I checked you out, partly because of concern for my own safety."

"I get it, but I've also seen your gun."

"True," Emily said and smiled. "I also read the notes on the hand-made Islamic prayer beads you found at the scene."

"You know about the prayer beads?" Jakob asked incredulously.

"Yes, and from what I've learned, I'm not going to hang a set from my rearview mirror. Anyway, I wanted to let you know what I did."

They stopped so Jakob could deposit the check at an ATM outside his bank.

When he returned to the car and had snapped his seat belt, Emily turned and looked directly into his eyes. "I want you to know that I'm impressed by your courage. You're different from most lawyers I've been around."

"Thanks," Jakob replied. "And you're different from any Uber driver I've ever met."

"In a good way?" Emily smiled.

"In every way," Jakob answered. "But if you want to hear about courage, I should tell you about my father."

During the rest of the ride to the office, Jakob described some of the persecution suffered by his father in the former Soviet Union. Emily listened attentively.

"I'd like to meet him," she said when he finished. "He sounds amazing."

"Next time my parents are in Atlanta, we'll get together. You and my mother can talk about the best brand of violas."

CHAPTER 27

H ana accepted the call from Bart Kendall.
    "I didn't hear from you about my proposal for participation
in the documentary," the producer said.

"I've been in Israel," Hana replied. "But I didn't forget. I was still
thinking about it."

"We begin filming the day after tomorrow," Bart said. "It will
take at least a week, so I can fit you in at your convenience. Your part
will involve a static shot, so we should be able to take care of it in two
to three hours."

"What do you mean by a static shot?"

"You would be talking to the camera, not moving around on a
location or a set."

During the conversation, Hana was sending up a prayer for direction. No answer came, but even a small opportunity to counter BDS
might be worth pursuing.

"Would you be asking questions or will I give a presentation?"
Hana asked.

"I'm not the narrator, so it would be a presentation with a lead-in
sentence or two introducing you. Prepare something and send it over.
We can work from there. You have my email, correct?"

"Yes. Would I have to sign a release or permission form?"

"Of course. Otherwise, we couldn't use your image or voice."

"Could you send over the release form before I make up my mind?"

"Sure, but it's routine stuff we use on all our commercial shoots."

The call ended. Inspired, Hana put together several paragraphs that included moral perspectives and economic reasons why the movement was off-base and counterproductive to peace in the region. She was about to send it to Bart when an email popped up with the release form attached.

Hana opened and read the two-page document. The first page granted Bart's company permission to use her image and voice in the project. There were no red flags. The second page looked fine until the last paragraph, which included the language "Producer retains the right to edit participant's role in the manner best suited to the goals of the project within his sole discretion." She immediately called Bart.

"Like I said, that's standard language," he said when she asked him about the sentence. "It would be an unnecessary step to obtain approval after a film has been edited."

Hana paused before answering to be sure of what she wanted to say. "Then I'm going to pass," she said. "I need to express myself and what I believe in strictly my own words. On an issue like this, it's not unreasonable to have input into what's edited out or how it's presented."

"Suit yourself," Bart said curtly. "I was willing to give you a chance to voice your opinion, and you rejected it." The producer's tone of voice reinforced Hana's decision.

The following morning, Hana told Daud about the project.

"I'm glad you turned it down," he said bluntly. "The producer of the documentary has an agenda. How did you meet this guy?"

"At church and then he took me out to dinner at a nice restaurant," Hana answered.

"What's his name?"

"Bart Kendall. I had no idea what he had in mind until the end, so he wasn't completely honest. You're not going to contact him, are you?"

"No, no. But you asked for my opinion, and I gave it to you."

"Oh, I talked to Mikael yesterday and asked him about you."

"What did he say?"

"That you needed to improve on your footwork if you wanted to be a better footballer. Otherwise, he recommended you switch to rugby."

Daud smiled. "Mikael always told the truth. What else?"

"He said you were a serious man everyone on the team respected."

That night Hana awoke from a nightmare in which she was surrounded by black shapes that rushed toward her and then retreated. She drank a glass of water in her bathroom before going into the living room to pray. One of the worst parts of the dream was a vague sense that Daud was present but not coming to her aid. She didn't want to place too much emotional weight on any person—her help came from the Lord—and she took the dream as a warning not to do so. After a short prayer, a sense of peace returned, and the disturbing aftereffects of the dream receded.

In the morning, she found herself more confident and relaxed during her Skype conversation with the investigator. Sometimes, a bad dream could have a good impact.

Hana had a productive day at the office working on several projects for Mr. Collins. Late in the afternoon, she received a text and a cute photo from Sadie via Ben's phone inviting Hana and Leon to come over for another visit at the townhome.

• • •

Jakob loosened his tie. It was eight thirty when he sent the last email and turned off his computer. No other lawyers remained in the office building, and he was about to request a different Uber driver because he assumed Emily was at school when she texted:

> Out of class. You said you were going to work late. Let me know
> if you need a ride.

Thirty minutes later Emily picked him up. She was wearing an evening gown with a string of pearls around her neck. Jakob did a double take when he slipped into the passenger seat of the car.

"No comments." Emily held up her hand. "We had a chamber music performance this evening. This is how a musician dresses when playing a viola in a Vivaldi piece."

"I thought you dressed up because I needed a ride after eight."

Emily grinned. "That's a comment."

In the close confines of the small car, Jakob caught a whiff of perfume. He took a deeper breath.

"Are you having sinus problems?" Emily asked. "That can cause a terrible earache during takeoff and landing. Do you have any of those soft things that screw into your ears to relieve pressure? They're either pink or orange, and they sell them at most drugstores."

"Are you a paid spokesperson for the company?"

"No, but you really should get some."

The formal outfit didn't have an impact on the former police officer's driving habits. She abruptly changed lanes in traffic. They stopped for a red light at an intersection not far from Jakob's apartment. Nearby was a commercial area with a couple of restaurants.

"Did you eat supper before the performance?" Jakob asked.

"No, I play better on an empty stomach."

"Would you like to grab a bite to eat? There's a great pizza place in the next block. It's next to a Laundromat."

Emily pressed her lips together tightly for a moment. When she did, Jakob noticed how much red lipstick she'd used. The light turned green. She stomped on the gas and suddenly lurched to the left as the car swerved into the parking lot.

"I've always wanted to eat here," she said as she whipped the car into a parking place.

"Seriously? It really is good, especially if you like thin-crust pizza."

Jakob held the door open for her as they entered the crowded restaurant. With Jakob wearing a tie and Emily in an evening gown, they were the best-dressed couple in sight. A young hostess looked them over with a puzzled expression on her face.

"It's prom night," Jakob said.

The hostess rolled her eyes and led them to a table for two beneath a large poster of the Atlanta skyline. They ordered individual pizzas. Jakob's featured meats; Emily went vegetarian.

"And before you ask, I eat meat," Emily said after the waitress left. "But in moderation. I'll probably ask for a bite of your pizza."

Emily looked up at the ceiling for a moment. Jakob followed her gaze and saw nothing.

"I like the music track they're playing," Emily said. "Classic rock guitar was incredibly innovative. That's Eric Clapton."

"I don't know much about him other than his name."

For the next ten minutes Emily delivered a lesson in music history covering the 1960s and '70s. Her passion for the subject shone through.

"Have you thought about teaching?" Jakob asked when she finished.

"That's the plan," she replied. "The competition for performance jobs is insane, and I'd rather work with kids than temperamental conductors."

"Kids can be temperamental, too."

"Yes, but I'd be in charge."

Their food arrived. Jakob slid his pizza toward Emily. "Select first," he said.

Emily carved off half a slice. Jakob then ate a big bite that was scorching hot. He quickly chased it with a gulp of beer.

"Are you okay?" Emily asked.

"I'm not sure," Jakob answered. "Do you remember when you called me brave?"

"Yes."

Jakob pointed at the pizza. "Right now, I'm afraid of this hot pizza."

Later at home, Jakob thought about his time with Emily as he logged on to the internet. She'd had a tough childhood living with an alcoholic father and a mother who'd suffered through three failed marriages. Instead of focusing on the pursuit of terrorists on the other side of the world, Jakob typed in the Uber driver's name. Two articles from the Atlanta paper popped up, both about her days working as an undercover officer combating sex trafficking. Emily's identity was revealed because she testified in the trial of two men from Thailand charged with kidnapping, aggravated assault, and other crimes based on the illegal transportation of teenage girls from Southeast Asia into the United States. The aggravated assault charges especially caught Jakob's interest. The men were violent predators who didn't hesitate to attack or maim those who opposed them. Detective Emily Johnson was part of the team that arrested them following a brief gun battle. She knew as much as or more than Jakob did about living under the threat of danger.

• • •

Saturday morning, Hana told Daud she was going to see Ben and Sadie. The investigator had already received a full account of the birthday party.

"It will be the middle of the night in Israel when I'm there, but I'd like to introduce you to Sadie," she said. "Would you send me a video telling her hello? She understands basic greetings in Hebrew, but it would need to be mostly in English."

"What exactly should I say?" Daud asked skeptically. "I rarely talk to little kids."

"Not much. I just want Sadie to put a face to a name. I'll tell her more about you myself."

"I'd like to hear that conversation."

"Girls only." Hana smiled. "It will also be good for Ben to see you."

"Should I say anything about Gloria?"

Hana paused. "That might make Sadie sad. She doesn't understand the lawsuit and won't be listed as a plaintiff on the pleadings."

"Why does she think you've dropped into her life?"

"She isn't analyzing it, just feeling the love."

"That's powerful," Daud said.

"I hope so."

It was five when Hana arrived at the Neumann townhome. Ben had picked up a Mexican take-out dinner. Sadie's tastes were simple; her desired fare was two basic tacos, but she was proud that she could tolerate a dash of mild hot sauce. Every time she took a bite, she fanned her open mouth with her hand.

"You don't have to put hot sauce on it," Ben said after the fourth display of hand waving. "The meat is seasoned."

"No, it's the way you're supposed to eat them," Sadie answered. "Marquita at my school told me. They're hotter than the spicy chicken Poppy buys me."

Hana and Ben were eating bite-size empanadas, chilaquiles, and delicately seasoned rice. When the meal was over, Hana took out her phone and showed them the video sent by Daud.

"I understand him!" Sadie squealed when he greeted her by name in Hebrew and asked how she was doing.

"Keep listening," Hana said.

Daud's deep voice continued in English: "Hana tells me you are a beautiful and smart girl. She enjoyed your birthday party and told me about it. I live in Jerusalem. I hope that someday I will meet you in person in Israel or in the United States. Please hug Hana and kiss her on the cheek. If you want to send me a video, I would like to see it. Bye-bye."

"Let's watch it again," Sadie said immediately.

The little girl held the phone in her hand and stared at the screen while the video replayed. After viewing it the second time, she returned the phone to Hana and gave her a tight hug followed by a kiss on the cheek.

"If you marry Daud, will you live with him in Israel or Atlanta?" Sadie asked.

"Who said I was going to marry him?" Hana asked in surprise.

"It happens," Sadie said matter-of-factly. "Let's make a video for him."

As soon as the video started, Sadie launched into a lecture explaining how Daud should treat Hana. Both Ben and Hana laughed so hard they were on the verge of tears.

"I'm serious," Sadie said when she'd finished and they stopped the recording.

"And right," Ben replied. "I'm sure Hana appreciates all the help you gave her."

"Absolutely," Hana said.

"Can I play in the backyard with Leon?" Sadie asked.

Hana and Ben stayed at the kitchen table.

"May I ask you a personal question about Daud?" Ben asked when they were alone.

"Yes."

"Sadie assumed you were dating him. Is she right?"

"We saw each other a couple of times when I was in Israel, and we've talked almost every day since I returned. Sadie is right. Daud and I are attracted to each other."

"Which is your business, not mine. My concern is that Daud's involvement in the case stays at the right level. It seems to Jakob and me that you're involving him in everything, instead of giving him a defined role."

"He has a defined role," Hana replied defensively. "He's investigating the case. Once that's complete, he won't have an active role. And don't worry about my personal feelings affecting my professional responsibilities."

After Sadie came inside, she and Hana sat in the living room so that Sadie could show off her literary skills by reading two picture books, both of which showed signs of frequent use. Written inside the front cover of one of the stories was an inscription from Gloria to Sadie: *To my precious Sadie Ann—May your heart find the same love of beauty and kindness as Katelyn. All my love, Mommy.*

"I didn't know your middle name was Ann," Hana said.

"I don't like it that much. That's why everyone calls me Sadie."

The book was about a little girl named Katelyn who helped her mother plant a flower garden. The mother became ill, and Katelyn faithfully tended the flowers, taking bouquets to her mother in the hospital. The child began delivering flowers to other people in the hospital, who were blessed by her kindness and shared bits of their lives with her. The watercolor illustrations were a perfect complement to the text. As Sadie turned the pages, Hana, sensing the mother would die and the last flowers Katelyn gave her would be placed on her grave, began to dread the outcome. However, the mother recovered, and the final scene was a year later when Katelyn took flowers to the hospital to celebrate the birth of her little brother. When Sadie finished, Hana noticed Ben standing in the doorway to the kitchen listening.

"I'd rather have a little sister than a brother," Sadie announced when she closed the book. "But that can't happen until Daddy gets married again."

"Let's read another book," Hana said without looking at Ben.

"Will you stay for my bathtime?" Sadie asked. "I don't need help except with my hair. It gets all tangled and angry."

"I'm not sure—"

"One more book and then Hana needs to take Leon home," Ben said. "He's a tired puppy and fell asleep on the floor."

• • •

In the middle of the night, Hana had a dream. She and Sadie, dressed in clothes from the 1940s, were standing next to each other on a train station platform. A train rumbled into the station and stopped. A conductor called for those who had tickets to board. Hana leaned over to Sadie, who was clutching a yellow ticket in her hand, and told her this wasn't their train. Hana opened her purse to check her own ticket. It wasn't there. Frantically, she rummaged through the purse but found nothing. The conductor issued a final boarding call, and Sadie calmly stepped forward. At that moment, a woman appeared at the top of the steps to the train car.

It was Gloria Neumann.

A smile on her face, Gloria held out her hand to Sadie, who ran up the steps to embrace her mother. They held each other with a fierceness reserved for mother and child. When Gloria lowered Sadie to the floor, the little girl looked back at Hana and blew her a kiss. The train pulled out of the station, leaving Hana numb with loneliness and abandonment. When the train disappeared from sight, Hana looked down at her hand. In it was her ticket. As she woke up, it took several seconds for her conscious mind to engage.

Hana got up and walked into the living room, then knelt in front of the sofa and closed her eyes. The images were so fresh and vivid, she felt on the verge of slipping back into the dream. She focused on a possible interpretation. The little girl might want to board the train to be with her mother, but her ticket was for a later departure. One likely meaning was like a punch in the stomach—the dream foretold Sadie's premature death. Hana buried her head in the fabric of the sofa and sobbed. Her breath came in gasps.

Twice before in her life she had cried like this during prayer. Hana knew they were tears of intercession, drops of salty water that cause heavenly ripples as large as tidal waves. The prophet Jeremiah once wrote: "Oh, that my head were a spring of water and my eyes a fountain of tears! I would weep day and night for the slain of my people." This night Hana wept not for a nation, but for a seven-year-old girl descended from the ancient Jewish prophet. She cried out from the depths of her spirit and asked the Lord God Almighty to protect the child's life until she reached the fullness of days allotted to her.

CHAPTER 28

Hana had trouble containing her excitement during her morning Skype session with Daud. In two days she would see him in Jerusalem. However, the investigator was in a serious mood.

"Is everything okay?" Hana asked.

"Yes, yes," he answered. "I'm under stress related to another matter and hope it won't spill over into the time when you arrive."

"I'll understand if you need to be working on something else. There will be things Jakob and I can do."

"Of course, but I want us to be efficient and productive. I've made progress with the man who holds a grudge against the Zadan clan. I'm certain he will meet with us and may be a key to unlocking information the Shin Bet didn't find."

"Good."

"But I'm not sure where Jakob Brodsky fits in. From what you've told me, he seems like a liability, not an asset," Daud said.

"Mr. Lowenstein has the same concerns, but Jakob has put his heart and soul into this case. We can make it work."

"He will need to be flexible."

"I'll be responsible for him," Hana said, knowing the job would fall to her anyway.

"What is the status of the police investigation into the physical attack and destruction of his car?"

"I've not heard anything new for several weeks."

"What did you decide about seeing your family during this trip?" Daud asked.

"They don't know I'm coming. If I'm able to squeeze in a visit to Reineh, it will be a huge surprise."

"I think keeping the trip confidential is a good idea."

"Me too." Hana checked the time. "Listen, I need to leave for work. I have a lot to do."

"Okay. I won't be available in the morning, so the next time we see each other will be at the airport."

Hana's heart leapt in anticipation. She spoke a formal farewell in Arabic that included the promise of a soon reunion. Daud smiled.

"I haven't heard anyone say that in a long time," he said. "My grandfather used to say that to my grandmother before he would leave for a week away from home."

"I think it is a lot better than 'bye,'" Hana replied in English.

During the month since returning to Atlanta, Hana had talked several times with Sylvia Armstrong at the US Attorney's Office in New York. None of the conversations yielded any more new information, but Mr. Lowenstein insisted that the lines of communication stay open. Armstrong called Hana again.

"Are you still scheduled to go to Israel?" she asked.

"Yes."

"My contacts inform me that your investigator has been active."

"That's why we hired him," Hana answered, glad about the favorable opinion of Daud's efforts from a third party.

"If you need help convincing the Israelis to work with you, let me know. I sent emails to several people this morning letting them know you're on the way and our interests are consistent."

"Thank you," Hana replied. "Can you provide me any names?"

"Yes, one name is Aaron Levy. He works in an antiterrorism unit in Tel Aviv and knows as much about the Neumann murder as anyone. Daud Hasan has already contacted him."

Hana didn't recall Daud mentioning that name in any of his reports.

"Okay," Hana said. "Anything else?"

"Safe travels."

After the call ended, Hana sent a quick memo to Mr. Lowenstein, Jakob, Ben, and Daud about the phone call. She expected Daud to respond with additional information about Aaron Levy, but he didn't.

The following morning, Hana arrived very early at the office. Janet was already at her desk.

"Why are you here now?" Hana asked.

"This is what assistants do when one of their bosses is leaving the country."

Hana thought about her backlog of work. She'd given up hope of having it all done and resigned herself to handling it remotely.

"There are a few extra things you can do," she said slowly.

"Bring it on."

As the two women were going over the projects, the phone buzzed. It was Gladys Applewhite.

"Good, you're here," Gladys said. "Mr. Lowenstein wants to meet with you first thing. He pulled into the parking deck and should be in his office in five minutes."

"I'll be there."

"Pep talk or thunderstorm?" Janet asked.

"I have no idea."

The senior partner's door was open and Gladys, who was on the phone, motioned for Hana to enter. Mr. Lowenstein was standing and drinking a cup of coffee.

"It sounds like Ms. Armstrong is cooperating."

"Yes, sir."

"Build on it. She could be more help than our investigator and a lot cheaper. Remind her that our tax dollars pay her salary."

"Are you serious?"

"No, but I talked to Armstrong's boss after I received your email. They want to help but expect reciprocity of information."

"Daud Hasan wants to protect the identity of some of his sources."

"You're in charge, not him. You'll be the clearinghouse."

Hana wasn't sure how to follow Mr. Lowenstein's orders. It was like trying to predict the weather a month in advance.

"And that goes double for Jakob Brodsky," Mr. Lowenstein continued, tapping his desk with his index finger. "You know I don't like him tagging along, and your comment about the investigator gives me an idea. Hasan can exclude Brodsky from meetings and interviews. The fact that Brodsky is Jewish should work for any situation in which Arabs are present."

Hana didn't want to mention that Daud had the same problem with Jakob.

"I understand."

"And your former involvement with security personnel at the airport would be another justification," Mr. Lowenstein said. "The Israeli authorities will likely be comfortable with you in the room and prefer to keep Brodsky out."

Once again, the older lawyer's ability to quickly come up with innovative ways to deal with a situation impressed Hana, even if she didn't like the ideas he gave.

"But how do I keep Jakob busy? He can't sit in a hotel room all day."

"Give him research tasks that he can do online or interviews with English speakers who aren't very important. And he can always be a tourist, even though I don't like paying for it."

"The money he and the client deposited in our trust account is funding the trip," Hana said and then braced for a negative reaction.

"Good point," Mr. Lowenstein said with a smile. "Hana, I wanted to tell you that I have the highest confidence in you. You've handled everything we've thrown at you superbly since you joined the firm. You may be tentative at first, which is good because you don't charge off in the wrong direction, but once you get your bearings you do impressive work. If Ben Neumann has a case, I believe you'll find a way to move forward."

"Thank you."

Mr. Lowenstein stood. "Copy me on everything you send out, no matter how minor it seems. I can separate the important from the trivial."

The senior lawyer escorted her to the door of his office. "Gladys, is there anything you want Hana to bring you from the Holy Land? I know you and the people who attend your church are interested in Israel."

"No, sir."

"If you change your mind, let her know."

Mr. Lowenstein returned to his office and closed his door.

"There's one thing," Gladys said to Hana.

"What? I'd be glad to pick something up for you or the congregation."

Gladys, a serious look on her face, spoke in a low voice. "I want you to be careful and come back safe and sound. That will be plenty for me. I'll be praying every day until I see you standing exactly where you are right now."

"Thank you," Hana said gratefully.

• • •

Jakob pressed down hard to close his large suitcase. The small carry-on bag containing his laptop leaned against the foot of the bed. Emily was scheduled to pick him up in ten minutes. Jakob bent over to shut another latch on the suitcase, then stood and hit the right side of his head on the corner of a chest of drawers. He caught his breath and winced sharply in pain. Feeling slightly nauseous, he dragged his suitcase to the front door, then made his way to the couch and sat down. He closed his eyes and tried to forget about the throbbing pain.

The sound of loud banging on the front door of his apartment startled him. Shaking his head to get rid of fogginess, he stumbled across the room and opened the door. Emily was standing on the landing outside his door.

"Why weren't you downstairs?" she demanded. "I waited five minutes, texted three times, and called twice."

"Uh, I must have dozed off on the couch," Jakob replied.

"Are you okay?" Emily asked, her frown turning into a look of concern. "You look pale. Did you pass out?"

"I'm not sure. I hit my head on the corner of a dresser."

"Is it bleeding?" Emily stepped closer for a better view.

Jakob touched the spot. There was nothing red on his fingers. "No, but it made me woozy. Come in. I need to eat a snack before we go."

Jakob bumped into the corner of the couch on his way to the kitchen. Emily followed. He opened the refrigerator and took out a yogurt.

"Would you like one?" he asked. "I have strawberry and peach."

"We need to get going soon."

"Okay, okay."

Jakob took a deep breath and felt steadier on his feet. Grabbing a plastic spoon, he headed toward the front door. Emily was in front of him and reached for his large suitcase.

"No, no," Jakob said. "I'll take that one if you can handle the carry-on bag."

Emily eyed him skeptically. "Sit down and eat your yogurt first," she said. "I'll make up the time on the way to the airport."

Jakob didn't argue. He peeled the top from the yogurt. "Are you sure you don't want one, too?" he asked.

"I'll grab a peach," Emily replied.

When the first slightly tangy bite hit Jakob's tongue, he felt mentally clearer. The second spoonful brought him more fully into reality. Emily returned with a peach yogurt and sat on the other end of the couch.

"I had a concussion spell," Jakob said. "No doubt about it."

"That worries me," Emily replied. "Does your head hurt now?"

"Just tender, and I don't remember what happened for a short time. I guess I just sat here on the couch."

Jakob leaned over and picked up his phone. Sure enough, there were multiple messages from Emily.

"You blew up my phone," he said.

"I didn't have any other option. If I'd known you'd hurt yourself, I would have come up here immediately."

Jakob moved his head from side to side to see if it bothered him. "I'm okay. Maybe I should start wearing a helmet around the apartment."

"I wish you weren't taking this flight," Emily said. "You should schedule an appointment with your neurologist."

Jakob ate another bite of yogurt. Emily's remained unopened.

"Eat your yogurt," Jakob said to her. "I shouldn't leave it in the refrigerator since I'm going out of town."

They ate in silence for a minute.

"Are you sure you should go to the airport?" Emily asked when they finished.

"Yes, the ticket is purchased and nonrefundable."

Jakob stood to convince himself that he could do so. The room didn't spin. He took a step and didn't wobble.

"Tell Hana Abboud to keep an eye on you," Emily said.

"She'll do that without being asked."

"And that you hit your head in the same spot."

"Sure." Jakob headed toward the door.

"Don't you want to throw these empty containers away?" Emily asked, picking up Jakob's yogurt. "They'll turn sour."

"Yes. I took out the rest of the trash earlier."

Jakob carried his large suitcase down the stairs without a problem. He hoisted it into the back seat of Emily's car. She placed the carry-on bag beside it. Jakob sat in the passenger seat and closed his eyes. Emily didn't turn on any music. They pulled out of the apartment complex onto a main road.

"Are you still with me?" she asked.

"Yeah."

Jakob opened his eyes. He touched the side of his head. It remained tender. "No dizziness, no blurred vision," he said with relief.

It was a fifty-minute drive to the airport. Emily slipped off the expressway twice to avoid common bottlenecks. The second time, she slowed for a moment and moved into the right-hand lane of a four-lane road. She then sped up and zigzagged back and forth between lanes for half a mile.

"I already know you can drive like a Formula One racer," Jakob said.

"I'm not trying to impress you. The same car has been behind us since we left your apartment. Nobody goes to the airport the way I do."

Jakob turned in his seat and looked behind them. It was a busy street.

"Which one?" he asked.

"The white Honda."

Jakob could see several white cars. Emily slowed and changed lanes. Jakob saw a distant car mimic her movement.

"That's a long way back. How did you spot it?"

"The driver is someone who knows what he's doing. I thought I lost him at a red light, but he showed up again."

They returned to the expressway and two miles later took the airport exit. Jakob turned around again.

"Keep looking straight ahead," Emily said. "If there's someone else in the car, he may be using binoculars."

"What are you going to do about this?" Jakob asked. "I don't feel good about leaving you."

"I'm staying at the airport until I get another passenger and then I'll see what happens. That should tell me if they're interested in you or me. You're about to enter the most secure zone in the city. You'll be fine."

Emily pulled to the curb. Jakob got out and glanced to the left. He didn't see the Honda.

"Be careful," he said.

"You be careful," Emily replied. "And don't worry. If the white Honda hangs around me, I'll call down the wrath of God through some of my former colleagues."

• • •

After checking her bag, Hana made her way to the gate. Jakob wasn't in sight. Hana sat down and opened the app for the doggie day care center. Leon and a brown puppy half his size were chasing each other around a plastic container of dog toys. Next she replied to three email messages. Her out-of-office notice would be up in the morning, but until then she wanted to handle what she could. The gate attendant began calling forward passengers on standby to let them know if there would be a seat for them on the flight to Newark. Hana leaned over and looked down the concourse. In the distance, she saw Jakob walking slowly in her direction. She waited until he came closer and waved him over.

"I was beginning to worry about you."

"You were right to do so," he said.

Jakob told her about the blow to his head and the car that followed him and Emily to the airport. "I didn't check in at the counter until I knew Emily had picked up another fare and determined the white car wasn't following her."

"What if someone is watching us now?" Hana glanced around.

"It's a weird feeling, isn't it? Not knowing."

The gate attendant announced it was time to begin boarding.

After the business-class passengers, Hana and Jakob were in the next section. When they stood up, Jakob paused for a moment and leaned on the handle of his carry-on bag.

"Are you okay?" Hana asked.

"Dizzy for a second. I have headphones and always sleep on airplanes. Hopefully I'll be better by the time we get to Newark."

Jakob sat in the aisle seat with Hana beside him. He took a pair of headphones from his carry-on bag.

"I'm not trying to be rude," he said, showing them to Hana. "I'll put them on after the announcements from the flight attendants."

"Go ahead."

During the two-hour flight, Hana reviewed everything on her laptop about the Neumann file and made notes detailing next steps. At one point, she noticed that a slightly built middle-aged man in the window seat was trying to read her computer screen. She tilted the computer toward Jakob.

"What language is that?" the man asked, clearly not picking up on her desire for privacy.

One of the reports from Daud was on the screen. Part of it was in Hebrew, part in Arabic.

"It depends," Hana replied cryptically. "What languages do you read?"

"Uh, English. I took Spanish in high school and struggled to make a C."

Realizing her suspicions weren't justified, Hana relaxed. "It's a combination of Hebrew and Arabic," she replied. "I live in Israel but work in Atlanta, so it's helpful to speak multiple languages. But my Spanish is terrible, probably worse than yours."

"I doubt that," the man said. "I wish I'd studied harder. My company offered me a couple of Spanish-speaking accounts, but I knew I couldn't handle it. The commissions would have been great."

"You could study now. Being motivated makes a difference."

"That's exactly what my wife told me. We live in San Antonio, and a working knowledge of Spanish would come in handy in day-to-day life."

For the next fifteen minutes, the man talked to Hana about his work and family. Finally, he stopped and yawned. "Well, I may get some shut-eye like your friend there," he said. "I've been up since four thirty this morning. This is my third flight of the day, and I still have to take a customer out for a late dinner when I get to New York."

The man closed his eyes, and in less than a minute his breathing signaled he was asleep. Sitting between two unconscious men, Hana was able to return to work.

CHAPTER 29

The change in air pressure inside the descending plane caused Jakob's ears to pop, and he woke up from a dream in which he was trying to swim laps in a pool but found himself stuck in the same spot, not making progress. He slipped off his headphones and turned to Hana, who was typing on her laptop.

"How long until we land?" he asked.

"The last announcement from the pilot said twenty minutes, but that was at least ten minutes ago. I'd better shut this down."

"What are you working on?" Jakob asked, rubbing his eyes for a moment.

"Our case. That's my entire focus for the next seven days."

They had a layover of two and a half hours in the Newark International Airport before leaving for Israel. Jakob had flown in and out of Newark many times, and to his relief, he felt physically and mentally normal as they joined the bustling throng of people always present in New York–area airports.

"I'm hungry," he said as they passed a cluster of fast-food restaurants. "Would you like to eat dinner?"

"Yes."

"I need a steak," he said.

"We don't have time to leave the airport," Hana replied.

"Turn right up ahead," Jakob said.

He led the way to a New York restaurant that sold aged steaks in the airport. Racks of red meat were on display inside huge refrigerated glass cases.

"This will prepare you for Israel," Hana said as they stopped to look at the steaks before entering the restaurant. "But there you have to be careful about buying meat that's been on public display without refrigeration. An aged steak isn't necessarily a good thing."

"That's why I'm going to load up on red meat now."

A young hostess took them to a table overlooking the tarmac. Hana ordered water, Jakob a glass of red wine. He held up his glass for a toast.

"To a successful trip."

"L'chaim," Hana responded.

"At least I know that much Hebrew," Jakob replied. "To life."

They touched glasses. The waiter came. Jakob ordered a large rib eye, and Hana selected a filet mignon. Several minutes later, their waiter arrived with the meals. The steaks had a perfect char on the outside. Jakob picked up his fork and knife.

"Do you mind if I pray over the meal?" Hana asked.

Jakob paused, his knife in midair. "So long as it's quick."

Hana closed her eyes. Jakob kept his eyes open and glanced around the restaurant. No one seemed to notice them.

"Lord, I ask you to direct our steps every moment of this trip," she said in an earnest voice. "We ask you to expose the deeds of darkness that caused Gloria Neumann's death and lead us to the truth about everything connected to her murder. Direct Daud Hasan in his investigation and show us who to talk to and where to go so that we can uncover the information and evidence we need. Make this a special trip in every way for Jakob and keep us safe from evil. In Jesus' name, amen."

Hana opened her eyes. Jakob stared at her. She immediately closed her eyes again.

"And bless this food," she added.

Hana picked up her fork and knife and cut into her steak. Past the char it was a deep red in the middle.

"Is that cooked enough for you?" Jakob asked. "We can send it back."

"No, it's delicious."

Jakob cut into his steak. It, too, was good. Several times, Hana checked her phone.

"Is there a problem?" Jakob asked.

"No," Hana said, shaking her head sheepishly. "I'm checking on my new puppy."

She handed Jakob her phone. A furry black-and-white animal was curled up asleep.

"What's his name?"

"Leon."

"As in Leon Lowenstein?" Jakob asked, raising his eyebrows.

Hana nodded slightly.

"Now I have information I can use against you," Jakob said with a confident grin.

Hana smiled in return. "I'm not worried," she said. "Mr. Lowenstein would be honored."

They finished the meal and made their way to the departure gate for the overseas flight. Hana spoke in Hebrew to a woman sitting next to them on a long row of seats. The conversation continued for several minutes.

"What was that about?" Jakob asked when Hana finished.

"Mostly her children and grandchildren. Her daughter lives in Portland, Oregon, and her son is located in Herzliya on the Mediterranean. Do you want to know more?"

"No, I just don't want to miss any important conversations."

"Daud knows we're going to have to speak a lot in English. If he struggles, I'll translate from Arabic or Hebrew."

"Okay."

Jakob started reading a newspaper.

Hana felt like a radar antenna picking up multiple signals as she listened to conversations in English, Hebrew, and Arabic. She loved the sounds of diversity. The gate attendant gave preliminary boarding instructions in English and Hebrew. The woman's Hebrew accent revealed that she came from the Tiberias region. Jakob closed the newspaper.

"Will you be able to fall sleep again?" Hana asked.

"Not until they turn off the cabin lights."

An older white-haired man with a cane in his hand and a name tag stuck to his shirt sat down next to Jakob.

"This is my first trip to Israel," the man said.

"Me too."

"I'm going on a tour with my church," the man continued. "Are you excited to visit the Holy Land? I've been saving five years for this trip."

"What's your itinerary?" Hana asked.

While they waited for their boarding group to be called, the old man took out a brochure and showed it to her. It was a typical ten-day excursion that began in Galilee, dropped down to the Dead Sea, and ended up in Jerusalem. Hana gave him several tidbits of information.

"And you'll love Jerusalem," she said with a smile.

"It almost makes me cry thinking about being where the Lord was crucified, buried, and rose from the dead," the man said, his voice cracking with emotion.

The gate attendant called out a boarding zone, and the older man shakily got to his feet to join his group members.

"Nice talking to you," he said. "Maybe I'll see you there."

After the man left, Jakob turned to Hana. "He seems like a nice guy, but he should be flying to a retirement home in Florida, not running all over Israel."

"He's a pilgrim," Hana replied simply. "And people like him have been visiting the Holy Land for two thousand years."

Hana and Jakob sat on the left side of the aircraft. A petite older woman from Netanya sat beside the window.

"If I bother you or crowd your space, punch me," Jakob said to Hana. "Don't put up with it."

They settled in. As the plane taxied away from the gate, Jakob slipped on his earphones, closed his eyes, and didn't open them during takeoff. Hana checked the movie selections for the flight and tried to get comfortable without getting too close to Jakob. The crew darkened the plane shortly after they were airborne for the nine-hour flight.

Jakob felt a nudge on his left arm and opened his eyes. Hana was pushing her dark hair behind her ears.

"If you want to take a bathroom break, you'd better do it now," she said. "Breakfast is coming in a few minutes."

Rubbing his eyes, Jakob made his way to the rear of the plane where he encountered a group of Orthodox and ultra-Orthodox men saying their morning prayers. He had to navigate his way through the bobbing heads and leather-wrapped arms to the lavatory. Returning to his seat, he could tell from Hana's eyes that she'd not rested very much.

"Did you sleep?"

"A couple of hours at the most. I don't think you woke up when I slipped past you to go to the restroom or stretch my legs."

"If I did, I don't remember it. Maybe the concussion is sending me into deeper realms of sleep."

"Seriously?"

"No," Jakob said and shook his head. "I've always been able to sleep at the drop of a hat. I had to chew gum to stay awake during civil procedure class in law school."

A male flight attendant was pushing a cart down the aisle offering kosher and nonkosher meals.

"Maybe I'll go kosher since I'm on my way to Israel and I'm

surrounded by all these holy men," Jakob said to Hana. "I've not seen the kind of religious action going on at the rear of the plane since the last time I took the train into Brooklyn."

The kosher breakfast was bland, even by airplane standards, and Jakob glanced enviously at the tiny link sausages on Hana's tray.

"Would you like one?" she asked.

Jakob speared a sausage with his fork and popped it into his mouth.

"It tastes better when it's forbidden, doesn't it?" Hana asked. "That's the way it was for Adam and Eve and the forbidden fruit."

"I'd have a tougher time turning down link sausage than a red apple," Jakob answered.

Now that he was awake, Jakob fidgeted as they completed the final leg of the flight. The plane descended over the Mediterranean, and in the light of early afternoon, he could clearly see the coastline south of Tel Aviv. Hana leaned back so Jakob had a clearer view.

"How does that make you feel?" Hana asked.

To his surprise, Jakob felt a touch of emotion. Even as a secular Jew, he couldn't deny the uniqueness associated with the reestablishment of a Jewish homeland after so long in exile. "A little more than I would have guessed," he said.

"You're not the first or last person to say that," she replied.

"How about you?"

"Like anyone who is coming home."

The plane landed at Ben Gurion Airport.

"Where did you work?" Jakob asked as they approached a security checkpoint.

"At the second level," Hana replied. "If there were questions about an individual, he or she was brought to us for more detailed interrogation."

"And tortured?"

"This is one of the worst places in Israel to joke," Hana answered, her face serious. "No one who works here has a sense of humor until they're in the parking lot to go home."

They separated at the security check because Hana was an Israeli citizen.

"Hope I see you on the other side," Hana said.

"I thought you said no joking allowed."

"It's not a joke," Hana answered with a smile.

Jakob selected a line with an attractive female officer and vowed, as Hana suggested, to keep his answers to a minimum.

"I'm an American lawyer working with an Israeli attorney on a case," he said when he stood in front of the glass-enclosed cubicle.

"What kind of case?" the woman officer asked.

"Personal injury. I'm a tort lawyer."

The woman gave him a puzzled look.

"Tort isn't a dessert," Jakob said. "That's spelled with an 'e' and is a French word."

The young woman smiled slightly. "Where are you staying?" she asked.

Jakob gave the name of the hotel in Jerusalem.

"Who else will you see while you're here?" the woman asked, keeping her head down.

"That will be determined by my Israeli cocounsel. We want to talk to witnesses and other people who may know something about our case."

"What is the name of the Israeli lawyer?"

"Hana Abboud."

The young woman looked up. "She's Arab?"

"Yes, from Reineh, but now working in Atlanta, Georgia, with an international law firm for the past eighteen months. She went to law school at Hebrew University. She also—"

"That's enough," the woman said, stamping Jakob's passport. "Have a good stay."

Jakob moved to the luggage area and saw Hana, who already had her bag.

"You made it," Hana said when Jakob approached.

"As soon as I mentioned your name, everything went smoothly. You're famous."

Hana raised her eyebrows. After retrieving their luggage, they stepped out into the sunny glare of a cloudless Middle Eastern sky. There was a line of taxis and minivans alongside the curb. Jakob heard someone call out and turned. About fifty feet away a muscular Arab man with closely cut black hair and wearing dark sunglasses started walking toward them. He was wearing a white, short-sleeved shirt and dark slacks. As he came closer, Jakob could see from the size of the man's arms that he spent a lot of time in the gym. The investigator took off his glasses and said something to Hana that Jakob didn't understand. She beamed in response. He turned to Jakob.

"Daud Hasan," he said in accented but precise English. "It is a pleasure to meet you."

"Jakob Brodsky."

"Come with me," Daud said. "My vehicle is in the airport security lot."

CHAPTER 30

I'll take your large suitcase," Daud said in Arabic to Hana.

"It's on wheels."

"Which will make it a lot easier on me. Also, after watching the video from Sadie three or four times, I'd better be nice to you or you'll report me to her."

Hana released her grip on the handle and walked beside him. Glad to be back in Israel, she was a bit nervous about whether the same explosion of chemistry that had marked her first meeting with Daud would continue.

"It's great to see you," he said. "The Skype calls were a poor substitute for the real thing."

Hana smiled. It was exactly what she needed to hear.

"I've missed you, too," she answered. "A lot."

They stopped to let several cars pass before crossing the street to the same security lot where Hana had parked on the rare occasions when she drove a vehicle to work. She recognized the car owned by one of the men in charge of her former unit.

"Avril Lieberman still drives the same car," Hana said, pointing to a white sedan with heavily tinted windows. "I was working here when he bought that car."

"He's a dinosaur," Daud replied. "But it's good that he doesn't like change. That's one reason I park here. He automatically renews my permit every year, even though I'm a private investigator."

Daud stopped in front of his dark green Land Rover and took out the key fob.

"I thought high gas prices forced everyone into a subcompact," Jakob said when he saw the vehicle.

"Not everyone," Daud said as he easily lifted Hana's heavy suitcase.

Jakob placed his suitcase beside hers. On the rear floor mat was a white license plate with green numbers.

"What's that?" he asked, pointing to the plate.

Daud lowered the gate and tapped the yellow plate affixed to the rear bumper. "I use the yellow Israeli plate when I am in a Jewish area and change to a Palestinian Authority plate when I travel in the West Bank. That way I have less chance of being hit by rocks on both sides of the line."

"Did you change plates on your car?" Jakob asked Hana.

"I never owned a car until I came to America," she answered. "When I lived here I used public transportation or rode with friends who had a car."

Daud opened the passenger door for Hana to enter and supported her elbow to help her up. The investigator's vehicle was higher above the ground than the Land Rovers driven by soccer moms in north Atlanta, and he maintained contact with her arm a split second longer than necessary. Hana settled in. Jakob sat behind her. Daud started the engine, which rumbled with power. He used an access card to leave the security lot.

"Does he speak any Hebrew?" Daud asked Hana in Hebrew with a nod of his head toward Jakob.

"English only, no Hebrew," she replied in the same language. "He's never been to Israel."

"I recognized two words," Jakob said from the rear seat. "You said 'English' and 'Israel.' I don't mind you talking about other matters in Arabic or Hebrew, but when it comes to me or the Neumann case, please use English."

"No problem," Daud replied with a smile. "That is the right thing to say, correct?"

"Yes," Hana answered, turning in her seat so she could see Jakob. "But avoid idioms when speaking to Daud. Contractions can be confusing, too. I've only gotten comfortable with them within the past year."

"Your English is phenomenal," Jakob said, realizing he'd accepted Hana's proficiency without considering how hard it was to achieve it.

"Contractions?" Daud asked.

"Combinations of words that are shortened like 'it's,' 'we'll,' 'I'm,' 'I've,' and things like that."

"That is okay," Daud replied. "I have been around Americans enough to understand the meanings even if I do not use them."

They left the airport and merged onto the expressway.

"How far is it to Jerusalem?" Jakob asked.

"Fifty-five kilometers," Daud answered. "It is a one-hour drive to your hotel."

Hana looked at her phone. It was four thirty Israeli time.

"Is there anything we could do this evening?" she asked Daud.

"Go to dinner and a movie," he replied, a serious expression on his face.

Hana glanced over her shoulder at Jakob, who pointed downward with his right thumb.

"I meant about the case," Hana said.

"I know what you meant," Daud replied. "We can eat dinner at a restaurant near your hotel and talk about what to do. No more jokes for the next week."

"Keep trying," Jakob responded from the back seat. "It's fun to see how Hana reacts."

"I'm ready," Hana said.

Daud glanced sideways. "We will see how ready you are."

The highway rose steadily higher. Jakob immediately liked Daud Hasan's style. The few times Jakob had hired a private investigator, he'd retained an older, retired police detective who never smiled and had the personality of a cactus. They passed a rail line coming out of a tunnel onto a series of graceful arched supports at least fifty feet off the ground.

"What is that?" Jakob asked.

"The track for the high-speed train that connects Tel Aviv and Jerusalem," Hana answered. "It opened while I've been away. The trip only takes thirty minutes."

"It is like a ride at a"—Daud paused—"carnivore."

"Carnival," Hana corrected.

"Yes," Daud said. "It is very fast, 160 kilometers per hour."

They continued to climb upward. The landscape was rocky with scrubby trees on the hillsides beside the busy highway.

"If you were a tourist, I would play a song for you," Daud said, glancing in the rearview mirror at Jakob. "Maybe 'Jerusalem of Gold.' Coming to Jerusalem for the first time is special."

They rounded another curve and more buildings came into view. Hana began to sing in a soft, clear voice.

"Who needs recorded music?" Daud said, catching Jakob's eye again. "You can hear a live performance of the song in the language it was written in."

The Hebrew words filled the car as Hana's voice grew louder. The hair on the back of Jakob's neck stood up as she reached a crescendo. Even without understanding what Hana said, he could feel both pathos and triumph in the combination of words and melody. The song ended, and the car became quiet. They reached the outskirts of the city.

"Welcome to the Holy City of Jerusalem," Daud announced.

"It's beautiful," Jakob said.

"For thousands of years most of the buildings in the city have been built with limestone taken from nearby quarries," Hana said. "When the sun hits the stones a certain way, they look golden. That's one reason for the title of the song."

"We are coming in through the Jewish areas, which are newer," Daud added. "My office and apartment are in an Arab area of East Jerusalem known as Beit Hanina. We will go there tomorrow in the morning."

"Daud's office is on the Israeli side of the security barrier," Hana added. "Nearby you can see the wall because it divides Beit Hanina."

"What do you think about the wall?" Jakob asked her.

"There is no doubt that it has saved lives by making it harder for terrorists to enter the Jewish areas," Hana replied. "But it is also a tragic reminder of the hatred that exists here. It deeply offends many Arab people because it divides families. It makes me sad every time I see it."

Jakob shut his mouth. Being with Hana in Israel was much different from talking to her in a high-rise office building in Atlanta.

"It does not make us angry to hear questions," Daud said. "It is common."

"But I don't feel like it's really any of my business," Jakob replied.

"If people do not ask questions, they will never have answers," the investigator replied.

Jakob knew he could rattle off scores of questions. Hana and Daud seemed willing to talk, but the intensely personal nature of the situation restrained him.

"Maybe later," he said.

"There are different kinds of Americans," Daud continued. "Some are afraid to talk honestly about real problems. Others think they know everything and have the right to tell us, both Arabs and Jews, what to do with our country."

"Is there another group of Americans?" Jakob asked.

"Yes," Hana said. "There are seekers of truth like you."

"What makes you say that?" he asked.

"Am I right or wrong?" she replied.

Jakob paused. "I hope you're right," he said.

"I am, until you prove me wrong."

They entered an older part of the city. "This is the German Colony, settled by German Christians in the late 1800s," Hana said. "It's a very expensive place to live. Our hotel is a couple of minutes away."

Hana liked riding with Daud as he smoothly wove in and out of traffic. Most of the cars on the road were small, and the Land Rover stood out. They reached their hotel, a two-story building with twenty-four guest rooms surrounding an interior open courtyard.

"This place was built during the time of the British Mandate between the two World Wars," Hana said to Jakob as they stopped in front of the entrance.

"Do you need me to go inside?" Daud asked her.

"No," Hana answered. "What time do you want to pick us up for dinner?"

Daud checked his watch. "Is an hour and a half enough time?"

"Perfect," Hana replied.

The investigator lifted Hana's luggage from the rear of the vehicle and drove off as she and Jakob entered the registration area. A middle-aged Arab man stood behind the desk.

"Ms. Abboud, you're on the first floor," he said after checking their reservations on a computer. "Mr. Brodsky, you are on the second floor."

A bellboy took Hana's bags to her room. She unpacked, showered, and put on a dark blue dress. It was still awhile before Daud would return, so she stepped into the courtyard. There were ten small tables. For now, she had the area to herself. She sat beside a bougainvillea bush covered in luscious red flowers. The winters in Atlanta were cold enough to keep the magnificent plants from surviving outdoors. Intending to review her notes about the Neumann case, she turned on her laptop, but, fatigued from the trip, she couldn't focus. She logged off the computer and closed her eyes.

When she did, the atmosphere around her thickened, but not due to heat or humidity. There was almost no moisture in the Jerusalem air this time of year, and the temperature grew cooler as the sun set. Hana relaxed and entered a state of acute inner alertness. All her senses came forward without any of them jostling for attention. She felt fully alive. It was a phenomenon she'd first experienced when sitting on the veranda in Reineh one evening with her great-grandfather Mathiu. He'd explained to her what was happening by using the Hebrew that best described the sensation—*kavod*—the invisible weight of God's glory.

The solitude of the courtyard became for Hana like the garden of the Lord, where in ages past he walked with Adam and Eve in the cool of the evening. Now it was her turn to spend time with the only One whose presence could complete her. She worshipped without words and without limitations. After several uncounted minutes passed, the enveloping love lessened.

"Abba," she whispered. "Thank you."

"Excuse me." A male voice forced her to open her eyes.

It was Jakob. Hana didn't resent the interruption. In fact, in that moment, his timing seemed perfect.

"Jakob, there is nothing that compares to God's presence," she said. "And no better place than Jerusalem to find it. When your moment comes, don't miss it."

Jakob blinked his eyes. "Okay," he said slowly. "But I have no idea what you're talking about."

Another male voice echoed across the courtyard. "Hana!" Daud called out in a deep voice. "Are you ready?"

Hana stood and ran her fingers through her long black hair. "I need to grab my purse."

CHAPTER 31

J akob followed Hana and Daud to a table for four in a back corner of the restaurant. They each selected a different lamb dish. There were only six other customers, tourists from a Western nation, in the restaurant. Jakob took a sip of mineral water.

"Is this private enough to talk?" Jakob asked.

"It depends on the language," Daud replied. "That group was speaking Dutch when we passed by them. I think they are interested in their conversation, not ours."

"Do you speak Dutch?" Hana asked as she opened her laptop.

"Only enough to recognize it."

Jakob saw Hana scroll through her notes. "What's the status of the man from Deir Dibwan who was willing to talk to you about the Zadan brothers?" she asked.

"You will meet him tomorrow morning in Ramallah, but it is not a good idea for Jakob to join us. Nabil will not open his mouth around an American Jew."

Jakob didn't protest.

"Ramallah?" Hana asked.

"I have documentation from a border patrol commander that grants me access to zone A," Daud answered. "The permission is broad enough to include you."

"What are you talking about?" Jakob asked.

"Because Daud and I are Israeli citizens, it's illegal for us to go into areas of the West Bank primarily under the control of the Palestinian

Authority," Hana said. "Ramallah falls within that zone. If we went without permission, we might have to pay a fine when we returned to this side of the line."

"And be interrogated," Daud added.

"But I could go without a problem?" Jakob asked.

"Yes," Daud answered. "But—"

"Being Jewish would be a problem once I got there," Jakob said, finishing the thought.

"Correct," Daud said.

"How long will it take you? I'd rather not stay at the hotel with nothing to do."

"Most of the morning," Daud answered. "We do not want to rush Nabil. He will want to extend hospitality before talking."

"What's his attitude toward women?" Hana asked.

"He will like you," Daud said with a smile. "But do not worry. I will be there the whole time. You are my personal assistant. That will impress him. Do not say anything about living in America. He will know from your accent that you come from Nazareth."

"Why is he willing to talk to either one of you?" Jakob asked.

"He has a claim against the Zadan family that has never been satisfied," Daud replied.

"A feud?" Jakob asked.

Daud looked at Hana, who explained.

"Yes," she said. "These disagreements can be very serious between families and go on for years."

"Hatfields and McCoys in the Middle East," Jakob said.

Daud and Hana both gave him a blank look. "Never mind," Jakob added.

"And what about the Israeli authorities who investigated the attack?" Hana asked Daud. "Any progress there?"

"I am still working on that. There are many levels. I want to go deep."

"What does 'go deep' mean?" Jakob asked.

"Deep or high is the same thing," Hana answered. "As you know, we want to gain access to intelligence information that connects the Zadan brothers to other terrorist groups. The Israeli police and Shin Bet secret service have a large network of people feeding them information. All of it is cross-checked for links. Only the men and women in charge see everything."

"And the security services do not want to tell us something that will put someone they work with in danger," Daud added. "That can be life or death."

"How will you go deep?" Jakob asked.

Daud shrugged. "Trade information for information with people who trust me. Maybe Nabil will talk about a lot of things, and I can separate the wheat from the, uh, chaff. Correct?"

"That's right," Hana said. "What about Aaron Levy, the man Sylvia Armstrong mentioned? Will we talk to him?"

"Yes," Daud replied. "That is already scheduled."

"With me present?" Jakob asked.

"Of course," Daud replied as if it were an unnecessary question.

"What about the computers seized by the police at the Zadan residence?" Jakob asked. "When we killed Osama bin Laden, the CIA got a ton of stuff from the computers captured in Pakistan."

"That is on my list," Daud replied. "I know who has the equipment."

"Where are they?" Jakob asked.

"The location is not important. I am working on getting the information downloaded onto a flash drive so we can review it," he said.

Jakob turned to Hana. "Do you think the US Attorney's Office has it?"

"No," Daud answered.

"Why do you say that?" Hana asked.

"Because that is what I have been told."

"That could be a bargaining chip for us with the US attorney," Hana said to Jakob. "And enable us to coordinate an exchange of more information."

"I like the sound of that," Jakob said.

The waiter arrived with their food. Jakob had ordered a roasted lamb dish. It was slightly crispy on the outside and filled with seasoned flavor on the inside. He was about to swallow his first bite when he noticed Daud and Hana with their heads bowed. Jakob stopped chewing. Daud prayed.

"God, grant us great success and supernatural wisdom in what to do and who to talk to. Keep us safe and bless this food. In Jesus' name, amen."

"It sounds like you and Hana read the same prayer book," Jakob said when everyone's eyes were open.

"We do," Hana replied, smiling. "It's called the Bible. You should check it out for yourself. Jews wrote almost all of it."

"There is more about God's interaction with the Jews in the Bible than any other topic," Daud added. "Some people argue that the Jews are no longer relevant. God disagrees. I agree with God."

"Wouldn't it be better for you if the Jews were irrelevant?" Jakob asked.

"No, because it would make me doubt that God's promises for the rest of us are true," Daud said.

"Do you believe this, too?" Jakob asked Hana.

"Yes, and a lot more."

After the meal, Daud drove them back to their hotel. The three of them stood beside the Land Rover. The nearby courtyard was illuminated by small gas lamps on ornamental posts.

"I will pick you up at seven thirty in the morning," Daud said to Hana. "Get a good night's sleep."

Hana yawned. "I will until my body thinks I've overslept. Jakob slept almost the entire flight."

"And I'll read for a while before going to bed," Jakob said. "Text me when you're on your way back from Ramallah."

Jakob turned and climbed the stairs to his room. Hana lingered.

"What do you think of him?" she asked in Arabic.

"He is a secular American Jew," Daud said with a shrug. "Is he a good lawyer?"

Hana gave a quick summary of what she'd read in the dossier prepared by Mr. Lowenstein.

"Maybe his name should be David," Daud replied. "It sounds like he wants to fight Goliath."

"Like you?"

"Maybe."

Daud motioned to a wooden bench in the courtyard. "I know you're tired, but can we sit for a minute?"

Hana joined him. One of the gas lamps caused the shadows to dance. It was her first time being alone with him since she'd arrived. She told him about her encounter with the Lord earlier in the evening in the courtyard.

"Nothing like that has ever happened to me," Daud said when she finished. "I guess I'm too pragmatic and analytical."

"Do you think I'm any different? I'm a lawyer. You can't get more pragmatic and analytical than that."

"No, you're very different from me," Daud answered. "And I'm very glad about it."

Hana smiled. "Thanks. A glory encounter isn't based on personality or temperament, though, but rather God's desire and our receptivity. Anyway, I took it as a kiss from the Lord upon my return home. Jakob showed up and broke in at the end, but that was okay because it gave me a chance to encourage him to experience God's presence while he's here. We should be praying for him."

Daud eyed Hana for a moment. "Every time we talk I learn

something new and wonderful about you. I've changed my mind about something important."

"What is it?" Hana asked as curiosity rose up within her.

"Could we make a quick trip to Reineh? I want to meet your family."

Hana hadn't brought a man home since the breakup with Ibrahim. She wanted to say yes but also felt guarded.

"They'll investigate you more closely than you do the people in your cases," she said.

"I'm ready."

"And persistent."

"There are things I must say or I'll explode," Daud said, speaking more rapidly. "I didn't want to do it while you were in America, but now that you're here, I have to. Tell me how you feel about me, and I'll be quiet."

Hana paused for a moment before answering. She wanted to choose her words carefully. Her attempt at caution vanished as she replied, "I'd rather be sitting on this bench with you than anyplace else in the world."

Hana closed the door to her hotel room, leaned against it, and kicked off her shoes. She wasn't totally surprised by Daud's intensity, but it was still a shock when he switched off whatever normally kept his conversations under tight control. At least he was open and honest, Hana decided as she prepared for bed.

She woke up in the middle of the night not because of her biological time clock or a call to prayer; rather, she was gripped by fear and gasping for breath. Her heart pounding, she sat upright and quickly scanned the room. A sliver of light shone through a crack in the curtain over the window, and with her eyes used to the dark she could clearly see the whole space. Nothing was out of the ordinary. Slipping out of bed, Hana made sure she'd locked and bolted the door. Going to the sink, she drank a few sips of water and tried to remember what she'd been dreaming. All she could recall was the sensation of drowning without the presence of water, and the ensuing panic caused by the inability to breathe.

Hana returned to the bed and turned on a light for her night watch. Five minutes later, she felt herself nodding off to sleep. Getting out of bed, she paced back and forth while she prayed. Fatigue soon overwhelmed her, and she lay down and fell asleep.

• • •

Jakob sat at a table in the courtyard eating a breakfast of fruit, yogurt, cheese, and samples of herring and pickled sardines from a large buffet table set up in one corner of the open area. He'd been awake since three and had logged in to his office computer to answer and send emails. The option of fish for breakfast was new, but he liked it. So far, everything about Israel was good.

He was eating a sardine when Hana came outside. The Israeli lawyer was wearing a long dark skirt whose hem fell to the top of her sandals and a modest dark blue top. He waved, and she came over to him.

"This breakfast is awesome," Jakob said.

"I'm going to start with caffeine," Hana replied. "I didn't sleep well." She returned with a large cup of black coffee.

"Why couldn't you sleep?" Jakob asked.

"It was one of those nights when I'm exhausted but sleep doesn't seem to be the answer. Also, I had a bad dream."

Jakob waited. Hana took a sip of coffee and changed the subject. "Have you decided what you're going to do this morning?" she asked.

"Go to Hurva Square."

"That makes sense," Hana said. "I did that when I was here to interview Daud. I've been there many times, but it was different seeing it through the eyes of the Neumann case."

"That's what I'm thinking. What are you expecting from the meeting with this Nabil guy?"

"It's hard to know, but Daud wouldn't have set it up if he didn't believe it would be worth our time."

"Will you ask questions, too?"

Hana shook her head. "Not directly. It wouldn't fit with my role as an administrative assistant. If I think of something, I'll ask to take a break as a signal for Daud to meet me in another part of the house or business for a quick conversation."

"I believe our investigator is using you as an attractive distraction."

"Maybe, but Daud will look out for me."

Jakob ate a piece of tangy sharp cheese. "Any other suggestions for me?" he asked.

"Don't wander down any dark alleys."

A horn honked. They could see Daud's vehicle through the opening in the courtyard to the hotel entrance.

"I know we're here because of a tragedy," Hana said, "but Jerusalem is also full of good surprises."

CHAPTER 32

Daud opened the passenger door for Hana.

"Perfect outfit," he said in Arabic. "And I brought some jibneh baida and fresh olives to go with your coffee."

Resting in the center console of the vehicle was a small bowl filled with pieces of fried white goat cheese surrounded by green olives. Hana took a bite of the cheese. "This is good. Who made it?"

"You don't think I did?"

"Do you have a goat tied up behind your apartment building?"

"No. I told a neighbor you were coming, and she insisted I bring some with me."

"Thank her."

"Maybe you can if we go to my apartment later in the week."

"I'd like that."

They rode in silence as Daud navigated Jerusalem streets crowded with commuters in small cars. In front of the big hotels, lines of buses waited for tourists to emerge for the day.

"We'll stop and change license plates as soon as we're through the checkpoint," Daud continued. "Is there anything you need on this side of the line?"

"Should I have a notepad?"

Daud gestured to the rear seat. "Already done. Nabil may not want you writing while he talks. Your main job is to smile at him."

"Jakob brought that up," Hana replied. "You don't have to remind me how I'm going to be viewed."

"Don't worry. Nabil will focus on the real reason we're meeting. I want you to hear and decide what you think." Daud stopped for a red light. "What are Jakob's plans for the day?"

"To go to Hurva Square and maybe the Kotel," Hana said.

Daud didn't respond. Instead, he picked up the phone and placed a call. Someone answered, and Daud spoke in rapid-fire Arabic. "Follow Brodsky everywhere he goes when he leaves the hotel and find out if he's being tailed. I know he's going to Hurva Square and the Western Wall. Take pictures if he's under surveillance, but don't step in unless there is a real danger. If that happens, just ease him into a safe place. Bye."

Hana's eyes widened. "Who was that?"

"A guy who works for me from time to time. If Jakob is a target of the terrorists, it would be a huge break."

"Why?"

"Because it could lead us to someone here who doesn't want their connection to the Zadan brothers exposed."

• • •

Jakob finished a leisurely breakfast. He took a picture of the courtyard and sent it to Emily with a brief description of the hotel. She didn't respond. Returning to his room, he worked remotely for almost an hour. He knew he could muddle through while away and hadn't put an out-of-office message on his email account. Logging off, he went downstairs and asked the concierge whether to use a taxi or a private driver service.

"Three of my cousins drive taxis," the middle-aged man replied. "They offer the best way to go and can take you to all the sites if you hire them for the day."

"All I want to do is go to Hurva Square and then walk to the Western Wall," Jakob answered.

"There is so much more to see, and my cousins can get you to places where tourists don't normally go." The man reached under the counter. "I have a brochure with options—"

"Let's start with Hurva Square."

"Okay," the concierge said and shrugged. "They only drive Mercedes Benz, so you will like the ride."

In less than ten minutes an aging white Mercedes pulled up to the hotel and stopped.

"It's Wahid," the concierge said. "He's the best of the best."

Wahid opened one of the rear doors for Jakob while his cousin barked orders that seemed to include a lot more than a request for a trip to Hurva Square.

"Hurva Square?" Jakob asked as soon as the driver was behind the wheel.

"Sure," the man replied in a voice that sounded more New York than Jerusalem. "I can't drive you directly to the square, but I will take you as close as possible."

"Are you American?" Jakob asked.

"Resident alien with a green card," the man replied. "I was born in Nablus and have a Jordanian passport but moved to Queens when I was kid. Whether I'm here or there, I drive a cab to put bread on the table."

Wahid's driving reminded Jakob of Emily Johnson. He zipped through the winding streets.

"What was your cousin telling you?" Jakob asked.

"About a family dinner at our uncle's house next weekend. He wants my wife to bring dessert."

Jakob relaxed. Wahid pulled to the curb and stopped. He handed Jakob his card and pointed up a small hill.

"Hurva Square is a five-minute walk that way toward the old Jewish Quarter. From there you can follow signs to the Western Wall. Text or call me, and I'll pick you up if you need a ride later. You can pay me now or we can run a tab at the hotel."

Jakob felt comfortable with Wahid. "Run a tab," he said. "I'm here for a week."

"Did Rafi try to sell you a tour package?"

"Yes."

"Ignore him. Call me directly. He'll still get his cut without the hassle. I tell him he's too aggressive for most Americans, but he's old-school."

Jakob exited the cab and entered a maze of narrow streets filled with pedestrians, not cars. An occasional small vehicle squeezed by. Blue signs affixed to the walls of buildings identified the streets. He passed an ATM machine set into a wall of Jerusalem stone and entered Hurva Square. The small open plaza was less than a hundred yards across. On the western side was the Hurva Synagogue, which had recently been rebuilt after its destruction by Arab Legion forces in 1948.

Jakob walked across the stone pavers to the snack and ice cream shop. Normally decorated in black and white, it was odd seeing the small sitting area in vibrant color. Two young families with children were relaxing in the shade of a solitary tree eating ice cream. Three young female IDF soldiers lounged nearby. Glancing around, Jakob saw no threats, only people walking past or stopping to look in shop windows on the opposite side of the square. He located the surveillance camera that most likely had captured the images of the attack on Gloria and Sadie Neumann and moved into position beneath it until he was standing in the spot where Abdul Zadan drew his knife. Though the blood on the stones had long since washed away, the call for justice remained. Jakob realized he was standing awkwardly close to one of the families eating ice cream and stepped away.

He made his way slowly around the square so that every detail lodged in his mind. If he ever had the opportunity to present the Neumann case to a jury, he wanted to take them to Hurva Square, not only in a grainy black-and-white video, but with descriptive words. A group of young ultra-Orthodox men entered, walking with purpose. Guessing they were on their way to the Western Wall, Jakob followed.

. . .

Daud and Hana were cleared through the security checkpoint between Israel and the West Bank. Two Arab Israelis with Israeli passports and riding in an expensive Land Rover didn't attract close scrutiny. Daud drove three hundred yards, turned into a narrow street, and stopped. Hana waited while he installed the Palestinian Authority license plate.

"Now I look like a prosperous businessman from Ramallah," he said as he backed out of the street and continued on the main road.

"Have you ever been caught doing that?" Hana asked.

"If you mean by the boys playing in the street, yes. Otherwise, no."

They headed north toward Ramallah, about ten miles from Jerusalem.

"Where are we meeting Nabil?" Hana asked.

"Not Deir Dibwan. It's too small. Nabil owns a tobacco store in Ramallah and wants to talk there."

"A hookah shop?" Hana guessed.

"Yes," Daud said, nodding. "But we'll talk in his office. The shop is off-limits to women."

"Could we drive through Deir Dibwan?" Hana asked.

"Maybe on the way back. There's not much to see, and I don't want to attract too much attention." Daud glanced at her. "You've seen plenty of villages like it."

Hana looked out the window. Some Arab villages in the West Bank struggled economically. Others prospered. Ramallah, the head-quarters for the Palestinian Authority, was booming with growth and modern development.

"There are lots of new buildings since I was here a few years ago," Hana said as they came into the city.

"Built with euros and dollars," Daud replied. "At least some of the aid money doesn't end up in the Swiss bank accounts of corrupt politicians. Nabil's shop is near the main square in an older building that used to be part of a monastery."

"When my great-grandfather came here in the 1920s, over ninety percent of the population were Christians," Hana said. "Back then, Ramallah was a Christian town. What is the percentage now? Twenty-five?"

"Or less. Many have moved to America like you."

"I'm not there permanently." Hana cut her eyes toward Daud.

They passed the educational complex for a girls' school founded in the 1860s by the Quakers. Now coeducational, it occupied a large modern campus.

"When I was in high school, we had debate competitions in Jerusalem with girls from the Friends School," Hana said.

"Did you win?" Daud asked. "And don't be humble."

"I won and lost. They had a lot of smart students."

Daud turned onto a street leading directly to the center of the city. They entered an area where many church buildings built in the 1800s still remained.

"We're almost there," Daud said as he turned onto a narrow street lined with different shops and parked alongside the curb. "It's better to walk from here."

Daud reached into the back seat and handed Hana a plain canvas bag. "This is your gear," he said.

"It's not my fashion style," Hana said, holding up the bag.

Daud chuckled. "It is today."

Hana checked to see what it contained. When she got to the bottom her eyes widened, and she slowly lifted out a Jericho handgun.

"Did you mean for me to have this?" she asked. "I do know how to use it."

"No." Daud snatched it from her and put it in the glove box.

"And that's the kind of mistake I rarely make. We'll leave it here. If I thought we'd be in danger, I wouldn't have brought you."

They walked side by side down the narrow sidewalk. Because of its mixed religious background, Ramallah was more liberal than most other towns and cities in the West Bank. Some women wore Western clothes; a few were concealed behind traditional Islamic burkas. A gold-and-red scarf covered Hana's head. Turning a corner, Hana and Daud reached the tobacco shop.

"Come inside, but stay by the door," Daud said as they entered.

The dimly lit shop was filled with the pungent fragrance of flavored tobacco. The strongest as well as the most popular flavoring was mint. Hana also picked up the subtle aroma of apples. Even though it was early in the morning, there were five or six hookahs in active use. The smoky atmosphere wasn't a place Hana would want to stay for hours, but it wasn't unpleasant, either. She stayed in the shadows by the door but knew her appearance attracted immediate attention. Daud talked to a man who worked at the shop. After a couple of minutes, he returned to her side.

"Nabil isn't here," the investigator said with frustration in his voice. "I confirmed the appointment with him after I left your hotel, but the man who runs the shop hasn't seen or heard from him since they closed last night. He called Nabil and woke him up. He claims he'll be here soon."

"What do we do?" Hana asked.

"Wait someplace else and hope he shows up. We can't stay in here."

They returned to Daud's vehicle. As soon as they were behind the tinted windows, Hana sniffed the edge of the scarf. Even within a short time, the fabric had absorbed the aroma of smoky mint.

"This might be for the best," Daud said. "If I see Nabil on the street, I'll ask him to join us in here. That way, there's less chance anyone will notice he's talking to me."

"Where did you meet with him before?"

"In the shop. I bought one of his most expensive hookahs. The purchase price will turn up on the expense account I submit to the law firm."

"And I'll take it back on the plane with me."

"Cradled in your lap," Daud said, smiling. "Your boss can put it in his office."

The side street had a lot of foot traffic. Hana watched the people passing by. "Where are they going?" she asked. "Not to the tobacco shop. It's tiny."

"This is a shortcut to the hisbeh produce market."

Daud received a phone call. Hana heard him say the name Mahmoud before exiting the vehicle to carry on the conversation privately. Daud paced back and forth in front of the Land Rover while he talked. Now that she knew the street led to the hisbeh, Hana noticed customers returning with baskets of fruit and vegetables. Daud slipped his phone into the front pocket of his shirt and walked rapidly down the street and out of sight. Hana checked to make sure the doors of the vehicle were locked.

Several minutes passed before Daud returned, accompanied by a tall man in his late fifties or early sixties. The two men approached the Land Rover and Hana heard the door locks click open. Daud opened the passenger door.

"Jemila," he said. "Please allow Mr. Abbas to sit in the front seat."

Hana slipped out of the car and into the rear seat. Nabil didn't seem to pay any attention to her. The two men sat in front.

"How do you like your hubbly-bubbly?" Nabil asked, using the local slang term for a hookah.

"It's the only one I use," Daud replied. "The rest of them are junk. Would you buy my old ones from me? I'll sell them cheap."

"They will have to be cheap."

"I'll bring them next time," Daud replied, checking his watch. "I know you're busy. Did you find out anything that will help me recover my money from the Zadan clan? I know Tawfik is young, but he should not have cheated my client."

"He's like his father, grandfather, and all who have gone before him," Nabil replied. "Tawfik's father swindled my brother in a whole-sale orange business, leaving him with all the debt. They are all liars, cheats, and fools who get themselves killed by the Jews. No mourners from our family went to their tent."

"Where does Tawfik get his money? You said he drives a big car and always has cash in his pocket."

"And never the same car," Nabil replied. "Maybe he leases them. I don't know. But the money is real. The problem is finding him when he's not surrounded by his family and powerful friends."

"What kind of friends?"

"No," Nabil said, shaking his head. "I will talk to you about Tawfik, but not them."

"If I don't know anything about them, how can I steer clear of them?"

"All you need to know is that they carry guns when no one else has them. Not homemade Carlo toys manufactured in a garage in Azzun, but Kalashnikovs and even new versions of the American M16."

"Have you seen these guns, especially the M16s?"

"No, no. But I know people who have. These guys are waiting for their moment to strike a blow for Allah. I think they're idiots."

"And Tawfik is one of them?"

"Maybe," Nabil said, raising one shoulder. "He's always been lazy. But Abdul was part of this group before he was martyred."

Daud was silent for a moment. Hana wanted to ask a question but knew she had to remain quiet.

"When would be the best time and place to catch Tawfik alone with a lot of money in his pocket?" Daud asked.

Nabil lowered his voice. "That's what I've worked on since the day we talked in the shop. Tawfik has a new girlfriend in Nablus. He eats with her family every week after Friday prayers. He's not religious, but they think he is because of what happened in Al-Quds when the American woman was killed by Abdul." Nabil paused. "If you catch him alone, he'll empty his pockets. He'll have money because he's seeing the girl."

"How much do you think I could get?"

"My family in Deir Dibwan say he brags about always having three to four thousand shekels in his wallet."

"He owes my client a lot more than that."

"And he has a Rolex watch. I've seen it with my own eyes. And a thick gold neck chain, not a thin one. I believe he will be wearing both of them when he sees the girl. He wants to show off for her."

Daud nodded. "Okay."

Nabil turned sideways. Hana could see the tobacco shop owner's face. He had bushy black eyebrows and a square chin.

"I wish I could be there to see a Zadan squirm," Nabil said. "But even so, this isn't a just revenge since I'm not doing it myself."

"Adopt me," Daud replied. "I can act as your son."

Nabil patted the leather armrest of the expensive vehicle. "You don't need a poor father like me."

CHAPTER 33

Following the group of young ultra-Orthodox men, Jakob rounded a corner and found himself at the top of a long set of stone stairs overlooking the Western Wall plaza. Even from a few hundred yards away there was no mistaking the massive size of the stones that made up the retaining wall for the enormous platform that once surrounded the temple built by Herod the Great.

It wasn't a special holy day in Judaism, and neither the plaza nor the area in front of the Kotel was crowded. Small groups and individuals milled about. To the right was the area reserved for women. Jakob could see that the men clearly had access to the best spots. Descending the steps, he passed the entrance to a local yeshiva and came to the security checkpoint. After passing through metal detectors and the watchful eyes of male and female guards, he walked across the plaza. Donning a cardboard kippah that he had grabbed from a large bin, he continued down the slightly sloping stone pavement to the holiest place in Judaism.

Ultra-Orthodox men of all ages stood in front of the Wall praying and reading from books written in Hebrew. Some of the men bobbed their heads and upper bodies back and forth. Jakob joined a group of tourists and listened to their female guide explain the history of the Wall. She pointed out the largest visible stone, which was forty-three feet long and weighed over five hundred tons. Archaeologists believed even more massive stones lay hidden from view.

Leaving the group, Jakob saw that the cracks between the stones were filled with tiny pieces of paper—prayers deposited as close as possible to the Almighty. A couple of times a year the papers were removed and buried in the Jewish cemetery on the slopes across the Kidron Valley from the Old City.

After traveling such a long distance to this unusual place, Jakob didn't want to miss anything it had to offer him. He didn't have any paper in his pocket, and he wasn't sure if he did what kind of prayer he would insert into a crack. He reached out and touched the stone in front of him. It was cool to his fingertips. He glanced up and down and then heard a voice that caught his attention. A few feet behind him a man was praying in Russian. Jakob glanced over his shoulder and saw a slender tourist about his own age with close-cut brown hair and wearing a white shirt and blue jeans. Like Jakob, he, too, wore a cardboard kippah on his head. His eyes closed, the young man was praying in a normal tone of voice to Jesus Christ. Not wanting to eavesdrop on a private spiritual moment, Jakob started to move away. But then he heard something that stopped him.

"Lord God," the man said, "hear my cry in this holy place. Speak to the Russian Jews and reveal to them the good news that Jesus Christ is their Messiah. Speak to them in Russia; speak to them in Israel; speak to them wherever they are found in a way that they may know the truth and be set free. May they believe and receive!"

The hair on the back of Jakob's neck stood up. The man paused. Jakob wanted to move, but his feet seemed stuck to the stone pavement. The man prayed a second time in a language Jakob didn't recognize. He then switched back to Russian.

"Heavenly Father, I pray that Russian Jews standing in this very place will believe that Jesus Christ is their Savior. They may wrestle with you like Jacob did when you changed his name to Israel, but they will come away from that encounter so transformed that they will, like him, have a new name."

At the mention of his biblical namesake, Jakob turned around and stared directly at the young man, whose eyes remained closed. The man switched again to a language Jakob didn't understand. But Jakob had heard enough that he did understand the purpose of the man's prayers. He walked gingerly past the Russian speaker. Every few steps as he moved away from the Wall, Jakob glanced over his shoulder. The man remained in the same place, never opening his eyes. Returning his cardboard kippah to a large bin, Jakob left the plaza and climbed the stone steps that led to the Jewish Quarter. He turned around at the top of the stairs and found the spot where he'd stood before the Wall. The man who had prayed in Russian was gone. Jakob carefully scanned the entire area. More people had arrived, and he couldn't spot the man wearing a white shirt and jeans.

Making his way back to the Jewish Quarter, Jakob felt different but wasn't exactly sure how. He reached Hurva Square and sat down on a stone bench across from the ice cream shop. This time his mind didn't return to the video of the attack on Gloria and Sadie Neumann. Instead, he watched the people passing by. Most of them were Jewish. Jakob had been around Jewish crowds in New York City, but never before had he felt any connection to other Jews beyond general membership in the human race. He knew some of the basic facts of Jewish history but had never personalized them at a deep level.

Today was different. As he watched the Jewish people moving across the square, something grew inside him. At first, he wasn't exactly sure what it meant. Then, suddenly, it hit him. He was a part of them, and they were a part of him. And with that realization, a floodgate opened, not of ethnic pride, but of an awareness of the sadness and success and tragedy and glory and pain and persecution and achievement and prejudice experienced by the Jewish people for thousands of years. Though many had died, others survived and thrived. And now they did so in their ancestral home. He looked down at the ancient stones of Jerusalem and saw them in a new way—as the foundation blocks for his own identity.

• • •

"Why didn't you ask him the name of the group Abdul Zadan joined?" Hana asked as soon as Nabil left and she had returned to the passenger seat. "He knew more than he let on. That could give us the big break we need for the case."

"Do you think it didn't cross my mind?" Daud replied testily. "But he'd already told me more than he intended to. I didn't want to make him suspicious about my true intentions. Interrogation is a dance, not a fight."

"Okay," Hana sighed. "I'm not trying to be critical. You were amazing. The conversation flowed so smoothly, and the final touch about him adopting you was brilliant. It opens the door to future communication."

"Thank you," Daud said. "Keep talking."

"I'm done," Hana replied. "Remember, pride goes before destruction."

Daud started the engine and pulled away from the curb. "Did you like your investigative alias?" he asked when they slowed to a stop in a line of traffic.

"Jemila has been a common name for women in our family," Hana answered.

"Jemila means 'beautiful.' Were they as beautiful as you are?"

Hana rolled her eyes. "With you, all conversation, whether interrogation or personal, is a dance," she said.

"I like that," Daud said, glancing at his watch. "We have time to swing through Deir Dibwan if you want to. It's just a few kilometers from here."

"Let's go."

It took less than thirty minutes to reach the town of slightly over six thousand residents. Houses shared space with ancient olive trees that stretched up the rolling hills.

"The village has been here a long time," Daud said as he turned off the main road. "But you can see that a lot of the houses are newer."

"And large," Hana said as they passed rambling multistory dwellings with flat roofs. "I guess many of the residents work in Ramallah."

"And the Zadan clan is prosperous," Daud said. "Nabil can say what he wants about them being liars and cheaters, but some of them worked hard to establish what they have here."

It was a familiar story to Hana. People drawn to fundamental Islamic beliefs didn't come from the lower class but from those prosperous enough to provide their children an education. Teachers planted seeds that bore fruit in radical terrorism activity, viewed by some as the highest and best expression of faith.

They turned a corner and came upon an expansive lot that featured a large new house surrounded by a wall. Red bougainvillea flowers peeked over the top of the enclosure in places. Daud slowed to a stop across the street. A new BMW was parked alongside the curb in front of the house.

"That's the Zadan compound," Daud said. "I watched the demolition video online. The house was rebuilt with money collected by the PA from places like Qatar. It's much nicer and bigger than the one that was destroyed."

The metal gate in the wall opened, and a young man in his late teens or early twenties came out. He glanced at the Land Rover before putting on a pair of sunglasses.

"It's Tawfik!" Hana said, sliding down lower in the seat.

"Don't worry," Daud replied calmly. "My windows are opaque to anyone standing five feet away."

"What if he comes over here?" Hana asked. "Go, go!"

"No," Daud replied calmly. "I'm going to talk to him."

Before Hana could protest, Daud opened the driver's-side door. He walked in front of the Land Rover and raised his hand. Tawfik stopped and looked in his direction. Crossing the street,

Daud began talking to the young man. Tawfik was well dressed and wearing what looked like a silk shirt and tailored trousers. His hair was carefully groomed. The young man listened to Daud for a few moments and then pointed to the left. Daud reached into his wallet and handed Tawfik his business card. The two men shook hands. Tawfik hopped into the BMW and left.

"Why did you give him your card?" Hana asked when Daud returned. "That seemed unnecessarily risky."

The investigator reached into his pocket, took out his wallet, and handed her a card that read "Fadi Wazir, East/West Trading Company, Ramallah." Below the name was an address in Ramallah and a cell phone number.

"It's a front company I use when I make contacts in the West Bank," Daud said.

"Is that the one you gave to Nabil?"

"No, I used a different one for him that's based in East Jerusalem. After hearing what Nabil told us about Tawfik, I suspect Tawfik is laundering money for a terrorist group. Otherwise, why would a twenty-year-old with no job drive a BMW and wear a five-hundred-shekel shirt? I told him I was looking for the home of a wealthy man who lives up the road. When he asked about my business, I told him I ship software used by hackers in Israel. That caught his attention, and he asked for my card. If he calls that number, it will appear on my cell phone with the name of my company so I know what it's about and how to respond."

"What if he wants to do a deal?"

"I'll set it up. I usually do sample shipments, which don't include everything needed. It's all approved by the Shin Bet. After that I can give the excuse that my supplier has either gone out of business or can't ship in quantity. A few times, I've delivered a complete product that allows backdoor access by the seller to the end user."

"Who is the seller?"

"A private company with government clearance. It's set up to protect me while serving the greater good. That's all I can tell you."

Hana's head was spinning. "You work directly with the Shin Bet?" she asked.

"What do the Americans say?" Daud answered with a smile. "I can neither confirm nor deny."

Hana's hunch about some kind of connection between Daud and Israeli security forces made sense. She knew not to pry further.

Daud continued, "I jumped out of the car to talk to Tawfik because it could be a huge break. If he places an order, it could lead us to information about the terrorist group linked to his brother."

Hana nodded. "True, but what about going to Nablus to catch him after he sees his girlfriend?"

"I had no intention of doing anything that could get me arrested or beaten up. If I'd met with Tawfik in Nablus, my goal would have been to have the same kind of conversation we just had."

"Nabil wouldn't like that."

"He'd never find out."

They drove away from the Zadan house. "Will we pass the house of the man you mentioned to Tawfik?" Hana asked.

"No."

"How did you know about him?" Hana asked.

"I had been to Deir Dibwan several times before you first contacted me," Daud replied. "This isn't totally new territory."

CHAPTER 34

Wahid picked up Jakob and drove him to the hotel. "Any other plans to go out later this afternoon or evening?" the taxi driver asked.

"No," Jakob replied.

"I'm here if you need me up until ten at night," Wahid said.

"Thanks," Jakob said as he got out. "And you'll let your cousin know I'm running a tab, right?"

"Already done."

Jakob went to his room and inspected himself in the bathroom mirror. He'd always thought he looked Russian, although that was hardly a monolithic image. One great beauty of America was the diverse appearance of its people.

Sitting on the bed with his legs in front of him and his back propped against a pair of pillows, Jakob waited for his laptop to boot up. He hadn't eaten lunch, so he popped a few handfuls of dry-roasted peanuts into his mouth. He sent Hana a text asking when they might return, but the message didn't show delivery.

There was a knock on his door. He got up and looked through the spy hole. A stocky man about his own age wearing a yellow shirt with dark hair and a black mustache stood on the landing with his hands in his pockets. Jakob opened the door.

"My name is Ensanullah," the man said in heavily accented English. "Daud Hasan sent me to take you to him."

"Daud didn't say anything about sending a driver when he left this morning."

"It has taken him longer than he thought in the West Bank."

The man pulled out his phone and showed Jakob a message in Arabic.

"I can't read that," Jakob said.

"Sorry, wrong message," the man replied.

He tapped his phone a few times and returned it to Jakob:

Pick up Jakob Brodsky at the hotel where he is staying in the German Colony and bring him to my apartment. Daud

"No," Jakob said as he returned the phone. "I'll need to talk to Daud first."

The man shrugged. "Okay. But I have been watching you since you left the hotel a few hours ago in the Mercedes taxi and went to Hurva Square, the Kotel, and back to Hurva Square. Daud asked me to take care of you and find out if you were being followed. I am, what do you call it, your guardian angel?"

Jakob's skepticism remained. His idea of angels didn't have thick black mustaches. "Get Daud on the phone," he said.

The man handed the phone to Jakob. After a couple of rings a male voice answered and began speaking in Arabic.

"Daud?" Jakob asked.

"Yes, it is me," the investigator replied. "Hana and I are going to meet you at my apartment in Beit Hanina. Ensanullah will drive you. If you arrive before we do, he will unlock the door, and you can wait for us. You may enjoy the coffee, wine, beer, and food."

"Did you tell this guy to follow me today?"

"Yes. He has been your security guard, but he did not see anyone or anything suspicious."

"Okay," Jakob said, relaxing. "I wasn't sure I could trust him."

"You can. He works for me. He is a professional."

Jakob ended the call and returned the phone to Ensanullah. "Let me grab my wallet and laptop."

A minute later they were descending the steps to the courtyard. When they passed the concierge station, Wahid's cousin ran out. "What's the matter?" the man demanded. "Did Wahid insult you? He should know better."

Jakob shook his head and answered, "No, no. This is a business associate. Wahid is a great driver."

They reached Ensanullah's car, a small compact, and got in.

"Wahid is not a great driver," Ensanullah said. "He could have gotten two traffic tickets when he was driving you to the Old City. I thought he knew I was following and wanted to lose me. But Daud told me you would go to Hurva Square, and I found you there."

Jakob didn't respond. They rode in silence to the eastern part of the city. Turning down a street, Jakob was suddenly confronted by the concrete security barrier that divided parts of the city in two.

"Where are we?" Jakob asked.

"Beit Hanina. On this side is Al-Jadida, the new village," Ensanullah said. "The older area is Al-Balad, the old village. My grandparents grew up in Al-Balad but live on this side now."

Jakob inspected Ensanullah's face for signs of emotion but couldn't see any. "Were they upset about moving?" he asked.

"My grandfather fought in the Jordanian army as a tank commander and was wounded in the leg and chest in the 1967 war. It happened not far from here when the Israelis captured this part of the city. How do you think I should feel about that? My grandparents have a modern apartment with air-conditioning, but it is not the place where my ancestors lived."

"Were they forced to move?"

"No," Ensanullah replied. "Life is better on the Israeli side for their bank account. My grandfather worked many years for the

Jerusalem utility company before he retired. Living in Al-Jadida, it is easier for him to go to Al-Aska on Fridays."

Several times during the day, Jakob had heard the call to prayer broadcast from minarets throughout the city. It was especially loud near the Western Wall because of the close proximity of the Al-Aska mosque. The tour guide had explained to her group that the famous Dome of the Rock was a shrine and not a regularly functioning mosque like the Al-Aska, which marked the spot where Muslims believed Muhammad prayed one night after miraculously traveling through the heavens on his horse, Buraq, from Mecca to Jerusalem.

As they drove, Jakob continued to ask Ensanullah questions about his family. The driver became more and more talkative. They passed the apartment building where his grandparents lived. Stopping for a moment, Ensanullah pointed to a second-story balcony filled with flowers in pots.

"That is their apartment. My grandmother has what you call the green thumb."

A few blocks later they entered an area of modern apartment buildings. After a couple of turns they reached the top of a small hill. Ensanullah stopped next to the curb in front of a four-story building. There was no sign of Daud's Land Rover.

"Daud lives in apartment 410 on the top floor," he said. "Here is a key. There is no elevator. Walk up the stairs. The code to enter the building is 311."

"You're not coming?" Jakob asked.

"No, I'm going to visit my grandparents before going home."

"Thanks for taking care of me today," Jakob said.

"Daud pays me well," Ensanullah said with a slight smile. "No tipping necessary."

Jakob laughed. Ensanullah was quiet for a moment. "You are a nice American Jew," the driver said. "Do not move to Israel. You will not like it here. Stay in the USA."

"That's my plan."

. . .

A kilometer away from the Qalandiya checkpoint for reentry into Israel, Daud stopped in an alleyway and changed the license plates on his vehicle.

"Have you ever forgotten to do that?" Hana asked when he was behind the wheel again.

"No, because I know the problems I would have if the plate didn't match the vehicle registration."

Daud handed a young female border patrol officer a piece of paper. She left to make a phone call.

"What's on the paper?" Hana asked.

"Written permission for us to break the law by going into Ramallah. That way, we can tell the truth when questioned."

There were lines of people on foot and in cars, buses, and taxis moving in both directions.

"Do they call every time?" Hana asked.

"They always check when I'm coming from this direction back into Jerusalem."

"Proceed," the young woman in the green uniform said in Hebrew when she returned with the letter.

Beit Hanina wasn't far from the checkpoint. Hana took her phone from her purse and sent a text to Jakob telling him where they were. He replied immediately:

I'm sitting on the balcony drinking his beer and enjoying the view.

She read the text.

"I told him to treat it like home," the investigator replied. "I won't charge one beer to your law firm, but two might be another story."

Daud pulled into a reserved parking space behind the hilltop building. "Is there anything you don't want to tell Jakob?" he asked.

303

"Or maybe I should ask if there is anything your boss doesn't want him to know?"

"I'm not going to play games with him," Hana replied. "That would be too hard to keep straight."

"Okay. But remember not to say anything about my connection with the Shin Bet. Just mention that I have access to sophisticated software that is in high demand on the black market."

Inside the apartment, Hana was more impressed by Daud's sense of style in person than when he had given her a virtual tour. The living area included a cream-colored leather sofa and several attractive lamps. Through the glass walls she could see Jakob sitting on the balcony that faced south toward Jerusalem. That side of the apartment overlooked a small grove of trees and manicured garden with a large fountain in the middle. Only plants that were well-watered remained vibrant in the dry climate. Hana joined him.

"Being a private investigator is the profession of choice in Israel," Jakob said when Hana appeared.

"It's probably the nicest unit in the building," Hana replied. "Come inside so we can talk."

Daud soon joined them in the living room. He placed a bowl of freshly cut fruit on a glass-topped table. Hana excused herself for a moment. When she returned, Daud was telling Jakob about the conversation with Nabil in Ramallah. The encounter sounded less colorful when told by Daud in his stilted English.

"Are you going to Nablus to ambush Tawfik?" Jakob asked.

"No, I do not have to go to Nablus to find him," Daud answered. "We went to Deir Dibwan, and I talked with him there."

"What!" Jakob burst out.

"Hana, please tell him while I eat some fruit," Daud said.

Hana relayed the encounter outside the Zadan residence, omitting Daud's connection with the Shin Bet.

"This is huge," Jakob said when she finished.

"I hope so," Hana said.

"What did it feel like seeing Tawfik in person?" Jakob asked her.

Hana realized then that everything had happened so quickly, she hadn't processed the encounter beyond a surface level. "I didn't feel anything," she replied. "My mind was totally focused on what Daud might be trying to accomplish."

"And I was hoping none of Tawfik's friends that Nabil mentioned would show up while we talked," Daud added. "They would be much more suspicious than he was. I think Tawfik is more interested in what money can buy than Islamic ideology."

"Let's hope so," Jakob replied. "How will you proceed?"

"I want to talk to you and Hana about that," Daud said, taking a drink from a bottle of mineral water. "I think I should wait at least a day before calling Tawfik if he doesn't contact me. I don't want to look too eager."

"Agreed," Hana replied. "Did you tell him the cost of the software?"

"Yes, which is half the price his organization can charge when selling it to criminal organizations and other fundamentalist groups."

"What does the software do?" Jakob asked.

"It makes a novice hacker an expert hacker."

"Is that a good idea?" Jakob asked, his eyes wide.

"Yes. There are bugs hidden in it that allow good people to know what the bad ones are doing."

It was Hana's turn to react with surprise. Daud was close to clue-ing Jakob in on the investigator's connections with the Israeli security network.

"Sounds risky," Jakob said. "What if a bug is discovered?"

"I run a risky business," Daud said and shrugged, taking another drink of water. "Tomorrow, I think we should visit my friend with access to the computers seized from the Zadan residence at the time of the attack. Based on what Nabil told us, I think we may find another piece of our puzzle."

"That's a good description," Hana said. "It sounded very American."

"Yeah," Jakob said. "Daud would fit perfectly in the US so long as he was working for the CIA or FBI."

Daud didn't respond. Hana eyed the investigator quizzically.

"Our next agenda item is deciding where to eat dinner," Daud said. "I think we should go to a good Arab restaurant. Ensanullah will drive you back to your hotel, and I will pick you up at seven o'clock."

"Ensanullah left," Jakob said. "He said he was going to see his grandparents."

"Grandparents?" Daud asked, raising his eyebrows. "That's not supposed to happen when I hire him for an entire day. I can call a taxi—"

"Let me take care of it," Jakob said. "I've met a driver who I'd like to use."

CHAPTER 35

Jakob and Hana rode in silence in the back seat of Wahid's Mercedes. Jakob assumed Hana was thinking about matters that couldn't be discussed in the presence of Wahid.

"Do you live in Atlanta, too?" the driver asked Hana, looking at her in the rearview mirror.

"Yes, but I grew up in Reineh near Nazareth."

"I know Reineh," Wahid replied. "I drove a fare there from Tel Aviv last week. It was a guy from California who had a business meeting with a company that manufactures irrigation supplies."

"He probably met with my father or one of my uncles," Hana responded.

"Small world, eh?" Wahid said. "What brings the two of you to Jerusalem? A big lawsuit?"

"Just checking some things out for a client," Jakob said. "But as you know, I spent most of my day as a tourist."

"Maybe, but not many American tourists go to Beit Hanina," Wahid answered.

Hana caught Jakob's eye and shook her head. They rode the rest of the way in silence. As soon as Wahid dropped them off, they sat down at a table in the courtyard, which at this time of the afternoon was deserted.

"I didn't think it would be a good idea to mention Daud to the driver," Hana said.

"I'm not stupid," Jakob said, touching the side of his head. "And every time I have a headache, it reminds me to be careful."

"Is your head hurting now?"

"No. Maybe the air here agrees with me."

Hana paused for a moment. "Any communication with your other driver in Atlanta?"

"Not since she assured me that she wasn't followed when she left the Atlanta airport."

"Okay," Hana said. "No news is probably good. Do you have any questions about what Daud did today in Ramallah or Deir Dibwan?"

"Are you asking me because you're willing to admit your personal involvement with Daud makes it tough for you to be objective?"

"Not really. I hired Daud to investigate and that's what he's doing. But my presence in Ramallah didn't make a difference today. I could have stayed here and gone to Hurva Square and the Kotel with you."

"Except that you wanted to spend every minute you could with Daud," Jakob replied with a grin. "Hey, I think he's doing a great job. No questions or concerns from me."

"Me too," Hana said as she stood up.

"Do you know what we should do now before it gets too late on the East Coast?" Jakob asked.

"What?"

"Call Ben Neumann and give him an update. I told him I'd be in regular communication with him."

"You're right." Hana nodded.

"We'll Skype from my room."

When they reached Jakob's room, he knelt in front of the door.

"What are you doing?" Hana asked.

Jakob stood and showed her a tiny piece of brown paper. "I positioned this paper so I'd know if anyone came into my room while I was gone."

"What about housekeeping?"

"I waited until after the room was cleaned."

"Did you see that in a movie?" Hana asked skeptically.

"Several times. It always works."

Hana sat in a chair by the window while Jakob reached Ben via Skype. After a couple of rings Ben's face came into view. Jakob positioned his computer so the client could see both of them.

"How's Sadie?" Hana asked.

"Filled with endless questions about your trip. Is there any way you can send a few pictures? She wants to know where you are and what you're doing. She's especially interested in photos of your nieces and your cousin Fabia."

"If that happens, it will be later in the trip," Hana replied. "Let us tell you about today."

As she talked, Hana could see shifting emotions move across Ben's face. The most dramatic came when she told him they'd seen Tawfik Zadan.

"You're sure it was him?" Ben asked.

"Yes. Daud talked to him."

Ben pressed his lips tightly together as he listened.

"Daud wants to move forward on a fake business deal with Tawfik as a way to find out more about the group he's working with," Hana said. "It may be the same organization connected to the attack on your family."

Ben took a deep breath and exhaled. "I'm not sure how I would handle being in the same room with any of these people," he said.

"We're a long way from that day," Hana replied. "Right now, it's still a lone-wolf attack by Abdul."

"That's not all," Jakob spoke up. He told Ben about their dinner conversation with Daud the previous evening.

"The computer data sounds promising," Ben said.

"Yes," Jakob said, glancing at Hana. "But if there was something incriminating, I wonder why nothing has been done before now by the Israeli authorities."

"They often take a long-term view," Hana answered. "They're

less interested in prosecuting a terrorist attack that's occurred than trying to prevent more in the future. That's especially true when the immediate perpetrator is dead."

"I can see their point," Ben said, rubbing his eyes. "Jakob, I received a call this afternoon from a woman named Emily Johnson who says she's been driving you around for the past few weeks. I let it go to voice mail and haven't answered her because I wasn't sure if you'd want me to talk to her."

"I have no idea why she would call you," Jakob said.

"Have you talked to her about the case?" Hana asked.

"She's aware that there may be a connection between the mugging and my work, and she knows about the explosive device, but I haven't violated attorney-client confidentiality."

Troubled, Hana decided not to challenge Jakob in front of the client.

"She's a former cop and has direct access to information whether I tell her or not," Jakob continued. "I trust her, but it's up to you whether you want to talk to her."

"All right," Ben said. "It helps to know that much. I'll mull it over."

"I vote against it," Hana said. "Let Jakob find out first why she called."

"Good idea," Jakob jumped in. "I'll text her."

"When will I hear from you again?" Ben asked.

"Hopefully tomorrow night," Jakob answered. "Is this a good time to call?"

"Considering the number of nights I suffer from insomnia, the answer is yes."

The call ended. Hana turned to Jakob. "It's my turn to ask if your personal connection with someone has affected your judgment," she said.

"Emily? Not at all."

. . .

They returned from dinner at a restaurant in East Jerusalem. Jakob had sampled some of the best that the local Arab cuisine had to offer. Most food in the Middle East grows from the same culinary tree, but the individual flair of a skilled chef allows room for unique expression. Hana enjoyed Jakob's enthusiasm, which made her pay more attention than usual to the familiar flavors.

"That was great," Jakob said as Daud pulled to a stop in front of the hotel. "I never knew eggplant could taste like that, and the baked kibbe was delicious."

"And the fish shakshuka was the best I've ever eaten," Hana added.

"That's the way they prepare it in Alexandria," Daud said. "Shakshuka is a way of cooking, not just an egg dish."

"When were you in Egypt?" Jakob asked. "Can Israeli citizens travel there?"

"Yes, with a visa," Daud answered. "And I've been there more times than I can count. My grandfather lived in Port Said before coming to the Negev."

"What time will you be here in the morning?" Hana asked.

"Nine o'clock," Daud replied. "First stop is the rendezvous with my friend who has access to the computers seized at the Zadan residence."

"Where will we meet with him?" Hana asked.

"I have to put the blindfold over your eyes to take you there," Daud replied with a grin.

Hana forced a smile but wasn't satisfied with his answer. "Will it be near Tel Aviv?" she pressed.

"Uri is supposed to let me know the details later tonight. This falls into what you would call the gray area. He is doing me a favor, and someday I will do him a favor. After talking to him, we will meet with some people who work in Israeli internal security regarding their investigation of Gloria Neumann's murder."

"Will we have to sign any confidentiality paperwork?" Jakob asked.

Daud looked at Hana. "Please explain."

Hana quickly did so in Arabic.

"No," Daud said to Jakob. "But they are not under the control of the American courts."

"Which means their cooperation will be voluntary at every level," Hana said. "That's where Sylvia Armstrong and the US Attorney's Office could help with exchange of evidence by official sources."

"That is all true," Daud said, looking at his watch.

"Time for me to say good night," Jakob said. "Hana, that doesn't apply to you. Enjoy the journey."

"What did he mean by 'enjoy the journey'?" Daud asked with a puzzled expression on his face after the door closed. "Do you want to go someplace?"

"Only the places God wants to take us," Hana answered.

Daud switched to Arabic. "On that we agree one hundred percent, but I had trouble understanding your mood this evening. Part of the time you seemed to be happy and having a good time. Then at other times, you seemed wrapped up in your own thoughts."

"It's hard to jump back and forth so quickly between the personal and the professional," Hana said. "When I was here before, we settled our business first and then focused on getting to know each other better. It makes me uneasy when we switch back and forth."

"This investigation is an excuse to spend time with you and be paid for it. It's the best of both worlds," Daud said with a twinkle in his eyes. "Look, lawyers like Jakob Brodsky and the US attorney in New York think a lawsuit is going to make a difference in eliminating Islamic terrorism. It may help in an isolated way, but you and I know the problems in this part of the world can't be litigated in a courtroom. Only the power of the gospel can make a lasting difference, because it changes the hearts and minds of men and women who believe it."

"You're right," Hana agreed. "I need to remember that."

"And don't make me guess what you're thinking and feeling. Whatever my skill is as an investigator, I'm still a man trying to understand a woman."

"You're doing great," Hana said and smiled. "Talking helps a lot."

"Does that mean you're enjoying the journey?"

"Yes, very much."

• • •

Jakob left his room for the hotel lobby to pick up a bottle of complimentary shampoo. At the bottom of the stairs outside, he saw Daud still standing beside his car with his phone to his ear. Hana was nowhere in sight.

"No, not yet," the investigator said in Russian.

Jakob froze in place and then moved back into the shadows.

"My way is the only way this is going to work," the investigator continued in the same language. "Everything will be good in the end. Don't worry."

Daud lowered the phone from his ear, opened the door of his vehicle, and drove away. Jakob continued to the lobby.

"I have shampoo options," the young woman behind the counter said. "Your hair is thick and wavy, so I recommend this one."

Shampoo bottle in hand, Jakob returned upstairs. The investigator had spoken Russian with a pure accent that was more Ukrainian than Muscovite. Clearly, he was a man of many talents.

• • •

Hana emerged from her room. She'd woken up early and sent a detailed memo to Mr. Lowenstein outlining what had happened so far in Israel. In her first draft, she emphasized that she and Daud had left Jakob behind when they traveled to Ramallah and Deir Dibwan, but the sentence didn't sit right with her, and she changed it to simply report what they did. Jakob was sitting at a small table in the courtyard and drinking coffee when Hana joined him.

"Is your body clock adjusting to the time change?" she asked when she sat down.

"Not very well. I've been up for hours."

"Me, too, but I've been working. I sent a memo to Mr. Lowenstein about the trip."

"Did he respond?"

"Not yet."

Jakob glanced over Hana's left shoulder as a couple staying at the hotel passed close by. He lowered his voice. "I heard from Emily. She's concerned about Ben and Sadie's safety. That's why she called him."

Hana's heart sank, and her morning appetite left. "What's going on?"

Jakob continued in a soft voice. "It's true that she wasn't followed when she left the airport after dropping me off for my flight. What she didn't say at the time was that she turned the tables on the car tailing me and followed it. The driver led her to a run-down apartment complex in East Point. She stayed for a few hours to see who came and went. It was an active place, and she took a bunch of photos."

Jakob handed his phone to Hana, who scrolled through the pictures. There were multiple shots of four Middle Eastern males in their twenties or thirties. Two men had uncut beards in a manner preferred by fundamentalists.

"Where's the connection with Ben and Sadie?" Hana asked. "East Point is across town from where they live."

"The following day, Emily took a break from driving customers and returned to the apartment. The car that followed us to the airport was gone, but a couple of guys left in a different vehicle. Emily tailed them all the way to the community where Ben and Sadie live. As you know, it's gated, so the men parked nearby. They were still there when Emily left an hour later."

"Has she reported any of this to the police?"

"Not yet. She has a call in to Detective Freeman to request increased police presence in the area."

"Ben wants to keep things normal for Sadie," Hana said as much to herself as to Jakob.

"Nothing has been normal for either one of them since they were in Hurva Square nearly four years ago," Jakob noted.

Anger rose up inside Hana at the cowardice of anyone who posed a threat to innocent little girls. She closed her eyes for several moments. "We have to let the police deal with it," she said, keeping her voice steady.

"That's what I said in the voice mail I left Ben this morning," Jakob replied. "I encouraged him to return Emily's phone call and to contact Detective Freeman directly."

"Okay," Hana sighed.

"Should we tell Daud about this?" Jakob asked.

"Yes," Hana answered. "You can tell him on the way to our meeting."

CHAPTER 36

After Daud picked them up, Jakob summarized his conversation with Emily.

"If this is some kind of terror cell operating out of the apartment, the American authorities should know about it," Daud said when Jakob finished. "Maybe they already do."

"Emily is going to talk to the police detective working on my case. He has contacts within Homeland Security."

"Leave it there," Daud said. "There is nothing more we can do from here except pray."

"Pray a lot," Hana said. "That's what I've been doing since Jakob told me."

"Ensanullah says he was the only one following you yesterday," Daud said, looking in the rearview mirror at Jakob. "That is good news."

"Where is he today?" Jakob asked.

"Not working for me any longer. I was upset with him for abandoning his post."

Jakob thought Daud's reaction was harsh but kept quiet because he didn't know the protocol in the investigator's world. They rode in silence for several minutes. Daud took an exit and turned off the main highway.

"Are we going to Ra'anana?" Hana asked.

"Yes," Daud replied.

They entered the outskirts of the modern city that was home to around seventy-five thousand people. They turned onto Ahuza Street, the main boulevard.

"This is nice," Jakob commented from the back seat.

"Which is why a lot of Jews from America and Europe settle here," Hana said. "It's the national headquarters in Israel for Microsoft and a bunch of other high-tech companies."

Daud turned onto a side street and parked in front of a shiny five-story apartment building. "Uri does not live here, but it is where we are going to meet him," he said. "Bring your laptop, Hana."

They took an elevator to the fourth floor. Instead of ringing the bell, Daud sent a text message. A few seconds later the door opened. Standing before them was a young Israeli man in his midtwenties wearing shorts, sandals, and a black T-shirt with a comic-book figure emblazoned on the front.

"Good to see you again," Daud said in greeting and then introduced Hana and Jakob in Hebrew.

Uri invited them into an open-concept apartment that was furnished in steel, black leather, and glass. He spoke several sentences in Hebrew until Hana interrupted.

"English, please," she said. "So Jakob can understand."

"No problem," Uri replied. "I spent two years in Chicago taking classes at Northwestern."

They sat in a living area adjacent to the small kitchen. A glass-topped table in front of them was bare except for a purple flash drive. Uri pointed to it.

"Everything on the three computers seized by the police at the Zadan residence in Deir Dibwan is on there," he said.

"Have you looked at it?" Daud asked.

"No, and I don't want to. I'm going to step out for a cup of coffee and pastry while you check it out. Text me when you're done."

Daud accompanied Uri to the door, where they spoke in low voices for a minute. Hana couldn't hear what was said. Daud returned. "We can open it on your computer," he said.

Once Hana's laptop was up and running, she inserted the flash drive. "I hope there's no virus lurking in this data," she said.

The three of them sat together on a leather sofa. A long list of files popped into view. Some were identified in Arabic.

"It's gibberish to me," Jakob said, sitting back.

"These are Abdul's financial records," Hana said as she clicked open one of the files.

It was a simple budget that included meticulous detail about the young man's income and spending habits.

"He worked at a coffee shop in Ramallah," Hana said, pointing. "These are his tips."

Abdul lived frugally and earmarked a percentage of his earnings each month for deposit into a separate bank account marked "Retirement."

"Not what you'd expect from a terrorist knowing he was about to go on what would likely be a suicide mission," Hana said to Daud and then translated the information for Jakob.

They followed the financial trail to the final entry for "Tips" recorded two days before Abdul's death. Importantly, there were no significant deposits from an outside source.

"It was life as normal until he and Tawfik went to Jerusalem," Hana said. "If this is true, he acted based on belief, not payment."

The files were segregated on the flash drive based on the computer they came from. Nothing from "Computer 101" revealed anything out of the ordinary. In fact, it couldn't have been more mundane. After thirty minutes, Hana moved to "Computer 201." It contained video files, mostly sermons by an Imam or religious leader. Hana turned on the sound and quickly heard the phrases "death to the Jews" and "jihad against the infidels" a couple of times.

"Do you recognize any of the speakers?" Hana asked Daud.

He nodded. "A few. They are mostly Egyptian or Saudi. The two at the bottom are from Gaza."

Hana clicked open one from Gaza. The video quality was inferior to the others and the audio scratchy. Another set of videos included home movies from the lives of the Zadan family. They sampled a few, which showed large gatherings of men, women, and children outside and inside for meals.

"Stop," Daud said. "That's Abdul and Tawfik as boys."

In the frozen frame the brothers looked to be around ten and six. They were each holding a soccer ball. Tawfik had a gap-toothed smile. Except for the Islamic garb of the adults, the picture could have been from a holiday gathering of Hana's family in Reineh.

"How many boys that age now will end up like them?" Jakob asked.

"It will not stop until—" Daud began but stopped.

Hana knew what Daud was thinking and suspected he'd not continued because Jakob wouldn't understand. She closed the video. They watched portions of another one, but it was more of the same. Jakob stood and stretched.

"I need a break," he said.

While he was out of the room, Hana leaned against the sofa and rubbed her eyes.

"You may not want to tell me, but what did you say to Uri at the door?" she asked.

"Uri isn't his name," Daud replied in Arabic. "And I was telling him that I think you are the most beautiful woman in Israel."

Hana rolled her eyes. "Neither one of those statements is true," she said.

"No, both of them are true." Daud glanced in the direction where Jakob had gone toward a bathroom. "I asked him if he was aware of any other information about the Neumann murder that might help us. He told me there was nothing in his department. The information taken from the computers was in an investigative file marked 'Inactive.' That's one reason he didn't mind sharing it with us."

"That makes sense," Hana said, leaning forward and moving the cursor arrow farther down the row of videos.

She stopped at one with the Arabic title *Meal with Brothers* and opened it.

Jakob returned to the living area and took his place beside Hana on the sofa. While in the bathroom, he'd figured out that the resident of the apartment was female. No male would maintain the inventory of beauty products laid out on the vanity and positioned in the shower. Maybe the apartment belonged to Uri's girlfriend.

"Let's take a look at this," Hana said, pointing to the computer screen. "That word means 'brothers.' It may show some faces we need to identify."

Daud was in the kitchen getting a bottle of water from the refrigerator when she opened the file. The first scene was a social gathering of ten men around a table. There were empty platters of food, coffee cups, and plates of pastries on the table.

"That's Abdul," Hana said, stopping the video and pointing to a clean-shaven young man at one end of the table. "And Tawfik is standing behind him. Based on their ages, this can't be long before the attack."

"What's the date?" Jakob asked.

Hana closed the picture and returned to the file name. "Twenty-six days before the attack," she said.

Daud rejoined them. Hana sat in the middle and continued the video.

"Is there sound?" Daud asked. "It looks like dinner is over."

"Not on this one, but it was shot from a fixed position, maybe on a tripod. The camera isn't moving at all."

"Fast-forward and see if anything changes," Daud said.

Hana advanced the video without any differences popping up

in the accelerated images. She stopped when there was less than ten minutes left. At that point, whoever was operating the camera picked it up and moved it closer to the table. A tall, light-skinned man with a carefully groomed beard and wearing glasses placed a laptop on the table.

"Stop!" Jakob said. "I recognize the man with the glasses."

Hana paused the video while Jakob told them about the jihadist who spoke English with an American accent.

"You do not know his name?" Daud asked.

"No, but he made an appearance on at least one blog site that mentioned Gloria's death. I'd have to check my computer to be more specific."

"Keep going," Daud said to Hana.

When the video resumed, the other men in the room gathered around the laptop placed on the table. Abdul was present, but Tawfik was no longer visible. The man wearing glasses pressed a few keys on the laptop and a video began to play. It showed the outside of a concrete house in a dusty setting. There were six people wearing black masks and standing in front of the house with their hands clasped in front of them as they posed for the camera.

"Can you enlarge it?" Jakob asked.

Hana tapped a button a few times until the image expanded to full screen. She froze it and pointed. "They're boys," she said.

"How can you tell?" Jakob asked.

"By how tall they are next to the car. It's a small import made in Poland. There are a lot of them in Israel."

Four men, not wearing masks but with their hands secured behind them, were brought into view by larger figures who were wearing black masks. The bound men glanced around in obvious fear. Hana suddenly reached forward and paused the video. "This could be an execution film!" she exclaimed.

"Go to the balcony," Daud said to her. "We will find out."

Hana left and Daud pressed the play button. The bound men were led into the house, after which the front door closed. One of the adult men in a mask talked for a few moments to the young men who were lined up before the front door. A second man handed each of the young men a pistol. Jakob felt his throat constrict. The front door opened, and the young men rushed inside. The images on the screen suddenly became blurry as the feed went to surveillance cameras placed inside the house. Figures ran past the cameras. There was a flash of light that Jakob assumed signaled gunfire. Because the video was silent, there was a surreal quality to it. Suddenly, the camera captured a bound man in the corner of a tiny room slumping to the floor with two young masked men standing in front of him and pointing their pistols in his direction. Jakob felt the same way he had when viewing the surveillance video from Hurva Square.

"Oh my God," he said.

One of the two masked young men lifted his mask, vomited, and then wiped his mouth with the back of his hand. For an instant, the side of his face came partially into view.

"It's Tawfik!" Jakob said.

Daud stopped the video, rewound it, and froze the image. "Maybe," he said. "The light is not good enough to be sure. There are a lot of boys who fit that description."

"Facial recognition analysis could prove it, but it looks like Tawfik to me," Jakob replied emphatically.

The video continued, showing chaos and mayhem in the house. One of the other hostages was shot in the back while running down a hallway. A masked boy knelt beside the body for a moment, stood, and raised his hands triumphantly in the air. The video ended with all the masked boys and men assembled in front of the house with their hands folded across their chests. The fate of the other two hostages wasn't revealed, but there was no doubt in Jakob's mind what had happened. The Caucasian man wearing glasses closed the laptop.

The video in the room continued. Abdul sat down and took a sip of coffee. Behind him, the Caucasian man gave Tawfik a hug. The expression on the young man's face couldn't be seen.

"That's it," Jakob said. "He's congratulating Tawfik."

Daud grunted. The video ended thirty seconds later.

"Let's watch it again," Jakob said.

They ran the video to the point of the death of the hostage and removal of the mask. Jakob paused it. "I'm sure it's Tawfik," he said.

"Possibly," Daud said. "But one thing is sure. The boys in the masks are well trained. They know what to do inside the house. It is not as chaotic as you might think. This is not just for propaganda. It is a training video."

"We need to bring in Hana and find out if she wants to see this," Jakob said.

"Okay," Daud reluctantly agreed.

• • •

Out on the tiny balcony, Hana could see people drinking coffee at a café across the street. Uri wasn't in sight. It was the type of place where a terrorist might launch a knife or gun attack. In her heart, Hana knew something terribly dark caused the men in the video to gather around the laptop, but she tried to hope she'd been wrong about what it revealed. The door to the balcony opened.

"You can come in now," Daud said, a sober expression on his face.

"What did you see?" Hana asked as she crossed the threshold.

Daud turned to Jakob. "You tell her," he said.

Hana sat in a chair and listened as Jakob described what they'd witnessed on the video within the video.

"I believe the boy who takes off his mask is Tawfik," he said. "Daud isn't sure, but the face can be analyzed and compared to what we have from the attack in Hurva Square."

Her heart no longer racing, Hana's analytical ability kicked in.

"Wouldn't the Shin Bet or government security forces have done that?" she asked Daud.

"ISIS and other groups have released several videos like this one," the investigator replied. "I am sure all of them have been evaluated by the Shin Bet or Mossad to identify participation by Israeli citizens or terrorists from the West Bank or Gaza. If that is Tawfik in the video, they probably know about it but have not acted."

"Even if Tawfik is in the video, what impact does that have on the Neumann case?" Hana asked. "We already know he's a terrorist because he was present when his brother killed Gloria and stabbed Sadie."

"I don't know," Jakob said after a moment passed. "Maybe it's another piece of a puzzle."

"The identification of the men around the table could be important," Daud said. "Especially the one Jakob recognized. He might provide a link to an organization."

"You're right," Hana said. "How can we find out who he is?"

"Let me work on that," Daud answered. "I will have to let Uri know about this. He may not want us to keep the flash drive."

"I thought he said it was inactive," Hana answered.

"That is true, but it does not mean you can publicize it in an American courtroom."

"If there's a chance we won't be able to keep it, I want to watch the entire sequence again," Jakob said. "There may be something we missed."

Hana resumed her place on the sofa and clicked open the *Meal with Brothers* video.

"Are you going to stay?" Jakob asked her.

"Yes," she answered grimly. "If I watched the video from Hurva Square, I should watch this, too."

This time they didn't fast-forward through any of it. They watched in silence until the man placed the laptop on the table.

"Can we capture an image of his face and keep it on Hana's computer?" Jakob asked Daud.

Daud thought for a moment. "Not without additional permission," he said.

The video continued. Knowing now what lay ahead, Hana steadied herself. The scene shifted to the inside of the house and the boys chasing the captives from room to room.

"This has been edited," Jakob said. "Someone pieced this together from all the surveillance footage inside the house."

"And from a body camera on one of the young men or adults," Daud added. "I saw pictures that moved with a person."

At that moment, an image came into view showing a young man going through a door opening and firing a shot down a hallway. The video reached the point of execution of the hostage by two young men who cornered the bound man in a small room that looked no bigger than a closet. Hana felt a deep sadness in the pit of her stomach.

"Here it comes," Jakob said. "Watch the young man on the left. He's going to take off his mask and get sick."

Hana forced herself to lean in closer. The camera was behind the young man when he raised the mask and vomited on the floor at the feet of the dead man. The young man raised his hand to his mouth and turned his head to the side for no more than a couple of seconds as he repositioned his mask. To her, he looked like thousands of Middle Eastern teenagers. She stopped the video and rewound it.

"We did that too," Jakob said.

Hana froze the frame and tried to remember any distinguishing details of Tawfik's appearance. The black-and-white image was simply too unclear to convince her of a match.

"I'm not sure it's Tawfik," she said.

"Look at the nose and chin." Jakob pointed.

Hana did so, but she wasn't convinced. "Inconclusive," she said and turned to Daud.

"At least let us save his image," Jakob said.

"No," Daud said, shaking his head. "We are on, what do you call it in English, shaky ice?"

"Shaky ground or thin ice," Hana replied.

"Both," Daud said. "This has to be dealt with carefully. Let me do my job."

It was another situation in which Hana had to trust Daud. She saw no other option. "Okay," she said, leaning back.

Daud took the flash drive from Hana's computer and put it in his pocket. "Wait here while I return this to Uri," he said to Hana and Jakob. "I will only be gone a few minutes."

The investigator left.

"How will we identify the Caucasian man wearing glasses in the video?" Jakob asked. "I'm sure Daud is right. He's either European or American."

"Through Daud's contacts or Sylvia Armstrong," Hana replied.

"Or I could call Detective Freeman with the APD," Jakob said. "He has access to a facial recognition database through Homeland Security and the FBI."

"That would be a place to start," Hana said. "Especially since you know him. I guess their database is worldwide in scope."

"And probably includes Tawfik, since he was present when Gloria, an American citizen, was killed."

"But we didn't capture the image of the man you think was Tawfik from the video."

Jakob looked directly at Hana. "Yes, we did," he said simply.

"How?" Hana raised her eyebrows.

"I saved the entire video on your computer while Daud went to the balcony to get you. I could tell he was worried about us seeing it, and I didn't want to lose it. Our obligation is to our client, not Daud's contacts."

"Wait—"

"Not that I believe we should disregard other interests," Jakob continued, speaking rapidly. "But I don't want to lose the chance to follow a great lead because of bureaucratic red tape. The video is on your computer, not mine, so you control what's done with it. Remember, Daud works for us, not the other way around. If you're not careful, he'll blur the lines."

Hana, remembering her conversation with Mr. Lowenstein, knew there was truth in what Jakob said. However, deceiving Daud wasn't part of her plan.

"I don't want to do this to Daud," she said.

"Which if it comes out is why you're not going to tell him what I did," Jakob replied with emphasis. "All we need to do is confirm or disprove Tawfik's presence in the video and identify the other men around the table. For all we know, this may be a propaganda film produced by a terrorist organization without any financial links to our case."

"Or it might be the key we've been hoping to find while we're here," Hana said.

"Correct. The first thing is to research these types of videos and see what's out there on the internet. That will be my job, not yours."

While they waited for Daud, Jakob began his research using Hana's laptop. Most of the execution videos were beheadings, but within ten minutes Jakob had found three videos of hostage executions involving prisoners being chased down inside buildings and executed. One of the videos involved young boys armed with assault rifles. Hana sat in the kitchen while he relayed information.

"These people are insane," Jakob said.

"In the same way as the Nazis," Hana replied.

The door to the apartment opened and Daud returned alone. Jakob lowered the top of Hana's laptop to turn it off.

"What did Uri say?" Jakob asked before Daud said anything.

"He had not watched anything on the flash drive," Daud replied.

"That is not his job. I told him about the execution video, and he wanted to know if ISIS produced it. When I told him there was no identifying information, he became nervous. He grabbed the flash drive and told me to forget that he had agreed to help me. I think Uri is concerned it might have taken place in Israel, which would mean the file is not as inactive as he thought. I think it was filmed someplace else."

Hana's mouth became dry, and she licked her lips.

"Now what?" Jakob asked Daud.

"We visit Aaron Levy," Daud replied. "But let me do the talking and do not mention what you saw here. Understood?"

Jakob shrugged. "Sure."

"Aaron Levy?" Hana asked. "Sylvia Armstrong mentioned him. She called and asked him to cooperate with us."

Daud spoke. "I know Aaron much better than she does."

CHAPTER 37

When they were back in Daud's vehicle, Jakob checked his phone for messages from Ben or Emily. There wasn't any communication via text or email from either one of them.

"Where are we going?" he asked Daud as they pulled away from the apartment building.

"Tel Aviv."

Sobered by the video, they rode in silence. Jakob saw a sign indicating it was twenty kilometers to Tel Aviv. The number of houses and the scope of commercial development along the road increased. They exited the expressway onto a side street and drove for several miles through a commercial area.

When they stopped for a red light, Jakob asked, "Will you mention the video we saw on the flash drive?"

"I am not sure," Daud said. "I must protect Uri. We served together, and I was his superior for almost two years before he went to the United States to study in Chicago."

Jakob nodded to himself. That explained Daud's reluctance to cause trouble for Uri. Serving together meant one thing—military service.

They turned into the parking lot for a nondescript gray three-story building. The only unusual feature was a guard shack in one corner of the parking lot. Two soldiers stood outside it.

"Why don't they have a gate on the parking lot?" Jakob asked.

"This is just the beginning," Daud replied.

Daud parked near the guard shack. Neither he nor Hana said anything to the young soldiers who casually eyed them without ordering them to stop. Inside the front door was a security checkpoint similar to a US federal courthouse. Daud spoke in Hebrew to the man who seemed in charge. He left them waiting outside the body screeners while he made a phone call. He returned shortly and processed them into the building.

"I came here once when I worked at the airport," Hana said. "We attended a training seminar on the second floor."

They took an elevator to the third floor and stepped into a hallway where they were greeted by another security officer wearing civilian clothes. They followed him to an office at the end of the hall. Aaron Levy, a short, balding man in his fifties, greeted them in Hebrew and then switched to British-accented English. There were three chairs in front of a plain metal desk. The office was devoid of personal items or photos.

"Daud told me about the lawsuit you want to file, and I also talked to Sylvia Armstrong with the US Attorney's Office," Levy began in a friendly manner. "She urged me to meet with you and said your government wants to assist private parties in recovering money damages from the terrorist organizations. We agree. The Arab Bank litigation obviously caught our attention. Where are you in the legal process?"

Jakob expected Hana to respond, but she was looking at Daud. The investigator nodded to her. "Go ahead," he said.

"At the beginning of the investigative stage," she said. "Which is why we are here. We have to bridge the gap between Abdul and Tawfik Zadan acting alone and connecting the murder to an organization with assets."

"Hana read the report you gave me," Daud said. "We wanted to know what else you have uncovered, either on the record or off the record."

"Everything I say is off the record. You will not be able to call me as a witness in an American court," Levy replied with an easy smile. "My government wouldn't allow it, and your government wouldn't make me."

Jakob didn't doubt the truth of the man's statement. Levy picked up a thin folder that was on his desk and slid it across to Daud. "There's not much in there, but you're welcome to it. We have kept our eyes on Tawfik Zadan since he was released from detention and believe he has been recruited by a terrorist group based outside Israel, but we have no proof this cell was connected to the attack that killed Mrs. Neumann. Our current hypothesis is that Tawfik attracted the group's attention because of what he and his brother did at Hurva Square."

"What can you tell us about them?" Daud asked.

Levy shrugged. "It's small. There are at least a few men involved who were associated with ISIS. I cannot tell you names or details for security reasons, but it is like a hurricane that hasn't yet fully formed. We are the weathermen closely watching it."

"Are you sure Abdul and Tawfik did not attend any planning meetings by a recognized group before the attack?" Daud asked.

Jakob was impressed. It was a great leading question that opened the door for Levy to talk about the video within the video.

"I wouldn't be surprised if they were associated with other Islamic fundamentalists. But that is not the same as an organization with a chain of command that plans and carries out attacks. We have no conclusive evidence of those types of links. This was a lone-wolf attack."

"Did you review the data from the computers seized at the Zadan residence?" Daud asked.

Jakob held his breath.

"Yes, and we found nothing relevant," Levy answered.

Jakob felt deflated. If the Israeli intelligence services couldn't find a connection between Abdul and a terrorist organization, how could he and Hana hope to do so, even with Daud's help? Daud told Levy about his encounter with Tawfik in Deir Dibwan. Levy seemed interested and entered a few notes on a tablet.

Hana turned to Jakob. "Tell Mr. Levy how you were attacked in Atlanta after you went public with your desire to file a lawsuit against those responsible for Gloria Neumann's death."

Jakob summarized basic facts about the attack at the apartment and the destruction of his car.

"That sounds like a chain of command with a strategy to me," Hana said to Levy when Jakob finished. "I believe there is an organizational connection to what's happened. It just hasn't been identified."

"Maybe, maybe not," Levy said equivocally. "We don't close our minds to new information."

"Did you tell Sylvia Armstrong the same things you've said to us?" Hana asked.

"Basically, yes," Levy replied. "But with additional details that are only shared at the governmental level."

"Is she going to drop her investigation?" Hana asked.

"You will need to ask her, but my impression is that the two of you share an equal zeal."

Back in the car, Hana quickly flipped through the documents in the folder Levy gave them. "There's not much here," she said.

"Any mention of the information copied from the computers seized at the Zadan residence?" Jakob asked.

Hana read a paragraph and translated it from Hebrew to English. It contained no mention of the video within the video or the identity of the participants at the "meal with brothers." It concluded with the statement "No relevant data found."

"Exactly what he said in his office," Jakob said.

"Aaron did not tell us a fraction of what he knows," Daud said. "This was his way of gently telling us we are wasting our time."

"Do you think we're wasting our time?" Hana shot back.

"No," Daud said with a shake of his head. "But part of my job is to interpret what I hear from others. I am not ready to give up. Not yet."

During the return trip to Jerusalem, Jakob received an email from Emily. She'd talked with Detective Freeman, who had agreed to investigate the apartment in East Point and notify patrol officers assigned to the precinct where Ben and Sadie lived of the situation. Ben turned down Emily's offer to drive him and Sadie. Jakob told Hana about the email and Emily's conversation with Ben.

"It's a common way to deal with a threat," Daud interjected. "Some of the bravest people I have known reject every effort to make them fearful or cautious. It does not mean they were careless. I think it helps them think more clearly."

"Is that the way you are?" Hana asked Daud.

The investigator shook his head. "No, I am paranoid and suspicious. That works best for me."

It was midafternoon when they reached the outskirts of Jerusalem. Hana felt like they'd already put in a full workday. They hadn't eaten lunch, and she was hungry.

"Let's stop for food," she suggested to Daud.

"But I want to take you out for an early dinner," he replied.

"Without me," Jakob piped up from the back seat. "I can tell when I will be a third wheel."

"Third wheel?" Daud asked.

Jakob quickly explained.

"Half of what Americans say to each other consists of idioms," Hana said. "I spend most of my time trying to catch up to the meaning of conversations. I understand the words but not how they are put together."

Daud turned to Hana and said in Arabic, "The sound of one hand clapping."

"Exactly," she replied and translated the phrase into English for Jakob. "What do you think it means?"

"Uh, that it takes a crowd to support something?"

"Not bad," Hana answered. "It means that cooperation from everyone is necessary. It's a phrase used to encourage teamwork."

"Repeat it again in Arabic," Jakob said.

Hana did so, and Jakob mimicked the words. To Hana's surprise, he did so almost perfectly.

"That's good," Daud said, glancing over his shoulder at him. "As a Jew you probably want to learn Hebrew first. We can add Arabic later."

They turned onto the city streets of Jerusalem. Daud's phone beeped, and after checking the identity of the caller, he answered it. Hana realized it was Tawfik, and in a whisper she told Jakob. Daud did more listening than talking, but there was discussion about where to meet.

"Yes, I will be there," Daud said as he ended the conversation.

"What did he say?" Jakob asked.

"Tomorrow, I will return to Deir Dibwan and meet with Tawfik to find out if we can do business with his organization," Daud replied.

"Why?" Jakob asked. "Aaron Levy says Tawfik's contacts developed after the attack in Hurva Square, not before."

"Aaron is probably right, but he is not the prophet that his ancestor was to Moses. Tawfik is interested in buying the software and wants to meet with me tomorrow at the Zadan family home in Deir Dibwan. He promised to bring his bosses."

Before the meeting with Levy, Hana would have thought this was good news. Now, she wasn't sure. "Is this going to be dangerous?" she asked.

"Maybe if I went to the Zadan house, but I told him we had to meet at a coffee shop that is in the middle of town."

"Okay, that makes sense. What will you show him?"

"A demonstration on a laptop I use in my business. That way if someone steals it, what they will find on the hard drive makes me look like I would fit in with the group on the *Meal with Brothers* tape. I may leave the computer running while I go to the restroom so they can look at it. That makes me seem more casual than professional."

"What about us?" Jakob asked.

"Tomorrow, you are both tourists," Daud answered. "It would not be smart for Hana to be with me at this meeting. A woman's presence would be suspicious."

They reached the hotel in the German Colony.

"What would be a good time to pick you up for dinner?" Daud asked Hana. "We are going to a nice place."

"Two hours?"

"See you then."

"Don't worry about me," Jakob said as they got out of the car. "I'll find something to eat at the convenience store a couple of blocks away. They sell an odd kind of potato chips."

"I will not worry about your diet," Daud called after him.

The Land Rover pulled away, and Hana and Jakob walked into the courtyard.

"What are you thinking that you didn't say in front of Daud?" Jakob asked.

"I'm still upset about you transferring the video to my laptop without his permission. At some point it's going to come out, and Daud is going to be furious."

"Let me tell you another American idiom: Don't borrow tomorrow's trouble. Take it a day at a time. At this point, I'd like to send the video to Detective Freeman and explain the situation. Hopefully, he has access to facial recognition software that will confirm or rule out Tawfik's presence."

Hana hesitated. "I'm not sure."

"This is the right thing to do for our client," Jakob replied. "Consider this: if any of the men around the table turn out to be militant fundamentalists, Levy's theory about Tawfik is wrong. The

Zadan brothers met with known terrorists prior to the Hurva Square attack. And if Levy is wrong about that, he could be wrong about Abdul. I believe Freeman will work within our guidelines."

"Okay," Hana surrendered. "But I want no part of any conversation with him."

Jakob held up his phone. "I have his personal cell number."

Thirty minutes later, they hung up the phone with the detective after making clear the type of help they needed and the restrictions on further transfer of the images. Hana sent the video and offered up a silent prayer.

"He'll get on it and give us an answer," Jakob said.

"I hope this was the right thing to do."

Hana left Jakob's room to get ready for her dinner date with Daud. Keeping a secret when she had a guilty conscience wasn't one of her strengths. There was a huge chance she would blurt out what she and Jakob had done before dessert.

• • •

Jakob dozed off while relaxing on his bed. He woke up to an incoming phone call and grabbed his cell from the nightstand. It was Detective Freeman.

"It's been a slow day, so I ran the facial comparison program we have at the department," Freeman said when Jakob answered. "Is Ms. Abboud available?"

Jakob sat up straighter in bed. Hana would have left already for dinner with Daud. "No, she's out for the evening, but go ahead."

"Okay. The young Arab man who removes his mask is a ninety-five percent match with Tawfik Zadan in the video you sent taken during the attack on Gloria Neumann. The only reason the percentage isn't higher is the fuzziness of the images. A defense lawyer might disagree, but we consider a match like this rock-solid evidence, especially when the two images are close in time chronologically."

"That's good, although I'm not sure what that does to help our case. We already knew Tawfik was radicalized, just not how deeply."

"And I sent the execution video to one of my contacts at Homeland Security."

Jakob almost choked. "We asked you specifically not to share it with anyone!"

"Ms. Abboud took that position, not you."

"What difference does that make? We can't risk it coming out that we obtained a copy of the video."

"Did you steal it?"

"Technically, no, since we viewed it with permission, but we didn't have authority to copy it to Hana's laptop."

"Don't burden me with technicalities. Do you want to know about the dossier my friend at Homeland Security sent me?"

"Yes," Jakob said immediately.

"The Caucasian man wearing glasses is a professional videographer hired by terrorist groups to produce high-quality material for website and publicity purposes. He's originally from Minnesota and became radicalized about fifteen years ago. My friend thinks it's likely he edited the video but may not have been present when the events actually took place. His birth name is John Caldwell, but now he goes by Latif Al-Fasi. He's a zealot, a true believer in violent jihad. Caldwell has a film degree from UCLA. He's cagey, which is why he sticks to editing the violent stuff, not producing it. His original content is limited to propaganda material."

"Where does he live now?"

"Overseas mostly, but he returns to the US occasionally through Canada. Caldwell has a teenage daughter who lives with her mother in Payson, Arizona, not far from Phoenix."

"Is there an arrest warrant out for him?"

"That wasn't mentioned in the material I received, but he's

obviously on Homeland Security's radar because of who he knows and what he does."

"That makes sense," Jakob said and paused for a few moments. "Even if Caldwell isn't currently wanted on criminal charges, he could be subject to civil liability for inciting terrorist activity. I wonder if he has any money."

"There wasn't anything in the materials about his financial status, but if he retained any capitalist genes, he's making money for his services."

Jakob turned on his laptop so he could later review what he'd saved about the videographer. "Can you send me a copy of the dossier?" he asked.

"No. And don't worry about me sending the execution video to Homeland Security. They already had it."

"Okay," Jakob sighed with relief. "Is there anything else that might help us in the dossier?"

"Addresses for known contacts with Caldwell have been redacted, so I can't pass those along. You'll have to get that from the feds yourself if they're willing to share."

"I understand."

"One other thing," Freeman said. "Emily Johnson, the detective turned music student, is acting too much like a vigilante for my liking. Some former cops have trouble turning off the juice when they no longer carry a badge."

"She's concerned about the Neumanns for good reason."

"I'm not so sure. I requested increased patrols in your client's neighborhood for the past twenty-four hours. None of the officers noticed anything suspicious. The apartment Johnson identified in East Point as a terrorist hangout is rented by a young couple with two small children. A big extended family of brothers, sisters, and other relatives visit a lot."

Freeman's words didn't shake Jakob's confidence in Emily. "Did you tell her this?" he asked.

"No, I'll let you do it. But she needs to rein it in."

"I'll talk to her. And thanks again."

"Hey, I'd enjoy seeing you bust any of these guys and drag them into court."

Wide awake, Jakob quickly made notes about as much of the conversation as he could remember and went online to see if there was any public information about John Caldwell, aka Latif Al-Fasi.

• • •

Hana had packed two nice dresses, one green and one blue, for the trip. She selected the blue one and was putting the finishing touches on her makeup when Daud texted that he'd arrived. She went to the hotel entrance, but there was no sign of the Land Rover. Daud got out of a large, dark blue BMW sedan parked alongside the curb and approached. He was wearing a green tie, a black jacket, and gray slacks.

"I didn't know you owned two cars," Hana said in Arabic.

"I bought this recently," he replied. "I don't drive it much so it won't get scratched."

He held the door open for her, and she slid onto the soft leather. Hana wasn't an expert on automobiles, but it was clearly an expensive car.

"This is very nice," she said when Daud was seated behind the wheel.

"It's been a dream of mine to own one for years," Daud replied.

They pulled away from the curb and into late-afternoon Jerusalem traffic.

"It's a bit early to go to a nice restaurant, but you said you were hungry," Daud said. "At least it won't be crowded."

She glanced out the window at the passing street scenes. Surrounded by the quiet ambience of the car, Hana felt like she was in a movie or a dream. People stared as the car swished past. They made their way northeast and began to climb in the direction of Mount Scopus and Hebrew University, where Hana had attended law school.

"Are we going to Mount Scopus?" Hana asked.

"Yes," Daud answered. "The restaurant there has my new favorite view of the Old City. I like it better than the traditional one from the Mount of Olives."

They navigated the winding streets until they reached a small building that seemed suspended over the edge of the hill. Daud stopped and handed his car keys to a valet. In the early evening light, the sun reflected off the stones of Jerusalem, the City of Gold. They stood in front of a small entrance framed with the same stones.

"This is gorgeous," Hana said. "Was this a house?"

"Two houses that the owner combined to make the restaurant."

The maître d' seated them in what was once a living room with large windows overlooking the city. Daud positioned Hana at the table so she had the best view.

"I never would have been able to eat at a place like this when I was in law school," Hana said, glancing at the prices.

"Which I hope makes it that much nicer now that you can," Daud replied. "Do you want me to order for you?"

Hana hesitated.

"Trust me," Daud continued. "Consider it a test."

"Okay," Hana said with a smile as she closed the menu. "But I'm sure everything is delicious."

Enjoying the view from the window, she remembered the incredibly stressful evening when she and Ibrahim had sat on a bench less than a quarter mile away and ended their engagement. With Daud, she was more mature and confident of what she wanted in life, in faith, and with a man.

Daud ordered a roasted rack of lamb dish for Hana and a beef entrée for himself. "How did I do?" he asked when the waiter left.

"That was my number one choice," Hana answered.

Daud smiled and looked at her in a way that made Hana catch her breath. He reached out for her left hand, and she gave it to him.

"Are you going to take me to Reineh to meet your father?" he asked.

Hana knew that was the precursor to a marriage proposal. Daud would never propose directly until he was sure he had patriarchal approval. Hana felt her head about to nod and barely stopped it.

"Is there anything else I need to know before I agree?" she asked. "I don't want any secrets between us." As soon as she said the words, she felt her own betrayal of trust about the video flash before her eyes.

Daud spoke before she could continue. "Only when it comes to my work," he replied. "There are things I do, people I meet, and places I go that I can't discuss with anyone. If you don't know, you're safer than if you do."

"That's understandable," Hana replied. "And I have a confession to make."

Hana haltingly told him what she and Jakob had done. Daud listened impassively as she stumbled to a conclusion.

"It was wrong, and there's no way for me to make it right," she said sorrowfully. "For me to ask you about secrets when I was hiding something from you was so hypocritical. I'm sorry."

"Let me ease your guilt," Daud answered, leaning forward. "After I dropped you and Jakob off at the hotel, I made a few phone calls. We weren't the first people to see the execution video. It's not on any public forum, but it's not a secret, either. There's no risk of anything coming back to cause problems for Uri if the detective in America watches it or passes it on to their security services."

Hana felt tears of relief form in the corners of her eyes. "But that doesn't excuse what I did," she said.

Daud shook his head. "That was Jakob Brodsky, not you. I do not blame you for failing to control him, even though you promised that you would. Your boss in Atlanta was right about him, and I'll keep that in mind the rest of the time we're together."

Hana took a sip of water.

"Look at me again," Daud said.

Hana willingly obeyed.

"Do you see any condemnation or criticism in my eyes?" Daud asked.

Daud's dark eyes were pools beckoning Hana to enter without fear. "No," she sighed. "And thanks."

"You're welcome," Daud said as a big smile formed on his face. "Making you happy is my number one job."

After eating, they lingered over dark coffee as the restaurant filled with other patrons and the lights of the city twinkled more brightly on the hill across from them. When they reached the hotel, Daud turned off the car's engine and turned in his seat toward her. "You never answered my question," he said.

"Which one?"

"About taking me to Reineh to meet your father."

"We will go before I return to America."

"Return temporarily to America?" Daud asked.

"You know I love it here," Hana answered easily. "America was never a final destination."

A large smile formed on Daud's face for the second time. Hana prepared to open the car door and get out. Daud reached out and touched her arm. She faced him as he leaned close and kissed her. They kissed a second time.

"I wish we could go to Reineh right now," Hana said softly as they parted.

Daud gently stroked her cheek.

"When will I hear from you tomorrow?" she asked.

"As soon as I'm on my way back to Beit Hanina from Deir Dibwan," Daud answered. "Hopefully by midafternoon."

"Be careful."

"Always."

CHAPTER 38

Jakob slept later than he had any other morning since arriving in Israel. When he rolled out of bed, it was eight o'clock, and the sun shone brightly around the edges of the curtains. After a quick shower and shave, he went downstairs to the courtyard. Hana was drinking coffee and eating a light breakfast. She smiled as he approached.

"You look happy," Jakob said when he sat down across from her.

"I am," she replied.

"Which means you had a good dinner with Daud last night. I ended up ordering room service, which was better than I expected and worse than I'd hoped."

"What do you mean?"

"The entrée that I can't pronounce was terrible, but dessert was delicious. Do you want to torture me with the details of your meal?"

Hana told him about the food. "But I put something else on the table," she said. "Isn't that the way you say it?"

"Yes."

"I confessed to Daud that you transferred the video file to my laptop and sent it to Detective Freeman."

"I'm not surprised," Jakob replied and then let Hana explain without interruption.

"I have a confession, too," he said when Hana finished. "I misjudged Detective Freeman. He ran a facial comparison analysis and confirmed that Tawfik is the one who lifts his mask in the execution video."

"That's good," Hana began. "It means—"

"And he sent the video without my authorization to a friend who works for Homeland Security. Daud is right. The video isn't secret. Homeland Security identified the Caucasian man with the laptop. He's an American named John Caldwell who converted to radical Islam a number of years ago and now goes by the name Latif Al-Fasi. He's a professional videographer who works for terrorist groups. It's likely he edited the execution video."

Hana's eyes widened as Jakob talked. "What else did he tell you about Al-Fasi or his contacts? If he works for known groups, it might be a way to tie them to the Zadan brothers."

"Not much except that he has an ex-wife and teenage daughter who live in a town called Payson near Phoenix, Arizona. The information about Al-Fasi's contacts was redacted from the dossier Freeman received." Jakob paused. "But while you were eating your fancy lamb dish, I researched John Caldwell, aka Latif Al-Fasi, through software I bought to track down deadbeat defendants. When I entered the name Caldwell for Payson, Arizona, I received a couple of hits, one for a woman named Valerie Caldwell, formerly married to John Caldwell. She has a sixteen-year-old daughter. Valerie's employer is a film production studio with offices in Los Angeles, Berlin, and several other European cities. Apparently, she's in the video business, too. Maybe that's how she and John connected in the first place."

Hana took a sip of coffee. "It's hard to imagine her providing information to us about her ex-husband," she said.

"The key word in your sentence is 'ex-husband.' If Al-Fasi is as radicalized as he seems to be, she may be willing to talk negatively about him."

"Unless she lives in fear," Hana replied. "Maybe Daud can find out who Al-Fasi works for."

"Ask him, but I'm not waiting."

"We should coordinate our efforts," Hana said quickly. "Daud is going to call me when he's on the way back to Jerusalem from Deir Dibwan. Let's discuss it then."

Jakob grunted noncommittally. He returned to the buffet and brought back a plate filled with fruit, cheese, and pickled fish.

"This should drive the memory of last night's supper from my mind," he said.

"I'm staying with my memories," Hana replied as she nibbled a piece of melon.

They sat in silence for a few moments. Jakob ate a piece of cold herring followed by a bite of sharp cheese.

"What's on our agenda while we wait for Daud?" he asked.

"I can take you anywhere you want to go in Jerusalem."

Jakob sampled the salmon, which was milder than the herring. "You're the expert," he replied. "Let's check out one of your favorite places."

"I'll think it over and let you know."

Hana left. After Jakob finished his meal, he returned to his room and continued his research into Latif Al-Fasi. This time, he focused on the Russian internet. Not surprisingly, there were multiple hits that included what he'd found before along with similar projects. The videographer was an active participant in the preparation of Islamic fundamentalist propaganda and figured prominently in photographs with groups throughout the Islamic republics of the former Soviet Union.

· · ·

Hana stood in front of the mirror brushing her hair and thinking about where to take Jakob. Visitors could spend a month in Jerusalem and barely dent what the ancient city had to offer. Planning an outing with Jakob was also a way to keep her from worrying about Daud.

She checked on Leon, who was happily playing with two other puppies at the doggie day care center, and then composed her daily email report to Mr. Lowenstein, bringing him up-to-date on the events of the past twenty-four hours. As she typed, she was struck by how much had happened. The past day had covered a rapid series of ups, downs, and unknowns. The hectic pace they'd been keeping gave her an idea of where to take Jakob. When she stepped out of her room to the courtyard, he was waiting for her.

"Do we need a driver?" he asked. "If so, I'd like to use Wahid, the concierge's cousin."

"That's fine with me."

"Where are we going?" Jakob asked.

"A place with as much history crammed into it as anyplace in the city. Today, it's mostly peaceful, but it hasn't always been that way."

"Surprises are fine. Where is Daud by now?"

"Probably near the checkpoint on the road to Ramallah."

Thinking about Daud made Hana's heart pound. When Wahid arrived, Hana greeted him in Arabic. Their small talk back and forth took Hana's mind off her worry. After several moments, both she and Wahid laughed.

"I want to be part of any jokes," Jakob said. "Especially if you're talking about me."

"No, no," Hana replied. "Not you."

"She's teasing me about my New York Arabic," Wahid replied. "And she sounds Lebanese to me."

Wahid pulled the taxi into traffic. They made their way along the edge of the Old City to the Damascus Gate and turned onto a side street.

"There's the bus station for the Arab part of the city," Hana pointed out. "The road we're on still goes to Damascus. It's been that way for thousands of years."

Wahid pulled to the curb and stopped. Hana and Jakob got out.

"You brought me to see a bus station?" Jakob asked as Wahid drove away.

"Follow me."

They walked along a narrow sidewalk with a high wall to their left. After less than two hundred feet they reached a line of tour buses parked close together. Joining a group of twenty or so American tourists, they turned into a narrow alley and approached a group of men and boys selling postcards, tiny olive-wood camels, and other Holy Land trinkets. Multiple tourist groups from other parts of the world were waiting to enter through a small door in the stone wall.

Mingling with the tourists, Jakob looked for the older man he'd met at the Newark Airport but didn't see him. The noisy sounds of the bus station receded.

"Here we are," Hana said. "This is one of the sites where Jesus may have been crucified and buried. It's called the Garden Tomb or Gordon's Calvary, after a British general who made it famous in the 1800s."

"One of the sites?" Jakob asked. "How many are there?"

"Two primary possibilities. There is a traditional site that was identified in the fourth century by Helena, the Roman emperor Constantine's mother. And this one. No one knows for sure where the historical events actually occurred, but I like this place."

"I'm not sure the historical events happened here or anywhere else."

"Just listen and see what you think. I came here the first time on a field trip with my school when I was six years old."

Jakob felt duped. He grumpily followed Hana to the window where she paid an admission fee. The entrance reminded Jakob of something from a county fair in upstate New York he'd attended when he was a kid.

"We'll hear the lecture with this group," Hana said, pointing to the Americans who had arrived at the same time.

"Will there be a test?"

Hana smiled in response. Once past the entranceway, they entered a pleasant, enclosed garden without any religious trappings.

Interspersed through the greenery were narrow paths. An older man with a British accent introduced himself to the group and began to speak in a matter-of-fact way about the garden. Archaeologists had excavated an enormous cistern, which was common for watering gardens in first-century Jerusalem. The guide then strung together a series of verses from the New Testament, which were completely unfamiliar to Jakob. Most of the people in the tour group followed along on their Bible apps.

"Do you believe everything he's saying?" Jakob asked Hana as the guide led the group along a path to a different part of the property.

"It makes sense based on what I've read and studied."

Now that he was inside the walls, Jakob could accept Hana's nostalgic attachment to the idyllic spot in the midst of the noisy city. The guide stopped at a spot that overlooked a small rocky cliff to the left and the raucous Arab bus station to the right. He began to explain the preferred method of execution among the Jews over two thousand years ago.

"They stoned people to death," the man said. "Most of the time they pushed the condemned individual off a high place or cliff and then threw rocks on the body until they were satisfied that the person was dead. This place was a quarry, so there were a lot of rocks available, which made it a logical place of execution."

The guide pointed to the rocky cliff. "Some believe the configuration of the caves looks like a skull. That means this could be Golgotha, which means 'the place of the skull,' referred to in Matthew 27:33 and Mark 15:22."

With a little imagination, Jakob could see a misshapen skull face in the rocks.

"It makes sense that the Roman occupiers would adopt the Jewish execution site for crucifixions," the guide continued. "However, the Romans wouldn't have crucified criminals or Jewish patriots on top of a hill. No, those crucifixions were performed along busy thoroughfares as a deterrent to anyone else thinking about defying their rule. The Damascus Road below has always been a major artery into and out of the city. Thousands of people would use it every day. The Romans would line posts alongside the road and use them over and over again to crucify condemned men, who were forced to carry a crossbeam to the place of their death. It says about Jesus in the Gospel of John that 'many of the Jews read this sign, for the place where Jesus was crucified was near the city, and the sign was written in Aramaic, Latin and Greek.' Many archaeologists believe the city walls at that time were located less than two hundred yards from where we're standing."

Something the man said caught Jakob's attention, and he leaned over to Hana. "Was Jesus a Jew?"

"Yes."

Jakob thought about his time at the Western Wall. "But you're an Arab—"

"Who believes in the Jewish Messiah, just like the people from the United States, Asia, South America, and Africa you'll see here."

"How is it possible for you to believe this?" he asked Hana.

"It's by faith—"

"No, I mean if Jesus was Jewish—" Jakob stopped, not sure where his mind was going.

"Along with all the initial first-century believers in Jesus, including almost every writer of the New Testament," Hana said. "For them and me, he is the king of our hearts."

The guide spoke: "And Jesus wasn't crucified up high on a hill, as is often depicted in paintings or movies. His feet were less than a meter above the ground, which made the contact between those suffering on the cross and their loved ones watching them die more intensely personal."

As the guide described the scene, Jakob saw it all—the dirty, awful stench of death and suffering and unwashed humanity, the cruelty of one of the most brutal execution methods ever devised by evil men, the unfathomable mockery of those who taunted Jesus and demanded that he perform a miraculous sign, and the anguish of the condemned man's friends and family, who saw a person they loved and respected dying, along with their hopes, before their very eyes. Jakob's own chest tightened as the guide described the slow, suffocating death experienced as a victim's ability to force air into his lungs painfully slipped away. He winced when he learned that a soldier thrust a spear into Jesus' side, causing a mixture of blood and water to gush forth.

Symbolically carrying the dead Jesus with them, the tour group silently followed the guide past the enormous cistern to an open area that overlooked an excavated hole in the natural rock. It was a tomb.

"This tomb is old enough to be from the first century. John 19:41–42 says that 'at the place where Jesus was crucified, there was a garden, and in the garden a new tomb, in which no one had ever been laid . . . They laid Jesus there.'"

While the man talked about other Bible verses, Jakob watched people stoop to enter the tomb, stay for a few moments, and leave.

"We don't know if this is the actual tomb," the man said in an understated British manner. "But one thing we do believe is that the tomb of Jesus Christ was empty on the third day, and it's been empty ever since. Jesus rose from the dead and offers new life to everyone who repents and puts their faith in him."

The group moved down some steps and lined up for a chance to enter the tomb.

"Do you want to leave?" Hana asked. "That's the end of the lecture."

"No, I want to look, too."

He and Hana joined the line. Jakob didn't speak. For some reason it didn't seem right to do so. When it was their turn, she motioned for him to precede her.

"You first," he replied.

Jakob waited at the bottom of two wooden steps that led to the entrance. Hana emerged.

"I'll wait for you near the exit," she said.

Jakob lowered his head and entered the tomb. He found himself in an antechamber neatly chiseled out of the soft rock. To his right there were two parallel burial slabs with about three feet between them. It was a simple yet profound scene. Not wanting to stay too long because other people were outside waiting to enter, he stared for several more seconds at the empty slabs. Turning around, he saw a sign on a wooden door that read "He Is Not Here, He Is Risen." Stepping into the bright sunlight, he slowly climbed the stone steps away from the tomb.

"What did you think?" Hana asked.

"It seemed quiet and mysterious. But not in a creepy way that I would have expected with an empty tomb. It was—" He stopped.

"Holy?"

"Maybe, but I'm not exactly sure what that means."

CHAPTER 39

Hana didn't try to pry any more information from Jakob. Clearly, the tour of the Garden Tomb had touched him, and the experience needed to percolate. They retraced their steps toward the main street, now lined with even more buses. Jakob sent a text message to Wahid asking him to pick them up. A large group of Asian tourists approached, followed by at least fifty men and women from an African nation wearing their native garb and enthusiastically singing a song in an unknown language.

"You're right," Jakob said to Hana. "A lot of people visit this place."

"From all over the world."

They reached the street and found an opening in the line of buses. Wahid arrived in about ten minutes.

"Where to?" asked the driver as soon as they were settled into the old Mercedes.

"I'm leaving it up to Hana," Jakob answered.

"Do you want to go to another Christian site?" Wahid asked.

"No," Hana replied. "I have two other places in mind."

Over the next few hours they visited a model of the city of Jerusalem as it had appeared in the first century. The 1:50 scale depiction at the Israel Museum complex covered almost half an acre and revealed how massive Jerusalem was at the time of Jesus of Nazareth. From there, they drove a short distance to Yad Vashem, the Holocaust memorial.

"We can only see a small part of Yad Vashem today," Hana said as they bought tickets. "Someday, you must return."

Hana took Jakob through a few of the many exhibits and displays that documented Hitler's Final Solution. He didn't say much but lingered the longest at the interactive videos with Holocaust survivors. They visited the Children's Memorial, an audiovisual remembrance of the 1.5 million children who perished in the Holocaust, and walked slowly through a large room of flickering lights reflected in multiple mirrors and heard the names, ages, and nationalities of individual children who died. The list of the dead ran twenty-four hours a day, seven days a week, fifty-two weeks a year.

"To hear those names again, you would have to come back in several months," Hana said when they were outside. "It takes that long to repeat them all."

"The names of Russian children especially touched me," Jakob replied soberly. "Who knows? I could be related to some of them."

Hana checked her phone. There was still no message from Daud.

"I can leave now," Jakob said as he watched her. "But you're right. I'll return."

While they waited for Wahid, Jakob told Hana about overhearing the man praying in Russian at the Western Wall. Chill bumps ran over Hana's arms, but she didn't blurt out that it was a divine encounter, perhaps with an angel.

"After visiting the Garden Tomb, I understand more what he was praying," Jakob said. "And realizing that Jesus was Jewish is a big deal to me."

"Why?"

"You know that I'm secular. But it's a huge leap for a Jewish person to consider the possibility that Christianity is true."

Jakob then told her about his experience in Hurva Square and the unexpected identification with his Jewishness.

"I hesitate to share that because—"

"I'm an Arab?" Hana finished the thought.

"Yes, but you're different."

Hana knew exactly what she wanted to say. "My heritage and ethnicity isn't the most important reality that defines who I am. I'm thankful for my background and what my family has accomplished, whether persecuted by the Turks or marginalized by Israeli society. But my relationship with God through Jesus is my core. I know that's a religious statement, but it's not just a belief or an idea; it transforms everything about who I am and how I relate to all people, regardless of who they are and where they come from."

"That's something else I can't get my head around," Jakob said as Wahid's Mercedes came into view. "At least not yet."

During the drive to the hotel, Hana kept checking her phone.

"Are you worried about Daud?" Jakob asked.

Hana didn't answer. Instead, she pointed at Wahid and shook her head. Jakob sat back and looked out the window. He'd not felt as emotionally spent since the end of a four-day jury trial that had kept him up most of two nights. He checked his own phone. There was nothing significant on his office email account or any messages from Emily.

"If you want a first-class dinner in Jerusalem, I know exactly where to take you," Wahid said from the front seat. "Not many tourists go there. It is very authentic Middle Eastern cuisine. If I make the reservations, you will have the best seats in the house with great views of the Old City."

"No, thanks," Hana replied.

"What's the name of the restaurant?" Jakob asked. "I might go by myself."

Wahid gave the name. Jakob glanced at Hana.

"Never heard of it," she whispered.

"It's only been open for six months," Wahid said. "Six months from now it will be so crowded even I will have a problem getting a reservation."

"You've sold me," Jakob replied. "But will I still be welcome if I come alone?"

Wahid smiled. "Only if you give a big tip."

As they arrived at the hotel, Hana called out, "There it is!"

"What?" Jakob responded, looking around.

"Daud's Land Rover," she said as she threw open the door and dashed out of the taxi.

"You see why I eat alone," Jakob said to Wahid.

"Yes. Next time when you come to Israel, bring your girlfriend."

"I need to work on that," Jakob answered.

"When do you think you'll be ready for dinner?"

"Seven o'clock."

Jakob found Hana and Daud embracing in the courtyard. She stepped away as Jakob approached. Several other hotel guests were watching.

Daud coughed into his hand. "Let's go to Hana's room," he said.

"Did you enjoy being a tourist?" Daud asked once they were settled.

"'Enjoy' isn't the right word," Jakob answered.

"Where did you go?" Daud asked, puzzled.

"The Garden Tomb, the first-century city model, and Yad Vashem. It's going to take time for me to process what I saw and heard. If she decides to quit the practice of law, Hana would make a great tour guide."

Hana and Daud laughed.

"Can you tell us about your day?" Jakob asked Daud.

"It was long but good," the investigator replied. "Tawfik was only present for the initial meeting at the coffee shop. Nabil is right. He is more of a playboy than a fundamentalist."

"But it's Tawfik in the execution video," Jakob said. "I was able to obtain the results of a police facial recognition program that confirms it."

"I will not debate that," Daud says. "Who knows? Tawfik may be trying to forget what he has done by drinking and partying. But the men he works for want to buy the software program. They did not seem interested in hiding who they are and their goals. They are committed to militant fundamentalist ideology. When I asked about Tawfik, the one in charge said he has known him since he was a boy. He mentioned Abdul with respect as a 'brother' in their cause."

"Do you believe they are linked to any identified terrorist group?" Hana asked.

"Maybe," Daud said and turned to Jakob. "People in the US do not realize there is jealousy and competition among terrorist factions. They compete for glory in the pursuit of jihad. But these men are different. They are businessmen interested in profits to fund jihad."

"Any names?" Hana asked.

"Mostly first names, which I do not believe are true."

"Whatever their names, this is exactly the sort of group we're looking for," Jakob said.

"Only if we can link them to Abdul prior to Gloria's death and bring them under the jurisdiction of a US court," Hana said cautiously. "They may have millions of dollars or euros in a Middle Eastern or European bank, but there has to be a way to connect their enterprise to America."

"I know, I know," Jakob replied. "But you have to admit this is a positive development. Good work, Daud. What's next?"

"I need to deliver the software and see if I can obtain more information about them. When I reach the end of that process, I will have to decide whether to deliver an encrypted product or walk away."

"Financial information or personal information?" Hana asked.

"Both," Daud replied.

Daud suddenly jumped out of his chair and flung open the door to the outside. No one was there.

"Did you see or hear something?" Jakob asked in alarm.

"Maybe, but I was wrong." Daud resumed his seat. "I've been

on guard all day. I will ask the group to provide proof of funds to complete the purchase from their bank or financial institution. I will do the same on my side for the receiving bank."

"Why would they care about your bank?" Jakob asked.

"Because of the reason we are sitting in this room. They know if they transfer funds to a bank that would disclose information to an unfriendly foreign government or lawyers wanting to sue them, the deal is not worth the risk. I have a bank account in Qatar that I will use. Qatar is a major state sponsor of terrorist groups. I would not be surprised if they also use a bank there or in the UAE."

"As an Israeli citizen, how were you able to set up an account in Qatar?" Hana asked. "It's not easy to do."

"It took effort," Daud acknowledged. "But it was not the hardest thing I have done. The address on the account is not my apartment in Beit Hanina."

"What about identifying the men you met with?" Hana asked.

Daud reached in his pocket and took out a SIM card. "I took at least forty photos with a hidden camera. Aaron Levy can help identify them."

"This sounds great," Jakob said, glancing at Hana. "Speaking of photos, we need to bring Daud up-to-date on John Caldwell, aka Latif Al-Fasi."

Daud nodded several times while Jakob talked. Jakob took that to be a sign of interest.

"I will ask Aaron about him, too," Daud said when Jakob finished.

"Will that do any good?" Jakob asked. "Levy should have known Al-Fasi was in the video transferred from the laptops seized at the Zadan residence, but he didn't tell us about it."

"Just be patient while I talk to him."

"I'll try," he said, standing up. "In the meantime, I'm going out to dinner alone."

"No, no," Daud replied. "I want you and Hana to join me for

dinner tonight at my apartment. I have already made arrangements for a private chef and his staff to prepare the meal."

"A private chef?" Hana asked, her eyes wide.

"I don't want to crash your party," Jakob said.

"Hana would prefer a chaperone, correct?"

"Uh, sure," Hana replied with a nod. "I know it makes no sense to an American, but Daud is right. I'd like you to be there, too."

"Wahid will be upset," Jakob said.

"Wahid?" Daud asked.

"Our driver for the day," Hana answered. "Jakob, tell Wahid that the three of us will eat dinner at this new restaurant later in the week. That will make him happy."

"Okay," Jakob said reluctantly. "But I have no experience as a chaperone."

"I will send Ensanullah to pick you up at six thirty," Daud said.

"I thought you had fired him," Jakob ventured.

"We worked through what happened. In our business, we need each other's help more than a disagreement."

CHAPTER 40

After Daud left, Hana made a short video and sent it to Sadie. She included a panorama of the courtyard and told the little girl how much she missed her. Before ending the recording, she asked Sadie to make a video and send it to her.

As she got ready for dinner, Hana thought about the extravagant expense of hiring a private chef and his staff to prepare a meal. She didn't love or hate money, but since landing her first job, she'd tried to live a lifestyle that didn't violate her conscience. Daud had a different filter, a fact they would have to discuss.

Hana put on the other nice dress she'd brought on the trip. It was green with a lower-cut back than she usually wore. A single strand of pearls hung around her neck. If she needed to dress up again during the trip, she decided she would have to buy a fancy new outfit. Hana stopped. How could she be concerned about Daud's extravagance and do the same thing herself? She straightened her shoulders and resolved to wear the blue dress again if the situation arose.

There was a knock at her door. Hana quickly threw a scarf around her shoulders before opening it. Jakob and a stocky young Arab man stood outside.

"I'm Ensanullah Al-Amuli," he said. "Daud sent me to fetch you and the American."

Hana introduced herself. She could quickly tell that Ensanullah didn't approve of the way she was dressed.

"I'm ready," she said in English.

Ensanullah was driving Daud's new BMW.

"What happened to your other car?" Jakob asked. "You drove me around in a subcompact."

"This belongs to Daud."

Jakob looked at Hana and nodded approvingly. "More proof that being a private investigator in Israel is the way to go."

Hana and Jakob sat in the rear seat. Ensanullah sped through the streets to Beit Hanina.

"If he wrecks, Daud will be furious," Hana whispered to Jakob.

"He's good behind the wheel," Jakob replied in a low voice. "He's been trained."

By the time they reached Daud's apartment, the sun was disappearing beneath the rooftops of the nearby buildings. Ensanullah parked in a private space behind the building. He held the door open for Hana. She clutched the scarf tightly around her and hoped it covered her bare back.

"Thanks," Jakob said to the driver. "I hope to see you again."

Ensanullah responded with a formal Arabic good-bye that included the phrase "May Allah be with you."

Hana translated.

"Say it again, please," Jakob said to Ensanullah.

He did so, and Jakob repeated the phrase with only a minor slip-up. Ensanullah smiled, and the two men shook hands. Hana and Jakob entered the apartment building.

"Ensanullah likes you," Hana said.

"So long as I stay in America."

As they climbed the stairs, Jakob told Hana about his previous conversation with the driver.

"Daud wouldn't work with Ensanullah if he didn't trust him," Hana said.

They reached the apartment and Jakob rang the bell. A teenage Arab boy wearing a tuxedo opened the door and ushered them in. The living area had been transformed into a dining room with a table set for three, covered with a white linen tablecloth, candles, and sparkling silver place settings. Daud appeared wearing a light gray jacket.

"Hana, you look beautiful," he said with a wide smile. "How was the ride with Ensanullah? Did he scare you?"

"I was worried about the car," Hana answered.

"I liked it," Jakob said.

"He is a very good driver," Hana said.

Several people were working in the kitchen. The chef, an older man with a large mustache, came out to greet them.

"Ali has everything prepared," Daud said. "He and his staff are going to leave, and I'll serve you myself."

"I told Daud I should wait on you," Ali said in English. "But he insisted that he do it himself. If he makes a mistake, blame it on him!"

With a wry smile, Hana answered, "I will."

Several minutes later the chef and his crew left. There were silver platters on the counters in the kitchen.

"What's on the menu?" Jakob asked.

"We will start with three appetizers," Daud replied. "Eggplant dip, cranberry labneh, and miniature meat pies."

"Let me help," Hana offered.

"No," Daud said and raised his hand. "This is the way I want to do this."

He returned to the kitchen. There was a knock on the front door.

"Please check that," Daud said. "It's probably Ali or one of his staff who forgot something."

Hana was sitting closer to the door than Jakob. When she opened it, several men rushed inside, knocking her to the floor. She ended up lying on her stomach with someone on her back forcing her face against the hard floor. Someone else grabbed her hands, forcing them together. Hana tried an evasive maneuver to break free and was able to kick one of the men very hard in the side of the head. He grunted and fell backward. However, two more replaced him, and before she could attempt anything else, her wrists were bound together with a plastic tie that cut into her skin, causing her to cry out in pain.

"Quiet or you die!" a male voice commanded in Arabic.

Hana closed her mouth and tried to wiggle free, but the hand on her head pressed down harder, smashing her face against the tiles. Other voices in the apartment were yelling in Arabic. She couldn't make out Daud's voice in the chaos of the moment.

"Stop! That's not—" She heard Jakob call out and then suddenly go quiet.

Someone flipped Hana onto her back and dragged her by her feet into the dining area. The table where she and Jakob had been sitting was flipped over. All the men were dressed in black. Hana looked around and saw a man with a red splotch on the side of his face. It had to be the man she'd kicked. He looked familiar, and she suddenly realized who he was—Tawfik Zadan. Another man standing nearby roughly forced her head downward.

"Look at the floor or I'll cut your eyes out!" he threatened in Arabic.

Hana fixed her gaze on the floor at her feet. Pieces of broken glass and china lay everywhere within her line of sight. A pair of hands tied a gag across her mouth.

"Bring him over here and put them back-to-back," another voice said.

She felt a body press against her back, followed by more plastic ties that bound her arms to the arms of the body behind her. The other person groaned. Hana suspected it was Jakob, but she dared not steal a look to find out. The men in the apartment continued to shout at one another about securing the area. There was still no sound of Daud, and Hana feared the worst. As the only real threat to the attackers, he would be the one most likely to be killed immediately. Hot tears stung her eyes and rolled down her cheeks as she kept her gaze fixed on the floor. The voices died down. A man with an unusual Arabic accent spoke.

"Do you have their cell phones?" he asked.

"Yes," another voice answered.

"Bring them here."

A moment later Hana heard the sound of splintering glass and plastic. The person bound to her jerked slightly.

"What—" he began.

"Quiet!" yelled a man in English. "Look at the floor! Gag him!"

"Okay, okay," Jakob mumbled.

Hana felt Jakob shift his weight against her and then grow still. Her heart, which had been pounding since she was knocked to the floor, began to slow down. Blinking back her tears, she focused on her sense of hearing. Men were moving around the apartment. She tried to remember details of the layout.

"Here are all the computers I could find," a new voice said. "They belong to Hasan."

The mention of Daud's name caused another wave of tears to flow from Hana's eyes.

"Bring him to me," the man with the unusual accent said.

Hana closed her eyes and offered a silent prayer of thanks that Daud was still alive.

• • •

The fuzziness that fogged Jakob's mind began to clear. He wasn't sure if he'd been knocked unconscious or merely stunned by a blow to the left side of his head. He heard the sound of breaking glass and mumbled. Someone gruffly ordered him to be quiet in English and to stare at the floor. Jakob twitched. He thought there might be blood running down the side of his face, but with his hands bound together he couldn't be sure. Jakob knew one of his fingers had been sliced by broken china in the initial melee because it was stinging with pain.

He suspected he was bound to Hana. As his mind cleared, he became more aware of his surroundings. Hana wasn't making a sound. Jakob didn't hear Daud.

At least eight men had crashed through the door of the apartment. Jakob saw them knock Hana to the floor, and he had jumped to his feet. Out of the corner of his eye, he saw Daud pull open a drawer in the kitchen and pull out a large knife. At that moment, Jakob's world went dark, whether for only a few seconds or longer, he didn't know. When he came to, his hands were bound behind him, and he was tied to Hana. He assumed the men were speaking Arabic. The most prevalent voice he heard came from the direction of the kitchen, but there were other voices calling out from different parts of the apartment. Jakob closed his eyes. If he died, he hoped there was something better beyond this life.

Suddenly, Jakob heard a sound that caught his attention and caused him to sit up straighter. Someone was speaking in Russian.

"Talk in Russian," the man said. "None of these men understand it. They do what they're told and believe it is for the glory of Allah and the goal of jihad."

"You've made a stupid mistake," another man replied. "And there's no turning back. This is going to change everything."

Jakob licked his lips. There was no mistaking the voice of the second speaker—it was Daud.

"I'm following orders," the first man replied. "And you're the one who flew too close to the flame."

"Anzor, I had everything under control. Weren't you paying attention yesterday in Deir Dibwan? I laid out a perfect plan that would eliminate the problem and keep everything hidden from the Israelis and the Americans. Now, my first priority is to find a way to protect my own cover. You'll have to deal with this mess without my help."

Jakob remembered the snippet of conversation in Russian when he had eavesdropped at the hotel and now wished he'd heard more.

"We pay you a lot of money for your services," Anzor replied. "And that gives my brothers the right to tell you what to do. If your cover is blown, you'll have to leave this fancy apartment and your expensive cars and go where they tell you for a new assignment. Do you have a problem with that?"

"If I do, I will take it up with them, not you."

"Don't get smart with me," Anzor replied. "I'm the one holding a gun."

"And you wouldn't dare use it because that would cost you your own head."

"Listen," Anzor said. "You'll escape and look like a hero."

"Who shouldn't have left himself open to a surprise attack," Daud answered. "At least let me handle that part of the operation. I know how the Israelis think better than you do, and I can figure out the best way to sell my story. You may have to give me a black eye to make it look genuine."

"Gladly."

"What's the plan for the hostages?"

"Do you care? I know you've been spending a lot of time with the woman."

"She means nothing to me."

"We'll kill her."

Daud was quiet for a moment. "I have a better idea," he said. "Throw her in the back of a truck and send her to your headquarters in the mountains near Vladikavkaz. She would be a great prize for a commander's harem."

Anzor laughed sharply. "Risky, but it would be a bold move. If she is as smart as you say she is, it will be easy for her to learn the language and live in submission without too many beatings."

"And the American Jew?" Daud asked.

"He dies. We'll make it look like an accident."

"Then finish the job properly," Daud replied. "It's been botched twice."

Nausea swept over Jakob—for himself, for Hana, and because of the level of deceit perpetrated by Daud. He strained against the bands binding his wrists, but the thick plastic didn't budge. The voices moved away as the two men left the kitchen. Jakob felt Hana trembling uncontrollably against his back. Even though she didn't speak Russian, she had certainly recognized Daud's voice.

• • •

When Hana realized that Daud was communicating with one of their captors in a foreign language, she hoped he was trying to find a way to save their lives. But as she continued to listen, something about his tone of voice didn't fit that scenario. Daud was intense and argumentative but sounded more frustrated than fearful. Hana began to tremble from the shock of capture. Daud and the other man moved away, continuing their conversation. Hana shut her eyes and prayed.

Suddenly, she and Jakob were grabbed and lifted to their feet. Upright and wobbly, Hana had a chance to view their captors. Tawfik was no longer in the room. She and Jakob were surrounded by four men, one of whom spit in her face and cursed her in Arabic as a loose woman. The spittle ran down her left cheek. Another man took out a long knife and pressed it firmly against her neck.

An incredible calm washed over Hana as the ancient Aramaic word for "peace"—*shlama*—echoed through her soul. She managed to stand more upright and stared into the man's eyes as she waited for his next act. Death might be an end, but she knew it was also a beginning.

And in that moment the grace of the martyrs was hers. One slash of the knife and Hana knew without a doubt she would be in a place of never-ending peace and joy. The man pressed the blade harder against her neck. But then, instead of slitting her throat, the man jerked the knife away and severed the plastic ties that bound her to Jakob.

Two men dragged her across the floor. Hana wasn't able to make eye contact with Jakob, who was dragged toward the bedroom nearest the front door of the apartment. Hana was hauled into another room and forced to the floor. Her arms were bound to the metal leg of a large chrome desk. The smaller of the two men slipped a black plastic tie over her ankles and pulled it tight. Standing up, he ran his fingers through his hair. Sweat was pouring down his face. The men turned off the lights and left her alone in the dark.

As her eyes adjusted, Hana inspected the room, which was Daud's home office. There was a single window in the opposite wall. The blackout blind was rolled down, and only a narrow sliver of light illuminated the edge. Computer cords were lying on the floor near her feet. Now that she was alone, her confidence in Daud began to return. The language he spoke to the other man sounded like Russian or another Slavic language, but she wasn't one hundred percent sure. Daud had never told her how many languages he spoke. It was one of the countless items to discover in a lifetime together.

As she sat motionless in the dark, Hana knew that Daud would do anything he could to save her life. Closing her eyes, she prayed for strength and courage no matter what she faced. She prayed the same prayer for Daud and Jakob. Time passed. The pain caused by the plastic ties became more familiar. The door opened and someone turned on the lights, temporarily blinding her. When she could see more clearly, two men stood before her. One was Tawfik, who touched the side of his face and glared at her. The other man was clearly Caucasian. He spoke to Tawfik in Arabic. "Remove the gag."

Hana felt the hands of the young man who'd been present when his brother killed Gloria Neumann press against the back of her head. Once the gag was gone, she took a few deep breaths through her mouth.

The man in charge spoke to her in Arabic. "Hana Abboud, you are going to live and not die," the man said. "But do not speak unless I give you permission to do so."

Hana nodded slightly. She recognized the speaker's accent because of her contact with immigrants who had flooded Israel after the collapse of the Soviet Union.

"Good. I am going to ask you some questions. Tell me the truth or you will suffer greatly. You will not die, but you will suffer so much pain that you will wish you were dead. I already know some of the answers to my questions, so do not try to trick me."

Hana's mouth was dry, and she wasn't sure she could speak without croaking out her words.

"Tell me where your family lives."

Hana had been prepared to answer any question, but the possibility of harm coming to her family suddenly kept her mouth shut.

"I'm not going to wait long," the man said.

"Reineh," she managed.

"And like you, they are Christian infidels."

"We believe that Jesus Christ is Lord."

At the profession of her faith, some of the calm Hana had felt when the knife threatened her throat returned. She studied the man's face more closely. He was in his thirties with sandy brown hair, narrow lips, and a clean-shaven face, unusual for a radical Muslim. He placed a cell phone on the glass table above Hana's head.

"I am going to record our conversation. Tell me everything you know about Gloria Neumann."

"I'm not sure what you mean—"

The man motioned to Tawfik, who took a cigarette lighter from the front pocket of his pants and flicked it on. He leaned over and held it close enough to Hana's nose that she could smell the flame. She strained backward with her head to the side to avoid getting burned.

"Tell me everything," the man repeated as Tawfik kept the lighter in front of Hana's face. "I'll decide whether it's important."

"Yes," Hana said.

"Good."

Tawfik released his thumb from the lighter, and the flame went out.

"Get her some water," the man said to Tawfik.

Tawfik returned with a bottle of water. The Caucasian man unscrewed the top and tipped the bottle up so Hana could take a drink. She savored the liquid in her mouth before letting it run down her throat.

"Start at the beginning and leave nothing out."

Hana started with the initial meeting at Collins, Lowenstein, and Capella. It was bizarre talking about the fancy conference room while bound and in pain. When she mentioned Abdul, Tawfik took a step forward, but the other man put out his hand to restrain him.

"Obey or you leave," he barked at Tawfik, who glared at Hana but stood still.

"Go ahead."

Hana talked about everything except Sadie. When the first sentence about the child formed in her mind, she quickly moved past it and did the same with each encounter, trying not to break the rhythm of her voice. Finally, she tossed in a comment that they had made a tactical decision not to include the child in a potential lawsuit because of her young age. Her interrogator remained silent. Several times he gave her another drink of water. After the third drink, he told Tawfik to leave.

"Relieve Achmed in the room where the Jew is held and tell him to go to the balcony."

"But I want to—" Tawfik began to protest, taking out the cigarette lighter.

"Go!"

With a final glare at Hana, Tawfik handed the lighter to Hana's interrogator and left the room.

"Tell me about your investigation," the man said.

When describing her initial trip to Israel to interview Daud and Sahir, Hana desperately wanted to shield Daud but instinctively knew it would be impossible to do so. She revealed everything except the budding romantic relationship between them. Upon shifting back to Atlanta, Hana left out Sadie's birthday party but included Jakob's interaction with Detective Freeman and Emily Johnson. She was beginning to summarize the investigation of the past few days when she heard a sound behind her and paused.

"Someone wants to see you," her interrogator said. "He's been listening the whole time."

A figure came into view to her left. To Hana's shock, it was Daud. He looked at her with such an absence of feeling that it made her wonder if he was another man. She felt a mixture of confusion and horror wash over her face. The man spoke to Daud in Arabic.

"Has she been telling me the truth?"

"She didn't tell you that she wants to marry me," Daud replied.

The man flicked on the cigarette lighter. "And I warned her of painful consequences if she left anything out."

"No!" Hana screamed.

"Do as you like," Daud said, his eyes dead.

The man held the flame close to Hana's bare right foot. She silently appealed to Daud, who seemed about to step forward but didn't. The man extinguished the flame and stood up.

Hana's eyes frantically went back and forth between Daud and her questioner as she struggled to absorb what was happening.

"Should we keep her here any longer?" the man asked Daud.

"Only until we finish questioning Brodsky," Daud said. "Something may come up that she's tried to hide from us. In that case, you should certainly teach her a stricter lesson."

"Daud, please," Hana started.

Before she could say anything else, Daud leaned over and struck Hana's jaw with the back of his hand.

"Don't speak to me!" he yelled.

Tears gushing from her eyes, Hana's lower lip trembled. The room became blurry. The two men left.

• • •

Jakob lay with his face to the floor. Out of the corner of his eye, he could see the feet of the man sent to guard him. The guard was wearing expensive Nike basketball shoes. Every so often, he nudged Jakob with his foot.

Jakob desperately wanted to live, but it was a hopeless situation. To distract himself, he thought about his parents, his friends, Emily, Ben, and anyone else who came to mind. He imagined how they would react to the news of his death. Whatever method these men used to kill him wouldn't be accepted as accidental. Too many people knew Jakob had been stalked like a hunted animal from one side of the world to another. Maybe someday those responsible would be brought to justice. Especially Daud Hasan, whose level of betrayal transcended all other manifestations of evil.

Jakob's guard jerked him to his feet and shoved him into a chair. The sudden movement, along with the effects of the earlier blow to his head, made the room spin for a few moments. When Jakob's vision stabilized, Daud stood in front of him flanked by two other men. One of the men looked familiar, and Jakob soon realized it was Tawfik Zadan.

"Tawfik," he said before he could stop himself.

"Shut up, Jewish swine!" Tawfik yelled at him in English.

Jakob closed his mouth. The other man spoke in heavily accented English. "You are a prisoner of the military arm of the Abu Azzam Brigade. I am Anzor Varayev, a commander of the army operating in Palestine."

Jakob's eyes darted from Anzor to Daud. Daud's expression revealed nothing. Anzor motioned to the investigator.

"I have interrogated Hasan and the woman," he said. "Now it is your turn. Tell me everything you know about the death of the American Jewish woman and the martyrdom of Abdul Zadan."

Knowing they had already decided his fate, Jakob's mind was racing through what to do and say. The only thought that came to his mind was to delay as long as possible.

"I will start at the beginning," he responded.

After fifteen minutes he was still describing his efforts to find cocounsel to assist in the case.

"Enough!" Anzor threw up his hand. "You are wasting my time. Gag him and take him to the room with the woman."

"Don't you want to hear about John Caldwell?" Jakob asked, desperately trying to come up with something that might catch Anzor's attention.

Anzor held up his hand to stop Tawfik, who was approaching Jakob. "What did you say?" Anzor asked.

"John Caldwell, also known as Latif Al-Fasi."

Agitated, Anzor turned to Daud and spoke in Russian. "Did you know about this?"

"No. I would have reported it to the brothers immediately."

Puzzled at Daud's denial, Jakob tried not to show that he understood the exchange between the two men. Anzor turned his attention to Jakob and spoke in English: "Tell me about this Latif Al-Fasi."

Jakob again tried to prolong the time needed to reveal the information. Anzor interrupted when he described the appearance of Al-Fasi on the video seized from the computer at the Zadan residence.

"I've told him to be more careful," Anzor said in Russian to Daud. "Is this true?"

"Yes," Daud replied. "But I was unaware that Al-Fasi had been identified. If this idiot found out, then the Israelis and Americans already know. Where is Al-Fasi?"

"In Los Angeles meeting with Simi Valley Productions, the company we use to transfer resources to fund our work in the West."

Anzor spoke to Jakob in English: "Hasan says you did not tell him about this. Is that true?"

It was a moment Jakob had been anticipating ever since Daud lied to Anzor about Al-Fasi. His internal debate had been fierce—contradict the investigator and it would deservedly put Daud's life in greater danger, or go along with the lie and see why Daud deceived Anzor. Jakob avoided looking at the investigator.

"I never trusted Daud," Jakob replied. "Hana Abboud was in love with him and believed everything he told her. I withheld the information."

Anzor grunted. "What else did you hide from Hasan?"

Jakob described how he had violated Daud's instructions and forwarded the video to Detective Freeman for evaluation. "I sent it to my detective friend in America, and he passed it on to Homeland Security. They identified Al-Fasi and sent the detective a dossier with information about him."

Anzor said a curse word in Russian. Jakob stopped.

"Go ahead," Anzor said curtly. "Leave out nothing."

"Ms. Abboud told Daud what I did even though I instructed her not to," Jakob said and stopped.

"Does she know about Latif Al-Fasi?"

"Yes."

Anzor looked at Daud and spoke in Russian: "Stay here. I'm going to ask the woman about this. I should have let her finish earlier before you interrupted."

Anzor left. Daud turned to Tawfik and said something in Arabic. Tawfik nodded. Daud then quickly left the room with a sideways glance at Jakob, whose heart was pounding out of his chest. Tawfik took a knife from his pocket and faced Jakob.

CHAPTER 41

Exhausted and devastated, Hana could barely mumble a prayer. Her jaw ached where Daud had struck her, but it wasn't the physical pain of the blow that penetrated to the core of her being. It was the malevolent intent behind it. Everything she had thought true about Daud was false. The door opened, and her interrogator returned. Hana shrank back.

"Tell me what you know about Latif Al-Fasi," he demanded in Arabic.

"Uh, he's an American who films and edits execution videos," she said.

"More! I'm losing patience with you!"

Hana spoke as rapidly as she could. "He appeared in a video on a computer seized at the Zadan house in Deir Dibwan. Men were hunted down by masked teenage boys and killed. It was a video within a video. I do not know if that makes sense, but—"

"How did you and the American Jew identify Al-Fasi?" the man interrupted.

"Jakob sent the video to a police detective in Atlanta, and the US authorities identified Al-Fasi."

The man stared hard at Hana for several seconds. "Did you report this to Daud Hasan?"

"Yes. It was yesterday or today. I can't remember exactly."

Rage flew across the man's face. Hana closed her eyes to avoid what she feared was coming. The man yelled something Hana didn't understand. She opened her eyes as he turned toward the door to leave.

At that instant a massive boom shook the walls of the apartment and caused pieces of the ceiling to fall. Hana's first thought was that someone had detonated a suicide vest. Her interrogator covered his ears with his hands and stumbled toward the door. Before he reached it, two men wearing helmets and military uniforms burst into the room. They knocked the man to the floor and one of them pressed the muzzle of a rifle to his head while the other grabbed his hands and secured them behind his back with metal handcuffs. Although her ears were still ringing loudly, Hana heard gunshots from elsewhere in the apartment.

The soldier holding the gun to the man's head looked at her and yelled something in Hebrew, but she couldn't understand what he said. The other man was emptying the Caucasian man's pockets. Hana saw the lighter along with a handgun. The soldier ripped off the man's shirt to determine if he was wearing a suicide vest.

"Who are you?" she called out in Hebrew.

The soldier pointed to a patch on his uniform. She recognized it as the insignia of a special forces unit in the IDF. Hana closed her eyes in gratitude. The dust swirling in the room made her cough. She heard more gunshots. Then everything grew quiet. Another soldier entered the room, knelt beside her, took a knife from his belt, and cut the ties binding her wrists, arms, and ankles. Hana cried out in pain, and the young soldier looked at her with concern.

"Thank you, thank you, thank you," she repeated.

The soldier left. Hana rubbed her wrists gingerly. The two soldiers jerked Hana's interrogator to his feet and dragged him from the room. He didn't make eye contact with her. The other soldier who had unbound her reentered the room and spoke to her. "Can you walk?" he asked in Hebrew.

"I think so," Hana answered as she rose unsteadily to her feet but then plopped back down onto the floor.

"Stay there," the man replied. "I'll send a medic."

Hana moved her legs carefully several times while she waited. A young Jewish woman entered the room and closed the door.

"What did they do to you?" the woman asked in Hebrew.

Hana explained, and the woman checked her. Anything other than minimal movement of Hana's hands caused shooting pains in her hands and wrists.

"I hope it's temporary nerve pain," the medic said.

"What about the American? Is he okay?"

"He was shot and is on his way to the hospital. I don't know the seriousness of his wounds, but he was conscious when I saw him."

Hana's lower lip trembled as she struggled to maintain her composure. "What about the terrorists?"

"Neutralized or in custody," the woman answered, rising from the floor.

The door opened, and a man entered. It was Daud. There was blood on the front of his shirt.

"No!" Hana screamed.

The medic spun around.

"It's not what you think," Daud said in Hebrew. "I contacted the Shin Bet and let them know we were hostages. That's why the soldiers are here."

"He's lying!" Hana said to the medic who stood between her and Daud. "I want to speak to your commanding officer!"

"I'll get him," Daud said and left the room.

"He betrayed us and struck me in the face," Hana said to the medic, frantically pointing to her cheek. "He needs to be arrested!"

"I don't know who he is," the woman answered. "Colonel Tarif is in charge of the operation."

Hana was trembling with rage and fear. Daud was such a smooth talker that she knew he could turn the situation in his favor.

A middle-aged Druze man with a thick mustache and wearing a military uniform entered the room. He spoke first to the medic. "Is she able to talk to me?" he asked.

"Yes," the medic answered.

"Leave us," the officer said. "And tell no one to interrupt."

The medic left the room and closed the door behind her.

"I'm Colonel Tarif," the man said to Hana in Hebrew.

"Don't believe anything Daud Hasan tells you," Hana said breathlessly. "He was collaborating with the terrorists who took us hostage. Arrest him immediately."

"I can't do that," the officer answered. "Mr. Hasan is authorized to be here."

"But he is working with the terrorists! Were you able to talk to Jakob Brodsky before they took him to the hospital? He saw it all and will verify what I'm saying!"

"One of my staff interviewed him briefly, but I can't tell you what he said."

"Then what can you tell me? You have no idea how manipulative and deceptive Hasan can be!"

"The area is secure, and you are no longer in danger."

"Not as long as Daud Hasan is free! It's not secure, and I'm still in danger!"

Colonel Tarif stepped to the door, opened it, and motioned to someone outside. Daud entered.

"What are you authorized to tell Ms. Abboud?" the colonel asked Daud, who eyed Hana cautiously.

Hana could not believe what was happening, but it was clear no one was going to listen to her. "Please, get me out of here," she begged Tarif.

"I was speaking in Russian to Anzor, the man in charge of the terrorists," Daud said to Hana. "He's originally from Chechnya. If Colonel Tarif and his unit hadn't arrived when they did, Jakob would have been killed and you would have been sent to Chechnya and—"

"What?"

"Been forced into a marriage with a commander in the local Islamic militia. It was my suggestion as a way to keep you alive until you could be rescued."

Hana stared at Daud. "I don't believe a word you're saying," she said, her voice trembling.

Daud glanced at Colonel Tarif. "Leave me with her alone."

"No!" Hana said to the officer. "Please, no!"

After hesitating a few seconds, the colonel turned away. "We'll need to go soon so you can be debriefed," he said to Daud.

"I understand."

Tarif left, leaving Hana glaring at Daud. "There's nothing you can say—" she began and stopped as Daud knelt down on the floor at her feet.

"I'm going to make sure you learn enough of the truth that you'll know I would never do anything to harm or hurt you."

"You hit me!" Hana responded, pointing to her face.

"I had to convince Anzor there was nothing between us to keep him from becoming suspicious of my loyalties and killing you."

"You convinced me of your loyalties!"

Daud looked down at the floor for a moment before responding. "I haven't been completely truthful with you from the first time we met. My role here is much more complicated than you or Jakob realized. I believed I could walk a tightrope and serve my country and your client, but I fell, and it almost destroyed us all. That's all I can say for now."

"I'm going to do everything I can to make you pay for what you've done!" Hana yelled. "Leave, now!"

Daud slowly rose to his feet and their eyes met. There was no lingering evidence of the deadly gaze he'd given her moments before, but the memory of it remained burned into her mind.

• • •

Jakob closed his eyes for a moment. A dead terrorist lay sprawled on the floor of the room. People in real life didn't die like they did in the movies. Even though the man had been fatally shot, his body continued to twitch. A medic knelt and checked Jakob's left leg. He cut away the cloth to reveal the wound left by a bullet that had nicked Jakob's thigh on its way into the abdomen of one of the terrorists.

After he was hit, Jakob had fallen to the floor and stayed there with his eyes closed until the shooting stopped. When he raised his head, Tawfik was gone, and the wounded terrorist was bleeding out on the floor. The time from the initial boom of the concussion grenades as the special forces troops burst into the apartment until the final gunshot was less than a minute.

An hour later, Jakob was receiving treatment in a military hospital. His left leg numb from multiple shots of anesthetic, he watched the Israeli doctor stitch up the wound.

"How many stitches did it take?" he asked the doctor, who had told Jakob he'd immigrated to Israel from New Jersey.

"About thirty."

Jakob thought about the thirty-seven stitches that closed the wound on Sadie Neumann's face.

"You'll be sore. Limit your activities for a couple of weeks and avoid lifting anything over fifteen pounds. I gave you a shot of antibiotic and will write a prescription. The nurse will provide written instructions about wound care. You won't be running any marathons for a while."

"I never wanted to run one," Jakob answered. "What about Hana Abboud, the other hostage? How is she?"

"They brought her in a few minutes ago."

"Was she shot or seriously injured?"

"She wasn't shot. I'm not sure about her medical status."

"I'd like to see her."

"I'll find out if that can be arranged."

The doctor left. Now that he was no longer in imminent danger of dying, Jakob missed his cell phone. Sitting on the bed, he felt completely isolated from the rest of the world. He touched his ears in a vain effort to stop the ringing and rubbed his eyes. There was no removing his memory of the scene in the apartment. A male nurse entered his cubicle.

"Mr. Brodsky? Do you want to see Ms. Abboud?"

"Yes," Jakob replied, preparing to lower his leg to the floor and stand.

"No, no," the nurse said, holding up his hand. "I'll bring her to you."

A few moments later the curtain was pulled back and Hana slowly entered. She was still wearing the green dress, but her fancy shoes had been replaced by hospital slippers. She shuffled forward. Her hair was a mess. Seeing Hana alive, Jakob felt hot tears rush to the corners of his eyes and stream down his cheeks.

"I don't know where those came from," he said, clearing his throat and wiping away the tears. "But boy, am I glad to see you."

Hana sat in a plastic chair and eyed the bandage on Jakob's thigh. He told her what had happened. While he talked Hana's face remained as impassive as a stone statue. He suspected she was experiencing shock.

"What about you?" he asked.

"After we were separated, I spent most of my time alone with the man they called Anzor until the soldiers came." Hana paused and gingerly touched the discolored place on her cheek.

"Daud did this to me. Now he wants me to believe he wasn't cooperating with the terrorists."

"I think he may be telling the truth."

Hana looked up. "Why?"

As best he could, Jakob pieced together the conversations he'd overheard between Daud and Anzor. He hesitated when he reached the part about plans for his death and Hana's enslavement in Chechnya but told her anyway.

"I already know," Hana said. "Daud admitted it but claimed it was a way to keep me alive."

"That wasn't clear to me at the time," Jakob said. "The key information had to do with Latif Al-Fasi. Daud didn't want Anzor to know that we'd identified Al-Fasi and linked him to Tawfik and Abdul. When I brought up Al-Fasi's name, Anzor stormed out of the room to question you about Daud's knowledge of the situation. That's when the soldiers arrived."

Hana slowly lifted her right hand and brushed a strand of hair away from her face. "I'm not sure what to think or feel," she said. "Daud claims he was some sort of double agent working for Israel. If that's the case, his cover is blown, because the terrorists who were captured will soon spread the word that Daud wasn't arrested."

"His life will be in danger every time he steps onto the street."

"You know what that feels like."

Jakob remembered Anzor's comment about Simi Valley Productions and told Hana about it. "That's something we should check out," he said. "It might be—"

"My mind can't go there yet," Hana interrupted. "I'm still in shock about Daud."

Jakob thought for a moment. He spoke slowly. "Even though I have questions, I suspect Daud is on the right side. I mean, somehow he got word to the government that we were hostages."

"Unless it came from someone else."

"Who?"

"I don't know!" Hana answered with frustration in her voice.

They sat in silence for a few moments.

"Are you spending the night in the hospital?" Jakob asked.

"No. As soon as they release me, I'll go back to the hotel."

It was a natural statement, but the normality of it jarred Jakob. "Are you sure that's a good idea?"

"Colonel Tarif, the commander of the soldiers, told me security officers will establish a secure perimeter around the hotel. He also asked me not to talk to anyone about what happened. I desperately want to call my family even if only to hear their voices—" Hana stopped as fresh tears coursed down her cheeks. Even in his own pain, Jakob wished he could comfort her.

"A specialist is going to check my ears that have been ringing like crazy," Jakob said, then stopped.

Hana wiped her eyes with the back of her hand. "My ears stopped ringing after an hour or so, but you were closer to the initial concussion explosions than I was."

Hana struggled slightly as she rose to her feet. Jakob eyed her with sorrow and pity. "Hana," he said, "I'm sorry I contacted Leon Lowenstein and dragged you into this mess."

"You didn't see this coming," she said and sighed. "And I made a choice, too. Mr. Collins and Mr. Lowenstein left it up to me as to whether to help you or not."

They were silent for a moment. Jakob was glad for the quiet of a safe place. "We'll find out the truth about Daud," he said.

Hana turned to go. "Don't bother. It won't make a difference."

CHAPTER 42

Every cell of her being exhausted, back at the hotel Hana slipped on a nightgown, crawled into bed, and pulled the sheet up to her chin. She woke several times during the night when she moved her hands or feet in a way that caused pain. Otherwise, she was blessed with no nightmares. In the morning, she took a shower and stood beneath the water a long time to cleanse body and soul. The warm, soothing water helped more than she thought possible. After getting dressed, she turned on the local news, which reported a raid on a terrorist cell in Beit Hanina that resulted in the death of an unidentified terrorist. There was no mention of what really took place.

Getting dressed, she cautiously opened the door of her room to a pleasant day with a clear sky. She made her way to the courtyard and sat alone with a cup of coffee and only a few pieces of fruit on a plate. She had no appetite. An Israeli man about her own age approached and spoke to her in Hebrew.

"Good morning," he said. "My name is Yosef. Aaron Levy sent me to see you. I'd like to talk to you if you feel up to it."

"Do you have any official identification?"

The man produced a card that looked genuine. He spoke with a Moroccan accent, possibly indicating a Sephardic heritage.

"Okay," Hana answered, returning the card. "Are you going to record our conversation?"

"With your permission."

"I guess so," she sighed. "You're polite for someone who's going to interrogate me."

"Not so much interrogate as discuss," he replied, leaning closer. "You are aware of sensitive information, and we want to manage it wisely. Have you spoken to anyone about what happened last night in Beit Hanina?"

"Only Colonel Tarif and Jakob Brodsky," she said, then paused. "And Daud Hasan, whom I don't trust."

"Would you be willing to keep what happened yesterday and last night confidential for the time being?"

"Is there a news blackout? The report on channel 2 didn't tell much at all."

"Our request isn't limited to media."

"There are people who need to know," Hana replied slowly. "I have family in Reineh, and I'm here working on a lawsuit for the husband of a woman who was murdered in Hurva Square."

"I know."

"How much do you know?"

"We know the salient facts, from either Mr. Hasan or our own intelligence gathering."

Hana remembered Daud's earlier comment that you could never assume privacy in Israel. She'd not known the scope of Daud's loyalties or where the lines fell. For all she knew, he could have bugged her room or her computer, synced with her phone, or done any number of other things to spy on her.

"Does Daud Hasan work for you?"

"Before I respond, you need to answer my question."

Hana hesitated, then asked, "How long is 'for the time being'? A week, a month, a year, forever?"

"Only until some immediate matters are resolved."

"About Latif Al-Fasi?"

"And other persons of interest to us," Yosef said, glancing behind him at some nearby hotel guests who were eating breakfast. "Please keep your voice down."

"I'm Israeli," Hana said. "And I'm loyal to my country."

"We have no doubt about that."

"What about Jakob Brodsky? He knows what I know, perhaps more since he understands Russian and could follow the conversation between Daud and the man called Anzor."

"I met with Mr. Brodsky before I came here. He's willing to work with us, so long as we provide information to assist with the lawsuit as soon as we can."

To Hana that sounded like Jakob—negotiating a deal she wasn't sure he would keep.

"Then I will give you a tentative yes," she said. "But only if you talk to me about Daud."

Yosef glanced over his shoulder again. There was no one within earshot. "Daud Hasan had a working relationship with our agency. I can't provide specific details. He managed the crisis last night in Beit Hanina according to a protocol that had been prearranged for any case in which he was in imminent danger. The threat was larger in scope than anticipated, so there had to be improvisation."

"How can you be sure he's not a double agent for the terrorists? Everything I saw and heard convinced me his allegiance lay with the men who held me captive."

"Ms. Abboud, he was good at his job," Yosef replied with a clear effort at sincerity. "When you and Mr. Brodsky were taken hostage, Daud sent a numbered text to a secure line that revealed what was going on and triggered the rescue operation. Otherwise, you'd be on your way out of the country and Mr. Brodsky would be dead."

"I wish I could believe you."

"That is your choice."

Hana stared at her untouched plate of fruit. "Did Daud's relationship with your agency end because of what happened last night?"

"I can't confirm or deny anything, but terrorists survived the assault and saw how he was treated by the soldiers who rescued you. Currently, the captured terrorists aren't allowed to speak to anyone on the outside, but that will end soon and the story will come out."

"What about Tawfik Zadan?"

"He was captured."

"And the man Anzor, the one who questioned me? I saw the soldiers subdue him."

"Also captured and placed in isolation for interrogation."

Hana thought about Daud. If Yosef was telling her the truth, circumstances existed that she would have to consider even if she severed their personal relationship.

"I would like to report that your tentative yes is no longer tentative," Yosef continued.

"Agreed," Hana replied after a moment had passed. "But you already knew that's where I would end up."

"I hoped so," Yosef said with a smile. "Thank you. For the time being, I will be your contact person."

He stood and handed Hana a card with only his first name and a phone number. "Put the number in your phone."

"My phone was destroyed last night."

Yosef took a cell phone from his shirt pocket. "Here is a replacement. The internal card in your phone was intact. Daud damaged the case without destroying the internal memory. All your contacts, photos, and so on have been uploaded."

It was identical to her previous phone.

"You work fast," she said. "Will you be listening to all my conversations?"

Yosef didn't respond. "Thanks for your cooperation," he said, standing up.

The agent left. After her first bite of fruit, Hana's appetite began to return. She returned to the buffet and added some cheese and yogurt to her plate.

. . .

It was the middle of the afternoon when Jakob was brought back to the hotel in a military car with heavily tinted windows. He, too, had a new cell phone, but his own clothes were gone, and he wore loose-fitting pants and a garish yellow shirt that looked like it had come from a charity closet. The military doctor who had authorized his release from the hospital loaded him up with antibiotics and potent pain medication.

"I'd rather have a clear head and endure some discomfort," Jakob said to the doctor. "I just got off pain meds a couple of weeks ago."

"Then take one before you go to sleep. It will wear off by morning."

The soldier driving the car stopped in front of the hotel. Jakob no longer had the key to enter his room and went to the front desk to request another one. Rafi, the concierge, saw him dragging his right leg behind him.

"Are you injured?" Rafi asked with concern. "I can call a doctor. They come to the hotel."

"I've already seen a doctor," Jakob answered, realizing how challenging it would be to maintain secrecy. "I'm on the mend now. I'll be running a marathon before you know it."

Rafi eyed him skeptically.

"Tell Wahid I won't be going out today," Jakob continued. "But I may text him tomorrow."

After getting the key, Jakob wanted to check on Hana before navigating his way up the stairs to his room. He knocked on her door and stood so she could clearly see him through the peephole. She opened it.

"Don't criticize the shirt," Jakob said before she said anything. "They had limited fashion options."

Hana stepped forward and hugged him tightly. For the second time in twenty-four hours, Jakob had to fight back tears.

"Enough," Jakob said when they parted. "Now I know what the

bond feels like between those who endure and survive a harrowing experience."

"Thank God we survived," Hana answered. "Come in. Where is the best place for you to sit?"

"With my leg propped up on the bed."

Hana arranged a chair for him, and he sat down and elevated his leg to the level of the mattress.

"I talked to a guy named Yosef who works for the secret police or whatever they call them," Jakob began. "He came by at the crack of dawn—"

"And then he came to see me," Hana said. "He told me you'd agreed to keep what really happened secret for a while."

"That's right. Did you ask him about Daud?"

"Yes. I'm slowly coming around to what you told me at the hospital."

Jakob listened as Hana summarized what she'd learned. "We've been minnows swimming with sharks," Jakob said, shaking his head. "But I think we got what we came for."

"The company in California?"

"Yes. If Simi Valley Productions is laundering money for the group connected to Abdul and Tawfik, they would be a target defendant." Jakob stopped talking for a moment before continuing. "I wonder if Daud already knew about that. Have you heard from him?"

"No."

"What else did Yosef say to you?"

"Not much. He gave me a cell phone with all my information transferred to it. They were able to retrieve the storage card."

"Me too." Jakob raised his eyebrows. "Which was much better than this ugly shirt and pair of baggy pants."

There was a knock on the door. They looked at each other.

"The IDF told me I was under protective custody," Hana said, getting up from her chair.

"I hope they do a better job than Daud did."

Hana looked through the spy hole. "It's Daud," she said, turning to Jakob. "What should I do?"

"I'm not going to make you do anything. If you want me to go outside and tell him to leave, I'll do it."

Jakob watched as Hana bowed her head for a moment before opening the door. She didn't say anything as the investigator entered. Daud remained standing. He was wearing a blue shirt and casual pants. Jakob could see a few cuts on the investigator's muscular forearms. Daud sat in a chair so that he faced both Jakob and Hana, who positioned herself at the end of the bed. Jakob could see that Hana was visibly trembling.

"I want to speak to both of you so you can understand," Daud began. "There is much—"

"It may be too soon for us to have that conversation," Jakob cut in, his eyes on Hana.

"No, I want to hear," Hana replied shakily. "Even if I can't control my body."

Daud looked at Hana and buried his head in his hands. The simple, unspoken act dispelled some of the tension in the room. Jakob started to speak but decided not to. They sat in silence until Daud raised his head.

"Maybe it would be better if you ask me questions," he said. "I am prepared to answer anything."

Jakob looked at Hana.

"You first," she said. "I'm still having trouble being in the same room with him."

Jakob winced at the third-person reference to Daud. "Why did Anzor and his men come to your apartment?" Jakob asked.

"Because he did not like the way I was handling the Neumann investigation. You heard what he said in Russian. He did not want to wait. He wanted to kill you and Hana."

"What was your plan?"

Daud rubbed his hands together and sat up straighter in the chair. "This was the big moment for a mission I had worked on for over a year," he said. "My job was to learn all I could about Anzor and his associates. I was picked because I speak Russian. My superiors saw the Neumann case as a way to make deeper inroads into the Chechen network. They suspected there was a relationship between them and the Zadan brothers, but they were not sure how everything fit together. Anzor knew about Jakob representing the Neumann family, so when I mentioned his name, it gave me credibility."

"My name?" Jakob asked.

"Yes, and they knew you were looking for other lawyers to assist you. When I told them that you had associated Collins, Lowenstein, and Capella in America, it greatly increased their concern."

"Because the firm could finance litigation?" Jakob asked.

"Yes."

"Were they behind the attack on me in Atlanta?" Jakob asked. "And planting a bomb in my car?"

"I thought so, but I was not sure until I talked to Anzor at my apartment."

"And mentioned the botched attempts on my life," Jakob said.

"Correct."

"But they didn't know about me?" Hana asked.

"Not at first," Daud said. "But I could not keep you hidden. I believed I could protect you and Jakob because I would know in advance what the terrorists might try to do to you."

"You were wrong," Hana said.

"Yes. I was wrong."

No one spoke for a few seconds.

"Go on," Hana said.

Daud took a deep breath. "The Chechens brought me into meetings that enabled me to identify more of their leaders. My instructions were to move forward with one more meeting before the three of us were removed from the situation and the terrorist cell neutralized."

"Who was your boss?" Jakob asked.

"I cannot tell you, but it was not Aaron Levy. When I left Deir Dibwan, Anzor and his men prepared for the attack." Daud paused. "I told him and the other leaders we were going to have dinner at my apartment."

"Why?" Jakob and Hana both exclaimed.

"To make him believe that I was in control. But they decided it would be easy to capture you at my apartment with my cooperation. They saw me as a mercenary collecting money, and I had to act as if I did not care what happened to either one of you." Daud looked at Hana. "When the terrorist held the knife to your throat, I had my hand on a gun I kept hidden beneath the counter in the kitchen. The man with the knife was one second away from death, but if I had shot him, I do not believe I could have neutralized all of them. We had to wait for Colonel Tarif's unit to arrive."

Jakob saw a tear run down Hana's cheek. "Do we need to stop?" he asked.

"No," Hana replied and shook her head.

Jakob looked at Daud, who seemed to be waiting for him to ask another question.

"Why didn't you want Anzor to know that we had identified Latif Al-Fasi? That's when I realized you might not be working with the terrorists."

"That was new information to us," Daud answered. "Anzor's group always called him 'the American.' I knew he played a role in propaganda and finances, but your friends in the US identified him from the video. That was another reason I was ordered to press forward with the mission—to find out as much as I could about Al-Fasi and his contacts. When you mentioned him by both his birth name and Islamic name, it shocked Anzor."

"Now, both the Israelis and the Americans are after Al-Fasi," Jakob said.

"Yes," Daud agreed.

"And that's one of the main reasons for Yosef's visit to both of us," Hana added.

"Maybe," Daud said. "I am no longer assigned to the mission."

Jakob looked at Hana. "I know we agreed to wait, but if we don't act fast, Simi Valley Productions won't have any assets. We have to figure out a way to convince a federal judge to issue a pre-lawsuit freeze—"

"Or you can let our two governments cooperate in a way that saves other lives," Daud said.

"Leaving our client with nothing?" Jakob replied sharply. "And me beat up and shot and Hana suffering from PTSD? Something is not right with this picture."

"Jakob, this is bigger than us," Hana said in a soft voice. "And I believe Ben will understand."

CHAPTER 43

"Should I go?" Daud asked Hana after Jakob left the room in obvious frustration.

Hana had listened to the revelation about Daud's role with the terrorist cell on two levels—the factual information, and the way the information touched her emotions.

"No, stay," she replied.

Daud resumed his seat across from her and waited. Hana was silent as she debated what to say next. "Let's not talk about the past for a few minutes," she said in Arabic. "What are your future plans?"

"Professionally?"

"For a man like you, doesn't that determine everything else?"

"Maybe in the past, but not now." Daud leaned forward. "My ability to work undercover is finished. Terrorist groups and their state sponsors will put a bounty on my head. I always knew the risk when I agreed to do what I did for our country."

For the first time since the assault at the apartment, Hana felt a hint of sympathy for Daud. But that response was followed by the stark reality that if she maintained any contact with him, her life would be placed in greater danger as well.

"What does the government do for agents like you once you've been compromised?" she asked.

"A desk job in Tel Aviv with an apartment in a secured area is one approach."

Hana had a hard time imagining Daud chained to a desk all day.

"But that's for Jewish agents," he continued. "For an Arab it's more complicated. I don't want to pretend that I'm Jewish when I'm not; and my faith is as real as you believed it was twenty-four hours ago, maybe more so."

Hana eyed him suspiciously. "What else was a lie?" she asked.

"My extravagant lifestyle," Daud responded. "I enjoyed my Land Rover, but I didn't care about the BMW or the fancy apartment. That was all for show because of the money I received from the terrorist groups. I knew it bothered you."

"How? I didn't say anything."

"Hana, you could never do my job. Your eyes reveal what's in your heart, and I can read your face better than a child's book of stories."

Everything about Daud that had attracted Hana to him in the first place clamored for her attention.

"Maybe that's true, but you didn't answer my question. What will the government do with you or for you?"

Daud looked directly at her. "You play a big role in that decision," he said. "With all my heart, I still want to visit your family in Reineh. If you say yes, then one option rises to the top of the list."

"What is it?"

"I could move to America for a while and work as a liaison between the Mossad and the CIA or the Department of Homeland Security until things settle down here. There might still be threats against me, but they would be harder to carry out. Also, I'm"—Daud took a deep breath—"a man who can protect himself."

"And be violent toward a woman?"

This time Hana could clearly read the anguish that swept across Daud's face. "That was the hardest thing I've ever had to do. I would rather have been shot myself than strike you in the face. And the look in your eyes when you believed I'd betrayed you will never leave me. But I had to convince Anzor that you and I weren't in love. That way, he was open to my suggestion to send you to Chechnya. Otherwise, you wouldn't have left the apartment alive."

"I would have been a slave."

"No, you would have been rescued before you crossed the borders of Israel. I would have made sure of it."

Hana remained skeptical. Daud continued, speaking rapidly. "Every moment, I was thinking about what to do to save you. Forgiveness is hard, and I know it's too soon to ask, but I won't rest until I make this right with you."

Daud lowered his gaze. Hana moved her right hand, and the pain that shot up her arm reminded her of her torment. But Daud's words rang true. Her heart and mind, which had been torn apart by the ordeal at the apartment, slowly began to come back together.

"You're hurt physically and emotionally," Daud continued. "I promise to be patient and not press you until you're willing to give me a chance."

Hana hesitated for a few moments before responding. "Yes," she said.

"You're willing to give me a chance?" Daud asked hopefully.

Hana shook her head. "No."

Daud's face fell, and his eyes reddened.

"I'm willing to give *us* a chance," Hana corrected. "Let's go to the courtyard and talk. There's a small tree with a table beneath it where I like to sit. It's the place where the Lord met with me the first night I was here."

. . .

They stayed in the courtyard until the sun moved below the roofline of the hotel, and a faint late-afternoon breeze touched their faces. At one point, Hana was so overcome by the fact they were safe that tears streamed down her cheeks. She quickly explained why.

"Do you ever cry?" she asked.

"Not since I was a boy," Daud confided. "And you know it's not in our culture for a man to show emotion. I almost cried when you told me there was no hope for us, but I believe it could happen in the right circumstance."

"What would that be?" Hana asked.

"Seeing you standing at the back of a church about to be my bride."

"Is that a promise?"

"Yes, a promise I can keep."

. . .

Jakob awoke from a long nap and stepped outside his room. Hana and Daud were sitting together in the courtyard. She glanced up and waved for him to come down.

"No!" he called out. "This is your time!"

"Our time!" she responded.

Jakob made his way down the steps and across the stone pavers to them. Daud pulled up two chairs, one for Jakob to sit in and one for his leg.

"How are you feeling?" Hana asked.

"Looking forward to taking a pain pill and sleeping through the night. I'm going to be okay."

Hana smiled.

"And seeing you smile makes me feel better than any pain pill could," Jakob continued.

Hana's smile broadened. "I'm finding my way out of a dark place."

They talked quietly for several minutes.

"Do you have any plans for tomorrow?" Jakob asked.

"Going to Reineh so Daud can meet my family," Hana answered.

"And leave me here all by myself?"

"You have Wahid. He can take you someplace if your leg lets you move about."

"I'm not going out tomorrow," Jakob said and then paused. "And the only place I want to go is home. I'd like to move my flight to Atlanta up to the day after tomorrow."

"I agree," Hana said. "I'll join you."

"Why should you rush back?" Jakob asked. "You deserve a vacation."

"I will be right behind you," Daud said. "I am going to set up meetings about a job in the States."

"Probably not the kind of job you can talk about, correct?" Jakob asked.

Daud nodded.

"Oh, I have another question," Jakob said. "Is Ensanullah a terrorist?"

"No," Daud quickly answered. "He is a good man. When I asked him to look out for you, he thought it was because you had made some organized-crime people in Israel mad by competing with them in business."

"Right now, I wish I was in the restaurant business," Jakob said and patted his stomach. "Do you think we could order take-out from the restaurant Wahid recommended?"

Two and a half hours later, they finished the meal delivered via Wahid. Three candles rested in the center of the table in the court-yard. Hana's wrists were sore, but she was able to use a fork and knife.

"I'm going to miss being your chaperone," Jakob said after he ate the last bite of a sticky sweet dessert pastry. "Actually, that's not true."

"But it was good to have this meal together," Daud said. "To me it was a celebration."

"A proper celebration will have to wait for later," Hana said. "Maybe in the US."

"Send me an invitation," Jakob said as he stood up and yawned. "Time for my pain pill. Don't expect to see me for breakfast."

"Let's call Ben before we leave," Hana said. "We can talk in generalities about the case, but I really want to see Sadie, even if it's only for a few moments."

"Okay," Jakob answered.

"Good night," Daud and Hana said as Jakob moved away.

"Are you tired of talking to me?" Daud asked her in Arabic as soon as Jakob was gone.

"No." Hana shook her head.

Daud reached out and gently touched the top of her hand without taking it in his. Hana didn't pull away.

"Would you like to take a drive?" he asked.

"Only if we don't go in the direction of Beit Hanina."

"I won't be able to go back myself for a couple of days, and I'll never spend the night there again."

"Where will you sleep?"

"There's a government apartment where I can stay."

They walked slowly to the front of the hotel. Hana didn't see either the Land Rover or the BMW.

"What are you driving?" she asked.

Daud pointed to a white subcompact with several dents in the metal and scrapes in the paint.

"This is the only vehicle I actually own," he said. "It's cleaner on the inside than it is on the outside."

He held the door for her. Hana glanced around as she entered.

"Where are the security men watching out for me?" she asked as she sat in the passenger seat that squeaked slightly.

"In the car with you."

"You're it?" Hana asked in surprise.

"My superiors are aware that no one would protect you as zealously as me."

To Hana's relief, nothing rose up in her heart to argue against Daud's words. He started the car, whose engine whined like a high-powered sewing machine. They made their way across the city and climbed Mount Scopus toward Hebrew University.

"I'm curious," Hana said. "Did the government pay for our dinner the other night at the nice restaurant near here?"

"No, and the chef at my apartment was on my tab, too. I normally spend so little on myself that I have a healthy bank account."

Daud stopped the car at a spot with a slightly different view of the Old City than the one at the restaurant. It was a warm evening, and they sat on stone steps leading up to a government building. Hana slipped closer to Daud and leaned against his shoulder.

"Thank you for doing that," he said after a few moments passed. "I don't blame you for your anger, but my insides have been in knots worrying about how you felt toward me."

"I've tried to reassure you."

"I know, but those were words; this is action."

Hana pressed a little harder against Daud's shoulder. They sat side by side in silence for several minutes. She felt a familiar peace settle on her. "Is God saying anything to you?" she asked.

"No," Daud replied. "But I'm saying a few things to him."

"Can you tell me?"

"That if it's his will, I want you to always be by my side."

• • •

The following morning, Jakob awoke earlier than expected. He didn't see Hana in the courtyard and knocked on the door of her room. She opened it wearing a casual dress and sandals.

"I've eaten breakfast," she said. "Get a cup of coffee, and we'll skype with Ben and Sadie. I've already sent them a text letting them know we'd be calling."

Jakob's leg was stiff, but it loosened slightly as he made his way across the courtyard to the coffee bar and returned to Hana's room. She had her laptop open and placed the call as soon as Jakob sat down.

"Let me talk about the case," Hana said.

"I'll be a potted plant," Jakob answered.

"What does that mean?"

"It's a famous saying by an American lawyer. Look it up later."

The call connected and Ben's face appeared on the screen. A second later, Sadie came into view and waved. When she did, Jakob saw Hana put her hand over her mouth. She looked at Jakob and shook her head. "I can't talk for a moment," she whispered.

"Good afternoon," Jakob said to Ben. "How are you doing?"

"Fine. How about you?"

Jakob glanced at Hana, who was still struggling with her emotions.

"Hana and I are having an unforgettable time. We're making progress with the investigation but want to put it together in an organized way."

"Hi, Hana," Sadie jumped in, holding up a doll. "Fabia says hi, too."

"Hello, Fabia," Hana managed. "I'm going to see the real Fabia later today. She is so excited that you named your doll after her."

"Send pictures," Sadie replied. "Where's Daud?"

"He's going to pick me up in a little while and go with me to meet my family."

Ben raised his eyebrows.

"Has he kissed you?" Sadie asked.

"You don't have to answer that," Ben cut in.

"It's wonderful seeing your face, Sadie," Hana said. "I'll give you a big hug and kiss as soon as I'm back in Atlanta."

Jakob could hear the tremble in Hana's voice but wasn't sure it was apparent to Ben and Sadie.

"And I'll shake your hand, Ben," he said.

Ben smiled. "I'll look forward to it."

The session ended. The last image was Sadie blowing kisses and vigorously waving good-bye. Hana turned to Jakob. "I'm glad you turned into a talking plant," she said. "I was about to burst into tears the whole time."

CHAPTER 44

After leaving Hana's room, Jakob ate a leisurely breakfast in the courtyard and spent a couple of hours taking care of business on his laptop. Feeling antsy, he sent a text to Wahid, who replied that he was in the area and could be there in fifteen minutes. Jakob went downstairs to wait for him, still not sure where he wanted to go. He slipped into the rear seat of the taxi.

"You're limping. What's up with your leg?" Wahid asked.

"Flesh wound," Jakob answered cryptically. "It's not too bad."

"My guess is an old soccer injury that you aggravated," Wahid replied. "I have one of those myself."

Jakob didn't correct him.

"Where to?" Wahid asked.

Jakob didn't want to go someplace new. Instead, he wanted to return to a place he'd visited and experience it after his ordeal. The obvious choice was Yad Vashem, the ultimate monument to Jewish suffering. But that didn't sit right with him. That left the Garden Tomb or the Western Wall.

"If you were sitting in my seat, would you go to the Garden Tomb or the Western Wall?" Jakob asked Wahid.

"That's not a fair question," the driver said, glancing in the rear-view mirror. "You'll pay me more to take you to the Garden Tomb because it's farther away."

"I'll pay the same rate to level the playing field," Jakob replied.

"You're a Jew, so it has to be the Kotel," Wahid answered.

"Let's go."

Wahid pulled away from the hotel.

"Did you know that Jesus was Jewish?" Jakob asked.

"Of course. You should let me take you to Bethlehem. It's a great half-day excursion, and I know the best place for olive-wood products."

"Keep it to the Kotel today."

Jakob stared out the window of the car as the driver navigated the streets toward the Old City. The stone buildings truly were unique. Wahid pulled to the curb. "How long before I pick you up?"

"I'm not sure."

"Text me. It may take me awhile if I have another fare."

"That's fine."

It was a short distance to the security entrance into the Temple Mount area. Today, Jakob was more aware of the diversity of the people milling about. There were ultra-Orthodox Jews who probably came every day, tourists from the four corners of the earth for whom it was a once-in-a-lifetime experience, and Arabs who called the Muslim Quarter home. Jakob passed through the security checkpoint with a group from Malaysia.

Walking across the broad plaza, he headed to the place in front of the Wall where he'd heard the man pray in Russian. With each step Jakob felt an increasing sense that he was walking toward something important. Being in this place at this time wasn't a random event; he had been appointed to be here. His heart began to beat a bit faster.

Donning a cardboard kippah, he made his way to the Wall. He recognized the massive stone before which he had stood only a few days before. This time he stepped back to the spot where the unknown man prayed behind him. After staring at the enormous stone for a few seconds, Jakob bowed his head and closed his eyes. Although there were other people within a few feet of him, he felt wrapped in a blanket of solitude.

Some of the words he'd heard during his first visit returned:

Heavenly Father, hear my cry in this holy place . . . I pray that Russian Jews standing in this very place will believe that Jesus Christ is their Savior . . . They may wrestle with you like Jacob, but they will come away from that encounter so transformed . . . May they believe and receive!

Once again the hair on the back of Jakob's neck stood up. This time he let the man's prayers wash over him not as a spectator, but with a heart open to receive each and every word. As he did, a striving, a wrestling that had been such an integral part of his identity that Jakob accepted it as an immutable part of his life, ceased. A weight lifted; peace came.

Jakob closed his eyes again, and though he wasn't physically present at the Garden Tomb, he remembered what he'd heard and sensed in that place—the mystery of sacrifice and the power of resurrection. A Jewish man named Jesus lived, died, and rose from the dead in the city where Jakob now stood.

The glorious truth overwhelmed him, and in the secret place of the human heart uniquely prepared to receive the life of God, Jakob Brodsky was born anew. Jesus Christ was his Messiah, and Jakob was one of God's twice-chosen people. He opened his eyes a second time and looked around, half expecting everybody within twenty feet of him to be equally touched. But no one else seemed affected. He took in a deep breath, exhaled, and stepped into a new reality. He was a Jew who'd come home, a man in the land of his ancestors whose heart was now the dwelling place of God's Son. And with that knowledge, a tear of joy and thankfulness escaped his eye and ran down his cheek.

· · ·

It was nine by the time Hana and Daud left Reineh. It had been a full day that started with introductions and ended with a banquet. They passed the last house in the village and turned south toward Jerusalem. Hana was tired, but it was a fatigue filled with satisfaction.

"You have a great family," Daud said as the vehicle's headlamps shone the way before them. "I didn't know what to expect. Could you tell I was nervous at first?"

"Yes, but only for about five minutes. When Uncle Anwar put his hand on your head and prayed for you, everything shifted. His words about God's call on your life touched everyone in the room."

"Especially me. Nothing like that has happened to me before."

"After Anwar prayed, my father relaxed and accepted you. I could see it in his face. My mother liked you from the first moment, and my cousins were jealous in a good way."

"Fabia cornered me and interrogated me as if she were working for the Shin Bet."

"I saw."

"Why didn't you rescue me?"

"She had to satisfy herself. It will take awhile for her to come around, but I believe she will once you talk to my father in detail about the future."

Daud glanced at her. "How long do I have to wait? I don't want to use an intermediary."

"Let me work on that part. When I return for my birthday, that will be my mission, to act like the spies Moses sent out."

"Bring back a good report. I don't want to spend forty years wandering in the wilderness."

Hana reached over and lightly touched Daud's hand. It was still such a new experience for her that it sent chills through her body.

"Trust me," she said. "I'm a lawyer who knows how to present her case."

Daud smiled. "I need a good lawyer."

"Yes, you do. Your employment contract needs a complete face-lift, and I'll do it for a reduced fee."

"Half your usual rate?"

"Or less."

They turned onto a major highway that connected the north with the rest of the country.

"What was going on at our first meeting at the steak restaurant that you didn't tell me?" Hana asked.

"Everything I said was true, but it wasn't the whole truth. I remembered you because of Ibrahim, and the first time I saw your picture on the law firm website, I knew I wanted to get to know you." Daud stopped talking for a moment. "And I would have been crushed if you'd turned me down and hired another investigator."

"You knew how you felt toward me from the beginning?"

"Before we sat down that first evening at the restaurant in West Jerusalem."

They rode in silence for several minutes. Hana thought about Daud, Jakob, and herself. "I believe the Lord brought you, me, and Jakob together," she said.

Daud glanced sideways at her. "I guess I'm okay including Jakob in that sentence, but I'm glad he's not with us right now."

Hana reached over and touched Daud on the arm.

"Me too."

They spent the rest of the drive talking about their dreams for the future.

• • •

The following morning, Jakob was having a final breakfast in the courtyard when Hana came out of her room. While she was fixing a plate at the buffet, Daud arrived. The investigator poured a cup of coffee and sat down with Jakob.

"How was the trip to Reineh?" Jakob asked.

Daud glanced in Hana's direction and smiled. Jakob held up his hand and said, "I think that answers my question."

Hana joined them. The look she gave Daud eliminated any lingering doubts in Jakob's mind.

"Good morning," Hana said to him. "How's the leg?"

"Stiff but functional."

"What did you do yesterday?"

It was Jakob's turn to look each of them in the eyes. Hana immediately raised her eyebrows. "I think it was something good," she said.

"Yes," Jakob answered. "More than good."

Hana began to cry as Jakob told them about his encounter with God at the Western Wall. He saw her whispering under her breath.

"What are you saying?" he asked.

"I'm so grateful to God that I can't express it silently in my mind," she said. "It has to come out." She took a tissue from her purse and wiped her eyes.

Jakob turned to Daud. "Why aren't you crying?" he asked.

"Do you remember what I told you at dinner your first night in Jerusalem?" Daud responded.

Jakob hesitated for a moment. They'd talked about a lot. "Oh, yeah," he said, nodding. "That God is bringing the Jews to Israel because he keeps his promises."

"Right. And another of his promises in the book of Zechariah is that someday the whole nation will recognize Jesus as their Messiah. You're blessed to be at the front of the line. This is a time of rejoicing, not mourning."

Jakob turned to Hana. "I've never felt so thankful in all my life."

"God put the thankfulness there," she answered with a sniffle. "Don't ever lose it."

Hana and Daud offered to let Jakob tag along for the day, but he refused.

"The two of you need time together without me," he said. "And I want to be by myself and process what's been happening to me."

After breakfast, Hana and Daud left. Jakob texted Wahid, who replied that it would be an hour and a half before he could pick him up. While he waited, Jakob used his phone to read the entire book of Zechariah. A lot of the language and images seemed obscure and metaphorical, but other phrases about God's loving intentions toward the Jewish people gripped Jakob's heart. He immediately recognized in chapter 12 the passage Daud was referring to during breakfast in the courtyard: "I will pour out on the house of David and the inhabitants of Jerusalem a spirit of grace and supplication. They will look on me, the one they have pierced, and they will mourn for him as one mourns for an only child."

When Wahid arrived, he apologized as Jakob got in the rear seat: "I had a quick trip to Bethlehem for a Chinese couple. They wanted to cram everything in before their tour group left for the Dead Sea."

"No problem. I'd like to go to the Jewish Quarter and Hurva Square."

"But not the Kotel? It's close by."

"No." Jakob shook his head. "And I won't stay too long. I have unfinished business."

Wahid gave him a puzzled look before pulling away from the curb. It was a short drive to the drop-off point for the Jewish Quarter.

"I'll stay around the Old City," Wahid said. "There are plenty of fares in this area."

Jakob's route took him down streets that were now familiar. Even though he was slightly dragging his right leg, he felt a lightness in his step that he knew was connected to his heart. He stopped when he reached the edge of the square. Just as before, most people were passing through on their way to another destination, but some were staying to shop, eat a snack, or sit and talk. He walked slowly around the edge of the small plaza. He paused in front of a shop window and saw a plaque with the phrase "Pray for the Peace of Jerusalem."

He stopped at the ice cream shop where Gloria Neumann was murdered. There was a vacant chair by itself, and he sat down. Today, the place of violence was a place of peace. But Jakob knew that could change in an instant. A single person filled with hate and revenge could be a messenger of death and destruction. With his eyes open Jakob took in the scene of the entire square and then in his imagination expanded his vision to include the whole city—and prayed for the peace of Jerusalem.

CHAPTER 45

As they neared Ben Gurion Airport, Hana's heart began to ache with loneliness even though Daud was sitting two feet away. She knew it was a feeling she would have to get used to, at least for a while.

"I will move quickly on locating a position in the United States," Daud said as if reading her thoughts.

"You won't have a problem finding work," Jakob offered from the rear seat. "I predict you'll have offers from several agencies."

"But not a job that is going to send you away for months on assignments so that you won't be able to come home," Hana interjected.

"Do you think I would do that?" Daud asked.

"No," both Hana and Jakob replied.

Daud laughed.

They were cleared through by the security guards at the entrance to the terminal, and Daud parked alongside the curb. Jakob took his suitcase from the trunk and, after shaking Daud's hand, stepped away from them. Daud lifted Hana's heavy bag and placed it on the walkway. They embraced and kissed. When they parted, Hana reached up with her right hand and placed it on Daud's left cheek and held it there for several seconds. He moved his face so that he could kiss her hand. She then placed her hand against her lips.

"Remember that," she whispered.

Daud nodded and touched his heart. "And remember that I always carry you in here."

Hana and Jakob entered the terminal. Two hours later they were sitting on the plane waiting for takeoff. Hana's heart was full and heavy.

Jakob took out his headphones. "Before I'm unconscious and while we're technically on the ground in Israel, I want to thank you for what you've done for me."

"You're welcome."

"And don't worry about how Mr. Lowenstein treats me when we're back in the States. If I can survive an encounter with Anzor Varayev, I can handle what your boss throws at me."

Eleven hours later they landed in Newark. After a two-hour layover they boarded a plane for the flight to Atlanta. By that point, Hana was exhausted enough to sleep. It was 10:35 p.m. when they stood in front of the baggage claim area at the Atlanta airport. Jakob was much more alert than she was.

"There's your bag," he said as a fresh group of luggage made its way around the conveyor belt. "I'll get it for you."

"I need to get home and go to bed," Hana said. "Have you heard from Emily?"

"Not since I confirmed the time for our arrival. She's never late."

"Jakob!" a female voice called out.

Hana and Jakob turned around as Emily Johnson ran up to them out of breath. She threw her arms around Jakob's neck and held on to him. He glanced over her shoulder at Hana and slowly put his arms around Emily.

"Are you okay?" Jakob asked after a few seconds passed.

Emily stepped away and smiled at him. "Yes, just relieved that you're home safe and sound and glad you didn't have any serious drama on your trip."

Hana and Jakob exchanged a glance. "There were a few bumps and bruises," Jakob admitted.

They moved away with their luggage. After a few steps Emily looked at Jakob. "What's wrong with your leg?" she asked. "Did you twist your knee?"

"No. It's going to be fine."

. . .

Hana retrieved her car from long-term parking. Once home, she collapsed in bed after taking a quick shower to wash away travel grime. She didn't expect to wake up in the night; however, at 3:33 a.m., she rolled over in bed and her eyes popped open. She closed them for a few seconds but knew heaven had knocked on the door of her heart. She slipped out of bed. Without Leon in the house, Hana didn't have to worry about waking up the puppy, and she spent several minutes walking through the house thanking the Lord for deliverance from death and the hope of love and joy in the future.

Sitting on the couch, she thought about the blessing she'd received from Anwar and read the passages in the Old Testament about Hannah, the mother of Samuel, and in the New Testament about Anna, the aged prophetess who, upon seeing the baby Jesus, proclaimed the redemption of Israel. Their testimony encouraged Hana's soul and stirred her spirit. She laid her hand on the pages and prayed for an impartation of the faith and vision and determination that rested on the two women. Feeling nothing, but confident she'd been obedient, Hana was about to lift her hand when an inner prompting stopped her. She stayed still before the Lord.

And in the silence of waiting, something began to build inside her like water slowly rising. It was a strength, an awareness, a reality. It crept higher and higher, filling her without creating an uncomfortable pressure. It was a resource, a reservoir, a fountain that she knew would, in the timing of the Lord, overflow from her life in moments of divine choosing.

In a split second, Hana saw scores of situations in which this would occur. The images vanished as quickly as they appeared, leaving her with expectation but no remembered details. It was enough. She bowed her head and, with joy and renewed commitment, dedicated herself to God's purposes accomplished through his grace.

In the morning, Hana drove to the doggie day care center to pick up Leon. She was shocked at how much he'd grown. When he wiggled all over in greeting, there seemed to be a lot more body in motion.

"What has he been eating?" she asked the young man who brought him out to her.

"Everything we put in front of him. He's having quite a growth spurt."

Running her fingers through the dog's fur was surprisingly therapeutic. Hana rested her hand on his head and stroked him during the drive home. Contact with a living creature filled with love was a comfort to her own soul. Shortly after she arrived home and filled Leon's dish with fresh water, her phone vibrated. It was Daud.

"I talked to Yosef," Daud said. "There have been more arrests, and the Chechen terrorist cell in the West Bank has been neutralized. It is okay for you and Jakob to talk about what happened in Beit Hanina so long as you avoid mentioning Colonel Tarif or the names of any other soldiers you may remember."

"I'll let Jakob know. How are you?"

"Missing you but glad it won't be long before I see you again."

They talked for an hour. Each conversation brought another layer of healing to Hana's soul. She considered telling him about her nighttime encounter with the Lord but sensed it was for another time.

"It's wonderful to hear your voice," she said as the call drew to a close.

Daud responded with a few lines from a famous Arabic love poem.

"That's enough," she replied with a smile. "You need to save something for the future."

"There is much more where that came from. I'm even writing a poem of my own."

• • •

Jakob and Ben sat in the reception area of Collins, Lowenstein, and Capella.

"How's Sadie doing?" Jakob asked.

"Every time I think I've answered all her questions, she comes up with another batch."

"Maybe she should become a lawyer," Jakob said.

"I'll leave that up to her."

"Has she talked to Hana since we got back?"

"No, but Hana is coming over for a visit tomorrow night."

The door opened, and Janet Dean entered. "Come with me, please," she said. "Ms. Abboud and Mr. Lowenstein are waiting for you."

Janet escorted them to the conference room where Jakob had first presented the Neumann case. Jakob's limp had lessened, and there was no sign of infection. His initial head injuries seemed far in the past.

Mr. Lowenstein shook Jakob's hand with genuine feeling. There was a tray with coffee and pastries in the middle of the table. The senior partner directed Hana and Jakob to the head of the table and positioned himself across from Ben.

"Hana, why don't you begin, and Jakob can jump in at any point," Mr. Lowenstein said. "Ben, we don't have anything in writing to give you today except a brief memo for the file. Once you hear their story, I think you'll understand why this is going to take time to sort out."

For the next hour and a half, Hana and Jakob took turns revealing what they'd not yet told the client. The cup of coffee in front of Ben grew cold because he forgot to drink it. Sitting in the comfortable conference room chairs in the middle of an American city, Jakob felt detached from the man who'd been bound, gagged, and threatened with imminent death in Daud Hasan's apartment. When Jakob summarized Daud's initial conversation in Russian with Anzor, Ben interrupted.

"The investigator was working for the terrorists?!" he asked in shock.

"Ultimately, no, but it looked that way until we were rescued."

Hana became emotional when she spoke, and Jakob filled in the blanks when he could. Eventually, Hana was able to describe her ordeal. Jakob moved on to the revelation about John Caldwell aka Latif Al-Fasi and Simi Valley Productions. Mr. Lowenstein pushed a stack of papers that lay in front of him across the table to Ben.

"This is the complaint for the lawsuit we're going to file against the production company. Our litigation staff worked late into the night putting it together. The first step will be to ask a federal judge in California to issue a temporary restraining order blocking the company from emptying its bank accounts and destroying records." Mr. Lowenstein paused. "Which may not be necessary because the FBI is raiding their corporate offices while we're having this conversation. They will lock down everything."

This was the first Jakob had heard about the latest development. "Will the feds shut us out, too?" he asked.

"Hana's number one priority at this point is to work with Sylvia Armstrong to keep that from happening," Mr. Lowenstein replied.

"I'm flying to New York in the morning to meet with her," Hana said and turned to Ben. "So I'll need to push back my time to see Sadie."

"She'll be okay," Ben said.

Jakob then described the rescue and subsequent conversations with Daud and Yosef.

"I'm glad you cooperated with the Israelis," Ben said. "It was the right thing to do."

"Two men living in Atlanta have been brought in for questioning," Jakob said. "Detective Freeman isn't sure if charges will be filed against them, but at least they're on the government's radar."

"The Chechen terrorist group in Israel has been decimated," Hana said. "Tawfik Zadan, Anzor Varayev, and the other men who broke into Daud's apartment and held us hostage will be prosecuted and sent to prison for a long time. Personally, I feel safer than I have since the attack on Jakob at the apartment. But not just because of those arrests."

"What do you mean?" Jakob asked.

Hana looked at him with a steely gaze that Jakob couldn't immediately interpret.

"Daud called me right before I stepped into this meeting," she said. "The FBI arrested Latif Al-Fasi this morning near Phoenix."

"Yes!" Jakob shouted.

"That's something else I'll discuss with Sylvia Armstrong," Hana said. "I'm confident Al-Fasi's next stop will be a jail cell in New York City."

"Hopefully, information obtained from Simi Valley Productions will lead to other defendants," Mr. Lowenstein said. "We'll be diligent and aggressive. You can count on it."

"Thanks for everything you're doing," Ben answered. "It's hard for me to take it all in."

"Did I forget anything?" Hana asked Jakob. "I don't want to leave out something important that happened in Israel."

"One thing," Jakob said. "You neglected to mention the date of your future marriage to Daud Hasan."

"Is that true?" Mr. Lowenstein asked in surprise. "You didn't mention it to me."

Hana gave Jakob a threatening look. "I didn't consider my personal life relevant to my report. Daud and I haven't set a date, but when we do, I'm not sure Jakob will be invited to the wedding."

"I'll still send a gift," he replied with a smile.

Jakob and Ben rode down together in the elevator. "What are you going to do next?" Ben asked when they reached the level for the parking deck. "Will you go to California when the lawsuit is filed and a hearing is scheduled in front of a judge?"

"I'm not sure. I know Hana will keep me in the loop, and I'll find the right spot to jump back in."

Ben dropped Jakob off at his office. After working a few hours, Jakob texted Emily and asked if she could pick him up after class so he could then take her out for a late dinner at a place of her choosing. He was ready to tell her what happened to his soul in Israel. Emily quickly responded and sent him a link to a restaurant with a note:

I've heard good things about this Indian place and want to check it out.

Jakob smiled. This time, he'd try something other than chilli paneer.

CHAPTER 46

Hana picked up Leon at doggie day care and drove directly to the Neumann house. As she led Leon down the sidewalk, he held his nose in the air as if enjoying familiar smells. He then turned onto the walkway for the correct address.

"You're smart," Hana said. "They've been teaching you a lot, and I didn't know you could read numbers."

Leon pulled excitedly on the leash while they waited for someone to answer the door. Ben opened it wearing jeans and a casual shirt.

"How was New York?" he asked.

"More steps in the right direction," Hana answered, looking past Ben's shoulder. "Where's Sadie?"

"Brushing her teeth."

"Here's a quick summary." Hana spoke rapidly: "The US Attorney's Office is going to charge Latif Al-Fasi under the anti-terrorism laws with conspiracy to commit murder in Gloria's death. Sylvia Armstrong believes they can present a strong case linking him to the Zadan brothers and the Chechen terrorist cell."

Ben slowly nodded. Sadie appeared behind her father.

"You look beautiful!" the little girl exclaimed when she saw Hana.

Hana leaned over, and Sadie gave her a long hug followed by a kiss on the cheek.

"And you smell good, too," Sadie said, talking rapidly. "Do you always wear the same perfume? My grandmother says that when you find one you really like it's okay to put it on every day. It's not like changing clothes. No one wants to wear the same clothes every day, except at my school where it's part of the rules." She paused to take a breath.

Leon pulled on the leash. The little girl grabbed Hana's hand. "Let me show you my room. It was a mess, but I cleaned it up."

"We need to let Leon play in the backyard," Hana replied.

Sadie led the way to the kitchen. "We got a new door," Sadie said. "This one has little wires in it that make it stronger. Isn't that right, Daddy?"

"Yes," Ben said and nodded. "And a new alarm system, although now I hope we don't really need it."

Sadie leaned over and scratched the puppy behind his ears. He wiggled in delight. "I'll play with you in just a minute," she said.

Ben released the dog into the backyard. Taking Hana's hand, Sadie led her down the hall and past the master bedroom with its photo of Gloria in her wedding gown. In the center of Sadie's bedroom was a white four-poster bed with a white-and-blue bedspread. A pile of stuffed animals huddled in front of the pillows.

"Where's Fabia?" Hana asked, looking around.

"We were playing hide-and-seek, and I haven't found her yet," Sadie answered. "Will you help me?"

Hana quickly looked around the room.

"Oh, she knows how to play," Sadie said. "She won't hide where you can see her without trying."

"Okay," Hana said. "Can she hide outside your room?"

"Not anymore," Sadie answered, shaking her head. "Daddy told me to stop hiding things in his sock drawer."

"Are you going to help me?"

"No, Fabia said that wouldn't be fair. If you have trouble, we can do hot/cold."

"What's that?"

"You don't know?" Sadie asked in surprise.

"That's why I need you to teach me."

Hana listened as Sadie explained the concept. It was new to Hana, and she filed it away to share with her nieces and nephews the next time she saw them.

"I'm going to start by looking under the bed," Hana said. She kicked off her shoes and got down on her knees so she could peer under the bed. There was a pink ballerina slipper, an orphaned green sock, and a hair bow, but no sign of Fabia.

"I don't see her," Hana said, sitting up.

"She doesn't like to hide under the bed," Sadie said. "That's a scary place, and she wouldn't want to spend the night there if I didn't find her."

"May I look in your dresser?" Hana asked.

"Yes, I'm not picky about it like Daddy."

Sadie certainly had plenty of socks, hair bows, and pajamas.

"I didn't have time to straighten up my drawers," Sadie said as Hana rummaged through the piles.

Hana's hand felt a piece of plastic that felt like a doll's leg. She pulled out the figure. It wasn't Fabia.

"That's the princess from *Frozen*," Sadie said. "All my friends have one. I haven't played much with her since I got Fabia. Nobody has a doll named Fabia."

The princess looked like she'd spent a couple of winters sleeping in the woods without a proper coat. One leg was loose in the socket and her ragged hair had been trimmed. Sadie could be rough on her dolls. Hana reached the bottom drawer without finding Fabia. On top of the dresser was a snow globe with several more characters from *Frozen* inside. The movie had been popular in Israel as well.

Beside the snow globe was a tiny Israeli flag on a small gold stand. Hana picked it up. "My mama bought that for me the day before she died," Sadie said matter-of-factly. "It's the last gift she gave me. It's the flag for Israel. Different countries have different flags."

Hana returned the flag to its place and reached for the closet doorknob.

"Be careful," Sadie said. "It's pretty full."

Hana opened the door slowly. A multicolored umbrella fell out, followed by a large wad of clothes.

"Are these clean?" Hana asked.

"I don't know," Sadie answered doubtfully. "I think Daddy should wash them again to be sure."

The small closet was a mess. Hana hesitated about digging around in the pile of clothes and toys. She saw a few broken potato chips and goldfish crackers on the carpet.

"You're getting colder," Sadie said.

Hana backed away and turned toward the nightstand beside the little girl's bed.

"You're getting warmer," Sadie informed her.

Hana looked underneath the nightstand. No doll. She reached for the brass handle on the single drawer.

"You're red hot," Sadie said.

Hana opened the drawer. Inside she found Fabia, who was lying on her back on a soft doll blanket. The doll's purse and a green hat rested beside her. She was wearing the outfit Hana had given Sadie as a birthday present.

"She looks comfortable," Hana said.

"She likes it in there. That way she can get into bed with me."

"May I take her out and hold her?" Hana asked.

"Yes, hold her next to your arm. It's the same color."

Hana did. It was a very close match.

"Put her back in her hiding place, please," Sadie said.

Hana laid Fabia on the blanket and carefully closed the drawer. "Does she always hide in the drawer?" Hana asked.

"No, that would be too easy."

"Do you ever hide from her?" Hana asked.

"Yes, I crawl all the way under the covers, but I can't stay there long."

"Why can't you stay very long?"

"I'm afraid of the dark."

Hana sat on the floor with her legs straight out in front of her and leaned against the bed. The little girl rested her head against Hana's right arm and shoulder.

"Do you think you could tuck me in one night?" Sadie asked in a small voice.

"I don't know. I'm sure your daddy does a good job."

"But would you like to do it?"

Hana's heart said yes, but she didn't want to overstep her role. "Maybe," she managed. "We'll see."

"When adults say that it usually means no," Sadie said with a pout.

"If I did tuck you in, would you sing a song for me?" Hana asked.

"Yes," Sadie said, brightening up. "If you'll sing again for me."

"Are you talking about when you fell asleep at my office?" Hana asked in surprise.

"I was fake asleep," Sadie replied with a smile. "I wanted to listen and I was afraid you'd stop if I opened my eyes. Will you sing a song right now? I'm not sleepy because I took a nap when I got home from school, so I won't have to pretend to be asleep."

"Okay."

Sadie nestled closer to Hana.

"I may shut my eyes so that I can hear inside what I should sing," Hana said.

Sadie nodded. Hana closed her eyes. And began to hum.

There is a haunting, plaintive cry inherent in the soul of Arab music that flows from the desire for eternal oasis in the midst of frequent drought. But the music also has roots in three thousand years of existence in the vast expanses of a world where the stars explode across the midnight sky and the sun dominates the noonday with unrelenting brightness. At times the sound can soar to places known only by psalmists whose worship was fashioned during long nights on solitary hills.

Hana let words from her Arabic heart language bubble up from within. At first, they were words of comfort that included snippets of phrases from the biblical psalms. Hana repeated them over and over with minor variations in melody until satisfied she'd tilled the soil, planted good seed, and watered it. It wasn't just a song for an afternoon; it was a declaration over the precious child's life.

And so Hana transitioned to words of promise for the future. She sang that Sadie would be an overcomer; that she would not stray from the path of God's will; that she would be a woman of grace; that she would know true love; that she would walk in light, not darkness. Hana paused. She knew where her heart wanted to go next, but religious and cultural boundaries held her back.

"Please, please don't stop," Sadie said. "It feels like you're telling a story, and it's not over."

Bursting all bonds and restraints, Hana sang with Hebrew words the message first announced to the Jewish people in their ancient language. A Messiah would come who would change them and change the world. She sang of deep longing and unrelenting love. She didn't try to form her thoughts into logical sentences but released words that communicated a sacrificial love deeper than human wickedness, a love that could bridge the chasm between heaven and earth, a love that restored what was lost and made everything gloriously new. She ended with a rising voice of triumph. Neither woman nor child spoke for a few moments.

"That was good," Sadie said, sitting up. "Did your mama sing that song to you?"

Hana gently kissed Sadie on the top of her head. "No, I made it up especially for you."

ACKNOWLEDGMENTS

I have wanted to write a book like this for over fifteen years. It wouldn't exist without the true story of my wife, Kathy, and the encouragement of the many who prayed before and during the writing process. I appreciate the consistent support for my novels I've received from Allen Arnold, Daisy Hutton, and Amanda Bostic at Thomas Nelson Publishing. The value of the input and advice for this story from my editors, Becky Monds, Jacob Whitlow, and Deborah Wiseman, is beyond words to thank. You know how much I appreciate you.

DISCUSSION QUESTIONS

1. Mr. Lowenstein encourages Hana to take the lead on the Neumann case because of her Israeli heritage. Do you think it was a wise decision for him to bring on a lawyer with a personal tie to the case? Why or why not?

2. Hana and Jakob Brodksy have a complicated relationship throughout much of the novel. What did you notice about their initial interactions, and how do you think they would interact if the story continued?

3. The Neumann family does not want Sadie involved in the court proceedings at all, even asking that her name be withheld. What do you think about this decision?

4. Hana and Jakob find themselves in many high-risk situations as they try to absolve Gloria's death. In what ways do they take responsible measures, and in what other ways do they put themselves in danger?

5. Hana's Uncle Anwar speaks a word of blessing over her when she visits, reminding her of Hannah in the Bible and telling her that he "prays she will pass the test." What do you think Hana's test was?

6. What do you think drew Jakob to visiting holy sites during his free time? Which places in or near the area would you be interested in seeing?

7. What was your reaction to Daud's deceptive act when confronting the terrorists? Would you be able to trust him again quickly, as Hana did?

8. Jakob experiences a spiritual moment at the Western Wall as he overhears a man praying for Russian Jews to know Christ, even mentioning his biblical namesake. When he looks for the man on his way out, he is nowhere to be seen. Given Jakob's faith background, what do you think he meant by feeling "different" after the incident?

9. What are your thoughts on the relevance of themes in *Chosen People* in today's world?

10. After Hana returns to the United States, how do you think Ben and Sadie Neumann's story changes moving forward?

IN A SMALL GEORGIA TOWN where racial tensions run high and lives are at stake, can one lawyer stand up for justice against the tide of prejudice on every side?

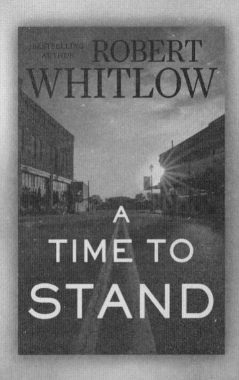

"Whitlow's timely story shines a spotlight on prejudice, race, and the pursuit of justice in a world bent on blind revenge. Fans of Greg Iles's *Natchez Burning* will find this just as compelling if not more so."

—*Library Journal*, starred review

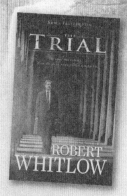
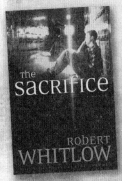

CONFESSION IS GOOD FOR THE SOUL, BUT IT COULD MEAN DEATH TO AN AMBITIOUS YOUNG LAWYER.

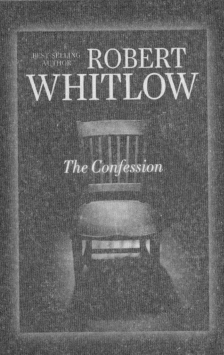

BEST-SELLING AUTHOR **ROBERT WHITLOW**

The Confession

"Christy Award winner Whitlow's experience in the law is apparent in this well-crafted legal thriller. Holt's spiritual growth as he discovers his faith and questions his motives for hiding his secret is inspiring. Fans of John Grisham will find much to like here."

—*Library Journal*

AVAILABLE IN PRINT, E-BOOK, AND AUDIO

THOMAS NELSON
Since 1798

BESTSELLING
AUTHOR
**ROBERT
WHITLOW**

A HOUSE
DIVIDED

"Highlights not only Whitlow's considerable skills as an author of
legal thrillers, but it is also a gripping story of family dynamics and
the burden of alcoholism."

—*CBA Retailers + Resources*

THOMAS NELSON
Since 1798

AVAILABLE IN PRINT AND E-BOOK

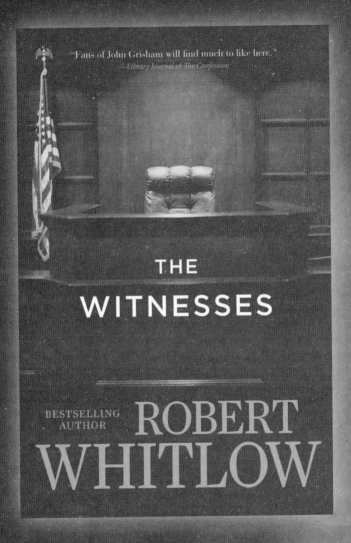

"Fans of John Grisham will find much to like here."
—*Library Journal of The Confession*

THE
WITNESSES

BESTSELLING
AUTHOR
ROBERT
WHITLOW

"Part mystery and part legal thriller, Whitlow's latest
novel is definitely a must-read!"
—*RT Book Reviews*, 4 stars

THOMAS NELSON
Since 1798   AVAILABLE IN PRINT AND E-BOOK

ABOUT THE AUTHOR

Photo by David Whitlow,
Two Cents Photography

Robert Whitlow is the bestselling author of legal novels set in the South and winner of the Christy Award for Contemporary Fiction. He received his JD with honors from the University of Georgia School of Law where he served on the staff of the *Georgia Law Review*.

• • •

RobertWhitlow.com
Twitter: @WhitlowWriter
Facebook: RobertWhitlowBooks